RAT QUEENS™

VOLUME EIGHT:
THE GOD DILEMMA

Shadowline®

image®

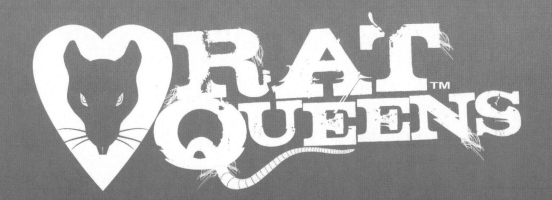

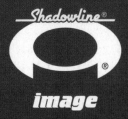

FIRST PRINTING: APRIL 2021

ISBN: 978-1-5343-1672-0

image COMICS PRESENTS

8

A
Shadowline®
PRODUCTION

RYAN FERRIER
writer / letterer

MORITAT
CASEY SILVER
artists, chapters 22–25

PRISCILLA PETRAITES
& MARCO LESKO
artists, chapter 21, original covers

MELANIE HACKETT
editor

MARC LOMBARDI
communications

JIM VALENTINO
publisher

KURTIS J. WIEBE
co-creator / consultant

TIM DANIEL
frame

Page 4 collage:
ROC UPCHURCH
Betty & Braga

MORITAT &
CASEY SILVER
Dee

STJEPAN SEJIC
Hannah

PRISCILLA PETRAITES &
MARCO LESKO
Molly

OWEN GIENI
Violet

RAT QUEENS created by Kurtis J. Wiebe and John Upchurch

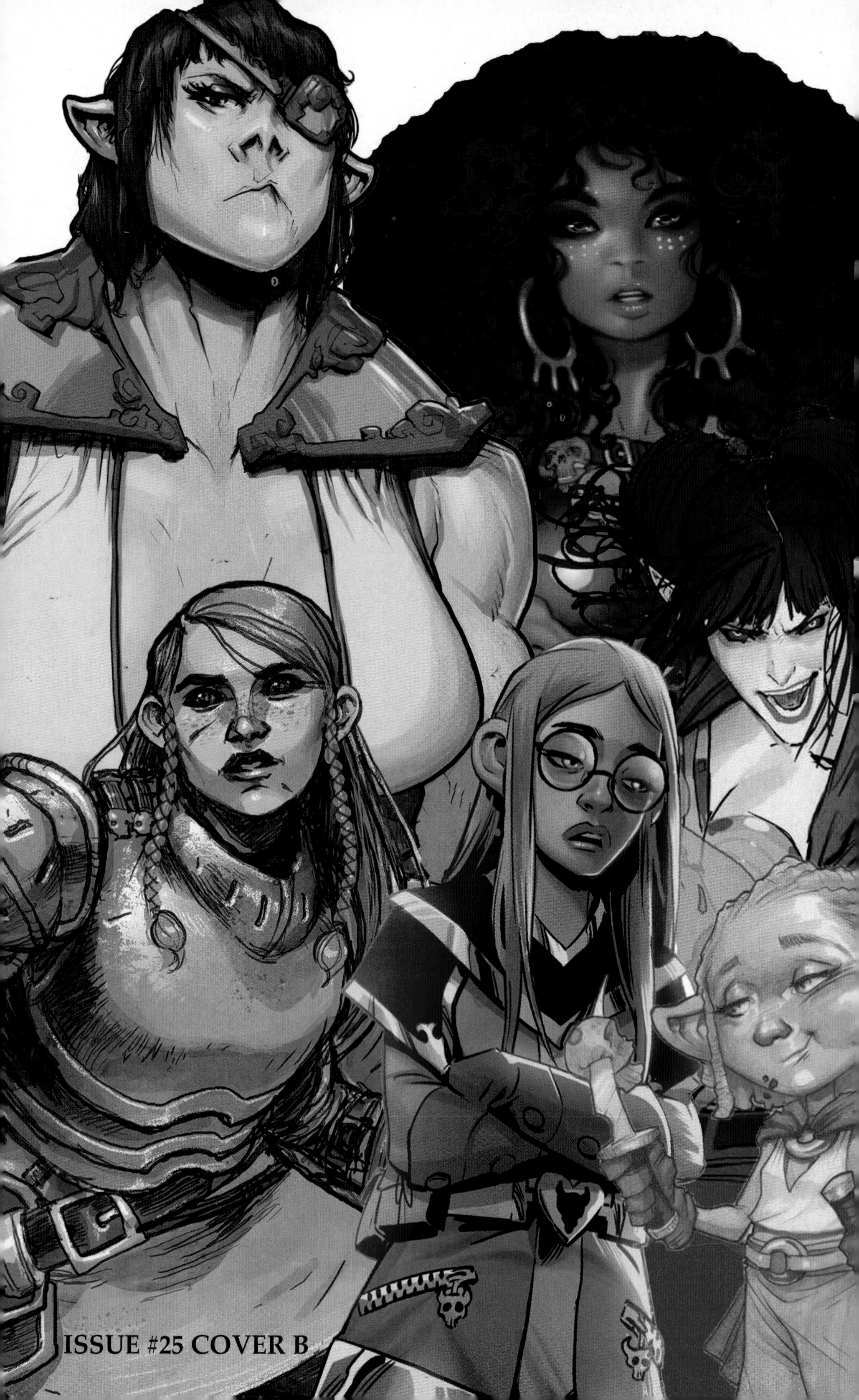
ISSUE #25 COVER B

CHAPTER TWENTY-ONE

ISSUE #21 COVER

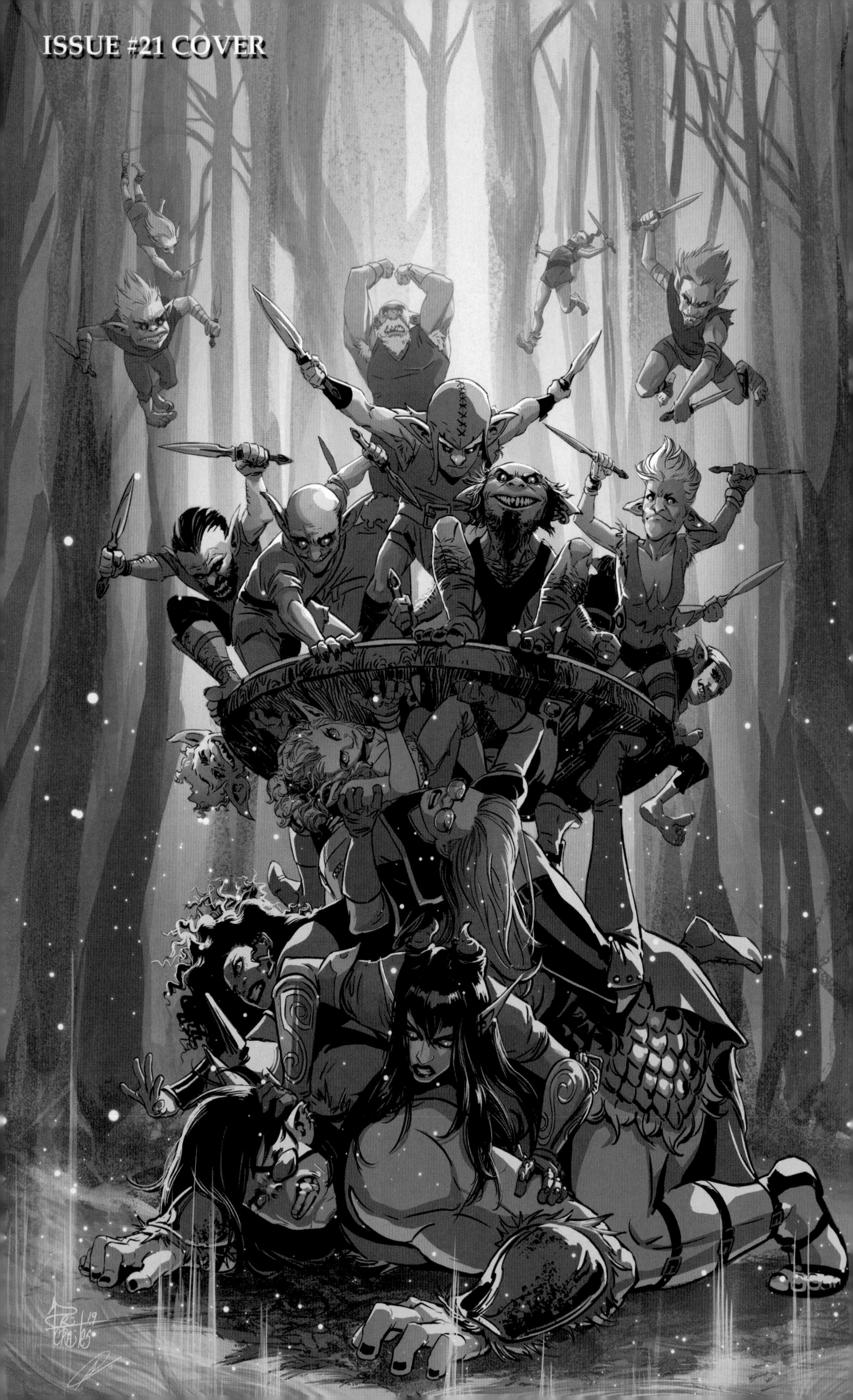

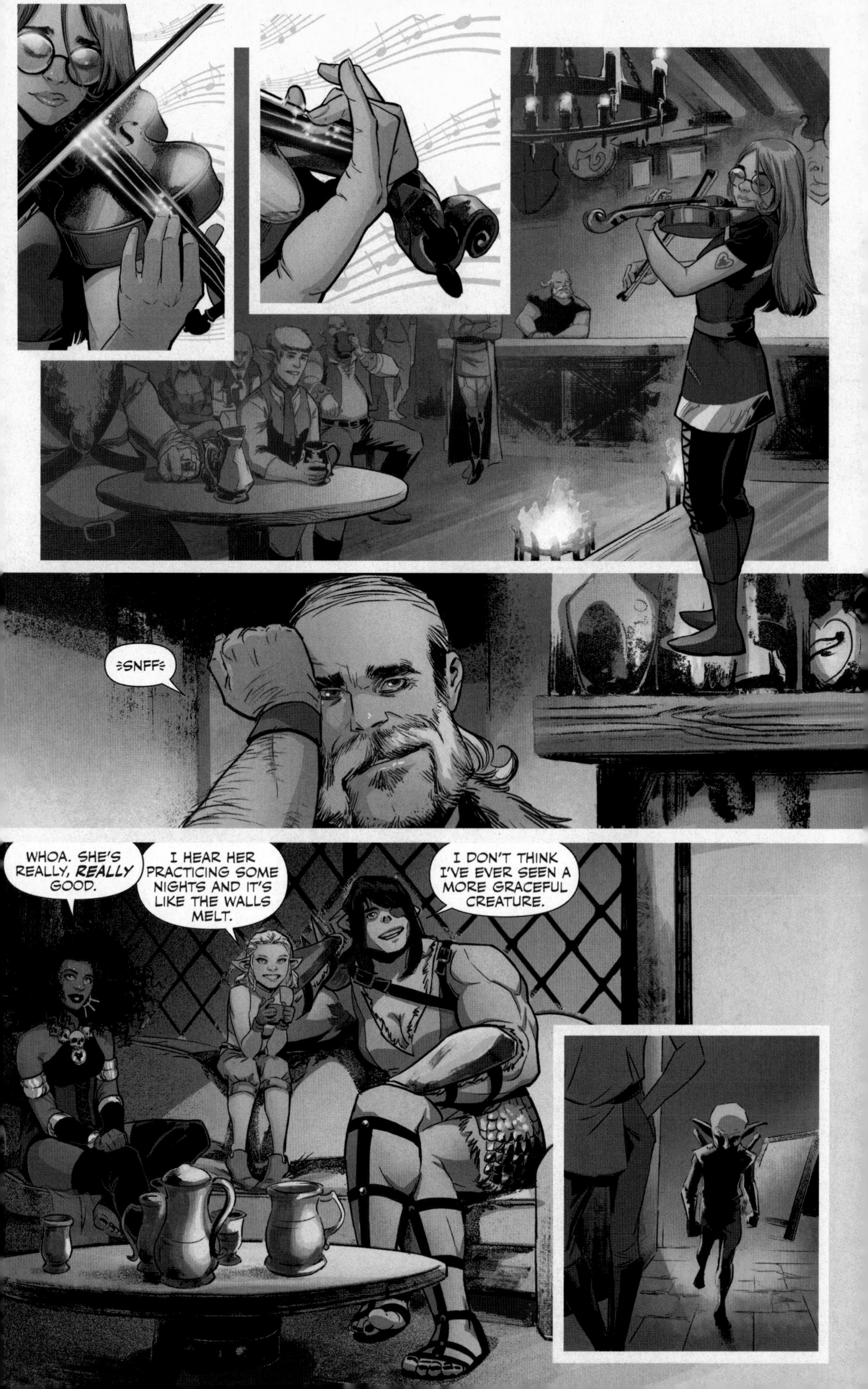
SNFF
WHOA. SHE'S REALLY, ***REALLY*** GOOD.
I HEAR HER PRACTICING SOME NIGHTS AND IT'S LIKE THE WALLS MELT.
I DON'T THINK I'VE EVER SEEN A MORE GRACEFUL CREATURE.

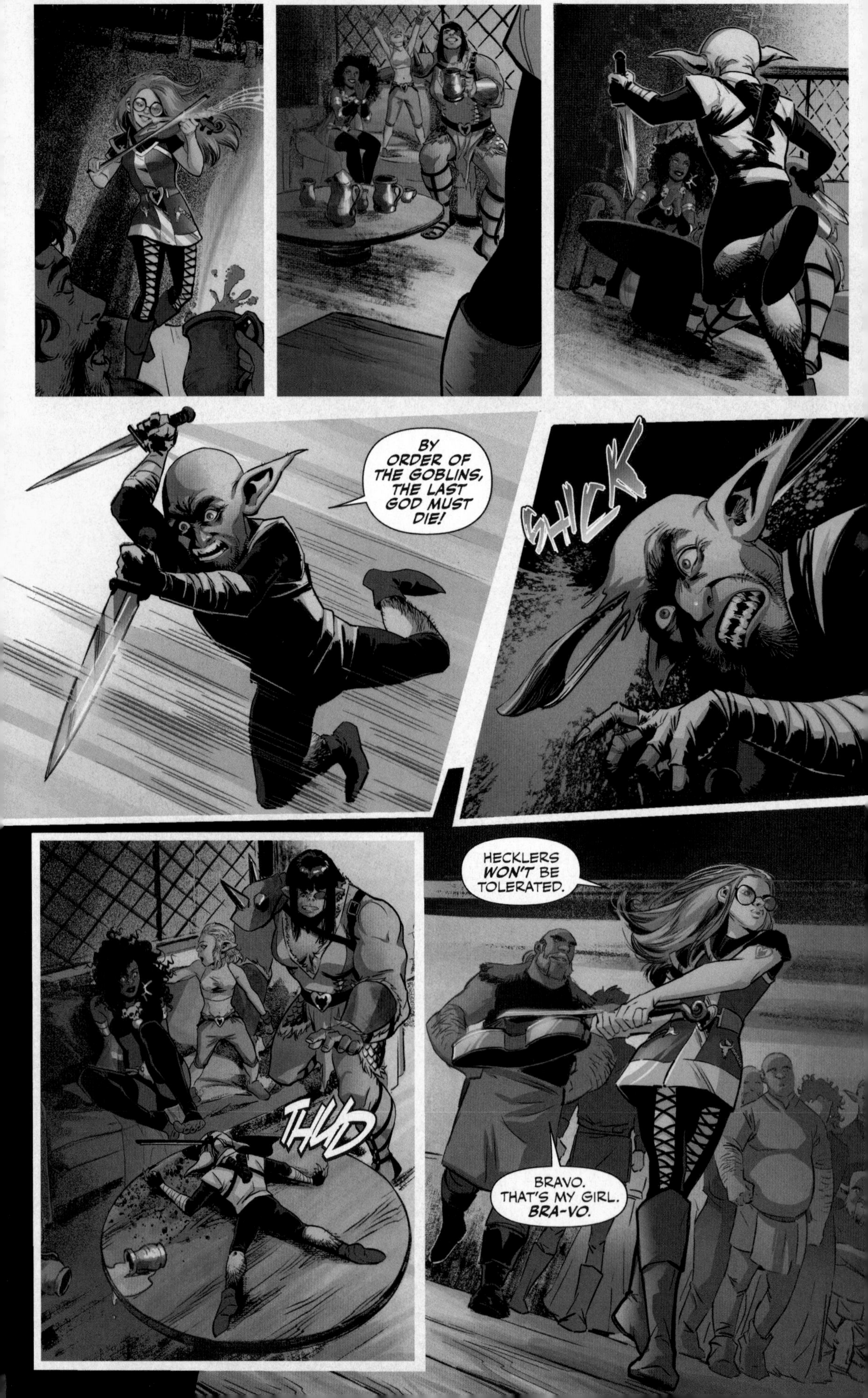
BY ORDER OF THE GOBLINS, THE LAST GOD MUST DIE!
SHICK
THUD
HECKLERS WON'T BE TOLERATED.
BRAVO. THAT'S MY GIRL. BRA-VO.

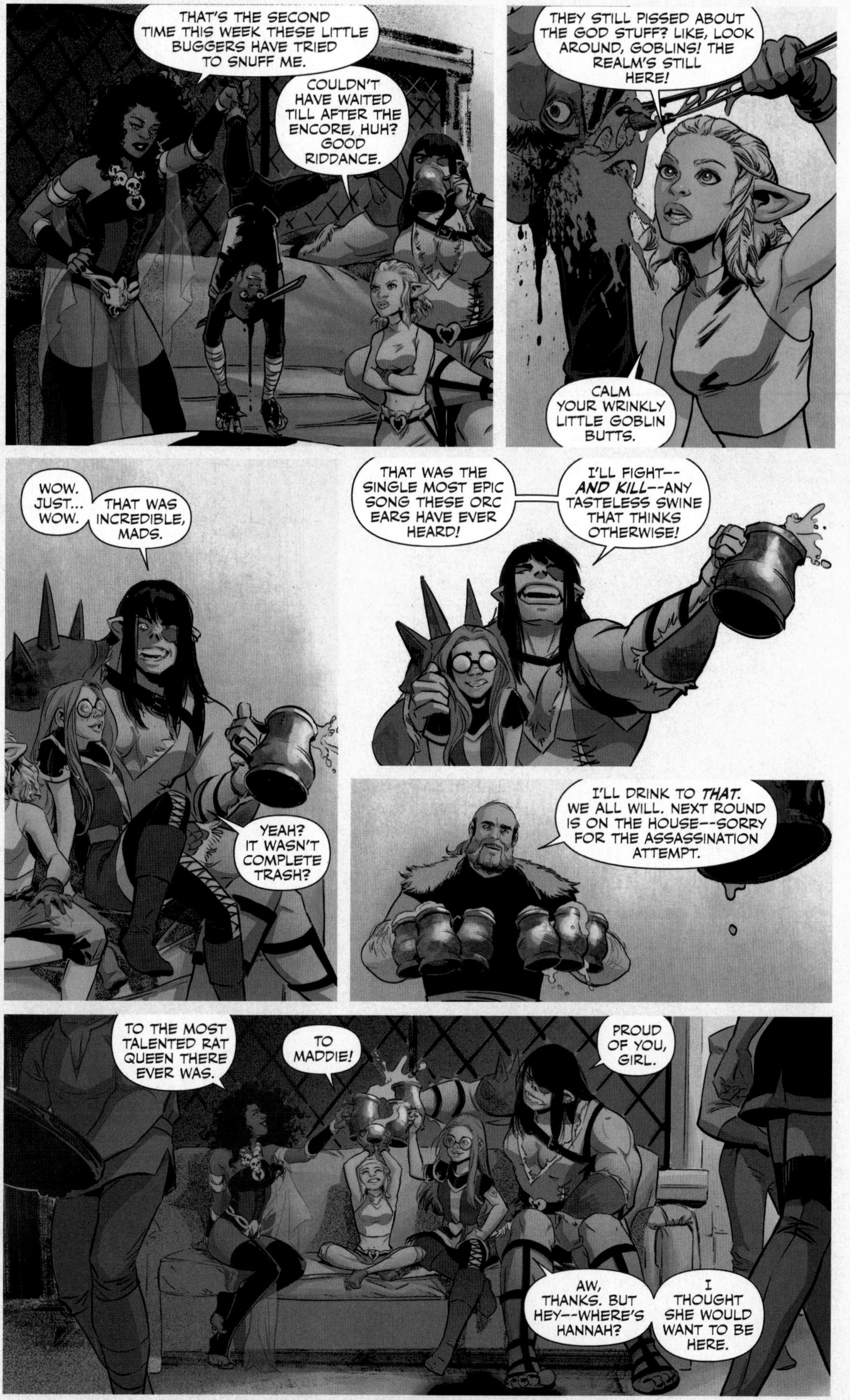
THAT'S THE SECOND TIME THIS WEEK THESE LITTLE BUGGERS HAVE TRIED TO SNUFF ME.
COULDN'T HAVE WAITED TILL AFTER THE ENCORE, HUH? GOOD RIDDANCE.
THEY STILL PISSED ABOUT THE GOD STUFF? LIKE, LOOK AROUND, GOBLINS! THE REALM'S STILL HERE!
CALM YOUR WRINKLY LITTLE GOBLIN BUTTS.
WOW. JUST... WOW.
THAT WAS INCREDIBLE, MADS.
YEAH? IT WASN'T COMPLETE TRASH?
THAT WAS THE SINGLE MOST EPIC SONG THESE ORC EARS HAVE EVER HEARD!
I'LL FIGHT-- AND KILL--ANY TASTELESS SWINE THAT THINKS OTHERWISE!
I'LL DRINK TO THAT. WE ALL WILL. NEXT ROUND IS ON THE HOUSE--SORRY FOR THE ASSASSINATION ATTEMPT.
TO THE MOST TALENTED RAT QUEEN THERE EVER WAS.
TO MADDIE!
PROUD OF YOU, GIRL.
AW, THANKS. BUT HEY--WHERE'S HANNAH?
I THOUGHT SHE WOULD WANT TO BE HERE.

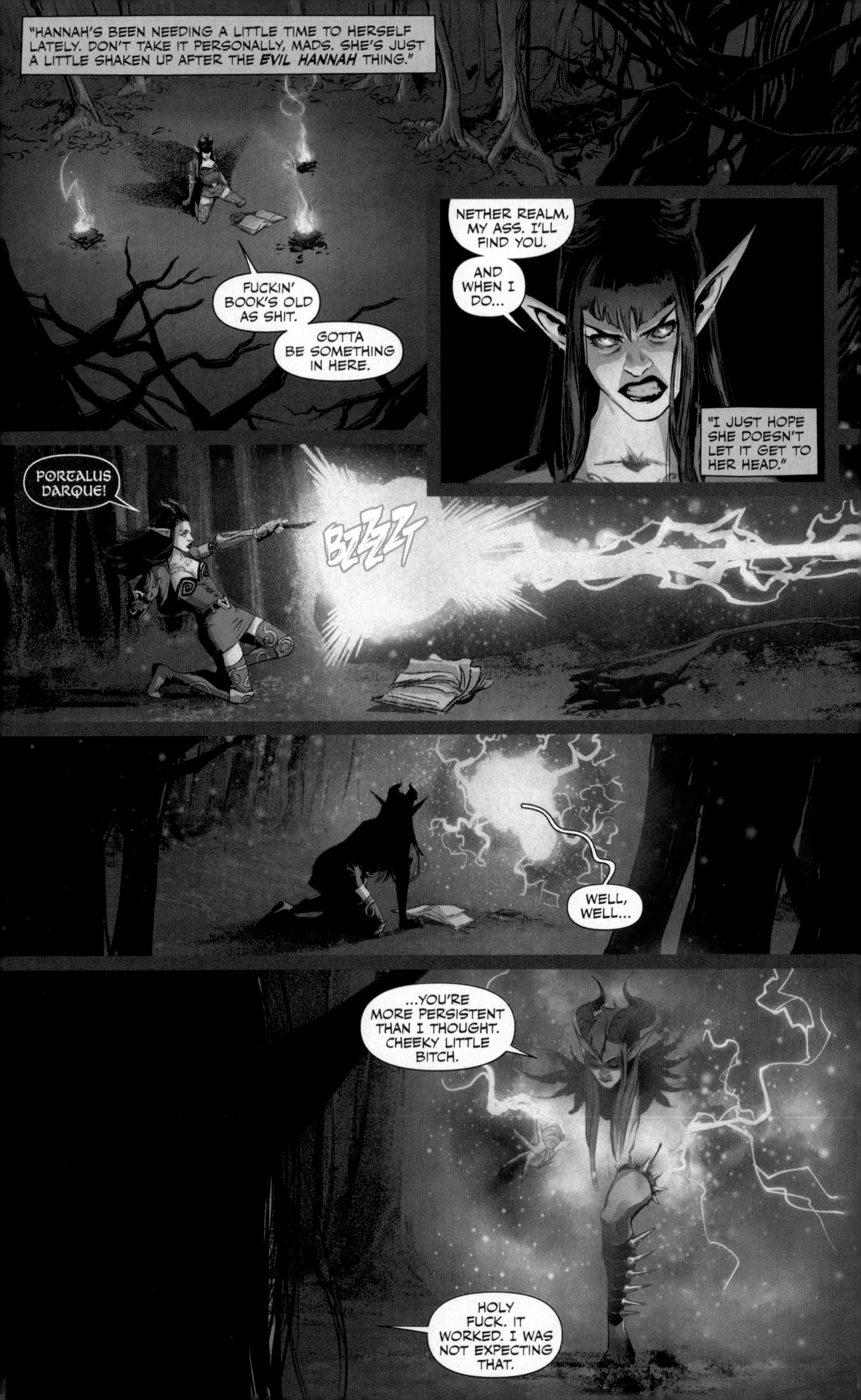
"HANNAH'S BEEN NEEDING A LITTLE TIME TO HERSELF LATELY. DON'T TAKE IT PERSONALLY, MADS. SHE'S JUST A LITTLE SHAKEN UP AFTER THE EVIL HANNAH THING."
FUCKIN' BOOK'S OLD AS SHIT.
GOTTA BE SOMETHING IN HERE.
NETHER REALM, MY ASS. I'LL FIND YOU.
AND WHEN I DO...
"I JUST HOPE SHE DOESN'T LET IT GET TO HER HEAD."
PORTALUS DARQUE!
BZZZZT
WELL, WELL...
...YOU'RE MORE PERSISTENT THAN I THOUGHT. CHEEKY LITTLE BITCH.
HOLY FUCK. IT WORKED. I WAS NOT EXPECTING THAT.

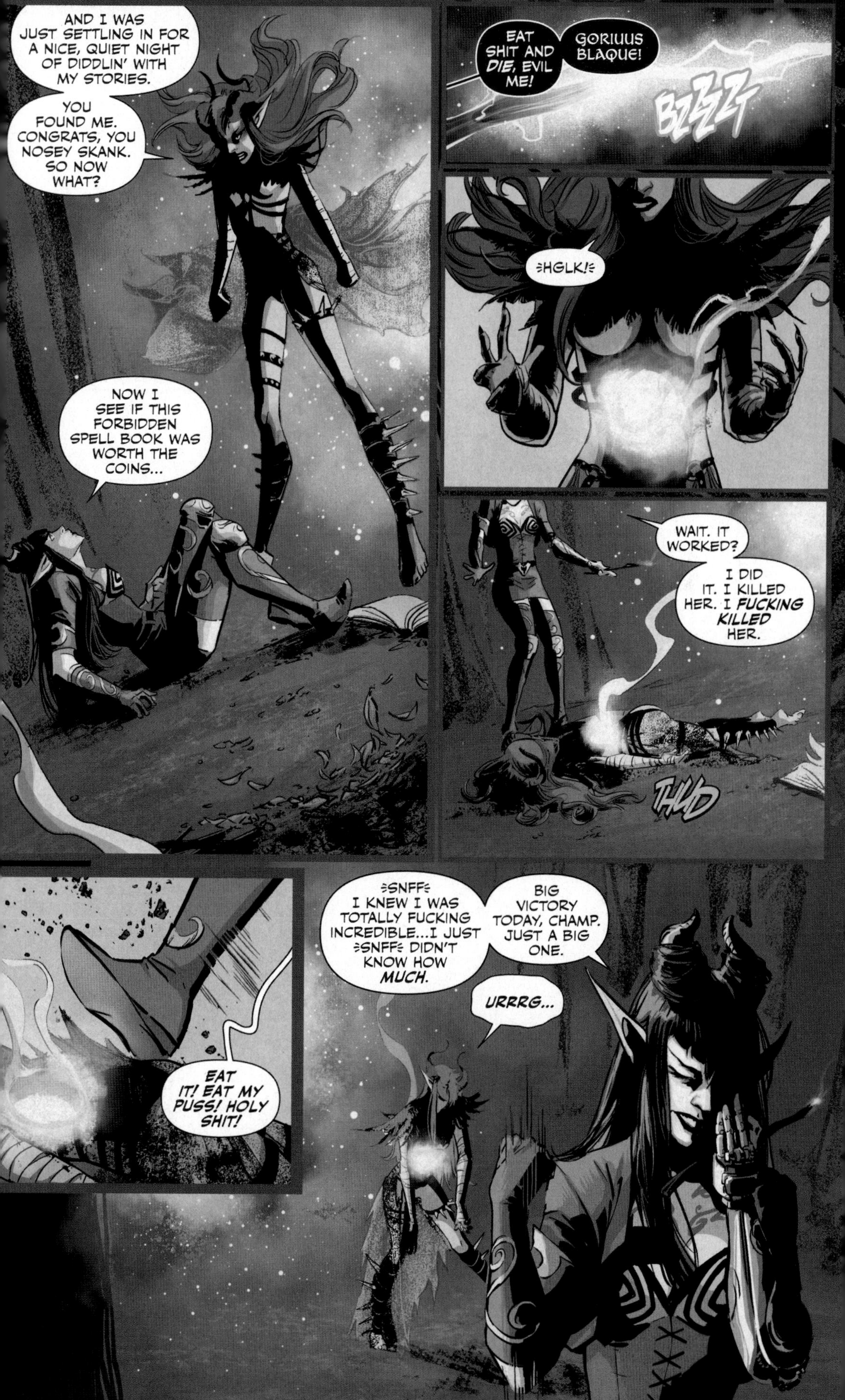
AND I WAS JUST SETTLING IN FOR A NICE, QUIET NIGHT OF DIDDLIN' WITH MY STORIES.
YOU FOUND ME. CONGRATS, YOU NOSEY SKANK. SO NOW WHAT?
NOW I SEE IF THIS FORBIDDEN SPELL BOOK WAS WORTH THE COINS...
EAT SHIT AND DIE, EVIL ME!
GORIUUS BLAQUE!
BZZZZT
HGLK!
WAIT. IT WORKED?
I DID IT. I KILLED HER. I FUCKING KILLED HER.
THUD
EAT IT! EAT MY PUSS! HOLY SHIT!
SNFF I KNEW I WAS TOTALLY FUCKING INCREDIBLE...I JUST SNFF DIDN'T KNOW HOW MUCH.
BIG VICTORY TODAY, CHAMP. JUST A BIG ONE.
URRRG...

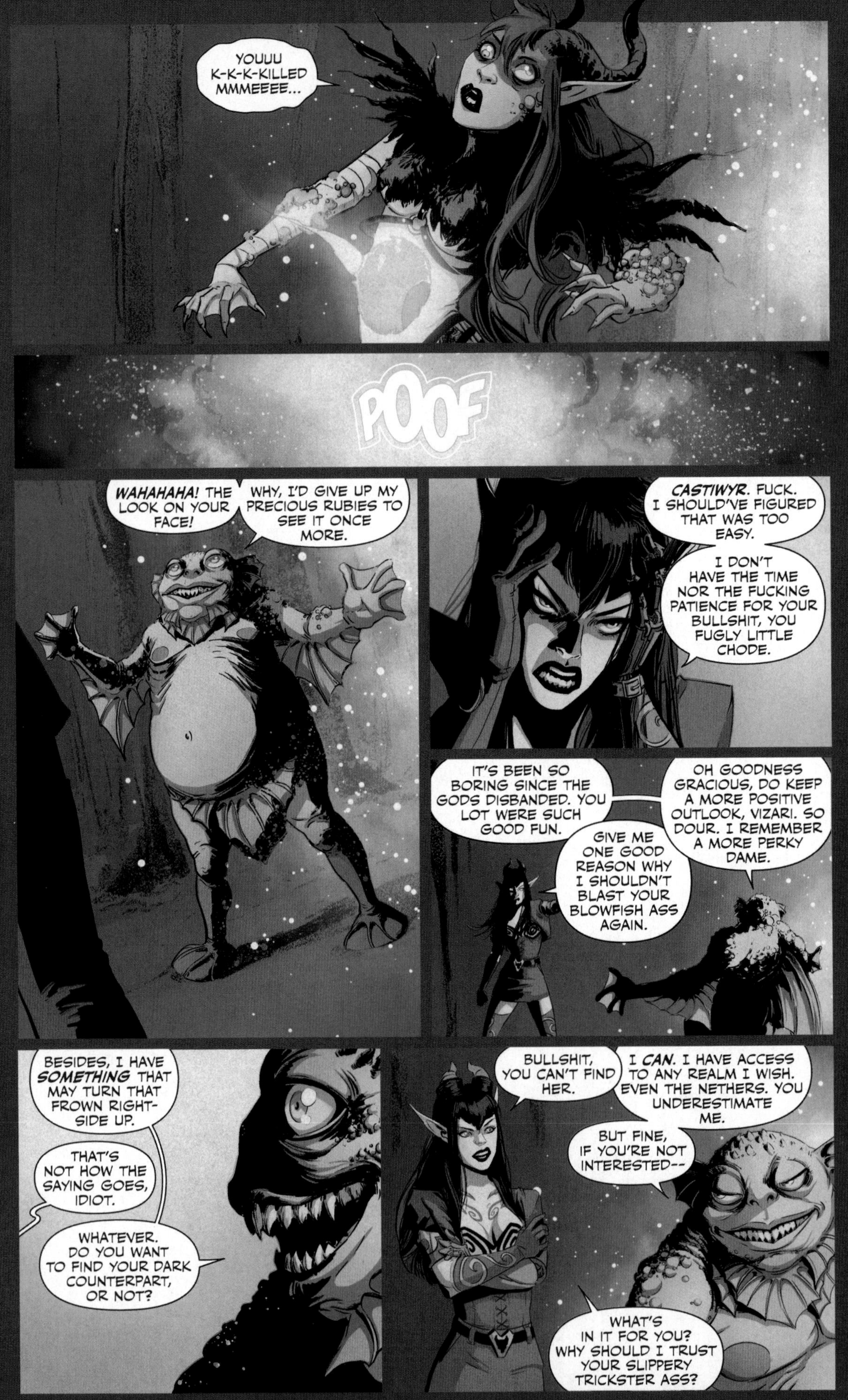
YOUUU K-K-K-KILLED MMMEEEE...
POOF
WAHAHAHA! THE LOOK ON YOUR FACE!
WHY, I'D GIVE UP MY PRECIOUS RUBIES TO SEE IT ONCE MORE.
CASTIWYR. FUCK. I SHOULD'VE FIGURED THAT WAS TOO EASY.
I DON'T HAVE THE TIME NOR THE FUCKING PATIENCE FOR YOUR BULLSHIT, YOU FUGLY LITTLE CHODE.
IT'S BEEN SO BORING SINCE THE GODS DISBANDED. YOU LOT WERE SUCH GOOD FUN.
GIVE ME ONE GOOD REASON WHY I SHOULDN'T BLAST YOUR BLOWFISH ASS AGAIN.
OH GOODNESS GRACIOUS, DO KEEP A MORE POSITIVE OUTLOOK, VIZARI. SO DOUR. I REMEMBER A MORE PERKY DAME.
BESIDES, I HAVE SOMETHING THAT MAY TURN THAT FROWN RIGHT-SIDE UP.
THAT'S NOT HOW THE SAYING GOES, IDIOT.
WHATEVER. DO YOU WANT TO FIND YOUR DARK COUNTERPART, OR NOT?
BULLSHIT, YOU CAN'T FIND HER.
I CAN. I HAVE ACCESS TO ANY REALM I WISH. EVEN THE NETHERS. YOU UNDERESTIMATE ME.
BUT FINE, IF YOU'RE NOT INTERESTED--
WHAT'S IN IT FOR YOU? WHY SHOULD I TRUST YOUR SLIPPERY TRICKSTER ASS?

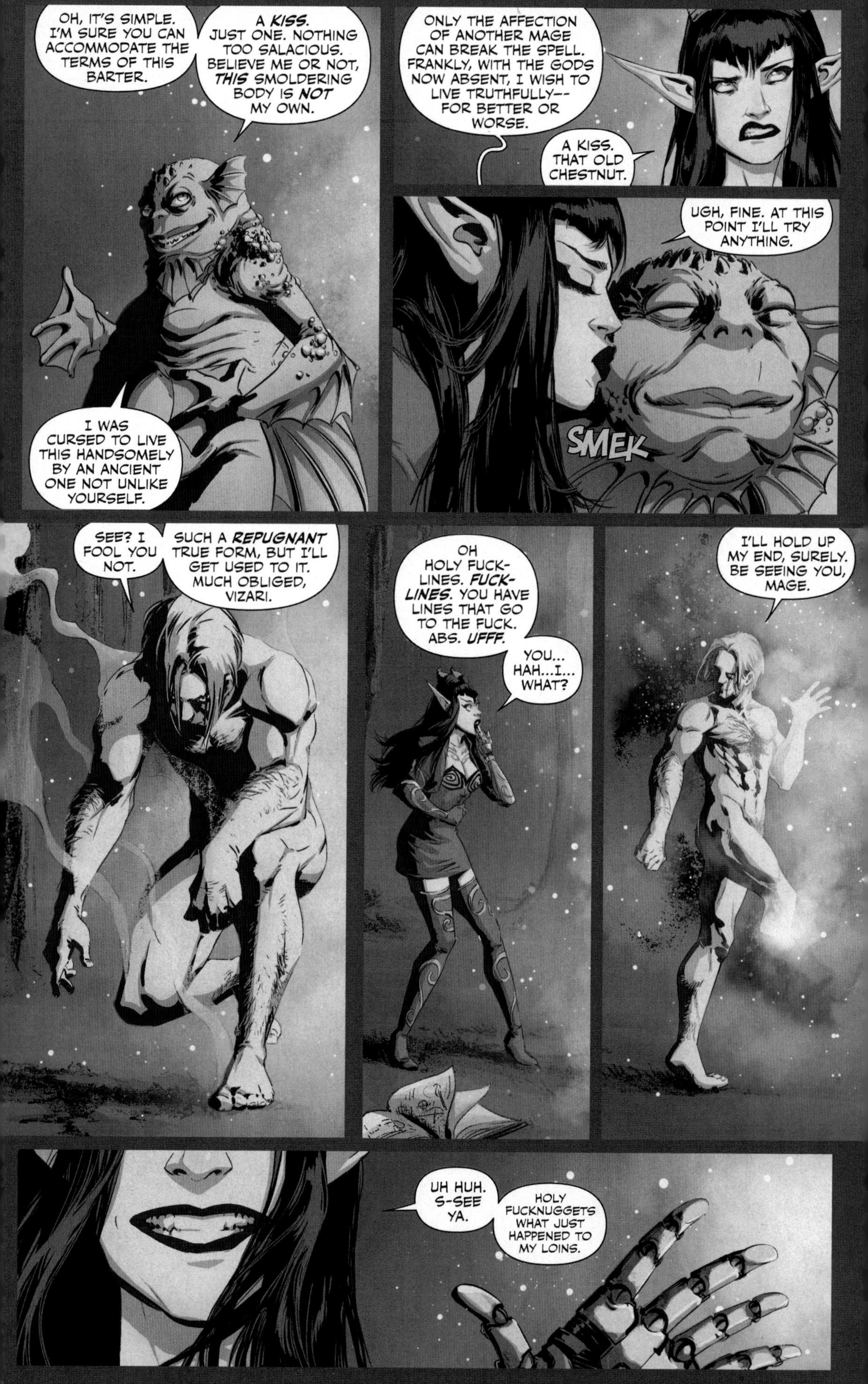
OH, IT'S SIMPLE. I'M SURE YOU CAN ACCOMMODATE THE TERMS OF THIS BARTER.
A KISS. JUST ONE. NOTHING TOO SALACIOUS. BELIEVE ME OR NOT, THIS SMOLDERING BODY IS NOT MY OWN.
I WAS CURSED TO LIVE THIS HANDSOMELY BY AN ANCIENT ONE NOT UNLIKE YOURSELF.
ONLY THE AFFECTION OF ANOTHER MAGE CAN BREAK THE SPELL. FRANKLY, WITH THE GODS NOW ABSENT, I WISH TO LIVE TRUTHFULLY-- FOR BETTER OR WORSE.
A KISS. THAT OLD CHESTNUT.
UGH, FINE. AT THIS POINT I'LL TRY ANYTHING.
SMEK
SEE? I FOOL YOU NOT.
SUCH A REPUGNANT TRUE FORM, BUT I'LL GET USED TO IT. MUCH OBLIGED, VIZARI.
OH HOLY FUCK-LINES. FUCK-LINES. YOU HAVE LINES THAT GO TO THE FUCK. ABS. UFFF.
YOU... HAH...I... WHAT?
I'LL HOLD UP MY END, SURELY. BE SEEING YOU, MAGE.
UH HUH. S-SEE YA.
HOLY FUCKNUGGETS WHAT JUST HAPPENED TO MY LOINS.

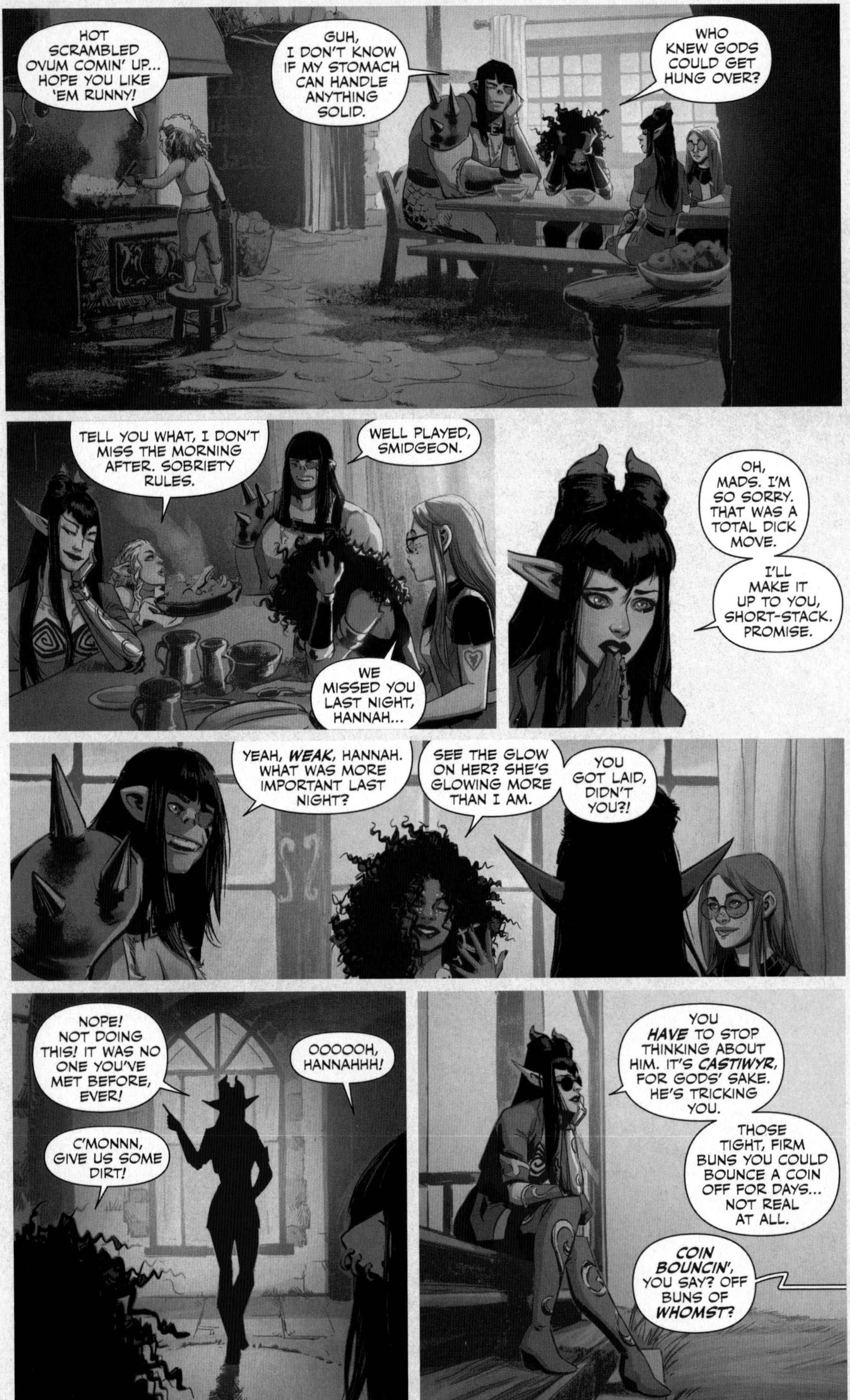

HOT SCRAMBLED OVUM COMIN' UP... HOPE YOU LIKE 'EM RUNNY!
GUH, I DON'T KNOW IF MY STOMACH CAN HANDLE ANYTHING SOLID.
WHO KNEW GODS COULD GET HUNG OVER?
TELL YOU WHAT, I DON'T MISS THE MORNING AFTER. SOBRIETY RULES.
WELL PLAYED, SMIDGEON.
WE MISSED YOU LAST NIGHT, HANNAH...
OH, MADS. I'M SO SORRY. THAT WAS A TOTAL DICK MOVE.
I'LL MAKE IT UP TO YOU, SHORT-STACK. PROMISE.
YEAH, *WEAK*, HANNAH. WHAT WAS MORE IMPORTANT LAST NIGHT?
SEE THE GLOW ON HER? SHE'S GLOWING MORE THAN I AM.
YOU GOT LAID, DIDN'T YOU?!
NOPE! NOT DOING THIS! IT WAS NO ONE YOU'VE MET BEFORE, EVER!
OOOOOH, HANNAHHH!
C'MONNN, GIVE US SOME DIRT!
YOU *HAVE* TO STOP THINKING ABOUT HIM. IT'S *CASTIWYR*, FOR GODS' SAKE. HE'S TRICKING YOU.
THOSE TIGHT, FIRM BUNS YOU COULD BOUNCE A COIN OFF FOR DAYS... NOT REAL AT ALL.
COIN BOUNCIN', YOU SAY? OFF BUNS OF *WHOMST*?

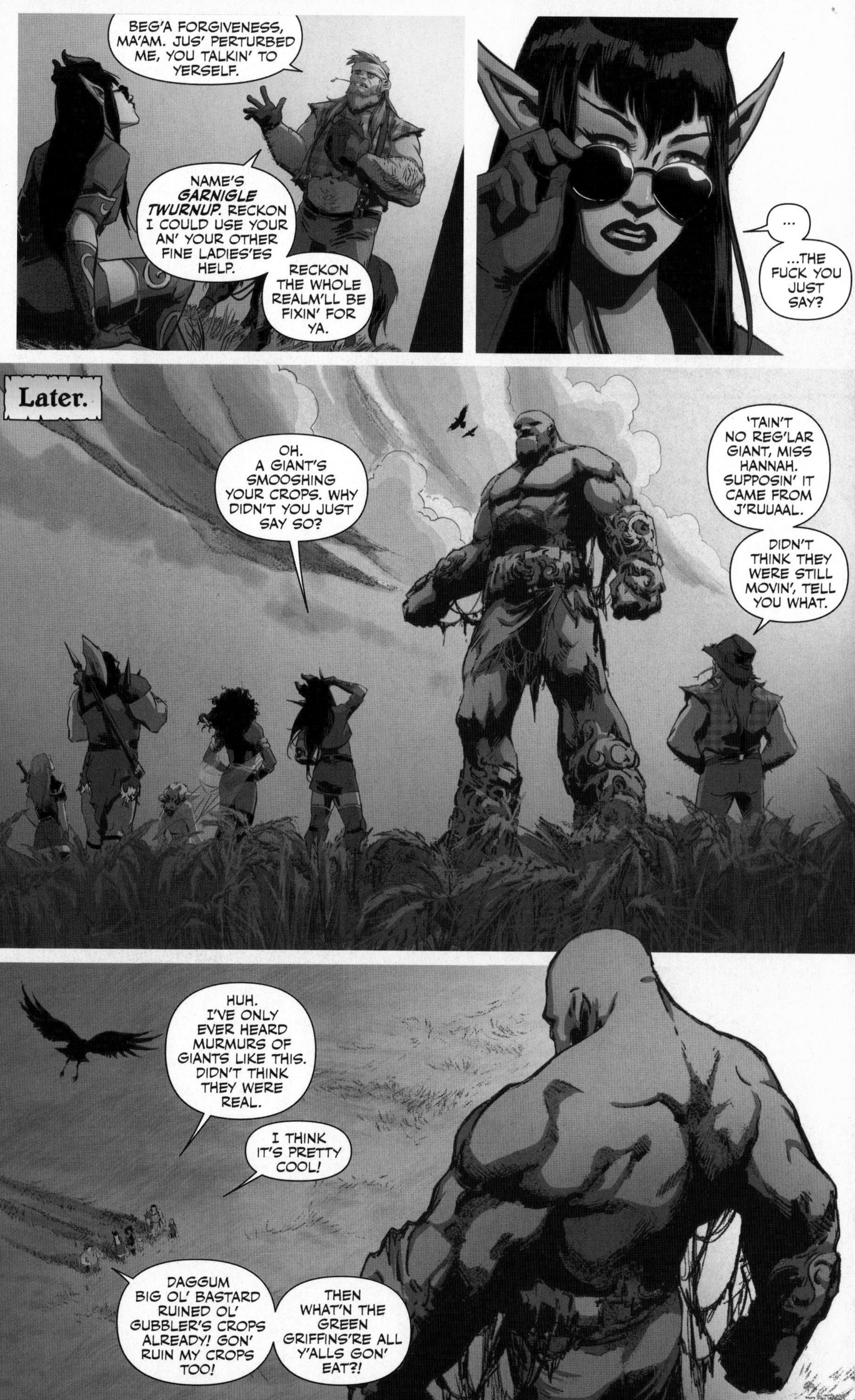
BEG'A FORGIVENESS, MA'AM. JUS' PERTURBED ME, YOU TALKIN' TO YERSELF.
NAME'S GARNIGLE TWURNUP. RECKON I COULD USE YOUR AN' YOUR OTHER FINE LADIES'ES HELP.
RECKON THE WHOLE REALM'LL BE FIXIN' FOR YA.
...
...THE FUCK YOU JUST SAY?
Later.
OH. A GIANT'S SMOOSHING YOUR CROPS. WHY DIDN'T YOU JUST SAY SO?
'TAIN'T NO REG'LAR GIANT, MISS HANNAH. SUPPOSIN' IT CAME FROM J'RUUAAL.
DIDN'T THINK THEY WERE STILL MOVIN', TELL YOU WHAT.
HUH. I'VE ONLY EVER HEARD MURMURS OF GIANTS LIKE THIS. DIDN'T THINK THEY WERE REAL.
I THINK IT'S PRETTY COOL!
DAGGUM BIG OL' BASTARD RUINED OL' GUBBLER'S CROPS ALREADY! GON' RUIN MY CROPS TOO!
THEN WHAT'N THE GREEN GRIFFINS'RE ALL Y'ALLS GON' EAT?!

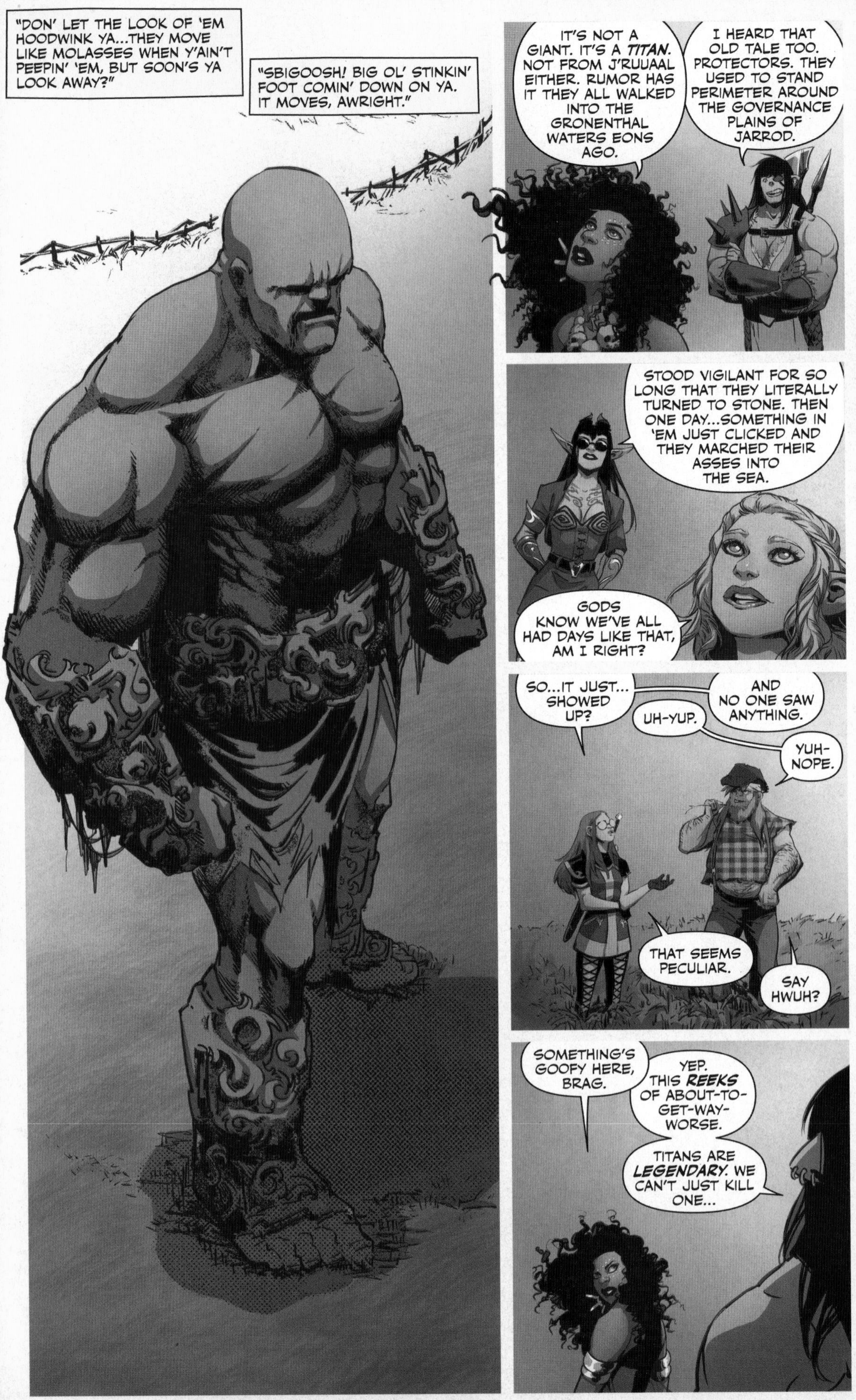

"DON' LET THE LOOK OF 'EM HOODWINK YA...THEY MOVE LIKE MOLASSES WHEN Y'AIN'T PEEPIN' 'EM, BUT SOON'S YA LOOK AWAY?"
"SBIGOOSH! BIG OL' STINKIN' FOOT COMIN' DOWN ON YA. IT MOVES, AWRIGHT."
IT'S NOT A GIANT. IT'S A TITAN. NOT FROM J'RUUAAL EITHER. RUMOR HAS IT THEY ALL WALKED INTO THE GRONENTHAL WATERS EONS AGO.
I HEARD THAT OLD TALE TOO. PROTECTORS. THEY USED TO STAND PERIMETER AROUND THE GOVERNANCE PLAINS OF JARROD.
STOOD VIGILANT FOR SO LONG THAT THEY LITERALLY TURNED TO STONE. THEN ONE DAY...SOMETHING IN 'EM JUST CLICKED AND THEY MARCHED THEIR ASSES INTO THE SEA.
GODS KNOW WE'VE ALL HAD DAYS LIKE THAT, AM I RIGHT?
SO...IT JUST... SHOWED UP?
AND NO ONE SAW ANYTHING.
UH-YUP.
YUH-NOPE.
THAT SEEMS PECULIAR.
SAY HWUH?
SOMETHING'S GOOFY HERE, BRAG.
YEP. THIS REEKS OF ABOUT-TO-GET-WAY-WORSE.
TITANS ARE LEGENDARY. WE CAN'T JUST KILL ONE...

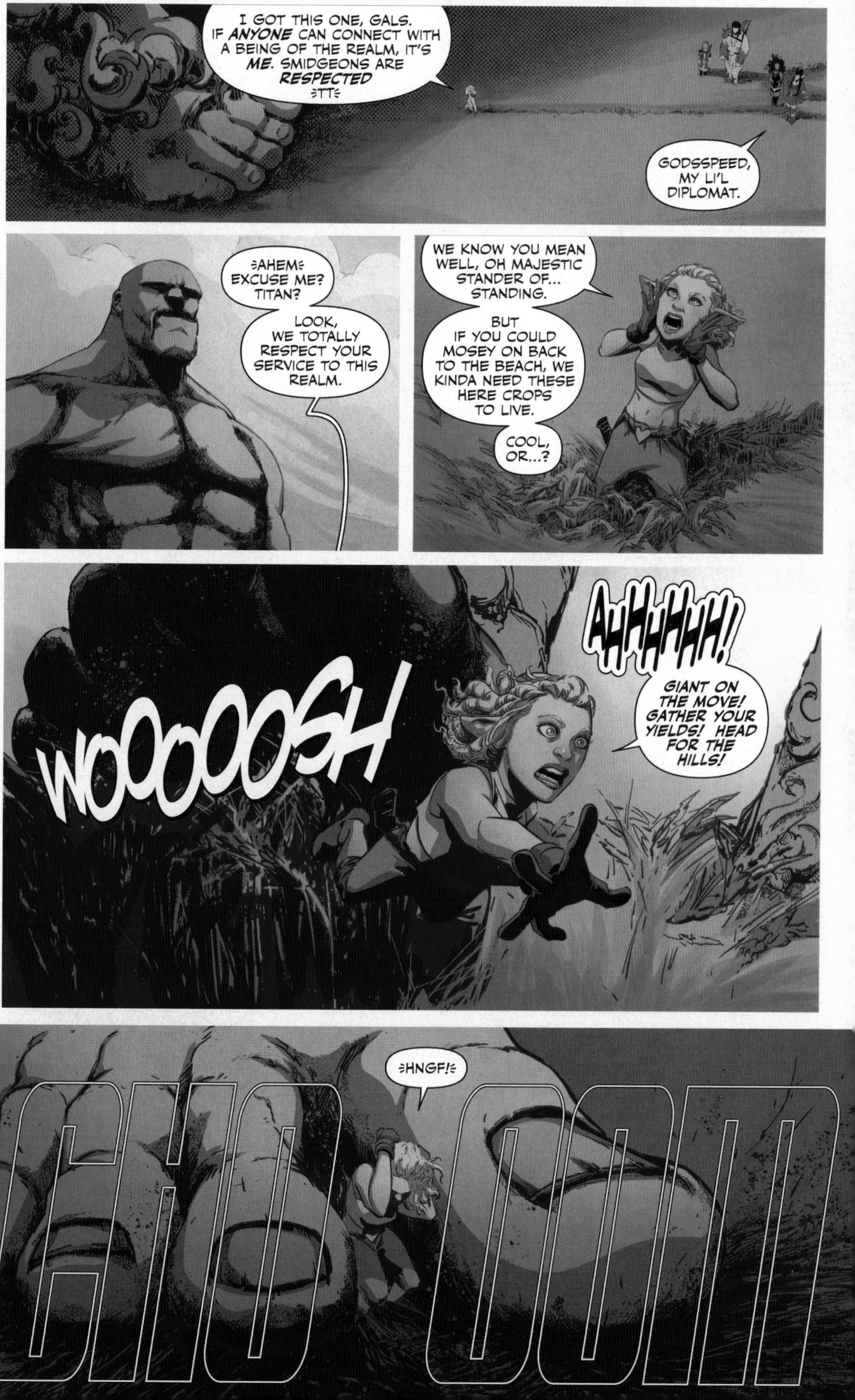
I GOT THIS ONE, GALS. IF ANYONE CAN CONNECT WITH A BEING OF THE REALM, IT'S ME. SMIDGEONS ARE RESPECTED
TT
GODSSPEED, MY LI'L DIPLOMAT.
AHEM EXCUSE ME? TITAN?
LOOK, WE TOTALLY RESPECT YOUR SERVICE TO THIS REALM.
WE KNOW YOU MEAN WELL, OH MAJESTIC STANDER OF... STANDING.
BUT IF YOU COULD MOSEY ON BACK TO THE BEACH, WE KINDA NEED THESE HERE CROPS TO LIVE.
COOL, OR...?
WOOOOOSH
AHHHHHH!
GIANT ON THE MOVE! GATHER YOUR YIELDS! HEAD FOR THE HILLS!
HNGF!
CHO OOM

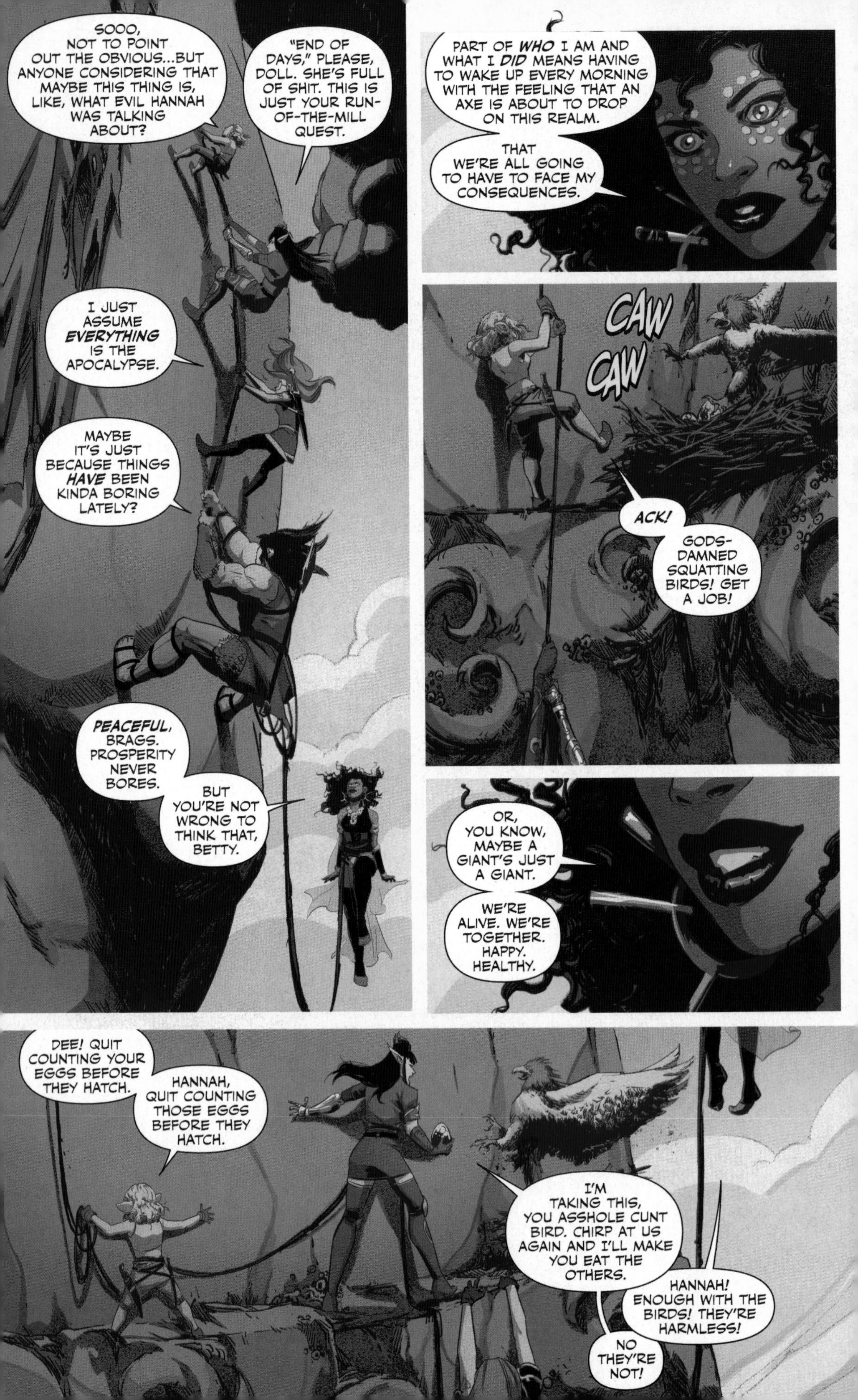
SOOO, NOT TO POINT OUT THE OBVIOUS...BUT ANYONE CONSIDERING THAT MAYBE THIS THING IS, LIKE, WHAT EVIL HANNAH WAS TALKING ABOUT?
"END OF DAYS," PLEASE, DOLL. SHE'S FULL OF SHIT. THIS IS JUST YOUR RUN-OF-THE-MILL QUEST.
I JUST ASSUME EVERYTHING IS THE APOCALYPSE.
MAYBE IT'S JUST BECAUSE THINGS HAVE BEEN KINDA BORING LATELY?
PEACEFUL, BRAGS. PROSPERITY NEVER BORES.
BUT YOU'RE NOT WRONG TO THINK THAT, BETTY.
PART OF WHO I AM AND WHAT I DID MEANS HAVING TO WAKE UP EVERY MORNING WITH THE FEELING THAT AN AXE IS ABOUT TO DROP ON THIS REALM.
THAT WE'RE ALL GOING TO HAVE TO FACE MY CONSEQUENCES.
CAW
CAW
ACK!
GODS-DAMNED SQUATTING BIRDS! GET A JOB!
OR, YOU KNOW, MAYBE A GIANT'S JUST A GIANT.
WE'RE ALIVE. WE'RE TOGETHER. HAPPY. HEALTHY.
DEE! QUIT COUNTING YOUR EGGS BEFORE THEY HATCH.
HANNAH, QUIT COUNTING THOSE EGGS BEFORE THEY HATCH.
I'M TAKING THIS, YOU ASSHOLE CUNT BIRD. CHIRP AT US AGAIN AND I'LL MAKE YOU EAT THE OTHERS.
HANNAH! ENOUGH WITH THE BIRDS! THEY'RE HARMLESS!
NO THEY'RE NOT!

HEADS UP, Y'ALL-- IT'S THE *HEAD*.

HOLY MOLY, I DON'T THINK I HAVE THE UPPER BODY STRENGTH TO GO ANY FURTHER.

SO, WHAT? DO WE...TALK... TO IT?

I DON'T THINK ANYONE'S HOME.

IT *IS* ALIVE. THE TITANS ARE LIVING STATUES NOW, BUT AT ONE TIME THEY WERE NORMAL, REGULAR FOLK.

SOMETHING ISN'T RIGHT WITH THIS ONE. I CAN FEEL IT.

POOR BASTARD'S MOUTH'S FULL OF SEA-JUNK.

NO, LOOK AT THE *VEIN* FORMATION ON THE STEMS, THAT'S ONLY FOUND IN CREATURES THAT--

WHOA. MADDIE. SHINFO--*SHITTY INFO*. IT'S JUST SEA-JUNK!

HOW WOULD *YOUR* TEETH LOOK WITHOUT BRUSHING FOR AN EON?

JUST LIKE BETTY'S, HEH.

HEY!

THWIP

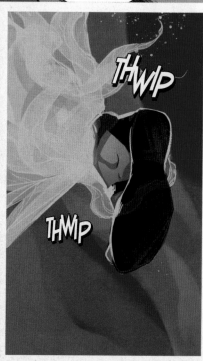

THWIP

THWIP

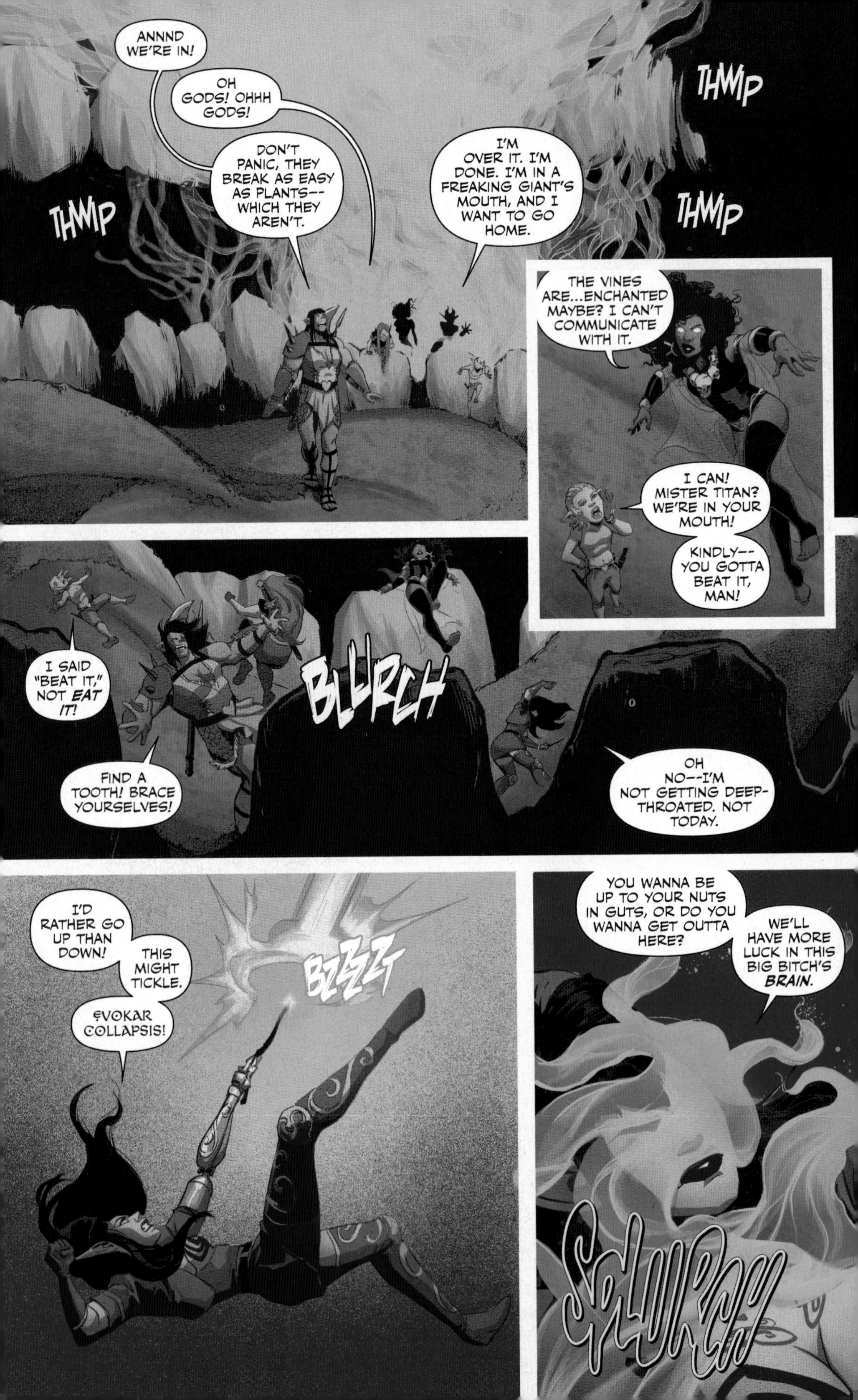
ANNND WE'RE IN!
OH GODS! OHHH GODS!
DON'T PANIC, THEY BREAK AS EASY AS PLANTS--WHICH THEY AREN'T.
THWIP
I'M OVER IT. I'M DONE. I'M IN A FREAKING GIANT'S MOUTH, AND I WANT TO GO HOME.
THWIP
THWIP
THE VINES ARE...ENCHANTED MAYBE? I CAN'T COMMUNICATE WITH IT.
I CAN! MISTER TITAN? WE'RE IN YOUR MOUTH!
KINDLY--YOU GOTTA BEAT IT, MAN!
I SAID "BEAT IT," NOT EAT IT!
FIND A TOOTH! BRACE YOURSELVES!
BLURCH
OH NO--I'M NOT GETTING DEEP-THROATED. NOT TODAY.
I'D RATHER GO UP THAN DOWN!
THIS MIGHT TICKLE.
EVOKAR COLLAPSIS!
BZZZZT
YOU WANNA BE UP TO YOUR NUTS IN GUTS, OR DO YOU WANNA GET OUTTA HERE?
WE'LL HAVE MORE LUCK IN THIS BIG BITCH'S BRAIN.
SPLURCH

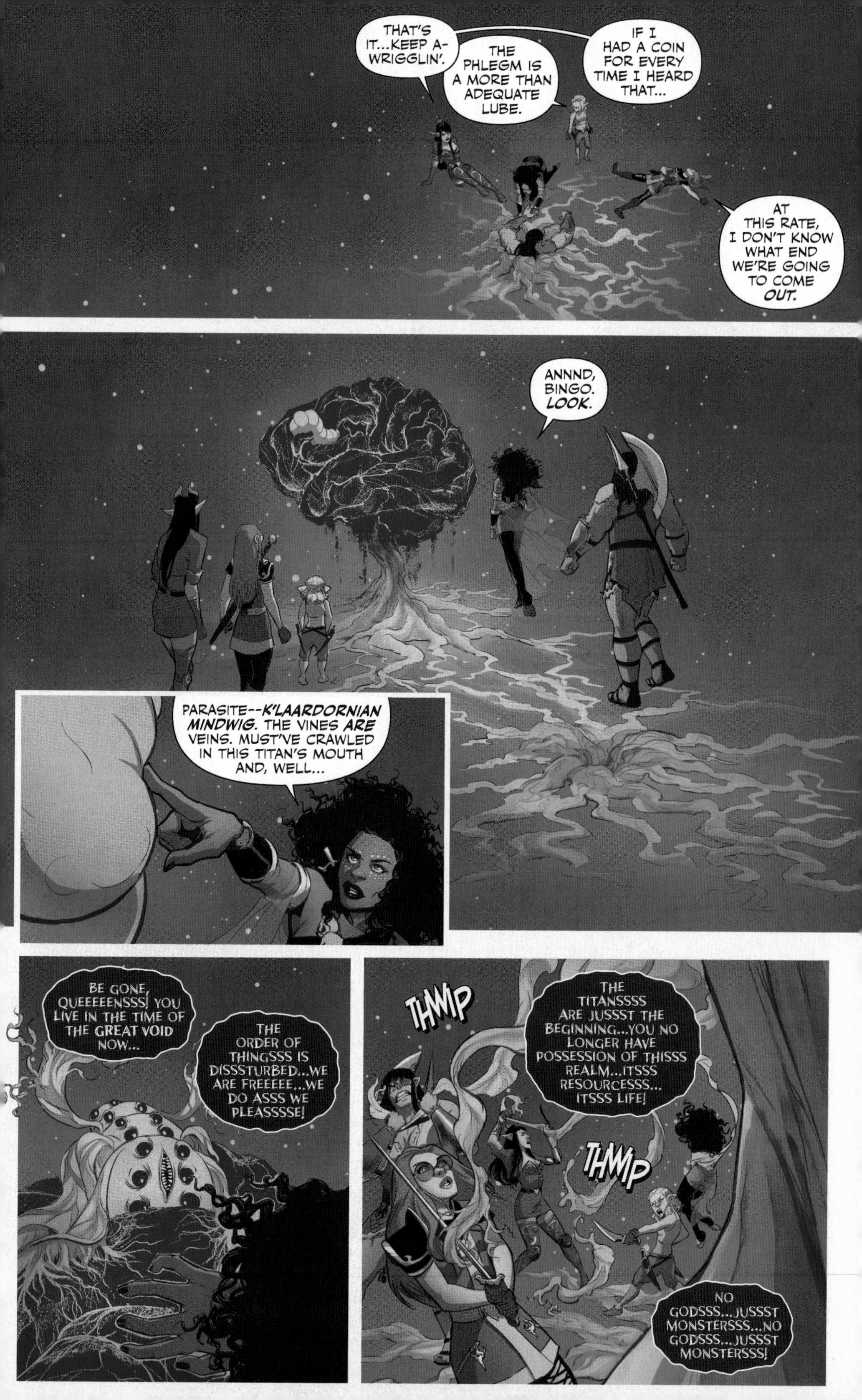
THAT'S IT...KEEP A-WRIGGLIN'.
THE PHLEGM IS A MORE THAN ADEQUATE LUBE.
IF I HAD A COIN FOR EVERY TIME I HEARD THAT...
AT THIS RATE, I DON'T KNOW WHAT END WE'RE GOING TO COME OUT.
ANNND, BINGO. LOOK.
PARASITE--K'LAARDORNIAN MINDWIG. THE VINES ARE VEINS. MUST'VE CRAWLED IN THIS TITAN'S MOUTH AND, WELL...
BE GONE, QUEEEEENSSS! YOU LIVE IN THE TIME OF THE GREAT VOID NOW...
THE ORDER OF THINGSSS IS DISSSTURBED...WE ARE FREEEEE...WE DO ASSS WE PLEASSSSE!
THMP
THE TITANSSSS ARE JUSSST THE BEGINNING...YOU NO LONGER HAVE POSSESSION OF THISSS REALM...ITSSS RESOURCESSS... ITSSS LIFE!
THMP
NO GODSSS...JUSSST MONSTERSSS...NO GODSSS...JUSSST MONSTERSSS!

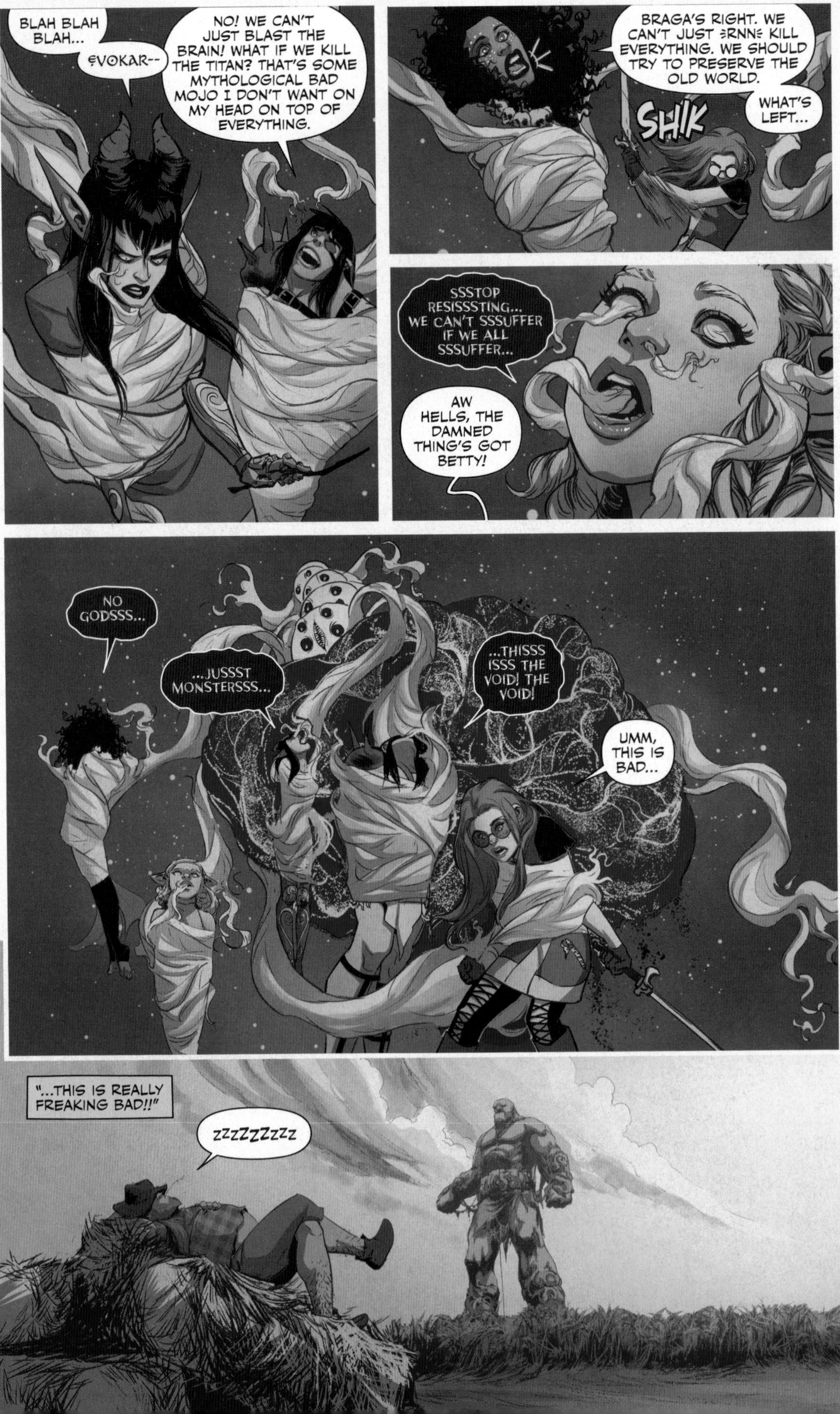
BLAH BLAH BLAH...
ƐVOKAR--
NO! WE CAN'T JUST BLAST THE BRAIN! WHAT IF WE KILL THE TITAN? THAT'S SOME MYTHOLOGICAL BAD MOJO I DON'T WANT ON MY HEAD ON TOP OF EVERYTHING.
BRAGA'S RIGHT. WE CAN'T JUST ƐRNNƐ KILL EVERYTHING. WE SHOULD TRY TO PRESERVE THE OLD WORLD.
WHAT'S LEFT...
SHIK
SSSTOP RESISSSTING... WE CAN'T SSSUFFER IF WE ALL SSSUFFER...
AW HELLS, THE DAMNED THING'S GOT BETTY!
NO GODSSS...
...JUSSST MONSTERSSS...
...THISSS ISSS THE VOID! THE VOID!
UMM, THIS IS BAD...
"...THIS IS REALLY FREAKING BAD!!"
ZZZZZZZZZ

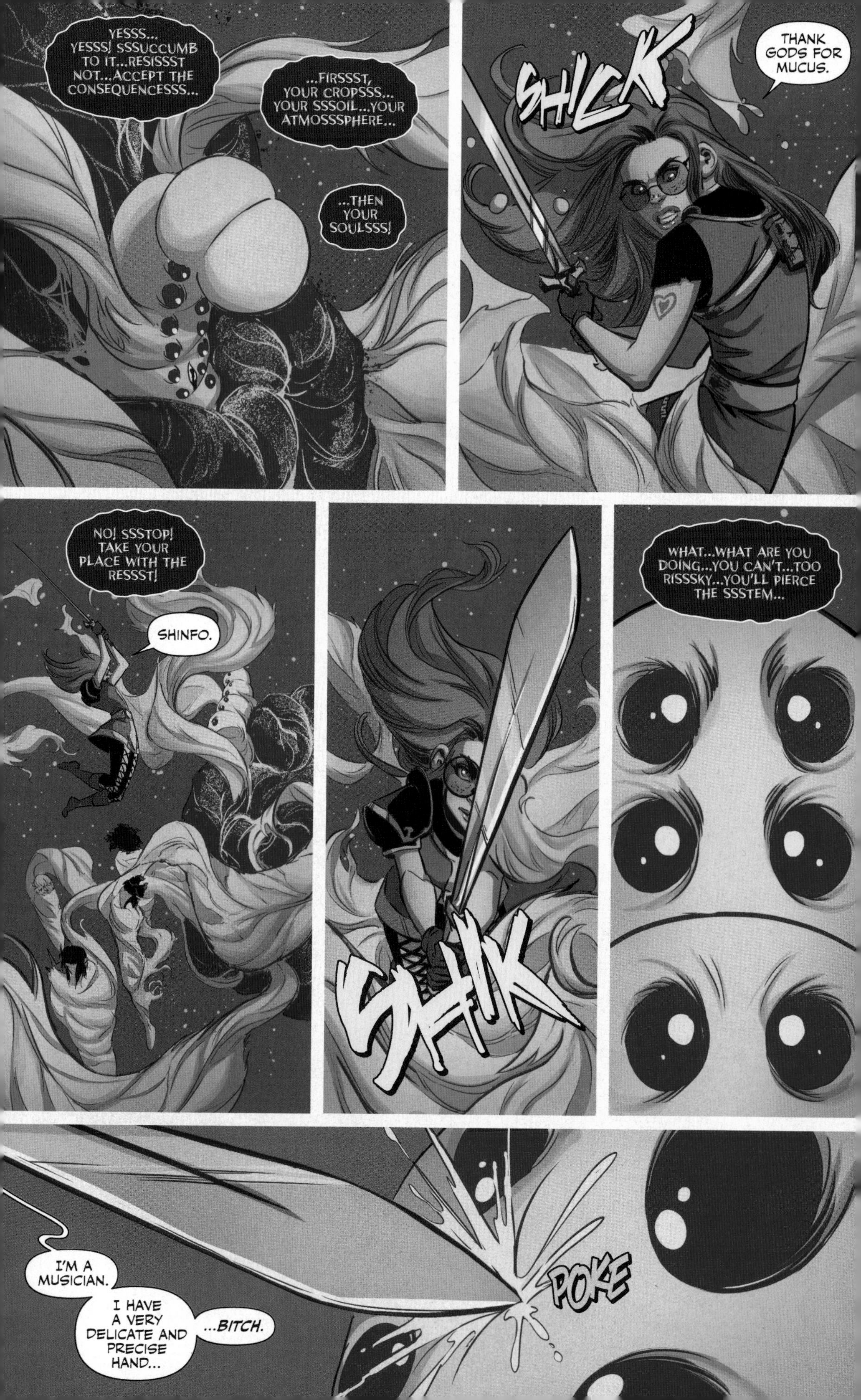

YESSS... YESSS! SSSUCCUMB TO IT...RESISSST NOT...ACCEPT THE CONSEQUENCESSS...
...FIRSSST, YOUR CROPSSS... YOUR SSSOIL...YOUR ATMOSSSPHERE...
...THEN YOUR SOULSSS!
SHICK
THANK GODS FOR MUCUS.
NO! SSSTOP! TAKE YOUR PLACE WITH THE RESSST!
SHINFO.
SHIK
WHAT...WHAT ARE YOU DOING...YOU CAN'T...TOO RISSSKY...YOU'LL PIERCE THE SSSTEM...
POKE
I'M A MUSICIAN.
I HAVE A VERY DELICATE AND PRECISE HAND...
...*BITCH*.

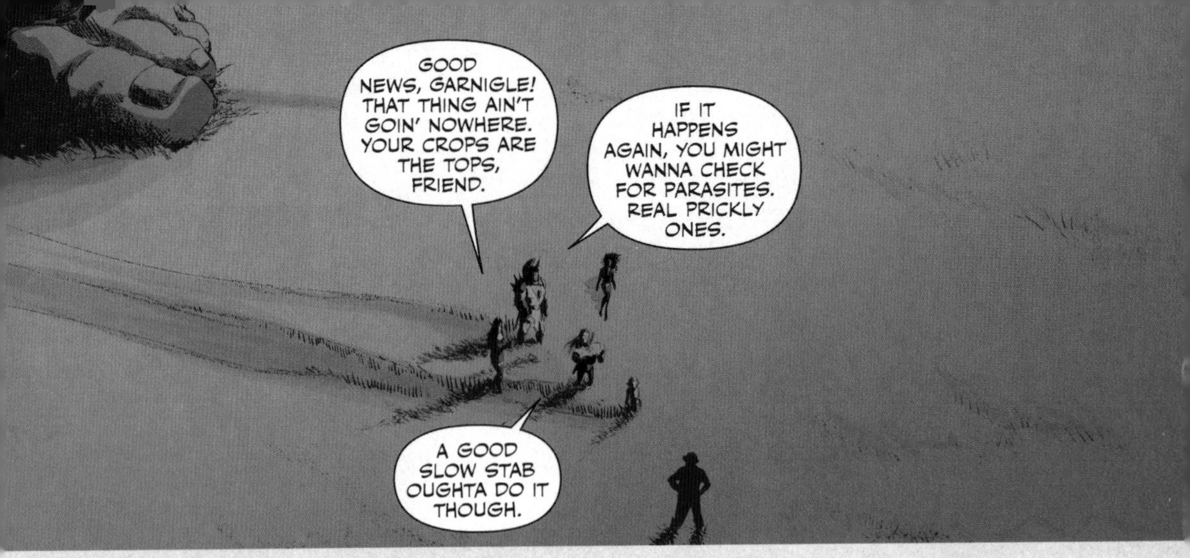
GOOD NEWS, GARNIGLE! THAT THING AIN'T GOIN' NOWHERE. YOUR CROPS ARE THE TOPS, FRIEND.
IF IT HAPPENS AGAIN, YOU MIGHT WANNA CHECK FOR PARASITES. REAL PRICKLY ONES.
A GOOD SLOW STAB OUGHTA DO IT THOUGH.

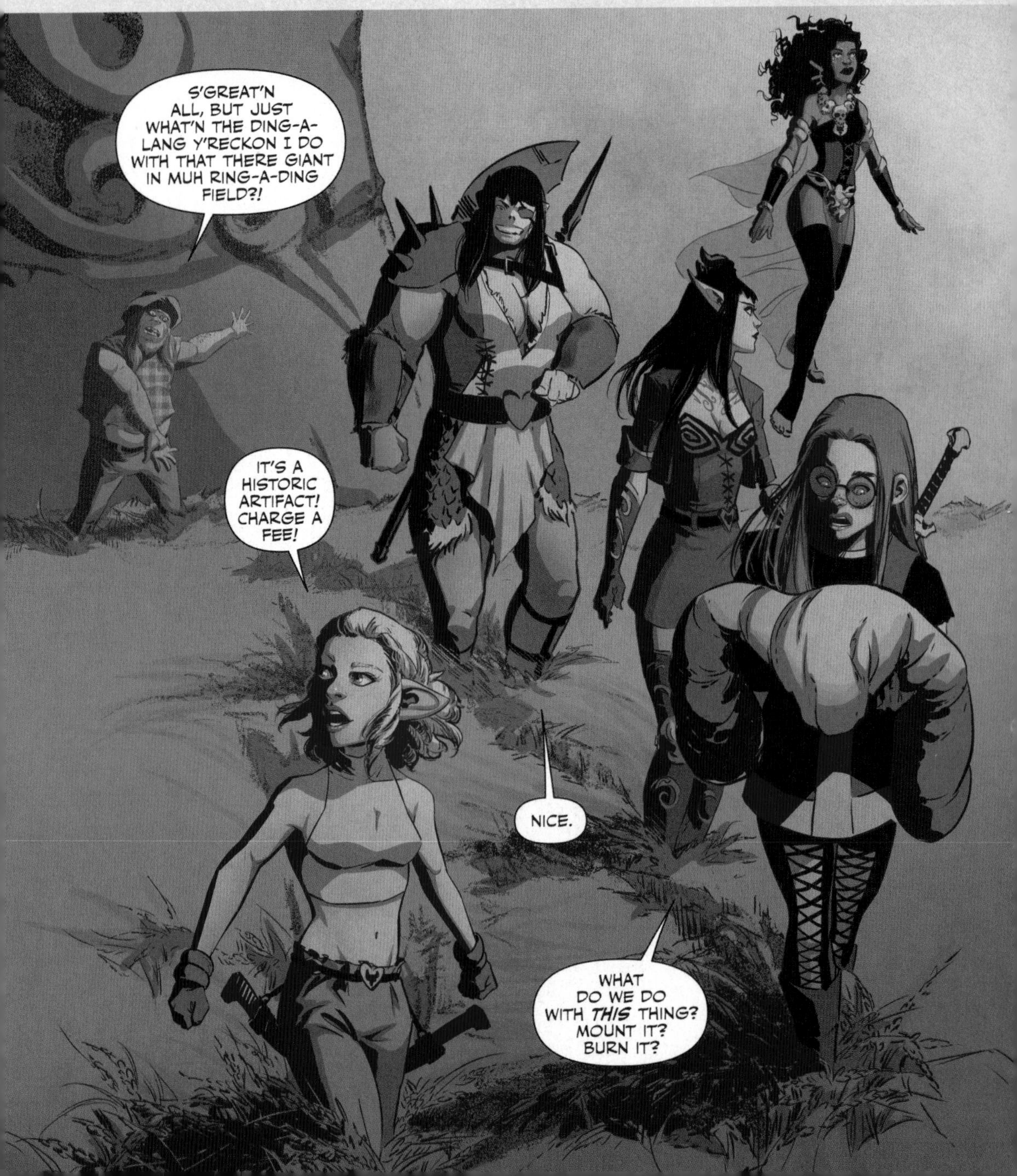
S'GREAT'N ALL, BUT JUST WHAT'N THE DING-A-LANG Y'RECKON I DO WITH THAT THERE GIANT IN MUH RING-A-DING FIELD?!
IT'S A HISTORIC ARTIFACT! CHARGE A FEE!
NICE.
WHAT DO WE DO WITH *THIS* THING? MOUNT IT? BURN IT?

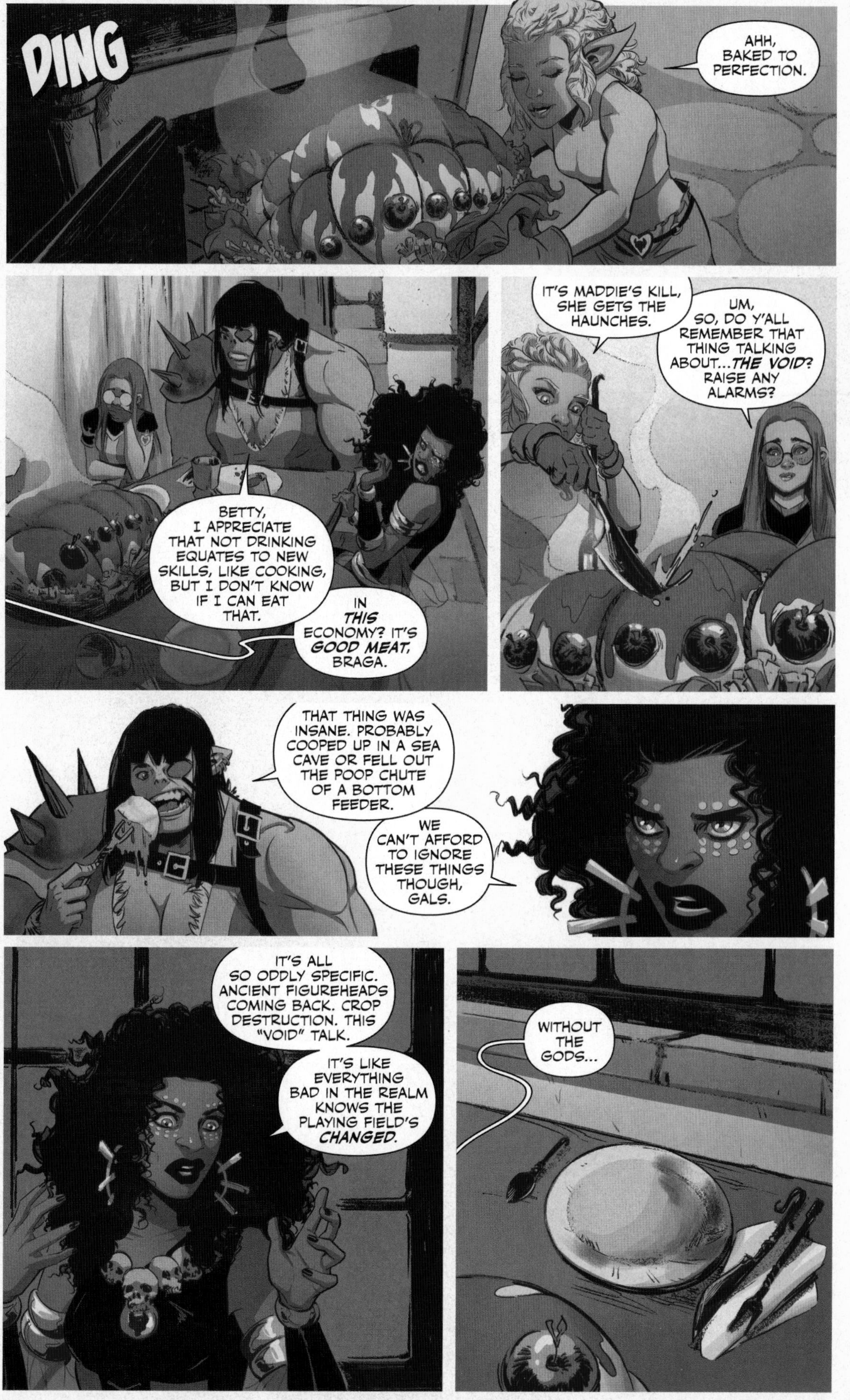
DING
AHH, BAKED TO PERFECTION.
BETTY, I APPRECIATE THAT NOT DRINKING EQUATES TO NEW SKILLS, LIKE COOKING, BUT I DON'T KNOW IF I CAN EAT THAT.
IN THIS ECONOMY? IT'S GOOD MEAT, BRAGA.
IT'S MADDIE'S KILL, SHE GETS THE HAUNCHES.
UM, SO, DO Y'ALL REMEMBER THAT THING TALKING ABOUT...THE VOID? RAISE ANY ALARMS?
THAT THING WAS INSANE. PROBABLY COOPED UP IN A SEA CAVE OR FELL OUT THE POOP CHUTE OF A BOTTOM FEEDER.
WE CAN'T AFFORD TO IGNORE THESE THINGS THOUGH, GALS.
IT'S ALL SO ODDLY SPECIFIC. ANCIENT FIGUREHEADS COMING BACK. CROP DESTRUCTION. THIS "VOID" TALK.
IT'S LIKE EVERYTHING BAD IN THE REALM KNOWS THE PLAYING FIELD'S CHANGED.
WITHOUT THE GODS...

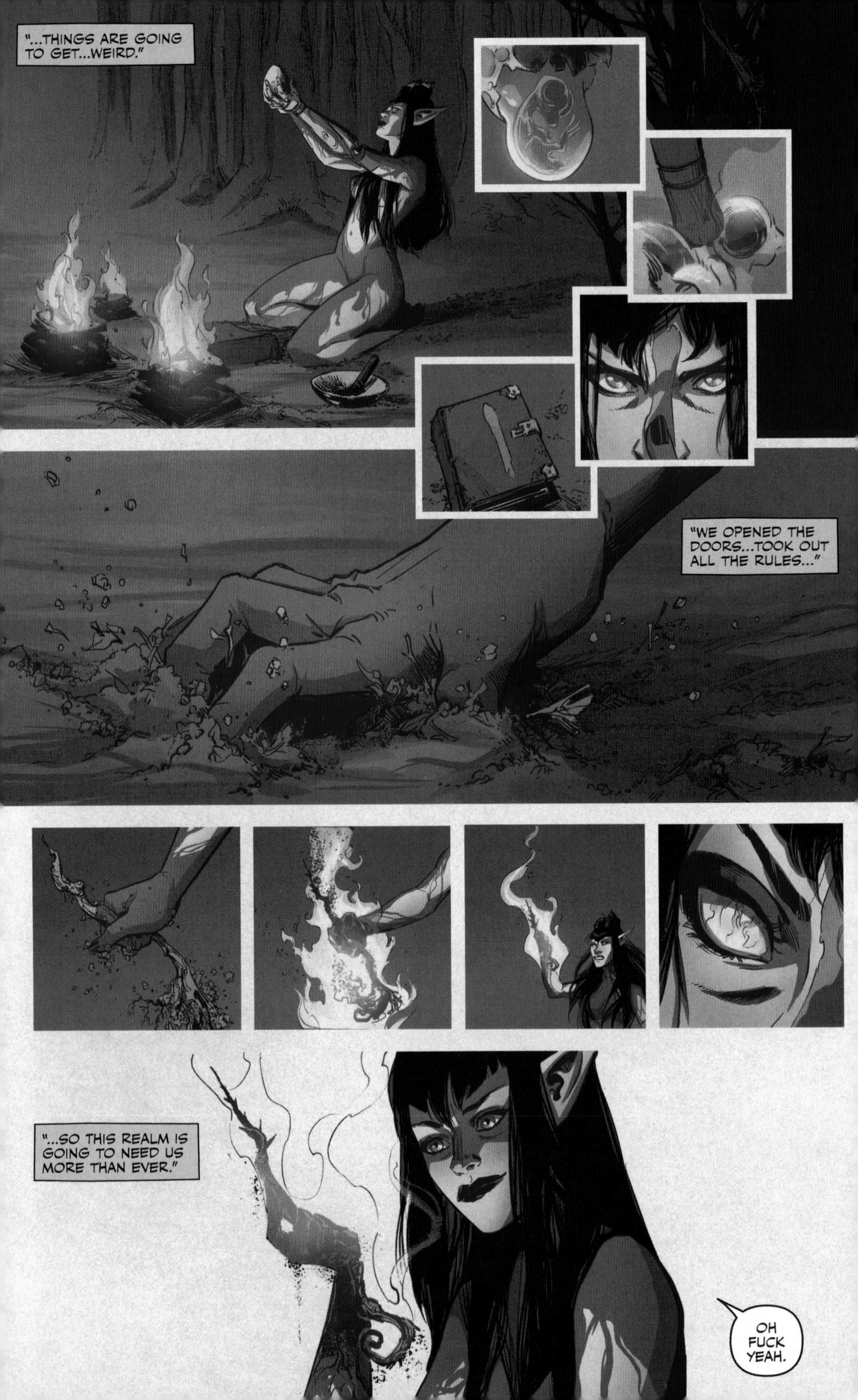
"...THINGS ARE GOING TO GET...WEIRD."
"WE OPENED THE DOORS...TOOK OUT ALL THE RULES..."
"...SO THIS REALM IS GOING TO NEED US MORE THAN EVER."
OH FUCK YEAH.

CHAPTER TWENTY-TWO

ISSUE #22 COVER

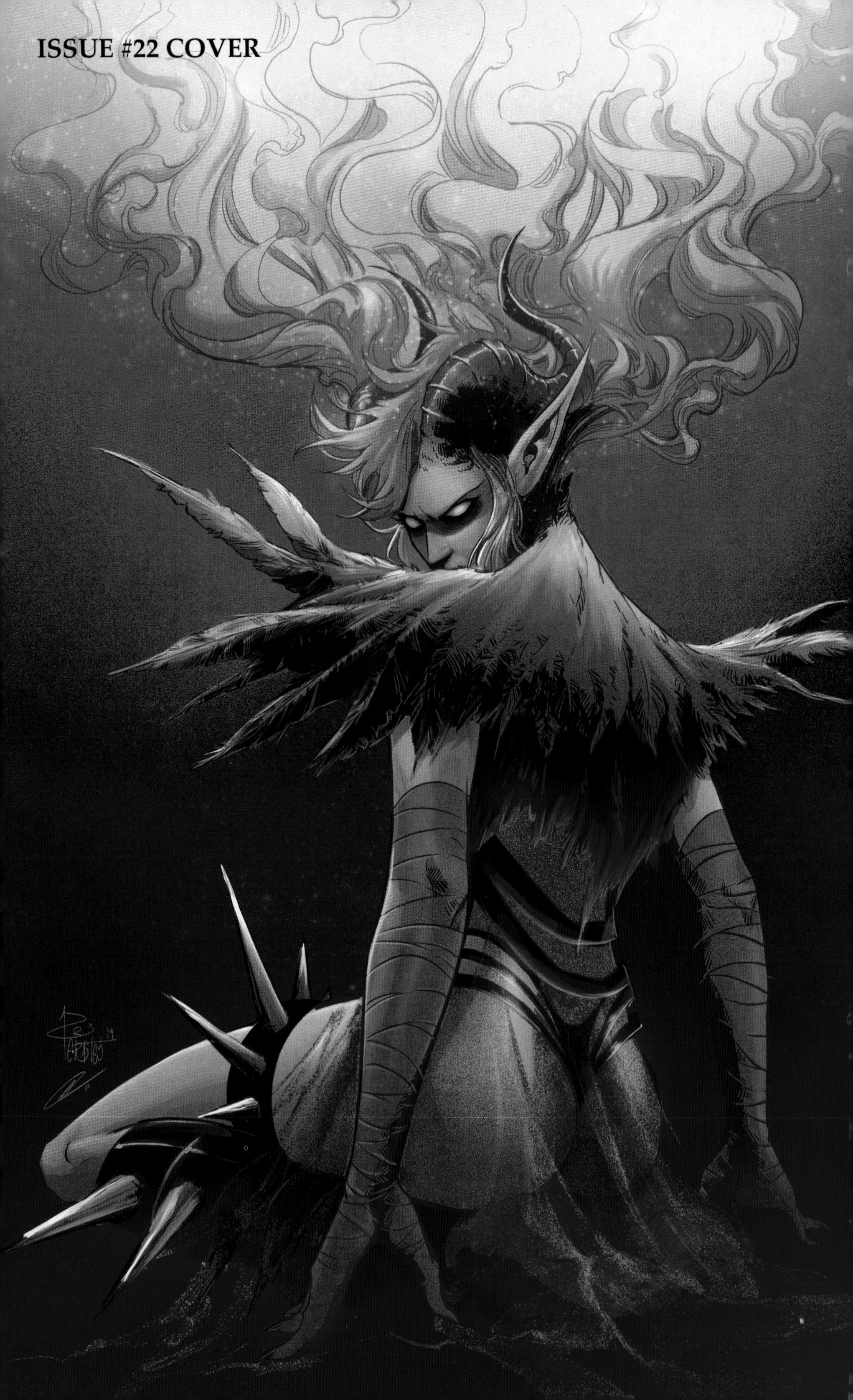

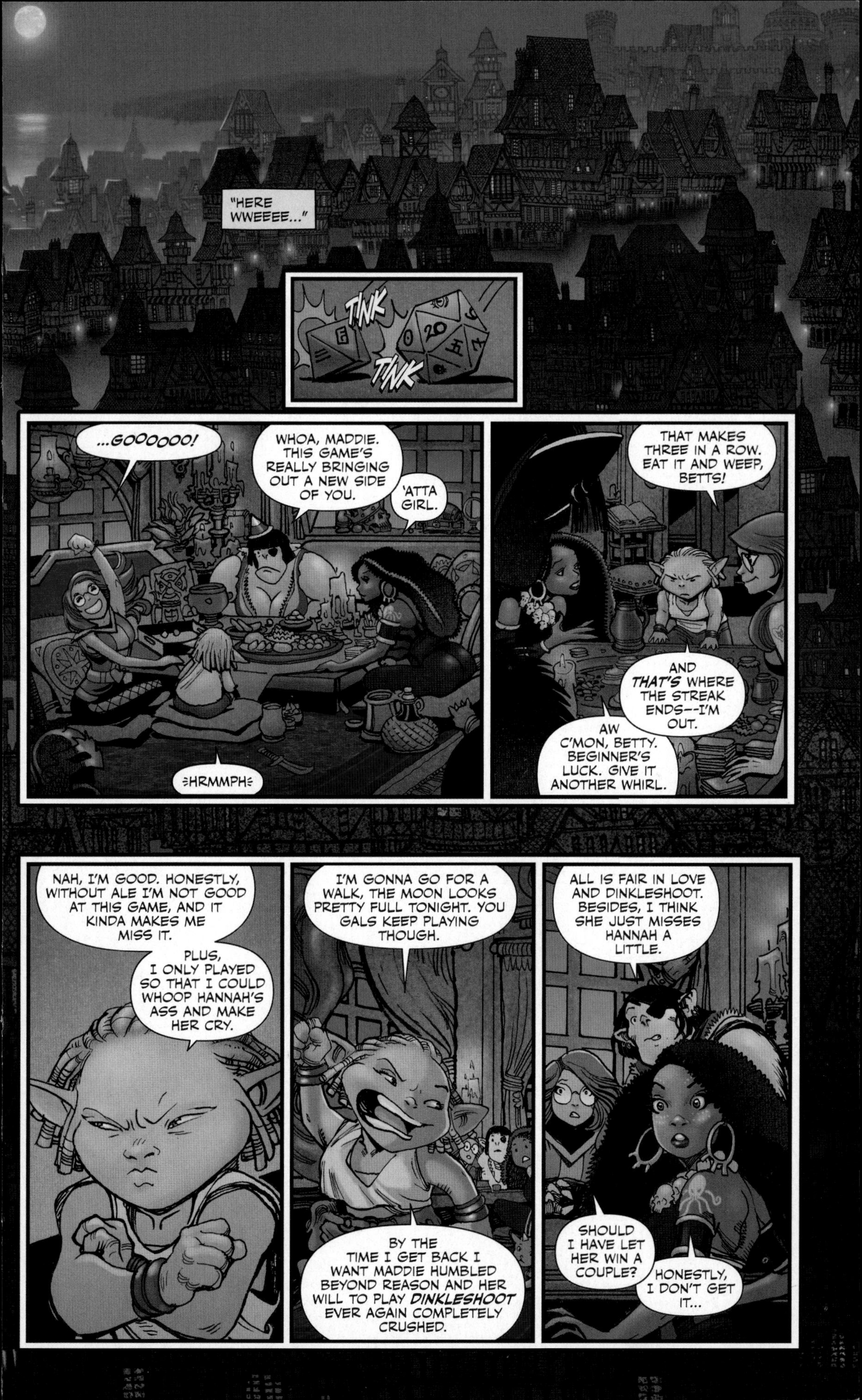

"HERE WWEEEE..."
TINK
TINK
...GOOOOOO!
WHOA, MADDIE. THIS GAME'S REALLY BRINGING OUT A NEW SIDE OF YOU.
'ATTA GIRL.
HRMMPH
THAT MAKES THREE IN A ROW. EAT IT AND WEEP, BETTS!
AND THAT'S WHERE THE STREAK ENDS--I'M OUT.
AW C'MON, BETTY. BEGINNER'S LUCK. GIVE IT ANOTHER WHIRL.
NAH, I'M GOOD. HONESTLY, WITHOUT ALE I'M NOT GOOD AT THIS GAME, AND IT KINDA MAKES ME MISS IT.
PLUS, I ONLY PLAYED SO THAT I COULD WHOOP HANNAH'S ASS AND MAKE HER CRY.
I'M GONNA GO FOR A WALK, THE MOON LOOKS PRETTY FULL TONIGHT. YOU GALS KEEP PLAYING THOUGH.
BY THE TIME I GET BACK I WANT MADDIE HUMBLED BEYOND REASON AND HER WILL TO PLAY DINKLESHOOT EVER AGAIN COMPLETELY CRUSHED.
ALL IS FAIR IN LOVE AND DINKLESHOOT. BESIDES, I THINK SHE JUST MISSES HANNAH A LITTLE.
SHOULD I HAVE LET HER WIN A COUPLE?
HONESTLY, I DON'T GET IT...

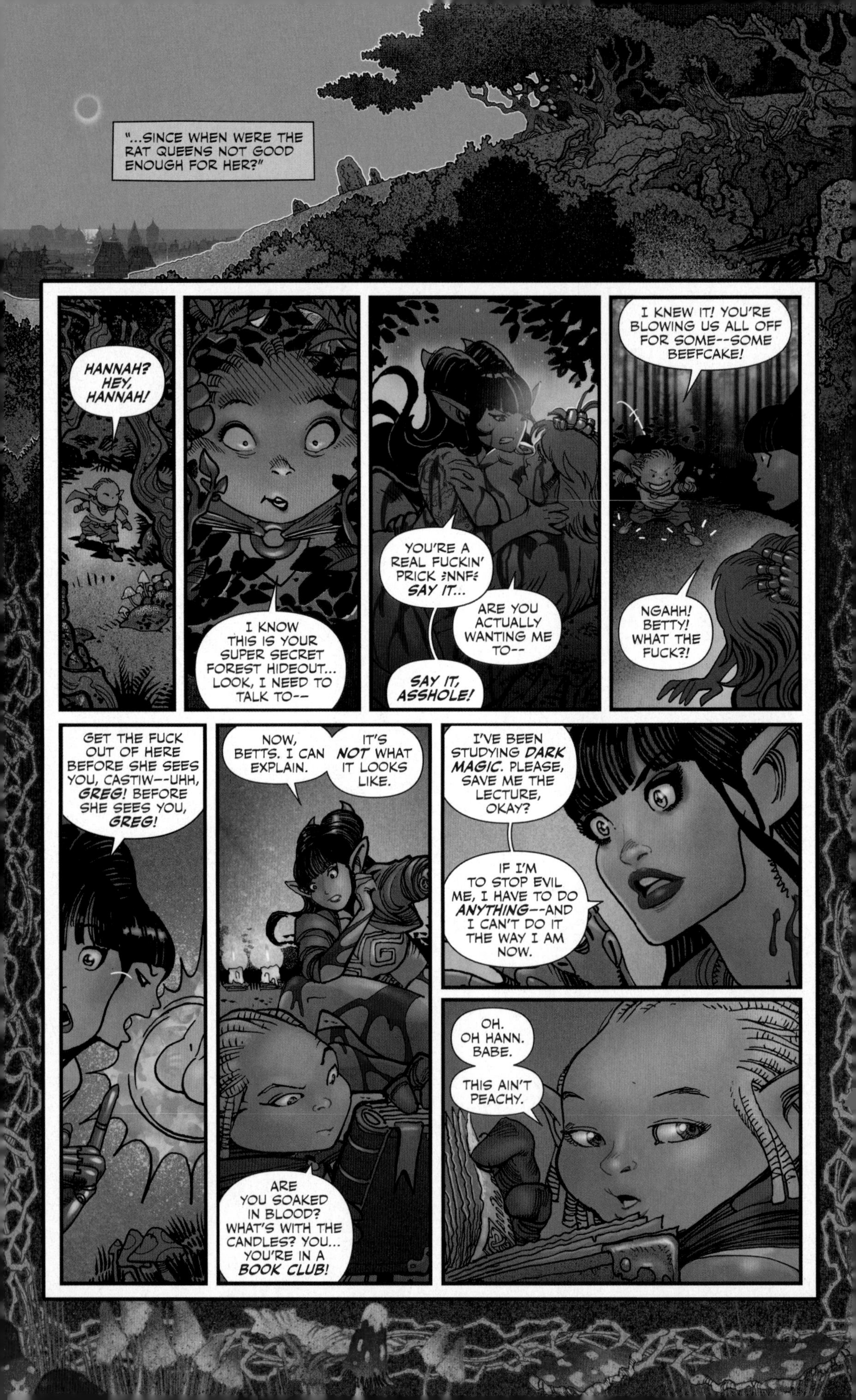
"...SINCE WHEN WERE THE RAT QUEENS NOT GOOD ENOUGH FOR HER?"
HANNAH? HEY, HANNAH!
I KNOW THIS IS YOUR SUPER SECRET FOREST HIDEOUT... LOOK, I NEED TO TALK TO--
YOU'RE A REAL FUCKIN' PRICK *NNF* SAY IT...
ARE YOU ACTUALLY WANTING ME TO--
SAY IT, ASSHOLE!
I KNEW IT! YOU'RE BLOWING US ALL OFF FOR SOME--SOME BEEFCAKE!
NGAHH! BETTY! WHAT THE FUCK?!
GET THE FUCK OUT OF HERE BEFORE SHE SEES YOU, CASTIW--UHH, GREG! BEFORE SHE SEES YOU, GREG!
NOW, BETTS. I CAN EXPLAIN.
IT'S NOT WHAT IT LOOKS LIKE.
ARE YOU SOAKED IN BLOOD? WHAT'S WITH THE CANDLES? YOU... YOU'RE IN A BOOK CLUB!
I'VE BEEN STUDYING DARK MAGIC. PLEASE, SAVE ME THE LECTURE, OKAY?
IF I'M TO STOP EVIL ME, I HAVE TO DO ANYTHING--AND I CAN'T DO IT THE WAY I AM NOW.
OH. OH HANN. BABE.
THIS AIN'T PEACHY.

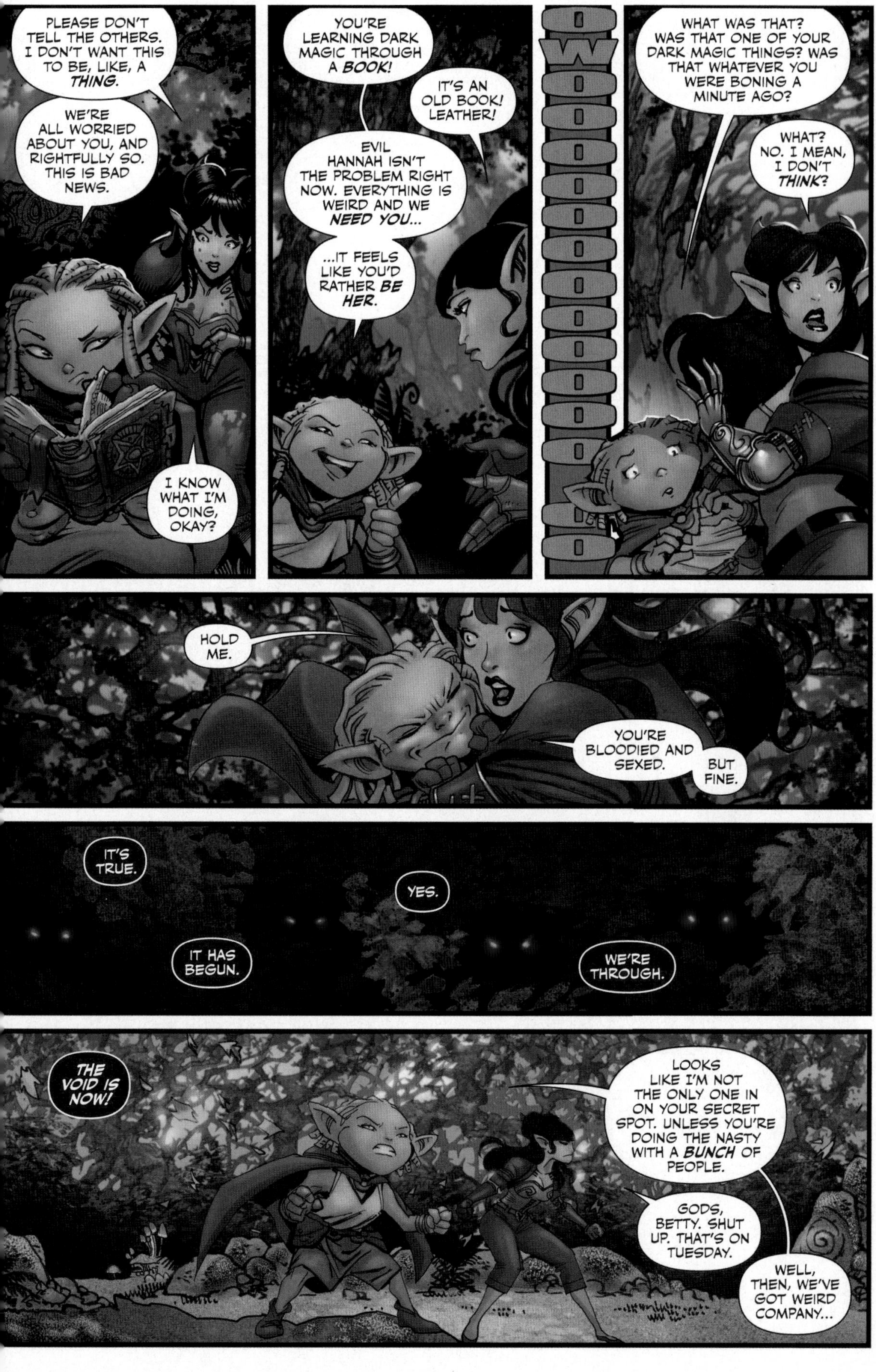
PLEASE DON'T TELL THE OTHERS. I DON'T WANT THIS TO BE, LIKE, A *THING*.
WE'RE ALL WORRIED ABOUT YOU, AND RIGHTFULLY SO. THIS IS BAD NEWS.
I KNOW WHAT I'M DOING, OKAY?
YOU'RE LEARNING DARK MAGIC THROUGH A *BOOK!*
IT'S AN OLD BOOK! LEATHER!
EVIL HANNAH ISN'T THE PROBLEM RIGHT NOW. EVERYTHING IS WEIRD AND WE *NEED YOU*...
...IT FEELS LIKE YOU'D RATHER *BE HER*.
OWOOOOOOOOOOOOOOOO
WHAT WAS THAT? WAS THAT ONE OF YOUR DARK MAGIC THINGS? WAS THAT WHATEVER YOU WERE BONING A MINUTE AGO?
WHAT? NO. I MEAN, I DON'T *THINK*?
HOLD ME.
YOU'RE BLOODIED AND SEXED.
BUT FINE.
IT'S TRUE.
IT HAS BEGUN.
YES.
WE'RE THROUGH.
THE VOID IS NOW!
LOOKS LIKE I'M NOT THE ONLY ONE IN ON YOUR SECRET SPOT. UNLESS YOU'RE DOING THE NASTY WITH A *BUNCH* OF PEOPLE.
GODS, BETTY. SHUT UP. THAT'S ON TUESDAY.
WELL, THEN, WE'VE GOT WEIRD COMPANY...

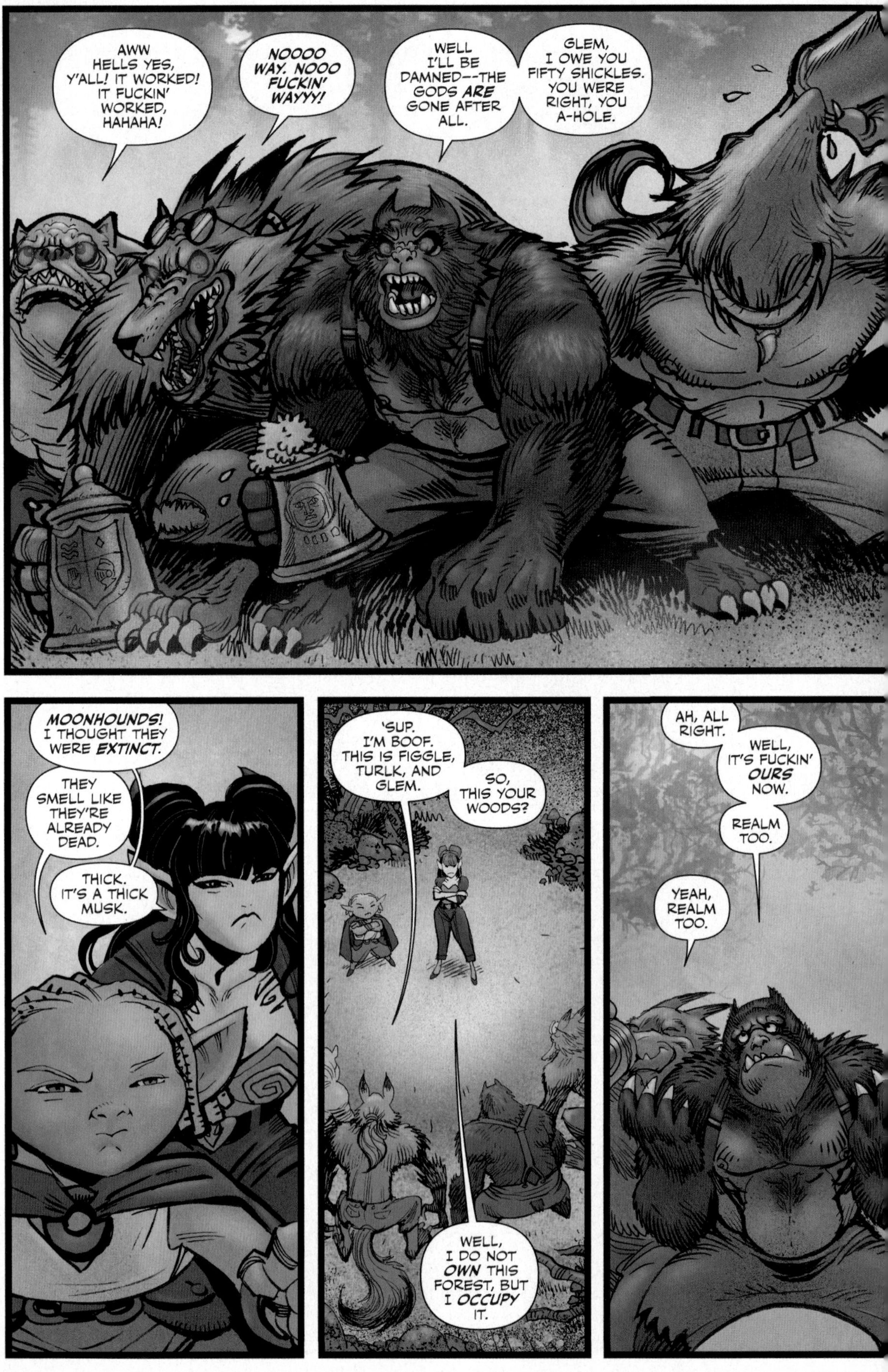

AWW HELLS YES, Y'ALL! IT WORKED! IT FUCKIN' WORKED, HAHAHA!
NOOOO WAY. NOOO FUCKIN' WAYYY!
WELL I'LL BE DAMNED--THE GODS ARE GONE AFTER ALL.
GLEM, I OWE YOU FIFTY SHICKLES. YOU WERE RIGHT, YOU A-HOLE.
MOONHOUNDS! I THOUGHT THEY WERE EXTINCT.
THEY SMELL LIKE THEY'RE ALREADY DEAD.
THICK. IT'S A THICK MUSK.
'SUP. I'M BOOF. THIS IS FIGGLE, TURLK, AND GLEM.
SO, THIS YOUR WOODS?
WELL, I DO NOT OWN THIS FOREST, BUT I OCCUPY IT.
AH, ALL RIGHT.
WELL, IT'S FUCKIN' OURS NOW.
REALM TOO.
YEAH, REALM TOO.

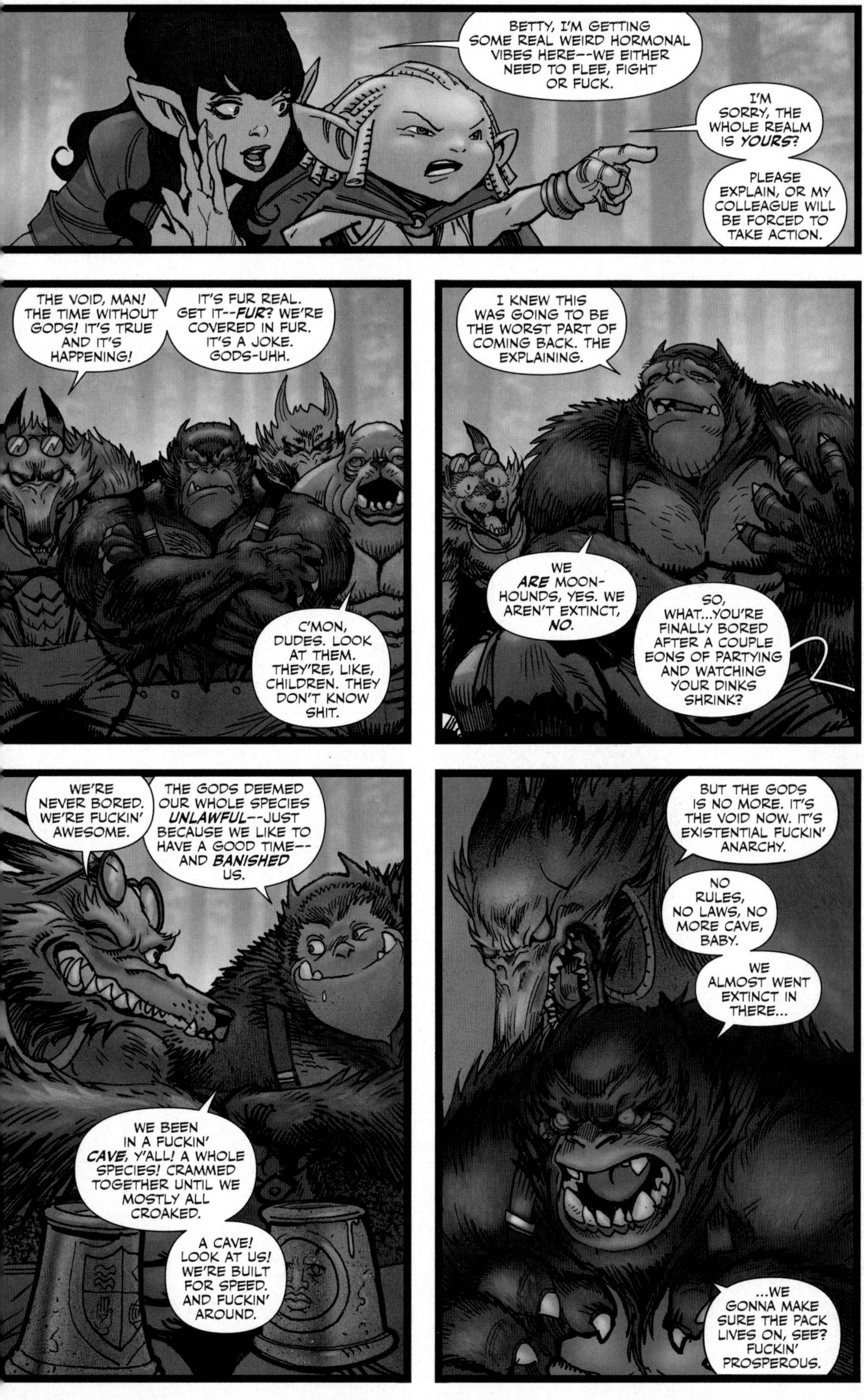
BETTY, I'M GETTING SOME REAL WEIRD HORMONAL VIBES HERE--WE EITHER NEED TO FLEE, FIGHT OR FUCK.
I'M SORRY, THE WHOLE REALM IS *YOURS?*
PLEASE EXPLAIN, OR MY COLLEAGUE WILL BE FORCED TO TAKE ACTION.
THE VOID, MAN! THE TIME WITHOUT GODS! IT'S TRUE AND IT'S HAPPENING!
IT'S FUR REAL. GET IT--*FUR?* WE'RE COVERED IN FUR. IT'S A JOKE. GODS-UHH.
C'MON, DUDES. LOOK AT THEM. THEY'RE, LIKE, CHILDREN. THEY DON'T KNOW SHIT.
I KNEW THIS WAS GOING TO BE THE WORST PART OF COMING BACK. THE EXPLAINING.
WE *ARE* MOON-HOUNDS, YES. WE AREN'T EXTINCT, *NO.*
SO, WHAT...YOU'RE FINALLY BORED AFTER A COUPLE EONS OF PARTYING AND WATCHING YOUR DINKS SHRINK?
WE'RE NEVER BORED. WE'RE FUCKIN' AWESOME.
THE GODS DEEMED OUR WHOLE SPECIES *UNLAWFUL*--JUST BECAUSE WE LIKE TO HAVE A GOOD TIME--AND *BANISHED* US.
WE BEEN IN A FUCKIN' *CAVE,* Y'ALL! A WHOLE SPECIES! CRAMMED TOGETHER UNTIL WE MOSTLY ALL CROAKED.
A CAVE! LOOK AT US! WE'RE BUILT FOR SPEED. AND FUCKIN' AROUND.
BUT THE GODS IS NO MORE. IT'S THE VOID NOW. IT'S EXISTENTIAL FUCKIN' ANARCHY.
NO RULES, NO LAWS, NO MORE CAVE, BABY.
WE ALMOST WENT EXTINCT IN THERE...
...WE GONNA MAKE SURE THE PACK LIVES ON, SEE? FUCKIN' PROSPEROUS.

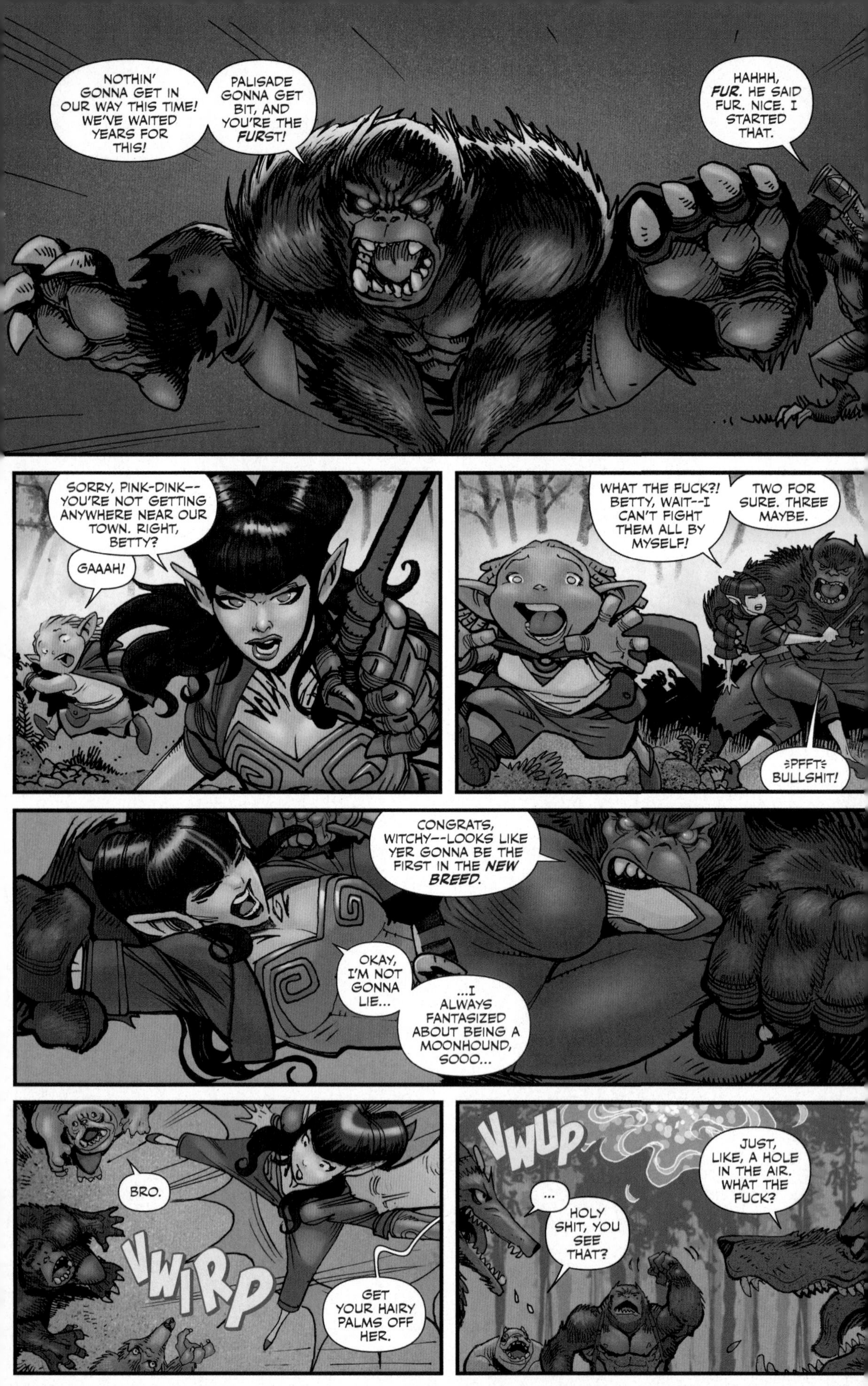
NOTHIN' GONNA GET IN OUR WAY THIS TIME! WE'VE WAITED YEARS FOR THIS!
PALISADE GONNA GET BIT, AND YOU'RE THE FURST!
HAHHH, FUR. HE SAID FUR. NICE. I STARTED THAT.
SORRY, PINK-DINK--YOU'RE NOT GETTING ANYWHERE NEAR OUR TOWN. RIGHT, BETTY?
GAAAH!
WHAT THE FUCK?! BETTY, WAIT--I CAN'T FIGHT THEM ALL BY MYSELF!
TWO FOR SURE. THREE MAYBE.
=PFFT= BULLSHIT!
CONGRATS, WITCHY--LOOKS LIKE YER GONNA BE THE FIRST IN THE NEW BREED.
OKAY, I'M NOT GONNA LIE...
...I ALWAYS FANTASIZED ABOUT BEING A MOONHOUND, SOOO...
BRO.
VWIRP
GET YOUR HAIRY PALMS OFF HER.
VWUP
...
HOLY SHIT, YOU SEE THAT?
JUST, LIKE, A HOLE IN THE AIR. WHAT THE FUCK?

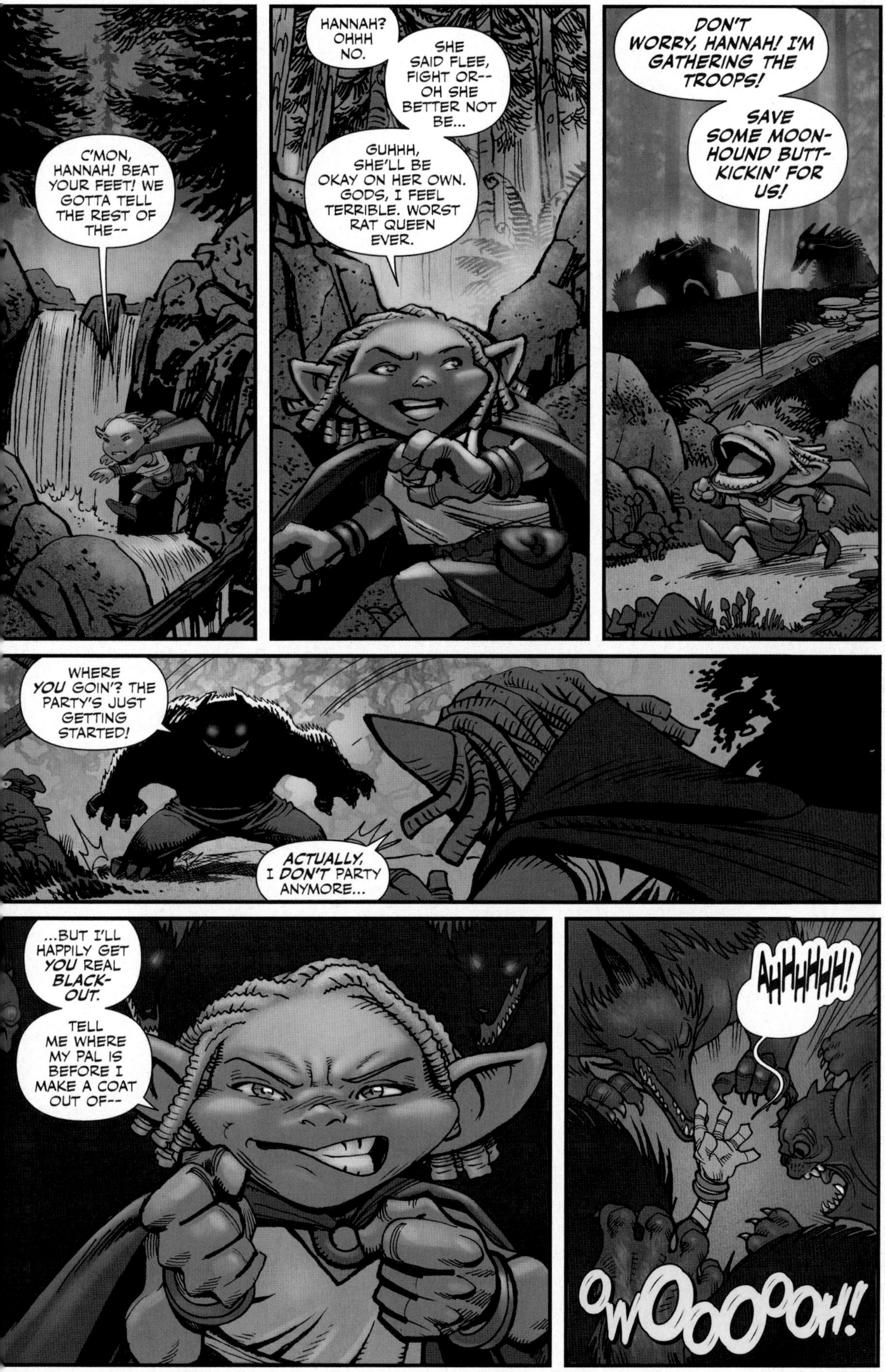
C'MON, HANNAH! BEAT YOUR FEET! WE GOTTA TELL THE REST OF THE--
HANNAH? OHHH NO.
SHE SAID FLEE, FIGHT OR-- OH SHE BETTER NOT BE...
GUHHH, SHE'LL BE OKAY ON HER OWN. GODS, I FEEL TERRIBLE. WORST RAT QUEEN EVER.
DON'T WORRY, HANNAH! I'M GATHERING THE TROOPS!
SAVE SOME MOON-HOUND BUTT-KICKIN' FOR US!
WHERE YOU GOIN'? THE PARTY'S JUST GETTING STARTED!
ACTUALLY, I DON'T PARTY ANYMORE...
...BUT I'LL HAPPILY GET YOU REAL BLACK-OUT.
TELL ME WHERE MY PAL IS BEFORE I MAKE A COAT OUT OF--
AHHHHHH!
OWOOOOOOH!

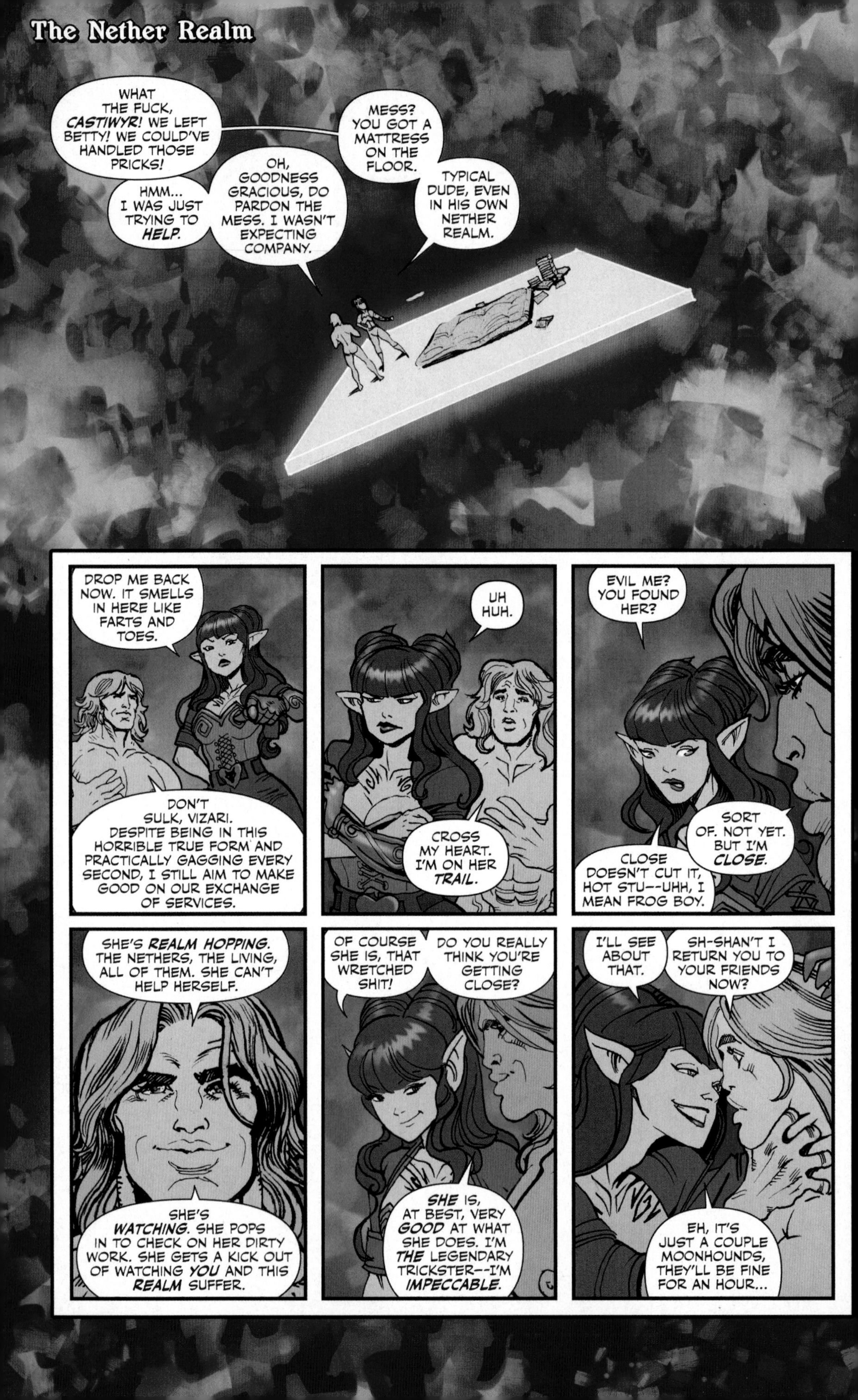
The Nether Realm
WHAT THE FUCK, CASTIWYR! WE LEFT BETTY! WE COULD'VE HANDLED THOSE PRICKS!
HMM... I WAS JUST TRYING TO HELP.
OH, GOODNESS GRACIOUS, DO PARDON THE MESS. I WASN'T EXPECTING COMPANY.
MESS? YOU GOT A MATTRESS ON THE FLOOR.
TYPICAL DUDE, EVEN IN HIS OWN NETHER REALM.
DROP ME BACK NOW. IT SMELLS IN HERE LIKE FARTS AND TOES.
DON'T SULK, VIZARI. DESPITE BEING IN THIS HORRIBLE TRUE FORM AND PRACTICALLY GAGGING EVERY SECOND, I STILL AIM TO MAKE GOOD ON OUR EXCHANGE OF SERVICES.
UH HUH.
CROSS MY HEART. I'M ON HER TRAIL.
EVIL ME? YOU FOUND HER?
SORT OF. NOT YET. BUT I'M CLOSE.
CLOSE DOESN'T CUT IT, HOT STU--UHH, I MEAN FROG BOY.
SHE'S REALM HOPPING. THE NETHERS, THE LIVING, ALL OF THEM. SHE CAN'T HELP HERSELF.
SHE'S WATCHING. SHE POPS IN TO CHECK ON HER DIRTY WORK. SHE GETS A KICK OUT OF WATCHING YOU AND THIS REALM SUFFER.
OF COURSE SHE IS, THAT WRETCHED SHIT!
DO YOU REALLY THINK YOU'RE GETTING CLOSE?
SHE IS, AT BEST, VERY GOOD AT WHAT SHE DOES. I'M THE LEGENDARY TRICKSTER--I'M IMPECCABLE.
I'LL SEE ABOUT THAT.
SH-SHAN'T I RETURN YOU TO YOUR FRIENDS NOW?
EH, IT'S JUST A COUPLE MOONHOUNDS, THEY'LL BE FINE FOR AN HOUR...

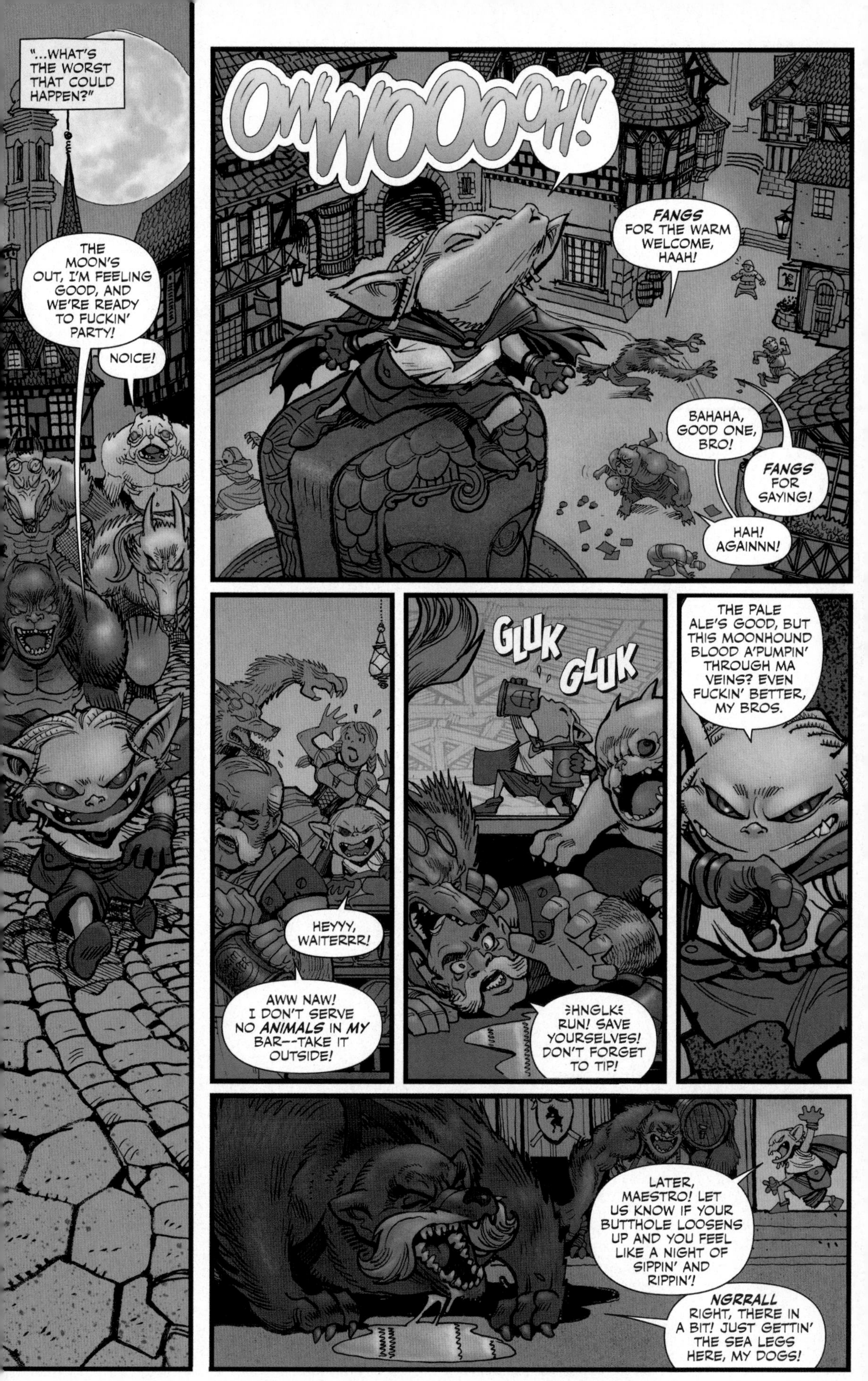
"...WHAT'S THE WORST THAT COULD HAPPEN?"
THE MOON'S OUT, I'M FEELING GOOD, AND WE'RE READY TO FUCKIN' PARTY!
NOICE!
OWWOOOOOH!
FANGS FOR THE WARM WELCOME, HAAH!
BAHAHA, GOOD ONE, BRO!
FANGS FOR SAYING!
HAH! AGAINNN!
HEYYY, WAITERRR!
AWW NAW! I DON'T SERVE NO ANIMALS IN MY BAR--TAKE IT OUTSIDE!
GLUK GLUK
HNGLK RUN! SAVE YOURSELVES! DON'T FORGET TO TIP!
THE PALE ALE'S GOOD, BUT THIS MOONHOUND BLOOD A'PUMPIN' THROUGH MA VEINS? EVEN FUCKIN' BETTER, MY BROS.
LATER, MAESTRO! LET US KNOW IF YOUR BUTTHOLE LOOSENS UP AND YOU FEEL LIKE A NIGHT OF SIPPIN' AND RIPPIN'!
NGRRALL RIGHT, THERE IN A BIT! JUST GETTIN' THE SEA LEGS HERE, MY DOGS!

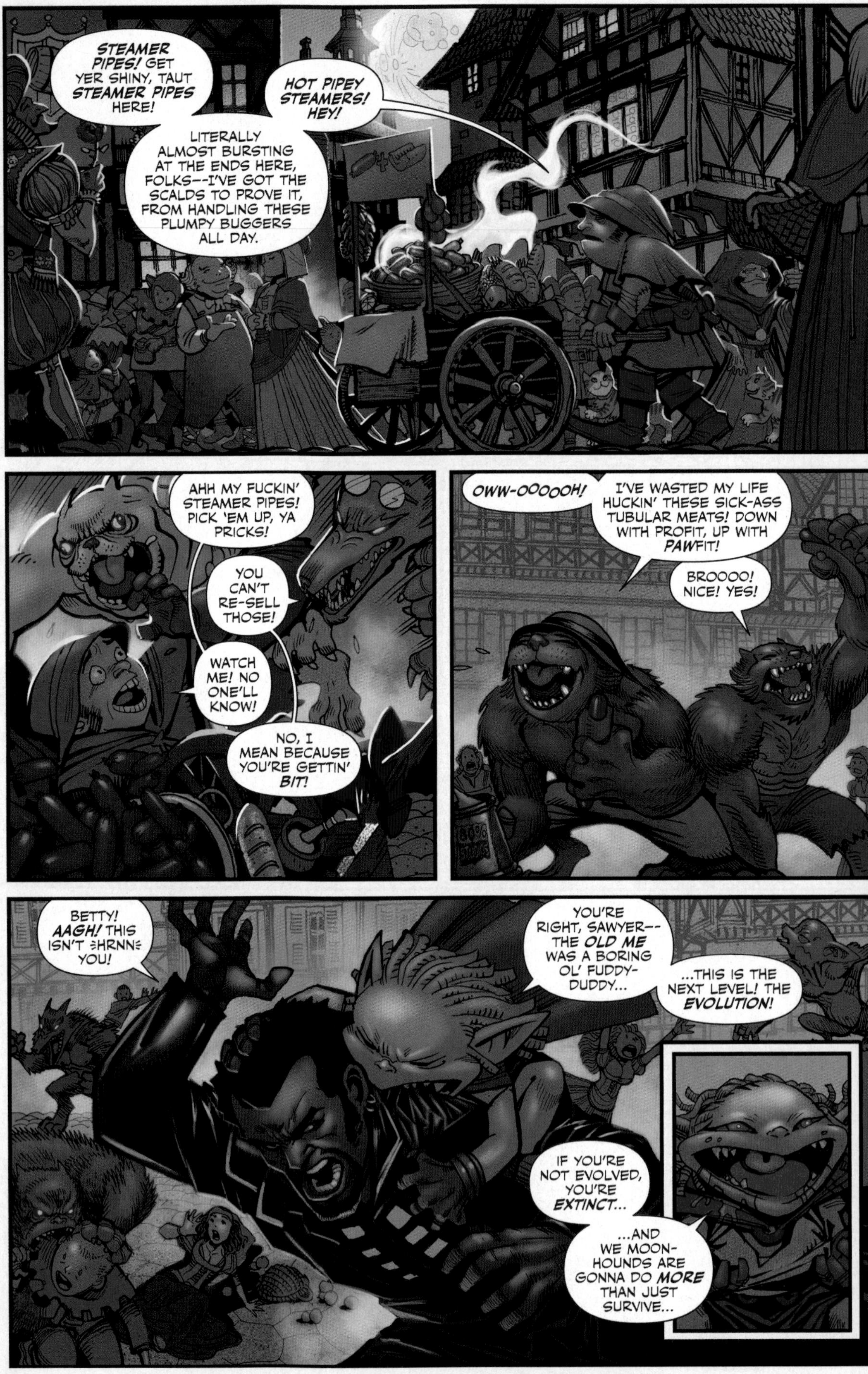
STEAMER PIPES! GET YER SHINY, TAUT STEAMER PIPES HERE!
HOT PIPEY STEAMERS! HEY!
LITERALLY ALMOST BURSTING AT THE ENDS HERE, FOLKS--I'VE GOT THE SCALDS TO PROVE IT, FROM HANDLING THESE PLUMPY BUGGERS ALL DAY.
AHH MY FUCKIN' STEAMER PIPES! PICK 'EM UP, YA PRICKS!
YOU CAN'T RE-SELL THOSE!
WATCH ME! NO ONE'LL KNOW!
NO, I MEAN BECAUSE YOU'RE GETTIN' BIT!
OWW-OOOOOH!
I'VE WASTED MY LIFE HUCKIN' THESE SICK-ASS TUBULAR MEATS! DOWN WITH PROFIT, UP WITH PAWFIT!
BROOOO! NICE! YES!
BETTY! AAGH! THIS ISN'T =HRNN= YOU!
YOU'RE RIGHT, SAWYER--THE OLD ME WAS A BORING OL' FUDDY-DUDDY...
...THIS IS THE NEXT LEVEL! THE EVOLUTION!
IF YOU'RE NOT EVOLVED, YOU'RE EXTINCT...
...AND WE MOON-HOUNDS ARE GONNA DO MORE THAN JUST SURVIVE...

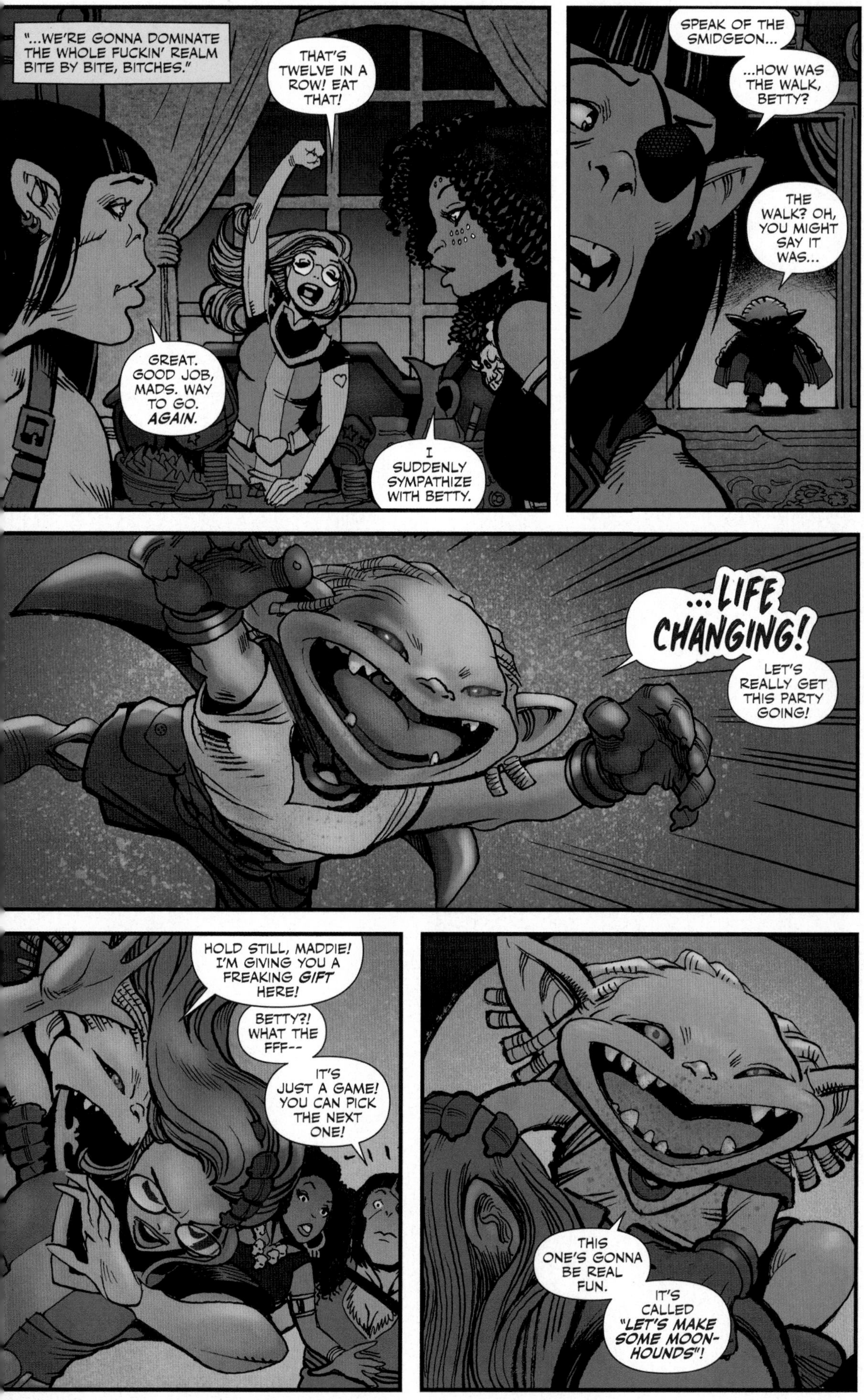
"...WE'RE GONNA DOMINATE THE WHOLE FUCKIN' REALM BITE BY BITE, BITCHES."
THAT'S TWELVE IN A ROW! EAT THAT!
GREAT. GOOD JOB, MADS. WAY TO GO. *AGAIN*.
I SUDDENLY SYMPATHIZE WITH BETTY.
SPEAK OF THE SMIDGEON...
...HOW WAS THE WALK, BETTY?
THE WALK? OH, YOU MIGHT SAY IT WAS...
...LIFE CHANGING!
LET'S REALLY GET THIS PARTY GOING!
HOLD STILL, MADDIE! I'M GIVING YOU A FREAKING *GIFT* HERE!
BETTY?! WHAT THE FFF--
IT'S JUST A GAME! YOU CAN PICK THE NEXT ONE!
THIS ONE'S GONNA BE REAL FUN.
IT'S CALLED *"LET'S MAKE SOME MOON-HOUNDS"*!

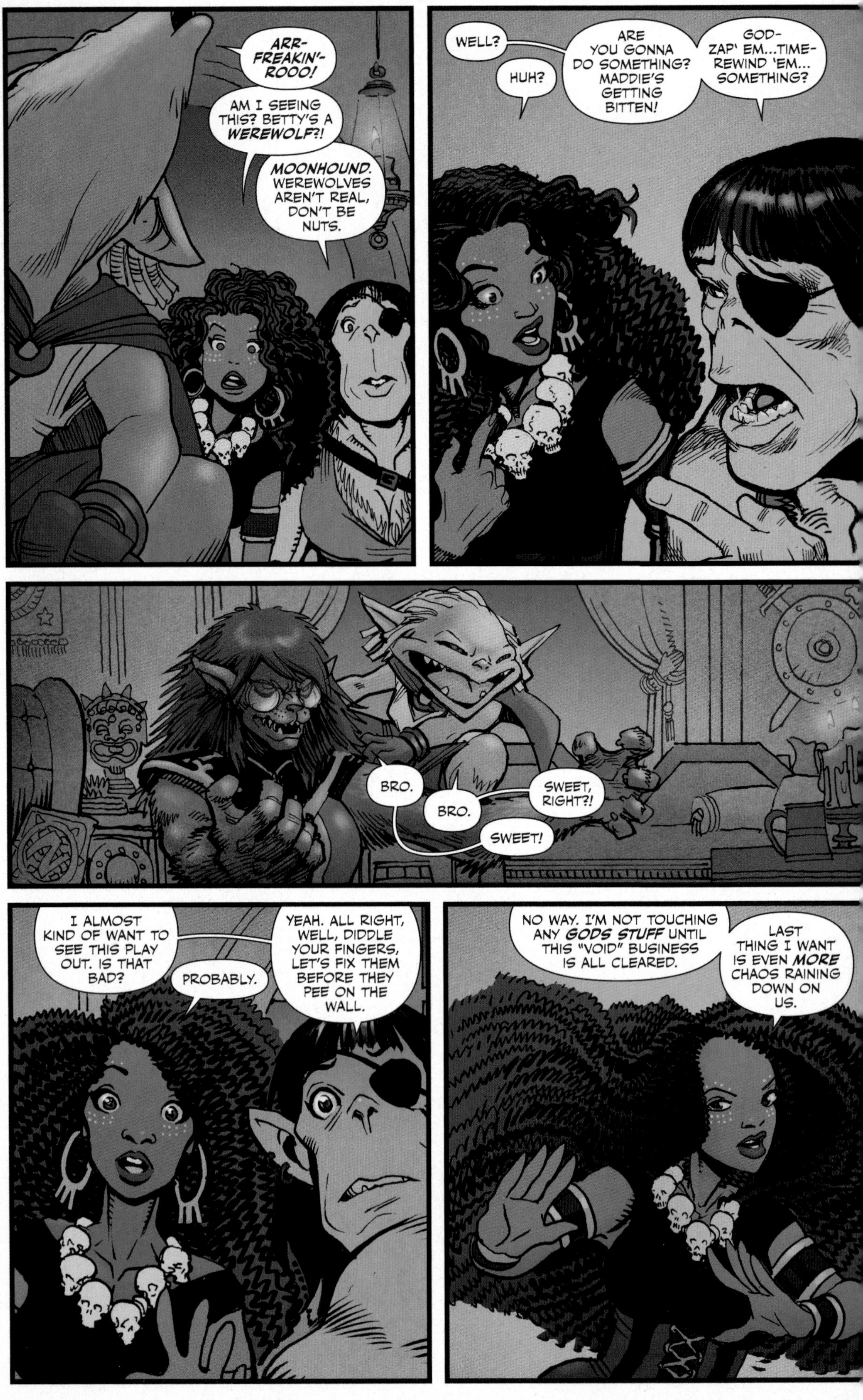

ARR-FREAKIN'-ROOO!
AM I SEEING THIS? BETTY'S A WEREWOLF?!
MOONHOUND. WEREWOLVES AREN'T REAL, DON'T BE NUTS.
WELL?
HUH?
ARE YOU GONNA DO SOMETHING? MADDIE'S GETTING BITTEN!
GOD-ZAP' EM...TIME-REWIND 'EM... SOMETHING?
BRO.
SWEET, RIGHT?!
BRO.
SWEET!
I ALMOST KIND OF WANT TO SEE THIS PLAY OUT. IS THAT BAD?
PROBABLY.
YEAH. ALL RIGHT, WELL, DIDDLE YOUR FINGERS, LET'S FIX THEM BEFORE THEY PEE ON THE WALL.
NO WAY. I'M NOT TOUCHING ANY GODS STUFF UNTIL THIS "VOID" BUSINESS IS ALL CLEARED.
LAST THING I WANT IS EVEN MORE CHAOS RAINING DOWN ON US.

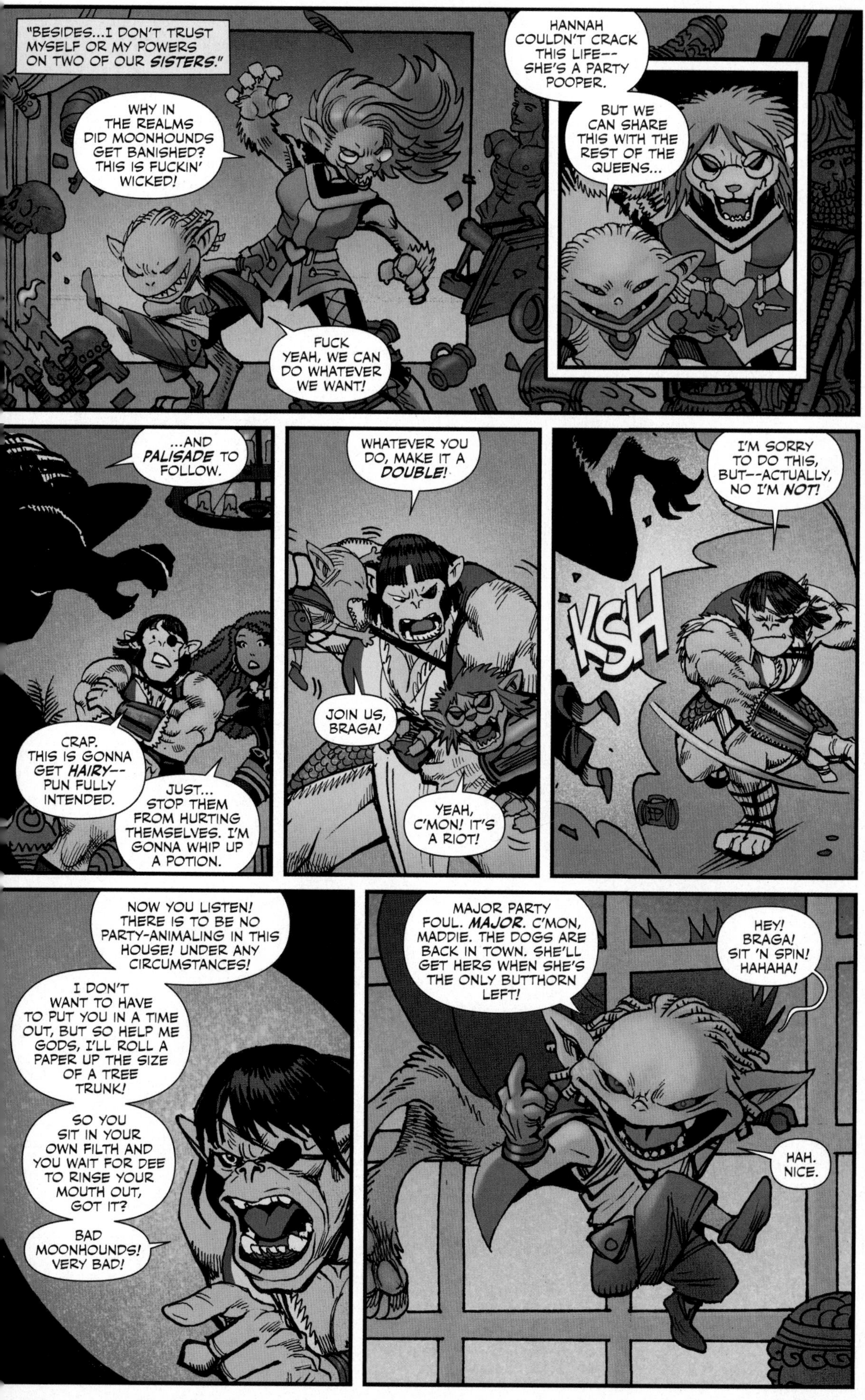

"BESIDES...I DON'T TRUST MYSELF OR MY POWERS ON TWO OF OUR SISTERS."
WHY IN THE REALMS DID MOONHOUNDS GET BANISHED? THIS IS FUCKIN' WICKED!
FUCK YEAH, WE CAN DO WHATEVER WE WANT!
HANNAH COULDN'T CRACK THIS LIFE-- SHE'S A PARTY POOPER.
BUT WE CAN SHARE THIS WITH THE REST OF THE QUEENS...
...AND PALISADE TO FOLLOW.
CRAP. THIS IS GONNA GET HAIRY-- PUN FULLY INTENDED.
JUST... STOP THEM FROM HURTING THEMSELVES. I'M GONNA WHIP UP A POTION.
WHATEVER YOU DO, MAKE IT A DOUBLE!
JOIN US, BRAGA!
YEAH, C'MON! IT'S A RIOT!
I'M SORRY TO DO THIS, BUT--ACTUALLY, NO I'M NOT!
KSH
NOW YOU LISTEN! THERE IS TO BE NO PARTY-ANIMALING IN THIS HOUSE! UNDER ANY CIRCUMSTANCES!
I DON'T WANT TO HAVE TO PUT YOU IN A TIME OUT, BUT SO HELP ME GODS, I'LL ROLL A PAPER UP THE SIZE OF A TREE TRUNK!
SO YOU SIT IN YOUR OWN FILTH AND YOU WAIT FOR DEE TO RINSE YOUR MOUTH OUT, GOT IT?
BAD MOONHOUNDS! VERY BAD!
MAJOR PARTY FOUL. MAJOR. C'MON, MADDIE. THE DOGS ARE BACK IN TOWN. SHE'LL GET HERS WHEN SHE'S THE ONLY BUTTHORN LEFT!
HEY! BRAGA! SIT 'N SPIN! HAHAHA!
HAH. NICE.

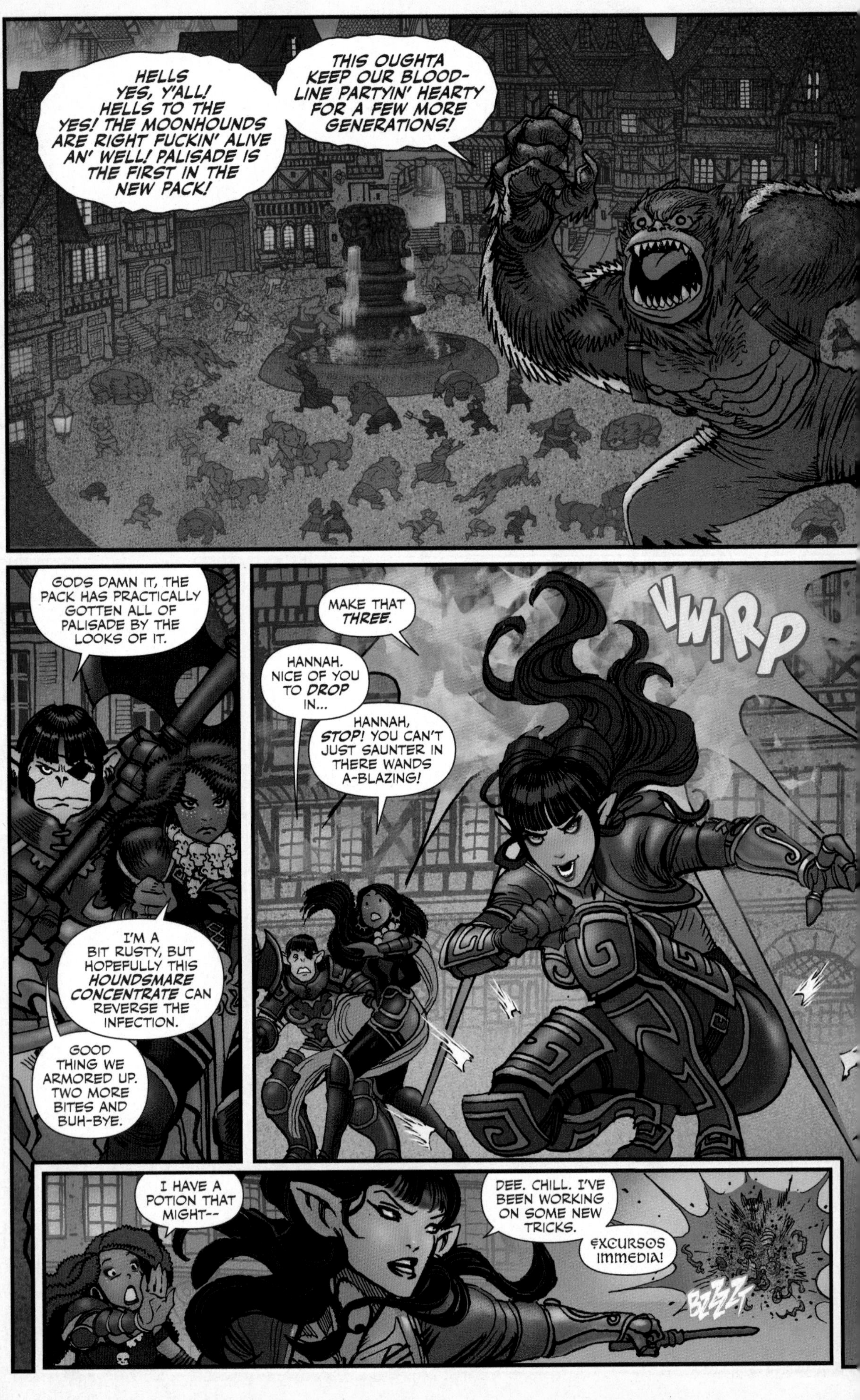
HELLS YES, Y'ALL! HELLS TO THE YES! THE MOONHOUNDS ARE RIGHT FUCKIN' ALIVE AN' WELL! PALISADE IS THE FIRST IN THE NEW PACK!
THIS OUGHTA KEEP OUR BLOOD-LINE PARTYIN' HEARTY FOR A FEW MORE GENERATIONS!
GODS DAMN IT, THE PACK HAS PRACTICALLY GOTTEN ALL OF PALISADE BY THE LOOKS OF IT.
I'M A BIT RUSTY, BUT HOPEFULLY THIS HOUNDSMARE CONCENTRATE CAN REVERSE THE INFECTION.
GOOD THING WE ARMORED UP. TWO MORE BITES AND BUH-BYE.
MAKE THAT THREE.
VWIRP
HANNAH. NICE OF YOU TO DROP IN...
HANNAH, STOP! YOU CAN'T JUST SAUNTER IN THERE WANDS A-BLAZING!
I HAVE A POTION THAT MIGHT--
DEE. CHILL. I'VE BEEN WORKING ON SOME NEW TRICKS.
EXCURSOS IMMEDIA!
BZZZZT

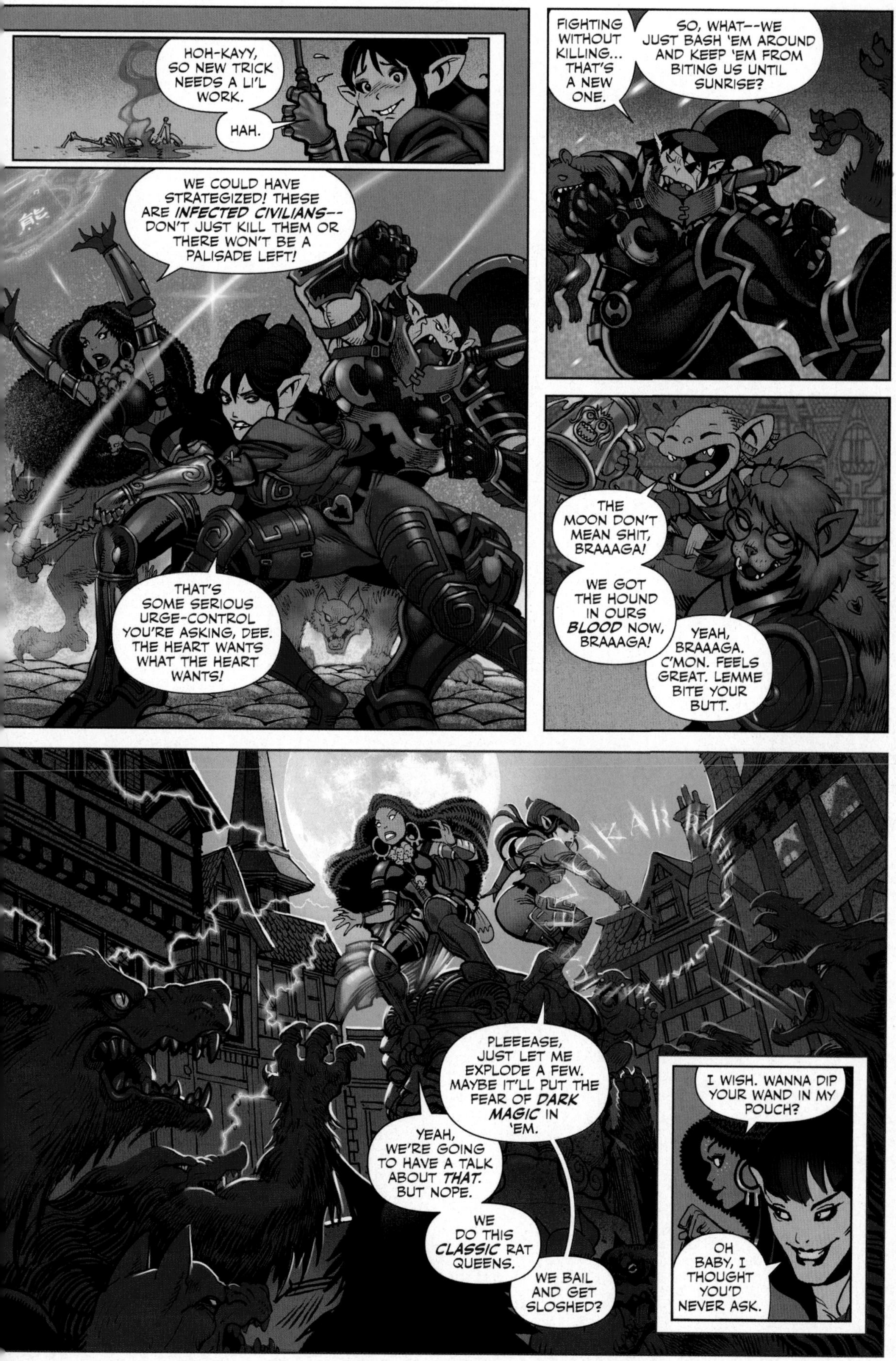
HOH-KAYY, SO NEW TRICK NEEDS A LI'L WORK.
HAH.
WE COULD HAVE STRATEGIZED! THESE ARE *INFECTED CIVILIANS*-- DON'T JUST KILL THEM OR THERE WON'T BE A PALISADE LEFT!
THAT'S SOME SERIOUS URGE-CONTROL YOU'RE ASKING, DEE. THE HEART WANTS WHAT THE HEART WANTS!
FIGHTING WITHOUT KILLING... THAT'S A NEW ONE.
SO, WHAT--WE JUST BASH 'EM AROUND AND KEEP 'EM FROM BITING US UNTIL SUNRISE?
THE MOON DON'T MEAN SHIT, BRAAAGA!
WE GOT THE HOUND IN OURS *BLOOD* NOW, BRAAAGA!
YEAH, BRAAAGA. C'MON. FEELS GREAT. LEMME BITE YOUR BUTT.
PLEEEASE, JUST LET ME EXPLODE A FEW. MAYBE IT'LL PUT THE FEAR OF *DARK MAGIC* IN 'EM.
YEAH, WE'RE GOING TO HAVE A TALK ABOUT *THAT*. BUT NOPE.
WE DO THIS *CLASSIC* RAT QUEENS.
WE BAIL AND GET SLOSHED?
I WISH. WANNA DIP YOUR WAND IN MY POUCH?
OH BABY, I THOUGHT YOU'D NEVER ASK.

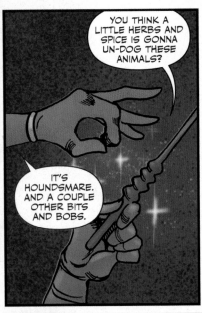

YOU THINK A LITTLE HERBS AND SPICE IS GONNA UN-DOG THESE ANIMALS?

IT'S HOUNDSMARE. AND A COUPLE OTHER BITS AND BOBS.

TOSSING IT ON 'EM ISN'T GONNA WORK, AND EATING WILL TAKE TOO LONG.

YOU CAN *BLAST* IT RIGHT INTO THEIR DAMN *SOULS*.

IT'S NOT AS COOL AS MAKING 'EM POP, BUT FINNNE.

WE SHOULD DO A TEST RUN. I DON'T WANT YOU TURNING EVERYONE INTO FROGS OR SOMETHING...

GOOD CALL. BETTY OR MADDIE?

HANNAH!

BETTY.

EVOKAR NEUTERALUS!

BZZZT

HOOOLY DOG'S BREATH, I'M NORMAL AGAIN. THAT WAS INSANE. I FEEL HUNG OVER!

WAIT... AM I ACTUALLY HUNG OVER?

AW, NO.

C'MON, DARLIN'. DON'T YOU KICK YOURSELF. IT DOESN'T COUNT.

BZZZT

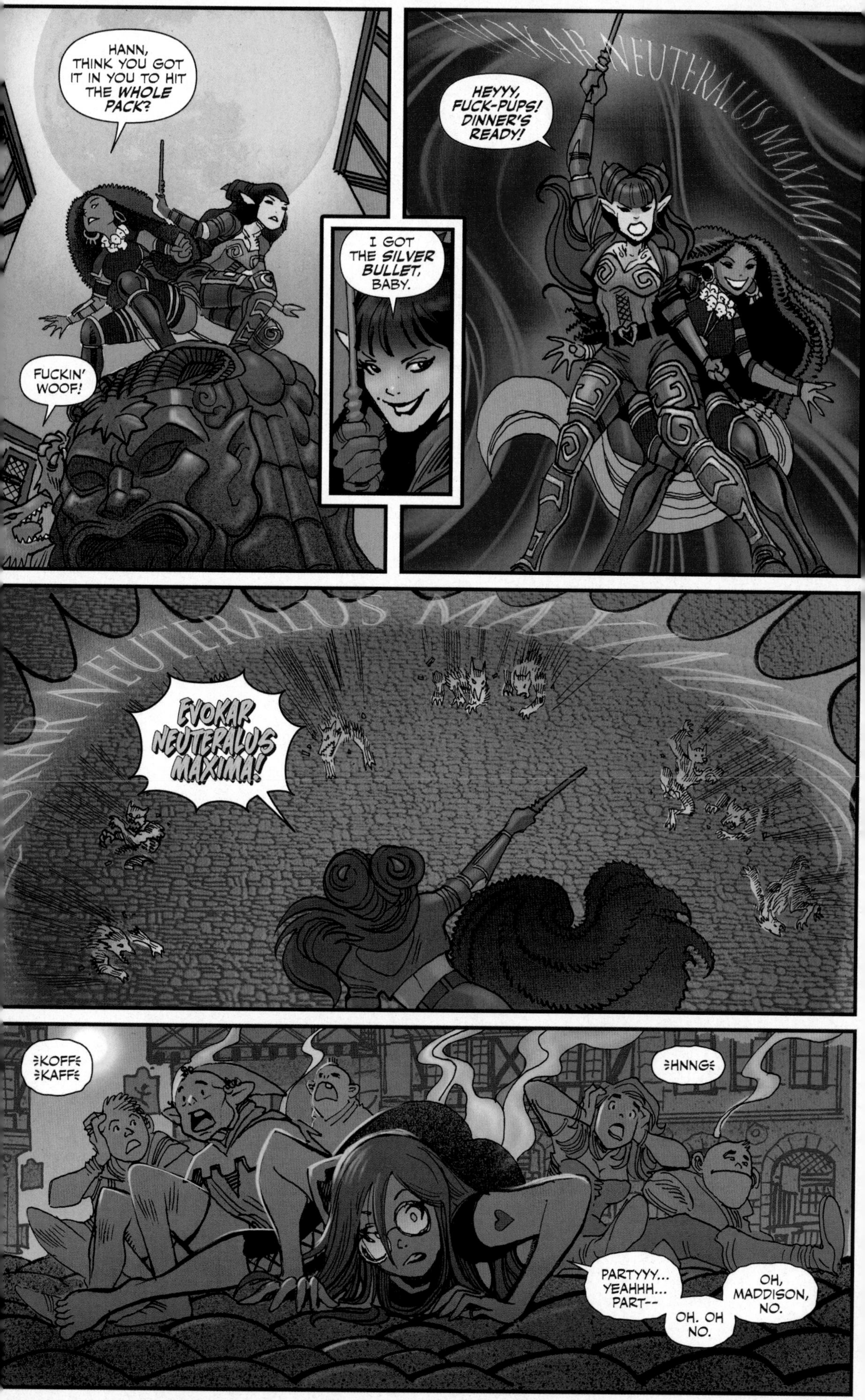

HANN, THINK YOU GOT IT IN YOU TO HIT THE *WHOLE PACK*?
FUCKIN' WOOF!
I GOT THE *SILVER BULLET*, BABY.
HEYYY, FUCK-PUPS! DINNER'S READY!
EVOKAR NEUTERALUS MAXIMA!
KOFF KAFF
HNNG
PARTYYY... YEAHHH... PART--
OH. OH NO.
OH, MADDISON, NO.

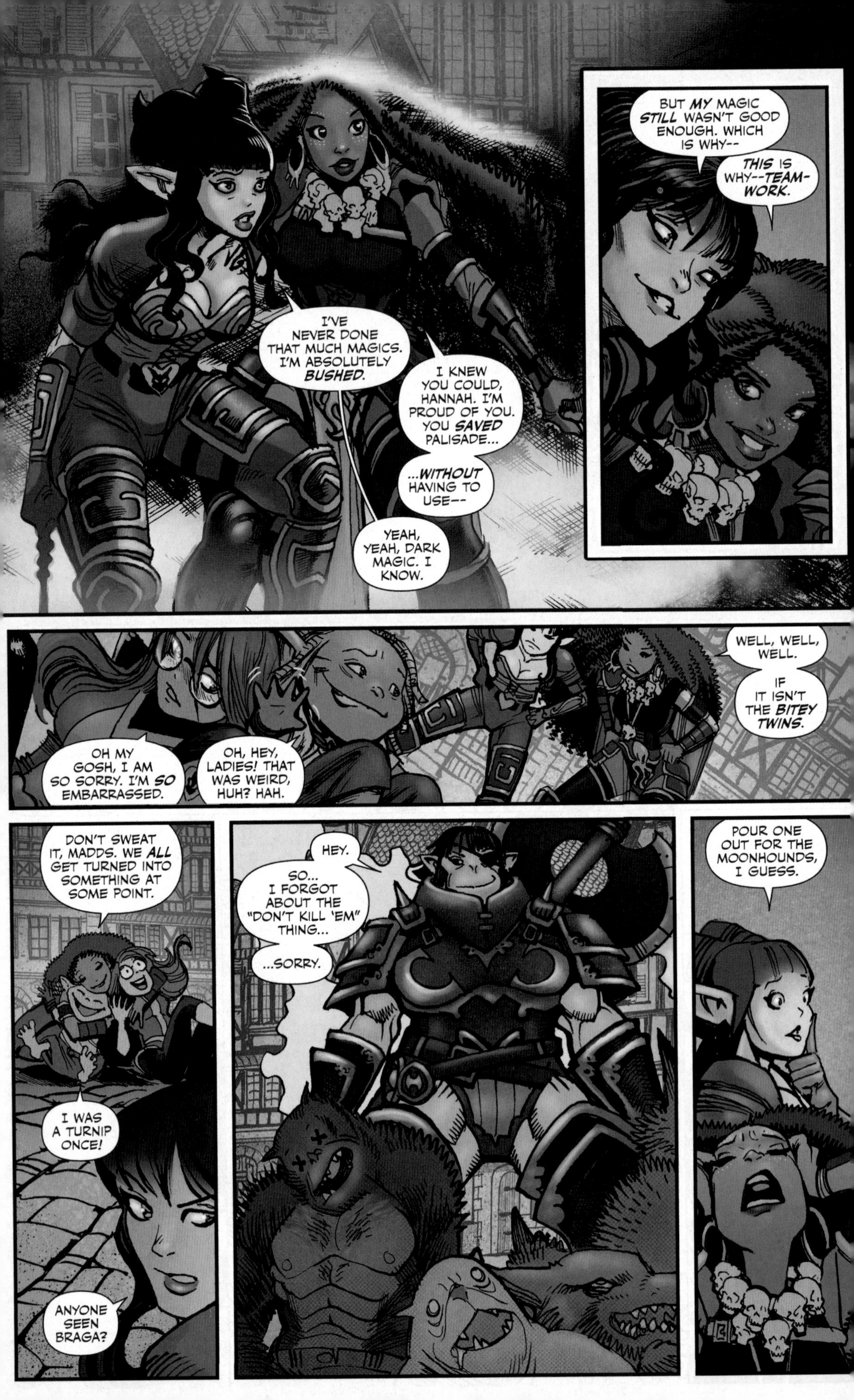
BUT MY MAGIC STILL WASN'T GOOD ENOUGH. WHICH IS WHY--
THIS IS WHY--TEAM-WORK.
I'VE NEVER DONE THAT MUCH MAGICS. I'M ABSOLUTELY BUSHED.
I KNEW YOU COULD, HANNAH. I'M PROUD OF YOU. YOU SAVED PALISADE...
...WITHOUT HAVING TO USE--
YEAH, YEAH, DARK MAGIC. I KNOW.
WELL, WELL, WELL.
IF IT ISN'T THE BITEY TWINS.
OH MY GOSH, I AM SO SORRY. I'M SO EMBARRASSED.
OH, HEY, LADIES! THAT WAS WEIRD, HUH? HAH.
DON'T SWEAT IT, MADDS. WE ALL GET TURNED INTO SOMETHING AT SOME POINT.
I WAS A TURNIP ONCE!
ANYONE SEEN BRAGA?
HEY.
SO... I FORGOT ABOUT THE "DON'T KILL 'EM" THING...
...SORRY.
POUR ONE OUT FOR THE MOONHOUNDS, I GUESS.

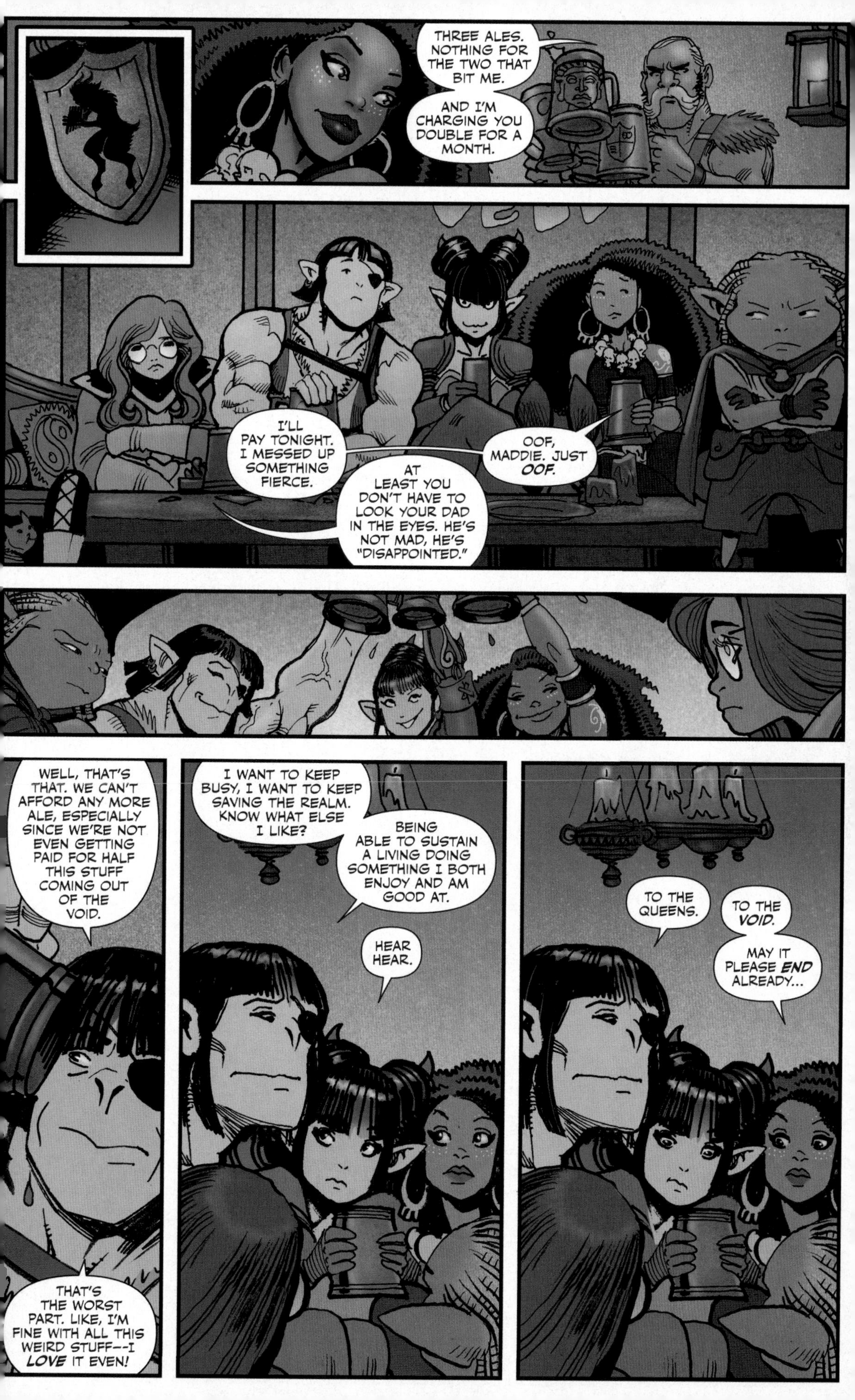
THREE ALES. NOTHING FOR THE TWO THAT BIT ME.
AND I'M CHARGING YOU DOUBLE FOR A MONTH.
I'LL PAY TONIGHT. I MESSED UP SOMETHING FIERCE.
OOF, MADDIE. JUST *OOF*.
AT LEAST YOU DON'T HAVE TO LOOK YOUR DAD IN THE EYES. HE'S NOT MAD, HE'S "DISAPPOINTED."
WELL, THAT'S THAT. WE CAN'T AFFORD ANY MORE ALE, ESPECIALLY SINCE WE'RE NOT EVEN GETTING PAID FOR HALF THIS STUFF COMING OUT OF THE VOID.
THAT'S THE WORST PART. LIKE, I'M FINE WITH ALL THIS WEIRD STUFF--I *LOVE* IT EVEN!
I WANT TO KEEP BUSY, I WANT TO KEEP SAVING THE REALM. KNOW WHAT ELSE I LIKE?
BEING ABLE TO SUSTAIN A LIVING DOING SOMETHING I BOTH ENJOY AND AM GOOD AT.
HEAR HEAR.
TO THE QUEENS.
TO THE *VOID*.
MAY IT PLEASE *END* ALREADY...

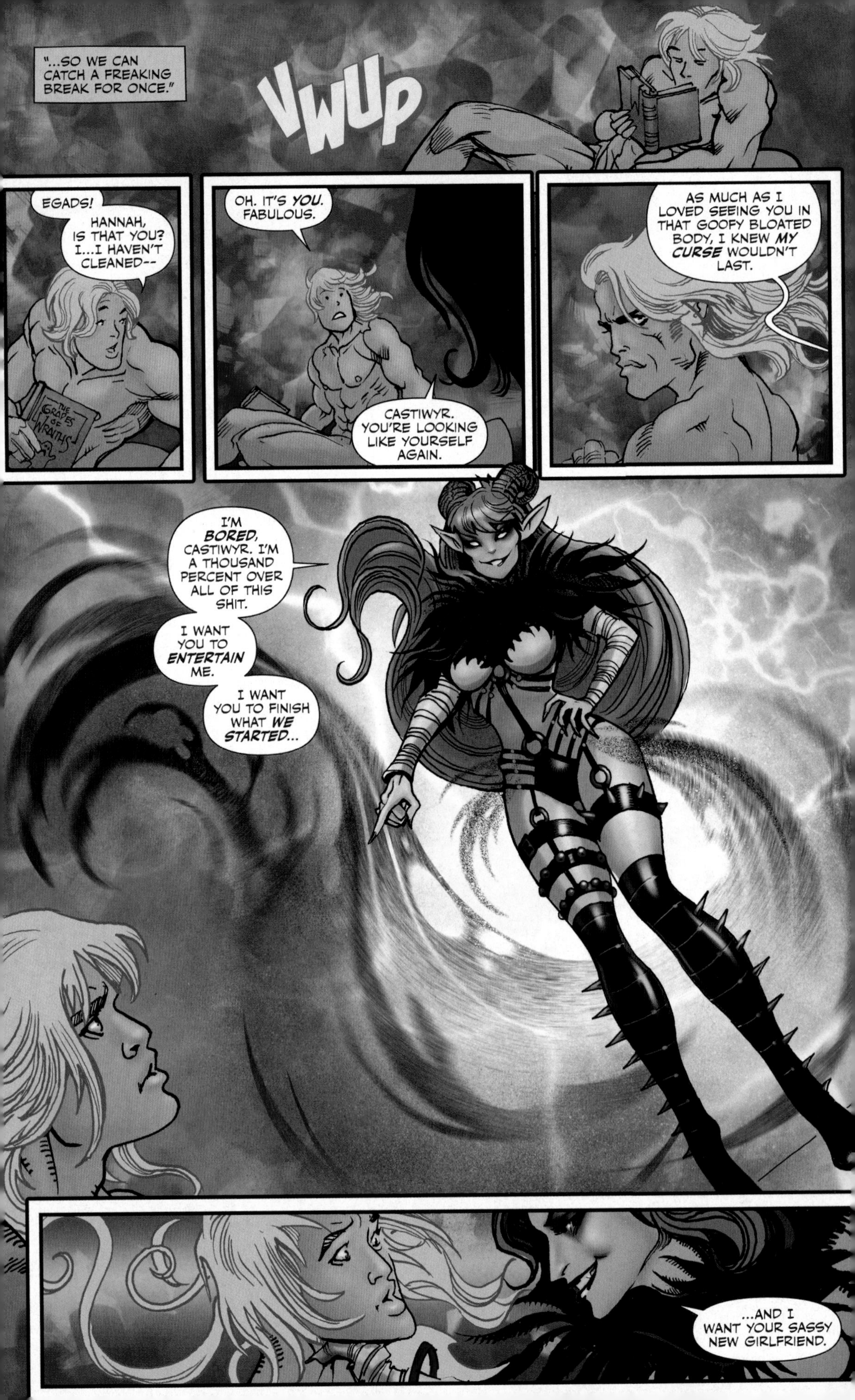
"...SO WE CAN CATCH A FREAKING BREAK FOR ONCE."
VWUP
EGADS!
HANNAH, IS THAT YOU? I...I HAVEN'T CLEANED--
THE GRAPES OF WRATHS
OH. IT'S YOU. FABULOUS.
CASTIWYR. YOU'RE LOOKING LIKE YOURSELF AGAIN.
AS MUCH AS I LOVED SEEING YOU IN THAT GOOFY BLOATED BODY, I KNEW MY CURSE WOULDN'T LAST.
I'M BORED, CASTIWYR. I'M A THOUSAND PERCENT OVER ALL OF THIS SHIT.
I WANT YOU TO ENTERTAIN ME.
I WANT YOU TO FINISH WHAT WE STARTED...
...AND I WANT YOUR SASSY NEW GIRLFRIEND.

CHAPTER TWENTY-THREE

ISSUE #23 COVER

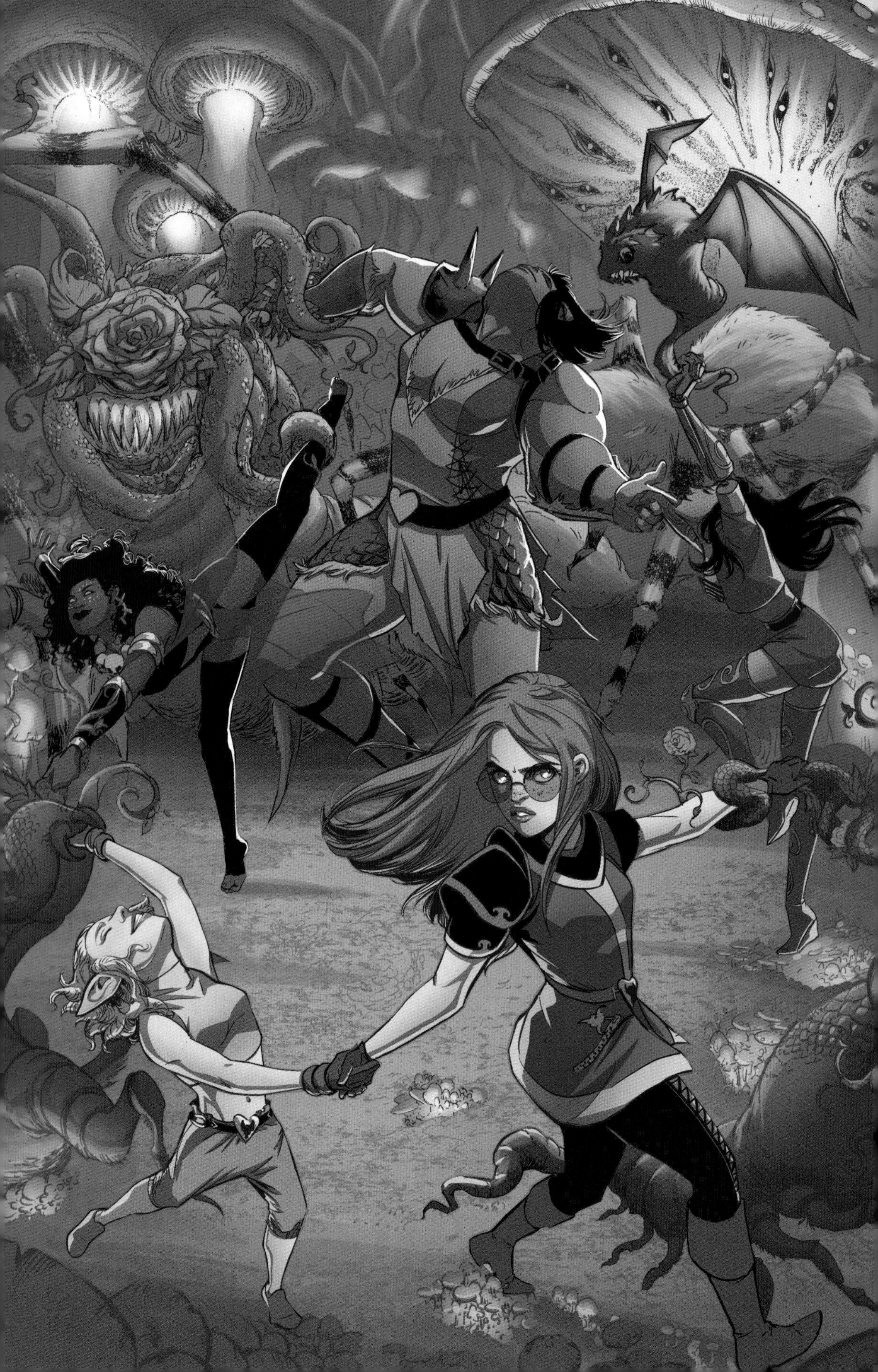

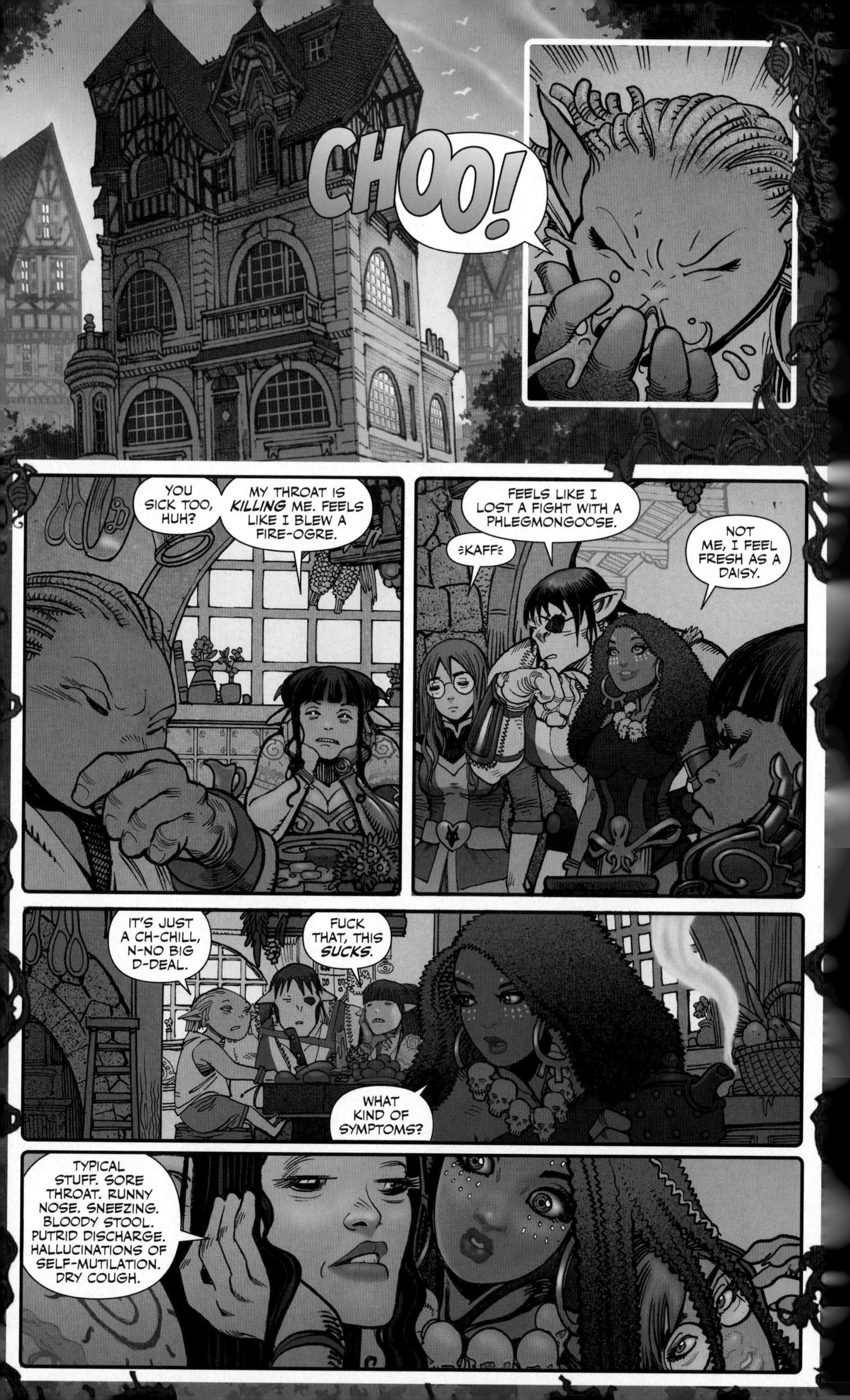
CHOO!
YOU SICK TOO, HUH?
MY THROAT IS *KILLING* ME. FEELS LIKE I BLEW A FIRE-OGRE.
FEELS LIKE I LOST A FIGHT WITH A PHLEGMONGOOSE.
KAFF
NOT ME, I FEEL FRESH AS A DAISY.
IT'S JUST A CH-CHILL, N-NO BIG D-DEAL.
FUCK THAT, THIS *SUCKS*.
WHAT KIND OF SYMPTOMS?
TYPICAL STUFF. SORE THROAT. RUNNY NOSE. SNEEZING. BLOODY STOOL. PUTRID DISCHARGE. HALLUCINATIONS OF SELF-MUTILATION. DRY COUGH.

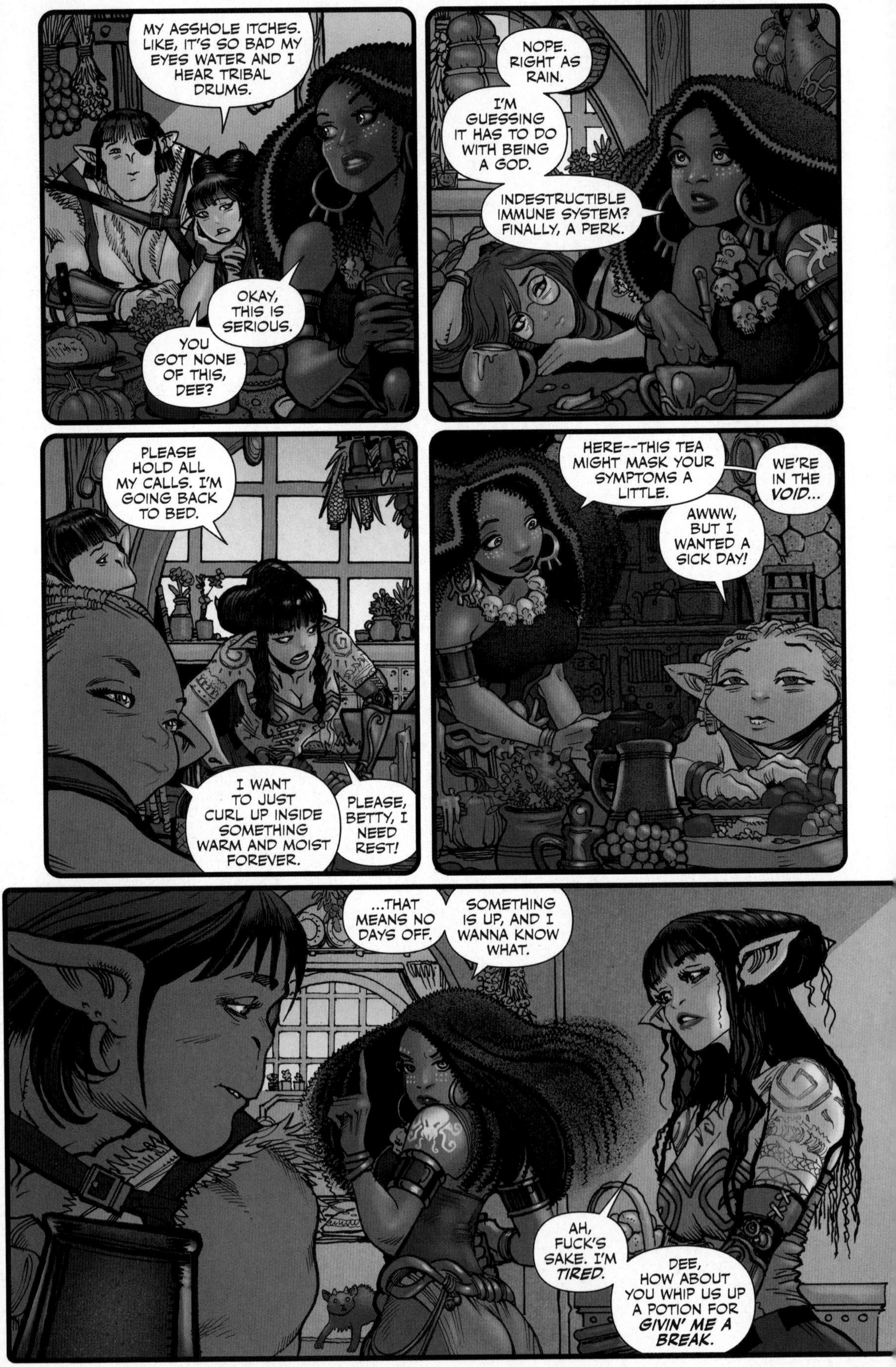
MY ASSHOLE ITCHES. LIKE, IT'S SO BAD MY EYES WATER AND I HEAR TRIBAL DRUMS.
OKAY, THIS IS SERIOUS.
YOU GOT NONE OF THIS, DEE?
NOPE. RIGHT AS RAIN.
I'M GUESSING IT HAS TO DO WITH BEING A GOD.
INDESTRUCTIBLE IMMUNE SYSTEM? FINALLY, A PERK.
PLEASE HOLD ALL MY CALLS. I'M GOING BACK TO BED.
I WANT TO JUST CURL UP INSIDE SOMETHING WARM AND MOIST FOREVER.
PLEASE, BETTY, I NEED REST!
HERE--THIS TEA MIGHT MASK YOUR SYMPTOMS A LITTLE.
AWWW, BUT I WANTED A SICK DAY!
WE'RE IN THE *VOID*...
...THAT MEANS NO DAYS OFF.
SOMETHING IS UP, AND I WANNA KNOW WHAT.
AH, FUCK'S SAKE. I'M *TIRED*.
DEE, HOW ABOUT YOU WHIP US UP A POTION FOR ***GIVIN' ME A BREAK***.

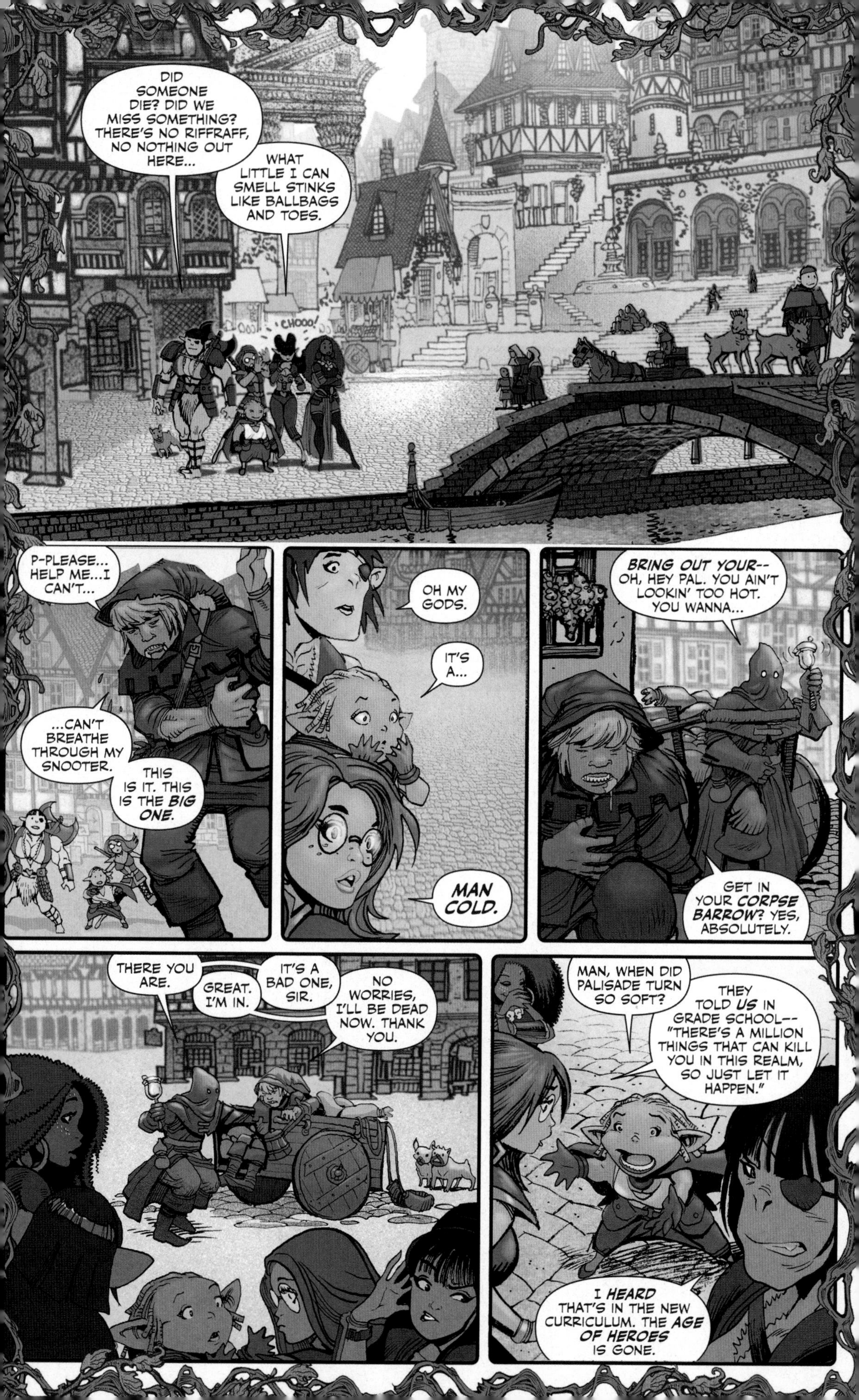
DID SOMEONE DIE? DID WE MISS SOMETHING? THERE'S NO RIFFRAFF, NO NOTHING OUT HERE...
WHAT LITTLE I CAN SMELL STINKS LIKE BALLBAGS AND TOES.
CHOOO!
P-PLEASE... HELP ME...I CAN'T...
...CAN'T BREATHE THROUGH MY SNOOTER.
THIS IS IT. THIS IS THE *BIG ONE*.
OH MY GODS.
IT'S A...
MAN COLD.
BRING OUT YOUR-- OH, HEY PAL. YOU AIN'T LOOKIN' TOO HOT. YOU WANNA...
GET IN YOUR *CORPSE BARROW*? YES, ABSOLUTELY.
THERE YOU ARE.
GREAT. I'M IN.
IT'S A BAD ONE, SIR.
NO WORRIES, I'LL BE DEAD NOW. THANK YOU.
MAN, WHEN DID PALISADE TURN SO SOFT?
THEY TOLD *US* IN GRADE SCHOOL-- "THERE'S A MILLION THINGS THAT CAN KILL YOU IN THIS REALM, SO JUST LET IT HAPPEN."
I *HEARD* THAT'S IN THE NEW CURRICULUM. THE *AGE OF HEROES* IS GONE.

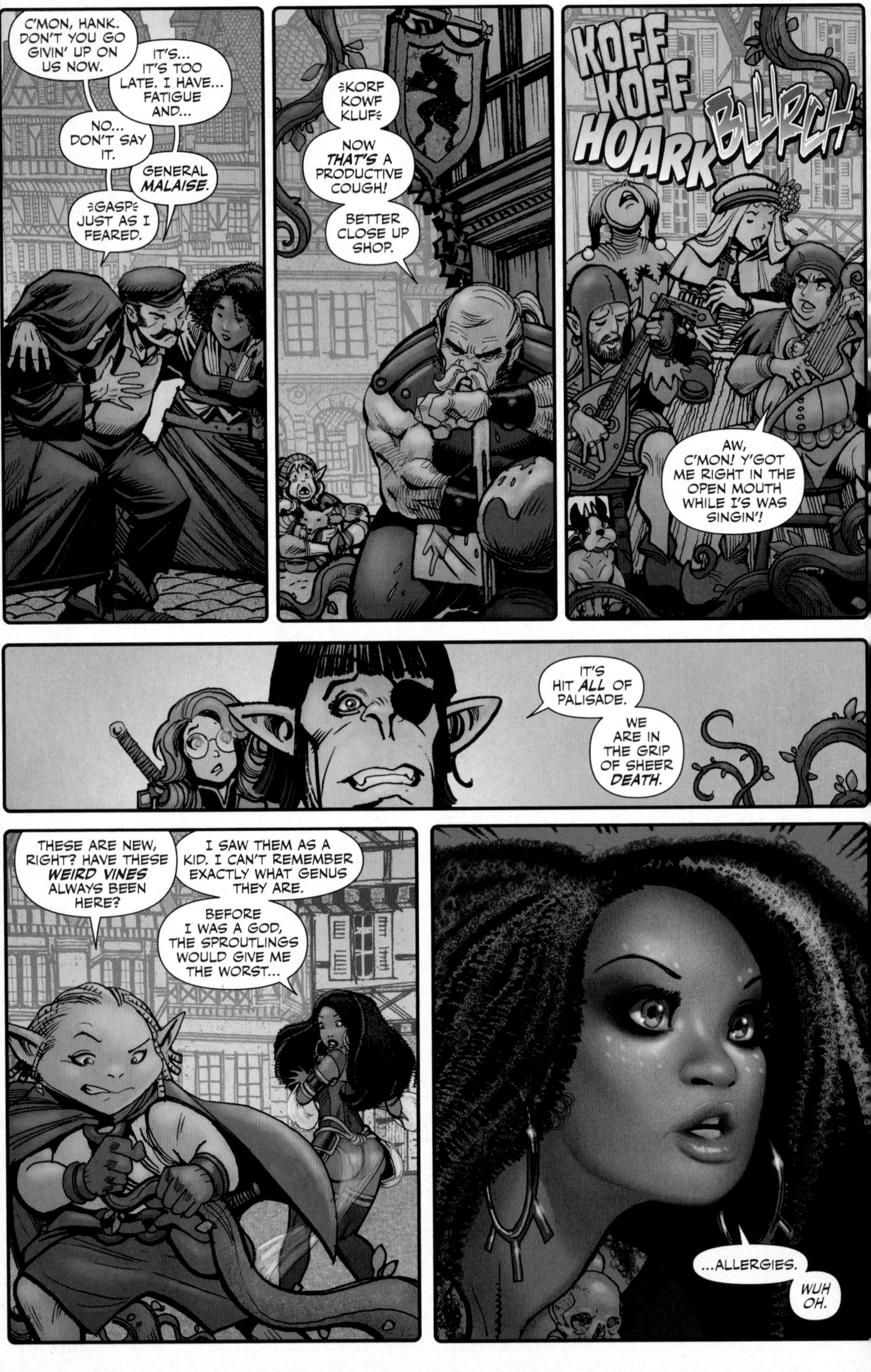
C'MON, HANK. DON'T YOU GO GIVIN' UP ON US NOW.
IT'S... IT'S TOO LATE. I HAVE... FATIGUE AND...
NO... DON'T SAY IT.
GENERAL *MALAISE*.
GASP JUST AS I FEARED.
KORF KOWF KLUF
NOW *THAT'S* A PRODUCTIVE COUGH!
BETTER CLOSE UP SHOP.
KOFF KOFF HOARK
BLURCH
AW, C'MON! Y'GOT ME RIGHT IN THE OPEN MOUTH WHILE I'S WAS SINGIN'!
IT'S HIT *ALL* OF PALISADE.
WE ARE IN THE GRIP OF SHEER *DEATH*.
THESE ARE NEW, RIGHT? HAVE THESE *WEIRD VINES* ALWAYS BEEN HERE?
I SAW THEM AS A KID. I CAN'T REMEMBER EXACTLY WHAT GENUS THEY ARE.
BEFORE I WAS A GOD, THE SPROUTLINGS WOULD GIVE ME THE WORST...
...ALLERGIES.
WUH OH.

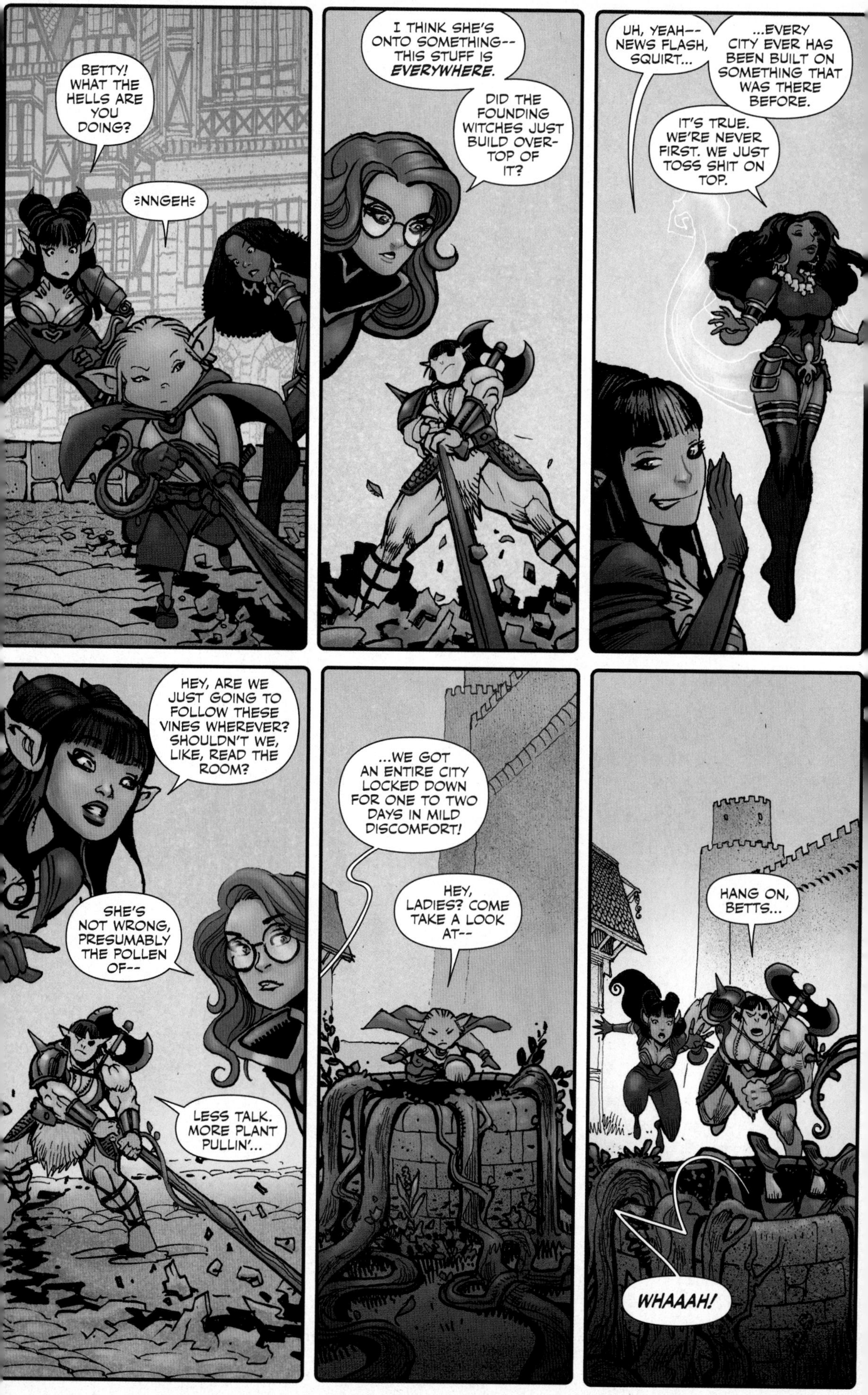
BETTY! WHAT THE HELLS ARE YOU DOING?
NNGEH
I THINK SHE'S ONTO SOMETHING-- THIS STUFF IS *EVERYWHERE*.
DID THE FOUNDING WITCHES JUST BUILD OVER-TOP OF IT?
UH, YEAH-- NEWS FLASH, SQUIRT...
...EVERY CITY EVER HAS BEEN BUILT ON SOMETHING THAT WAS THERE BEFORE.
IT'S TRUE. WE'RE NEVER FIRST. WE JUST TOSS SHIT ON TOP.
HEY, ARE WE JUST GOING TO FOLLOW THESE VINES WHEREVER? SHOULDN'T WE, LIKE, READ THE ROOM?
SHE'S NOT WRONG, PRESUMABLY THE POLLEN OF--
LESS TALK. MORE PLANT PULLIN'...
...WE GOT AN ENTIRE CITY LOCKED DOWN FOR ONE TO TWO DAYS IN MILD DISCOMFORT!
HEY, LADIES? COME TAKE A LOOK AT--
HANG ON, BETTS...
WHAAAH!

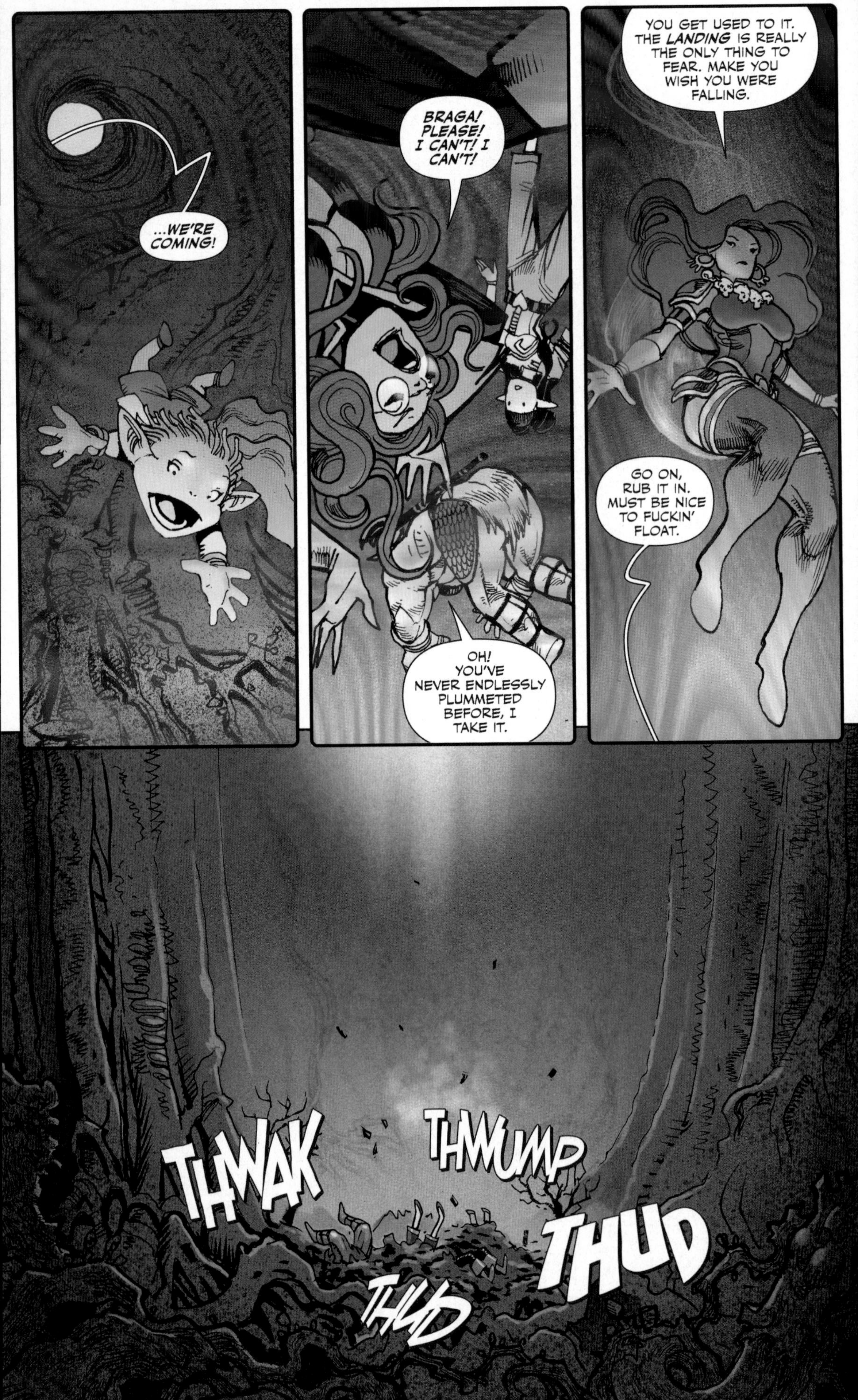

...WE'RE COMING!
BRAGA! PLEASE! I CAN'T! I CAN'T!
OH! YOU'VE NEVER ENDLESSLY PLUMMETED BEFORE, I TAKE IT.
YOU GET USED TO IT. THE LANDING IS REALLY THE ONLY THING TO FEAR. MAKE YOU WISH YOU WERE FALLING.
GO ON, RUB IT IN. MUST BE NICE TO FUCKIN' FLOAT.
THWAK
THWUMP
THUD
THUD

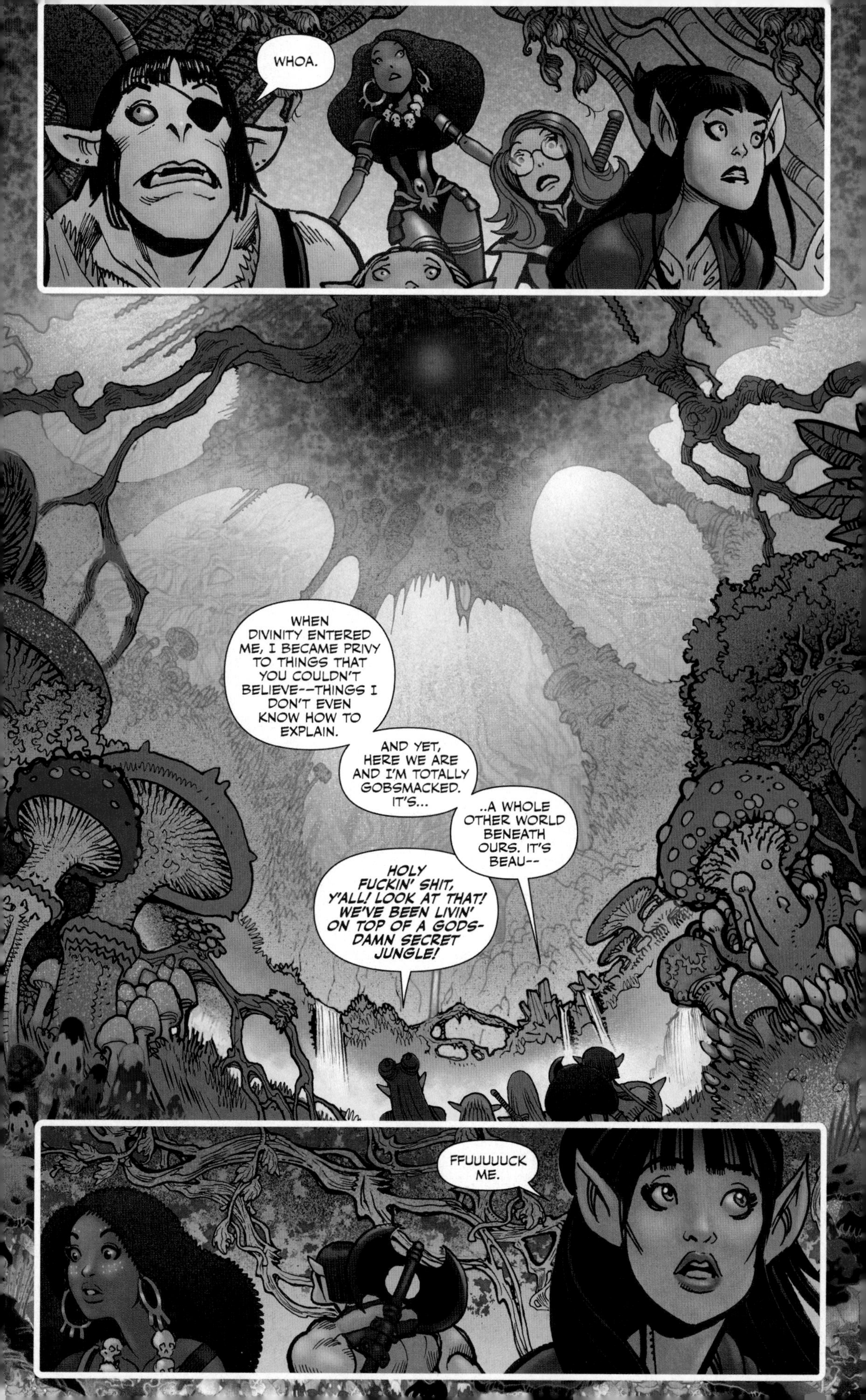
WHOA.
WHEN DIVINITY ENTERED ME, I BECAME PRIVY TO THINGS THAT YOU COULDN'T BELIEVE--THINGS I DON'T EVEN KNOW HOW TO EXPLAIN.
AND YET, HERE WE ARE AND I'M TOTALLY GOBSMACKED. IT'S...
..A WHOLE OTHER WORLD BENEATH OURS. IT'S BEAU--
HOLY FUCKIN' SHIT, Y'ALL! LOOK AT THAT! WE'VE BEEN LIVIN' ON TOP OF A GODS-DAMN SECRET JUNGLE!
FFUUUUUCK ME.

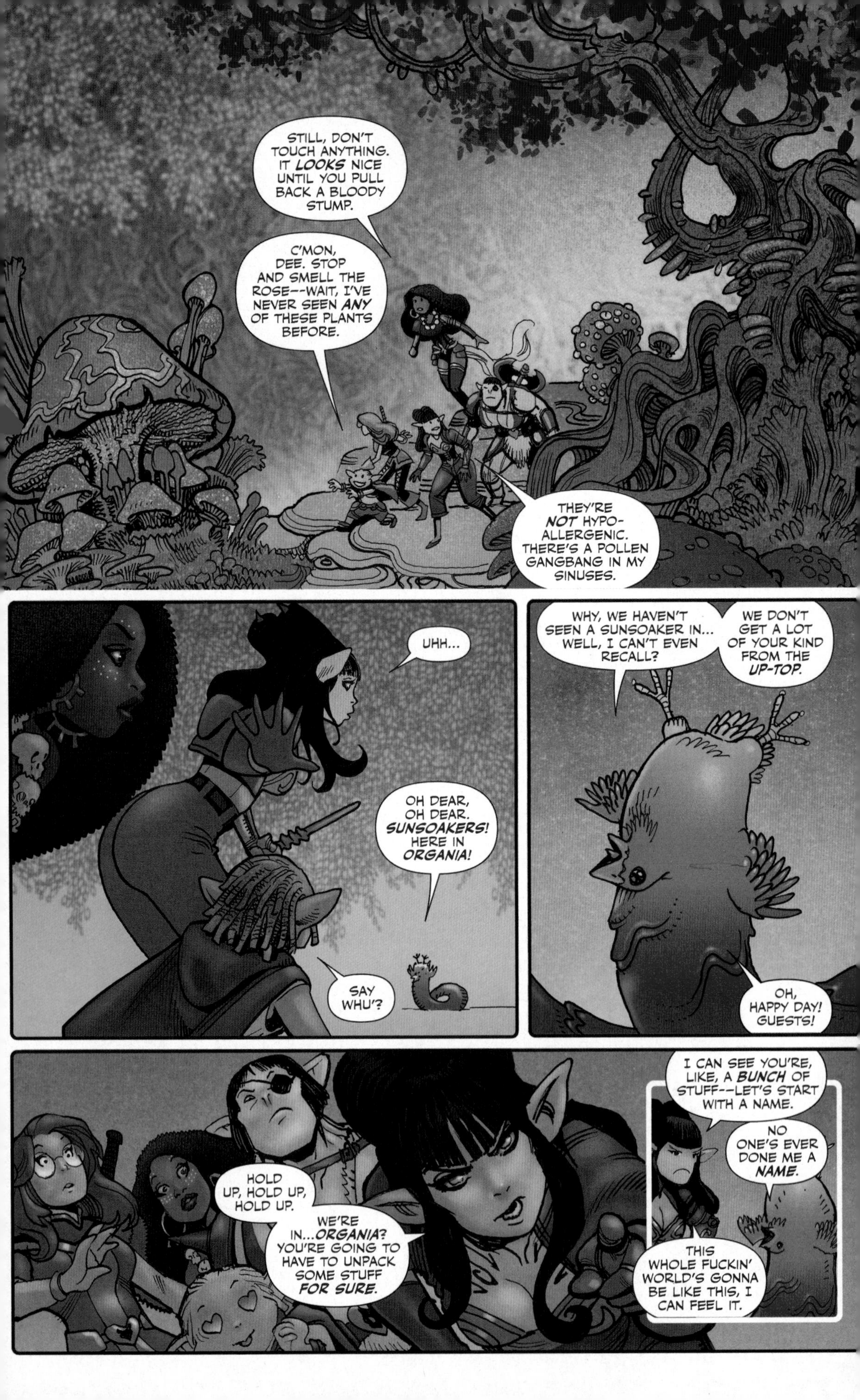

STILL, DON'T TOUCH ANYTHING. IT LOOKS NICE UNTIL YOU PULL BACK A BLOODY STUMP.
C'MON, DEE. STOP AND SMELL THE ROSE--WAIT, I'VE NEVER SEEN ANY OF THESE PLANTS BEFORE.
THEY'RE NOT HYPO-ALLERGENIC. THERE'S A POLLEN GANGBANG IN MY SINUSES.
UHH...
OH DEAR, OH DEAR. SUNSOAKERS! HERE IN ORGANIA!
SAY WHU'?
WHY, WE HAVEN'T SEEN A SUNSOAKER IN... WELL, I CAN'T EVEN RECALL?
WE DON'T GET A LOT OF YOUR KIND FROM THE UP-TOP.
OH, HAPPY DAY! GUESTS!
HOLD UP, HOLD UP, HOLD UP.
WE'RE IN...ORGANIA? YOU'RE GOING TO HAVE TO UNPACK SOME STUFF FOR SURE.
I CAN SEE YOU'RE, LIKE, A BUNCH OF STUFF--LET'S START WITH A NAME.
NO ONE'S EVER DONE ME A NAME.
THIS WHOLE FUCKIN' WORLD'S GONNA BE LIKE THIS, I CAN FEEL IT.

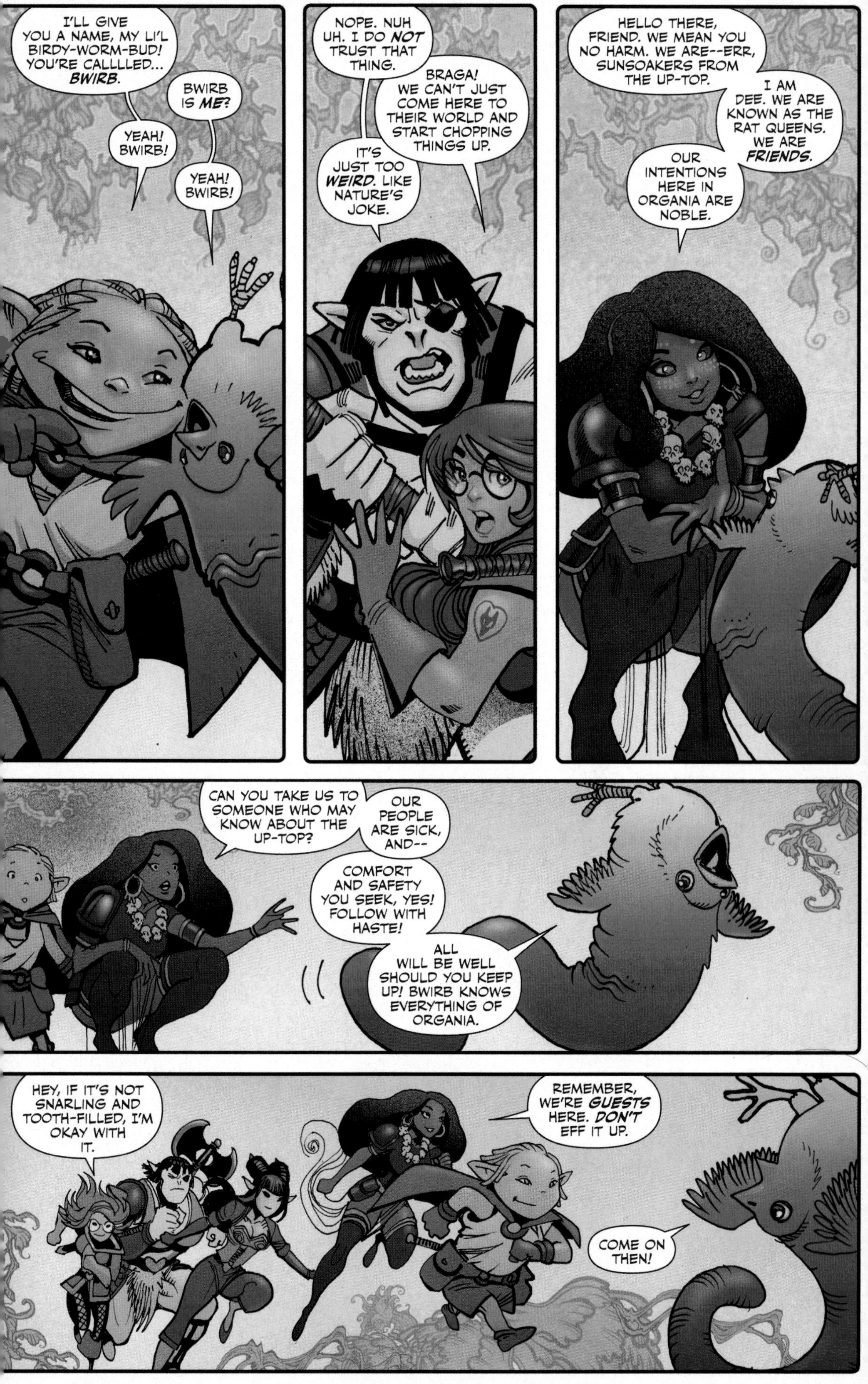

I'LL GIVE YOU A NAME, MY LI'L BIRDY-WORM-BUD! YOU'RE CALLLLED... *BWIRB*.
BWIRB IS *ME*?
YEAH! BWIRB!
YEAH! BWIRB!
NOPE. NUH UH. I DO *NOT* TRUST THAT THING.
BRAGA! WE CAN'T JUST COME HERE TO THEIR WORLD AND START CHOPPING THINGS UP.
IT'S JUST TOO *WEIRD*. LIKE NATURE'S JOKE.
HELLO THERE, FRIEND. WE MEAN YOU NO HARM. WE ARE--ERR, SUNSOAKERS FROM THE UP-TOP.
I AM DEE. WE ARE KNOWN AS THE RAT QUEENS. WE ARE *FRIENDS*.
OUR INTENTIONS HERE IN ORGANIA ARE NOBLE.
CAN YOU TAKE US TO SOMEONE WHO MAY KNOW ABOUT THE UP-TOP?
OUR PEOPLE ARE SICK, AND--
COMFORT AND SAFETY YOU SEEK, YES! FOLLOW WITH HASTE!
ALL WILL BE WELL SHOULD YOU KEEP UP! BWIRB KNOWS EVERYTHING OF ORGANIA.
HEY, IF IT'S NOT SNARLING AND TOOTH-FILLED, I'M OKAY WITH IT.
REMEMBER, WE'RE *GUESTS* HERE. *DON'T* EFF IT UP.
COME ON THEN!

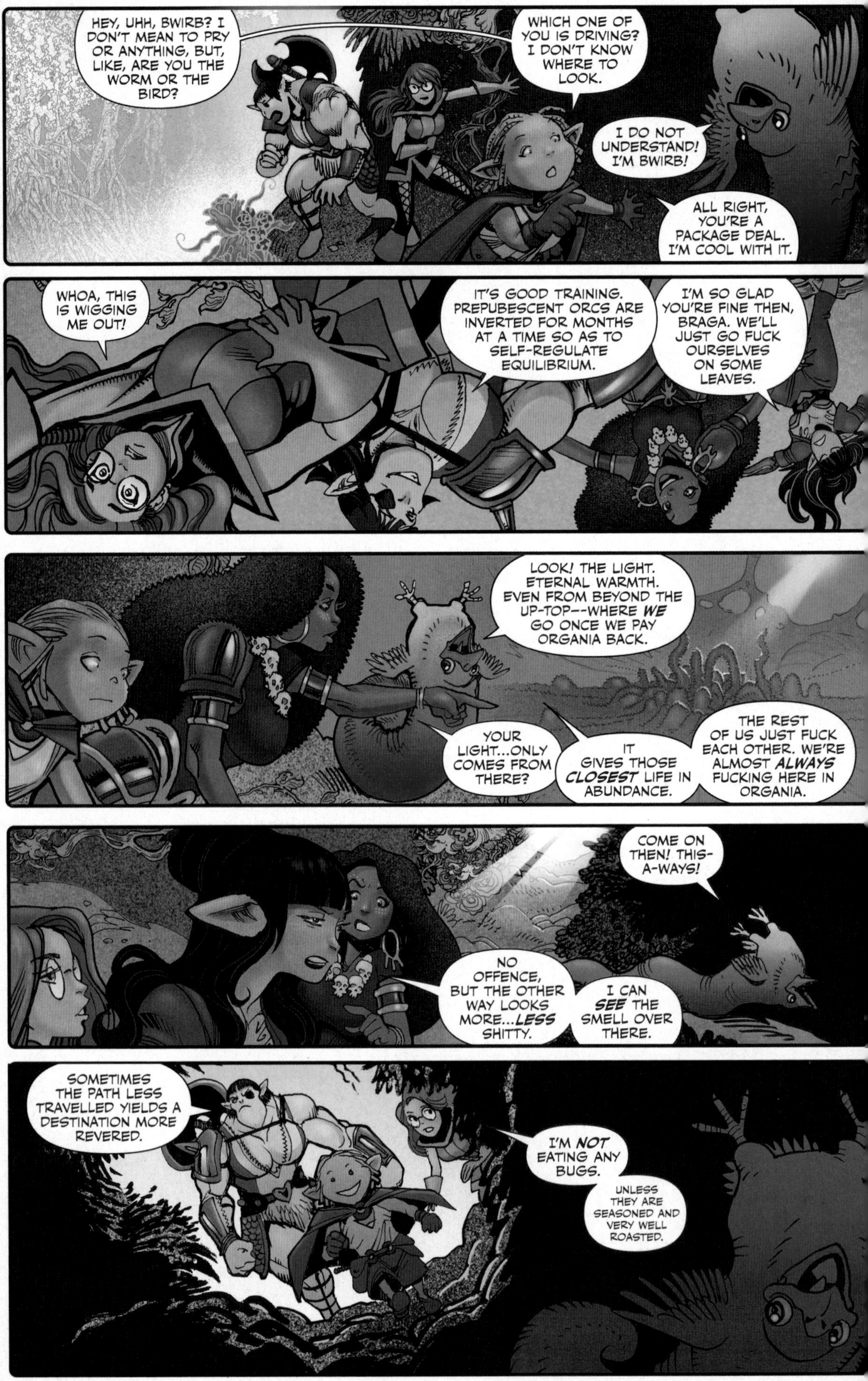
HEY, UHH, BWIRB? I DON'T MEAN TO PRY OR ANYTHING, BUT, LIKE, ARE YOU THE WORM OR THE BIRD?
WHICH ONE OF YOU IS DRIVING? I DON'T KNOW WHERE TO LOOK.
I DO NOT UNDERSTAND! I'M BWIRB!
ALL RIGHT, YOU'RE A PACKAGE DEAL. I'M COOL WITH IT.
WHOA, THIS IS WIGGING ME OUT!
IT'S GOOD TRAINING. PREPUBESCENT ORCS ARE INVERTED FOR MONTHS AT A TIME SO AS TO SELF-REGULATE EQUILIBRIUM.
I'M SO GLAD YOU'RE FINE THEN, BRAGA. WE'LL JUST GO FUCK OURSELVES ON SOME LEAVES.
LOOK! THE LIGHT. ETERNAL WARMTH. EVEN FROM BEYOND THE UP-TOP--WHERE WE GO ONCE WE PAY ORGANIA BACK.
YOUR LIGHT...ONLY COMES FROM THERE?
IT GIVES THOSE CLOSEST LIFE IN ABUNDANCE.
THE REST OF US JUST FUCK EACH OTHER. WE'RE ALMOST ALWAYS FUCKING HERE IN ORGANIA.
COME ON THEN! THIS-A-WAYS!
NO OFFENCE, BUT THE OTHER WAY LOOKS MORE...LESS SHITTY.
I CAN SEE THE SMELL OVER THERE.
SOMETIMES THE PATH LESS TRAVELLED YIELDS A DESTINATION MORE REVERED.
I'M NOT EATING ANY BUGS.
UNLESS THEY ARE SEASONED AND VERY WELL ROASTED.

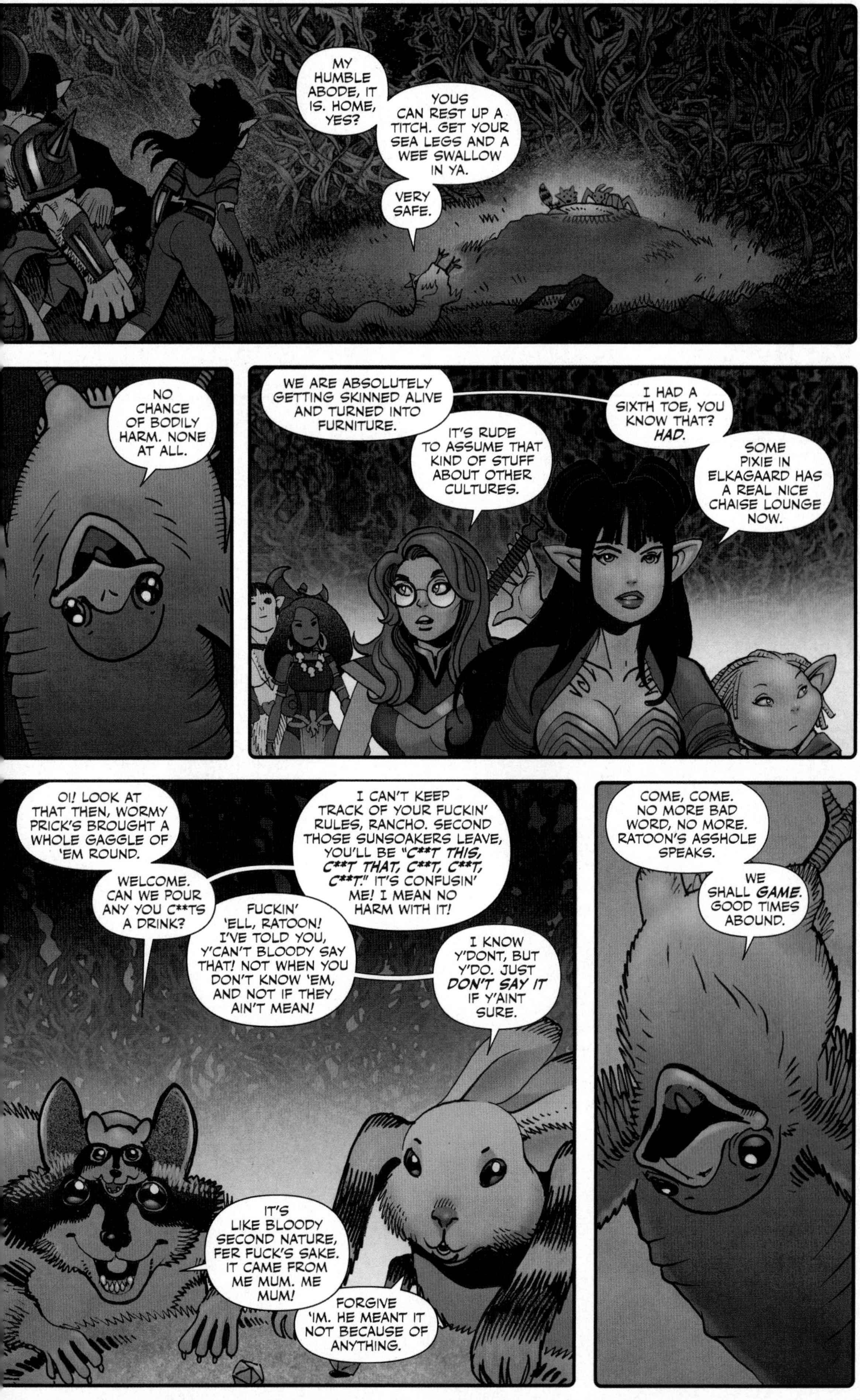
MY HUMBLE ABODE, IT IS. HOME, YES?
YOUS CAN REST UP A TITCH. GET YOUR SEA LEGS AND A WEE SWALLOW IN YA.
VERY SAFE.
NO CHANCE OF BODILY HARM. NONE AT ALL.
WE ARE ABSOLUTELY GETTING SKINNED ALIVE AND TURNED INTO FURNITURE.
I HAD A SIXTH TOE, YOU KNOW THAT? *HAD*.
IT'S RUDE TO ASSUME THAT KIND OF STUFF ABOUT OTHER CULTURES.
SOME PIXIE IN ELKAGAARD HAS A REAL NICE CHAISE LOUNGE NOW.
OI! LOOK AT THAT THEN, WORMY PRICK'S BROUGHT A WHOLE GAGGLE OF 'EM ROUND.
WELCOME. CAN WE POUR ANY YOU C**TS A DRINK?
I CAN'T KEEP TRACK OF YOUR FUCKIN' RULES, RANCHO. SECOND THOSE SUNSOAKERS LEAVE, YOU'LL BE "*C**T THIS, C**T THAT, C**T, C**T, C**T*." IT'S CONFUSIN' ME! I MEAN NO HARM WITH IT!
FUCKIN' 'ELL, RATOON! I'VE TOLD YOU, Y'CAN'T BLOODY SAY THAT! NOT WHEN YOU DON'T KNOW 'EM, AND NOT IF THEY AIN'T MEAN!
I KNOW Y'DONT, BUT Y'DO. JUST *DON'T SAY IT* IF Y'AINT SURE.
IT'S LIKE BLOODY SECOND NATURE, FER FUCK'S SAKE. IT CAME FROM ME MUM. ME MUM!
FORGIVE 'IM. HE MEANT IT NOT BECAUSE OF ANYTHING.
COME, COME. NO MORE BAD WORD, NO MORE. RATOON'S ASSHOLE SPEAKS.
WE SHALL *GAME*. GOOD TIMES ABOUND.

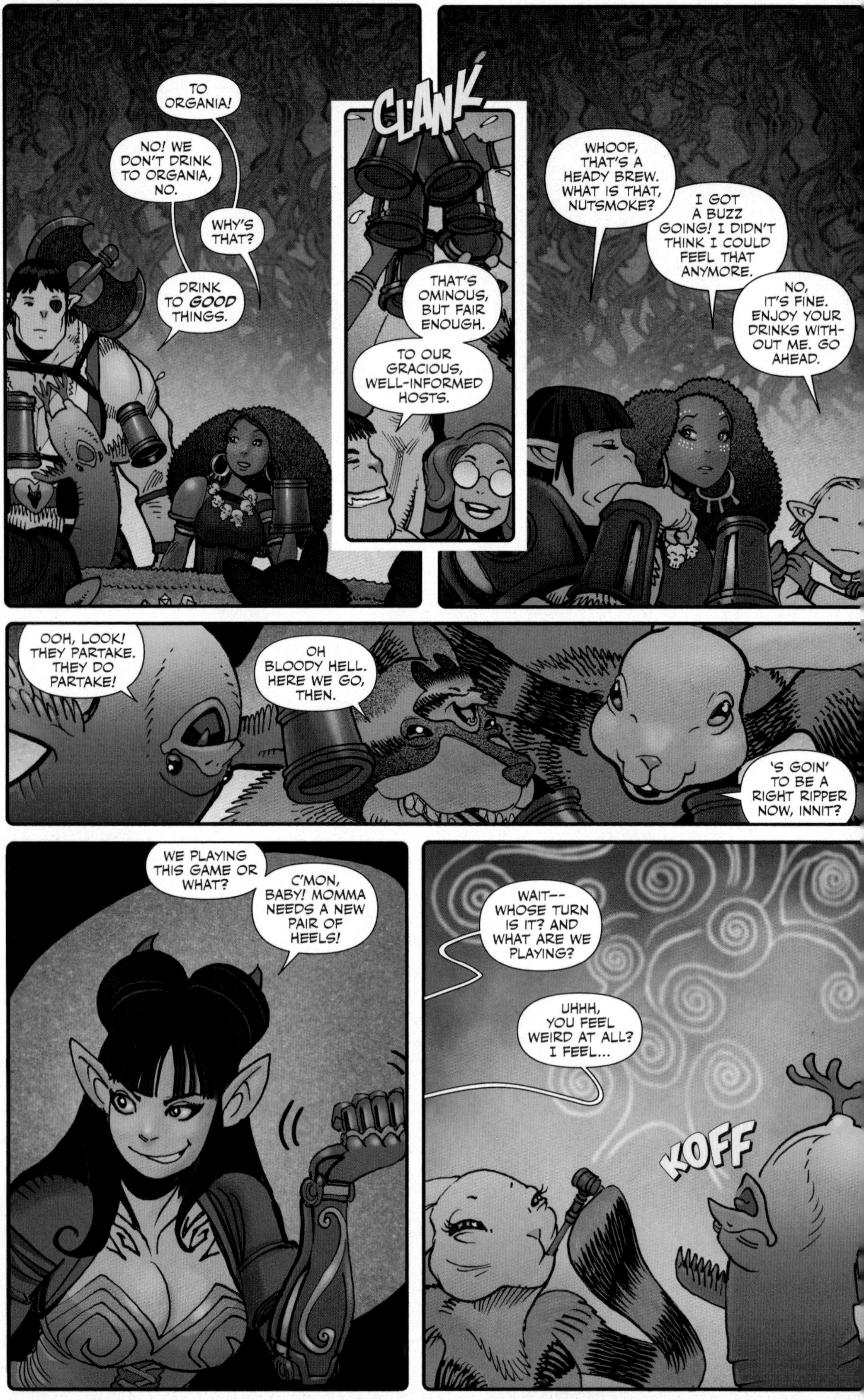

TO ORGANIA!
NO! WE DON'T DRINK TO ORGANIA, NO.
WHY'S THAT?
DRINK TO **GOOD** THINGS.
CLANK
THAT'S OMINOUS, BUT FAIR ENOUGH.
TO OUR GRACIOUS, WELL-INFORMED HOSTS.
WHOOF, THAT'S A HEADY BREW. WHAT IS THAT, NUTSMOKE?
I GOT A BUZZ GOING! I DIDN'T THINK I COULD FEEL THAT ANYMORE.
NO, IT'S FINE. ENJOY YOUR DRINKS WITH-OUT ME. GO AHEAD.
OOH, LOOK! THEY PARTAKE. THEY DO PARTAKE!
OH BLOODY HELL. HERE WE GO, THEN.
'S GOIN' TO BE A RIGHT RIPPER NOW, INNIT?
WE PLAYING THIS GAME OR WHAT?
C'MON, BABY! MOMMA NEEDS A NEW PAIR OF HEELS!
WAIT-- WHOSE TURN IS IT? AND WHAT ARE WE PLAYING?
UHHH, YOU FEEL WEIRD AT ALL? I FEEL...
KOFF

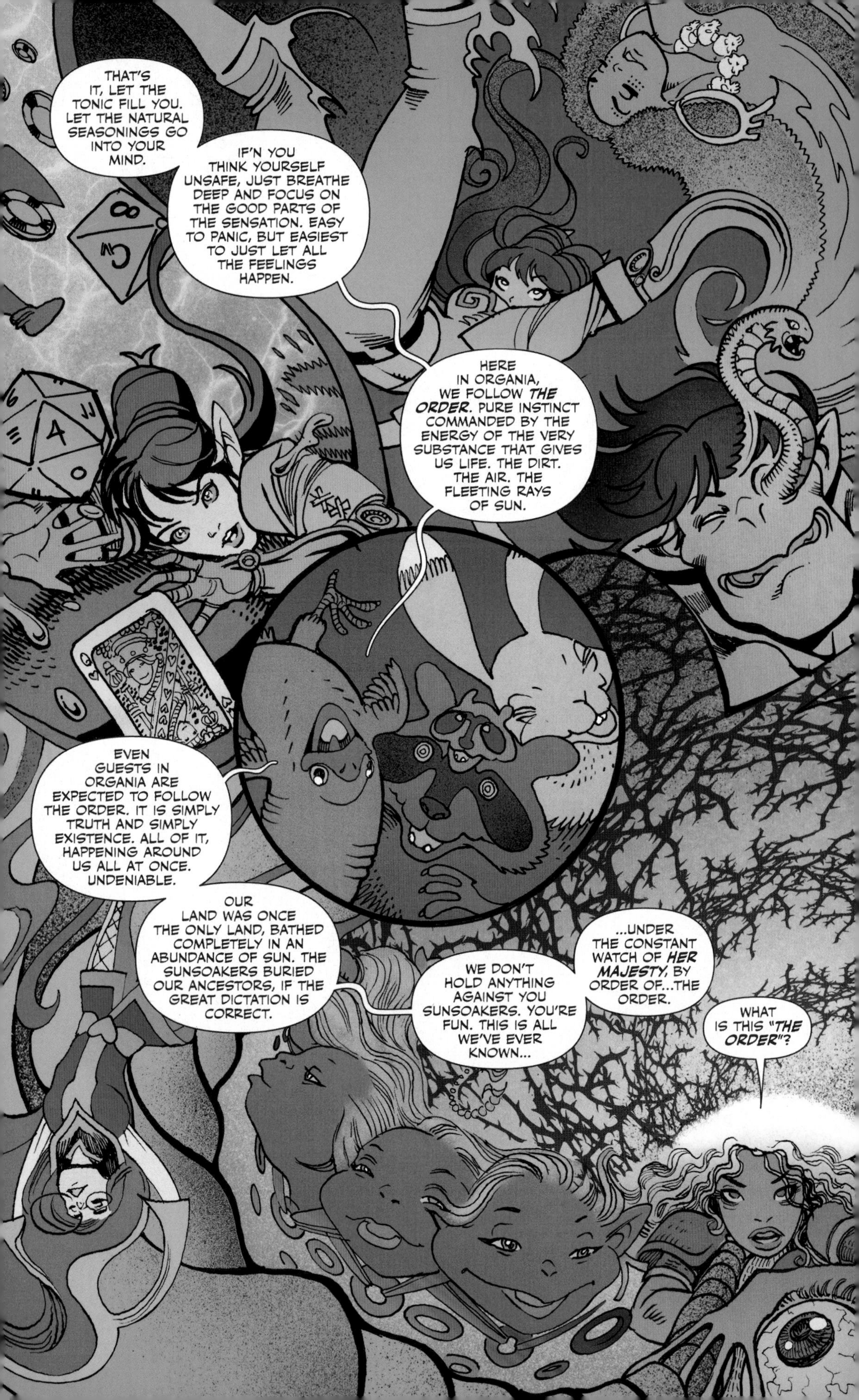
THAT'S IT, LET THE TONIC FILL YOU. LET THE NATURAL SEASONINGS GO INTO YOUR MIND.
IF'N YOU THINK YOURSELF UNSAFE, JUST BREATHE DEEP AND FOCUS ON THE GOOD PARTS OF THE SENSATION. EASY TO PANIC, BUT EASIEST TO JUST LET ALL THE FEELINGS HAPPEN.
HERE IN ORGANIA, WE FOLLOW *THE ORDER*. PURE INSTINCT COMMANDED BY THE ENERGY OF THE VERY SUBSTANCE THAT GIVES US LIFE. THE DIRT. THE AIR. THE FLEETING RAYS OF SUN.
EVEN GUESTS IN ORGANIA ARE EXPECTED TO FOLLOW THE ORDER. IT IS SIMPLY TRUTH AND SIMPLY EXISTENCE. ALL OF IT, HAPPENING AROUND US ALL AT ONCE. UNDENIABLE.
OUR LAND WAS ONCE THE ONLY LAND, BATHED COMPLETELY IN AN ABUNDANCE OF SUN. THE SUNSOAKERS BURIED OUR ANCESTORS, IF THE GREAT DICTATION IS CORRECT.
WE DON'T HOLD ANYTHING AGAINST YOU SUNSOAKERS. YOU'RE FUN. THIS IS ALL WE'VE EVER KNOWN...
...UNDER THE CONSTANT WATCH OF *HER MAJESTY*, BY ORDER OF...THE ORDER.
WHAT IS THIS "*THE ORDER*"?

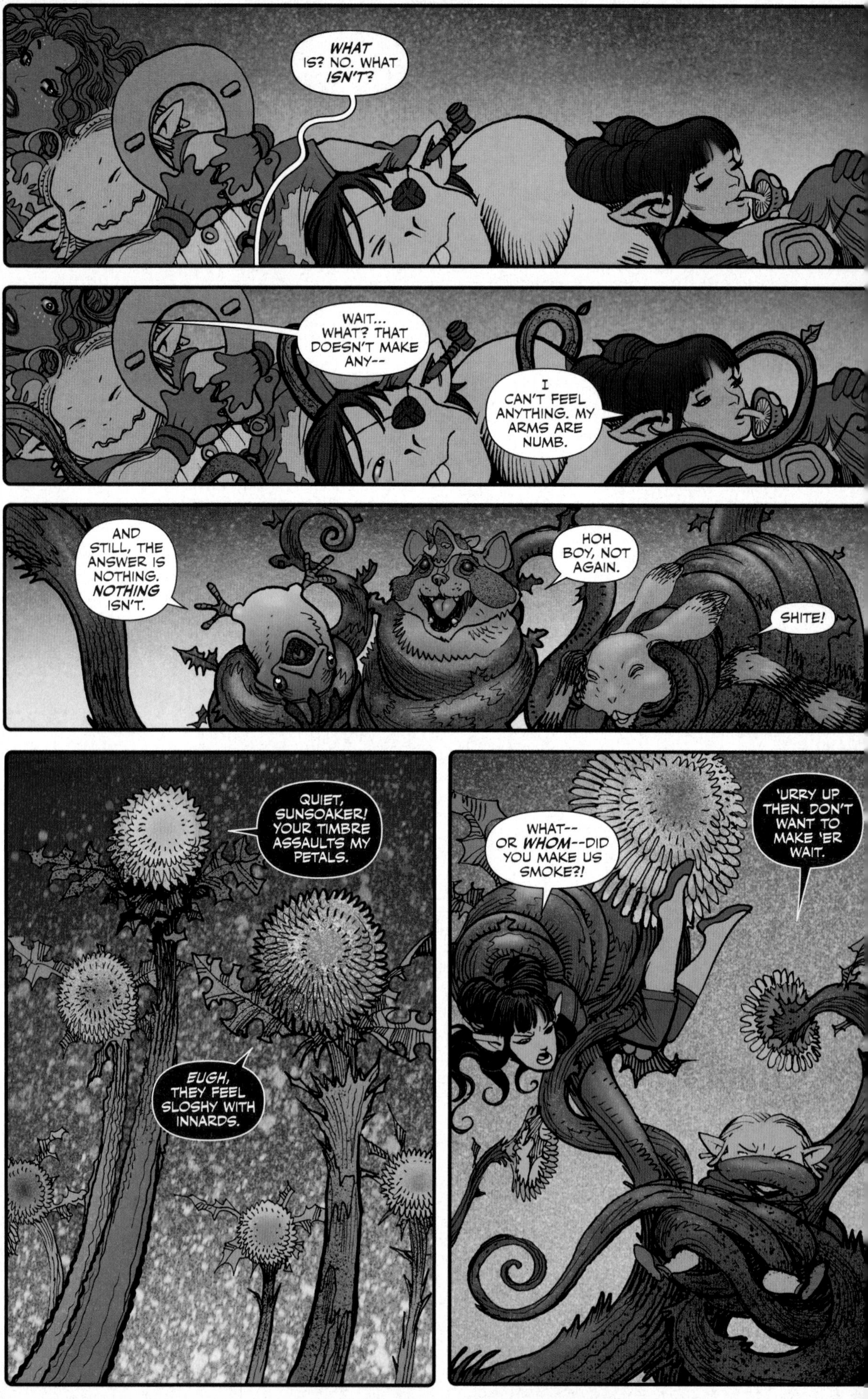
WHAT IS? NO. WHAT ISN'T?
WAIT... WHAT? THAT DOESN'T MAKE ANY--
I CAN'T FEEL ANYTHING. MY ARMS ARE NUMB.
AND STILL, THE ANSWER IS NOTHING. NOTHING ISN'T.
HOH BOY, NOT AGAIN.
SHITE!
QUIET, SUNSOAKER! YOUR TIMBRE ASSAULTS MY PETALS.
EUGH, THEY FEEL SLOSHY WITH INNARDS.
WHAT-- OR WHOM--DID YOU MAKE US SMOKE?!
'URRY UP THEN. DON'T WANT TO MAKE 'ER WAIT.

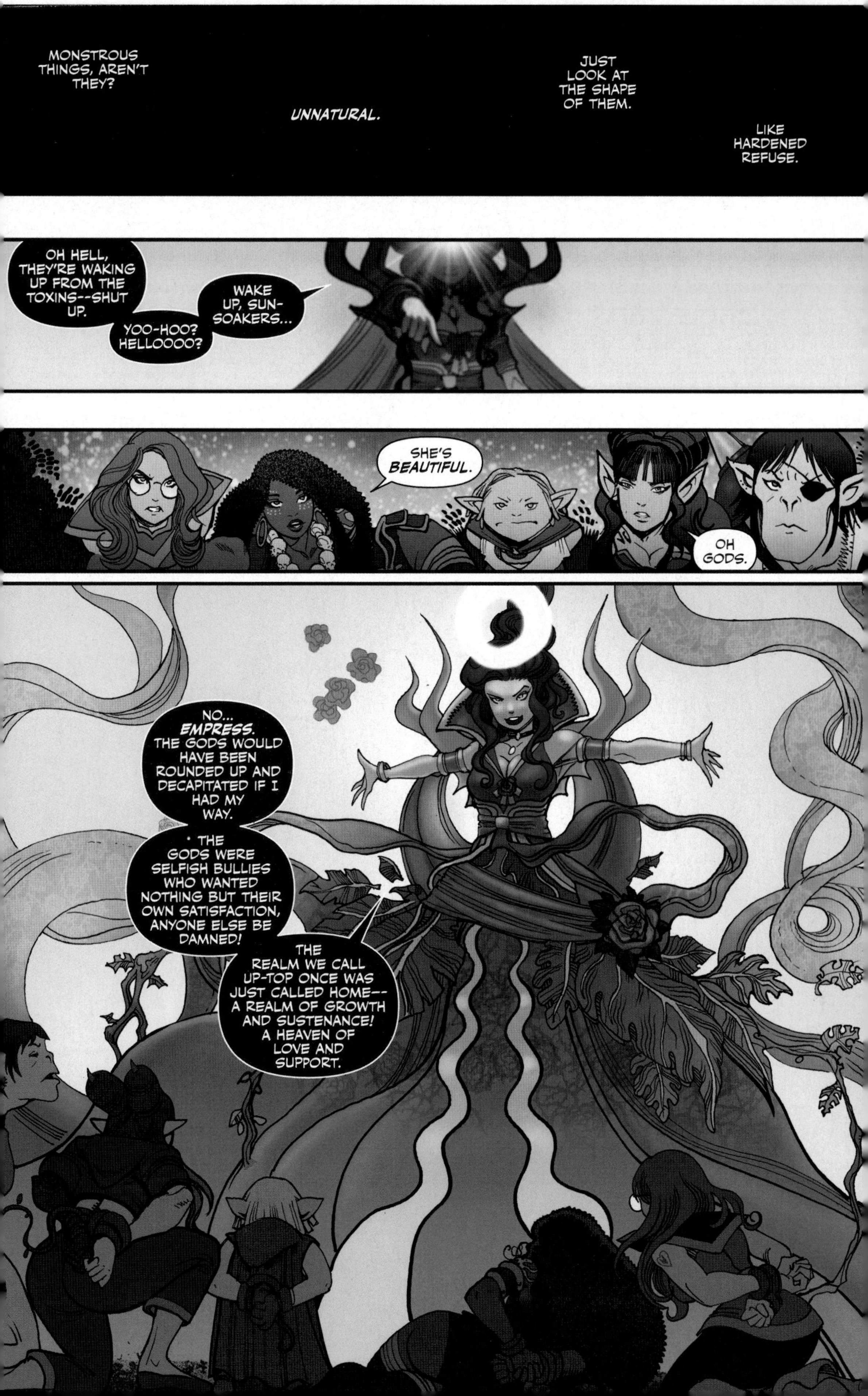
MONSTROUS THINGS, AREN'T THEY?
UNNATURAL.
JUST LOOK AT THE SHAPE OF THEM.
LIKE HARDENED REFUSE.
OH HELL, THEY'RE WAKING UP FROM THE TOXINS--SHUT UP.
YOO-HOO? HELLOOOO?
WAKE UP, SUN-SOAKERS...
SHE'S BEAUTIFUL.
OH GODS.
NO... EMPRESS. THE GODS WOULD HAVE BEEN ROUNDED UP AND DECAPITATED IF I HAD MY WAY.
THE GODS WERE SELFISH BULLIES WHO WANTED NOTHING BUT THEIR OWN SATISFACTION, ANYONE ELSE BE DAMNED!
THE REALM WE CALL UP-TOP ONCE WAS JUST CALLED HOME-- A REALM OF GROWTH AND SUSTENANCE! A HEAVEN OF LOVE AND SUPPORT.

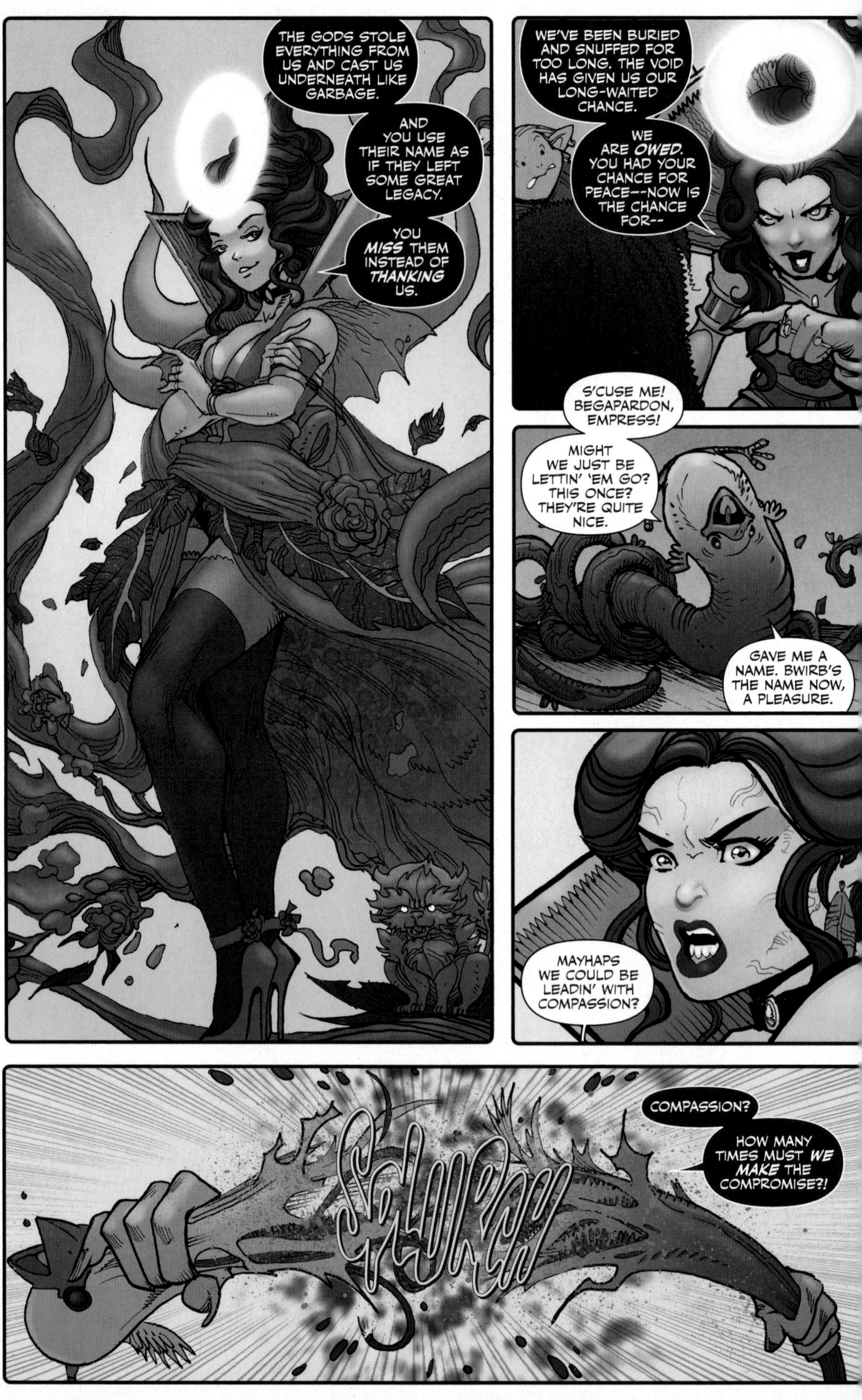
THE GODS STOLE EVERYTHING FROM US AND CAST US UNDERNEATH LIKE GARBAGE.
AND YOU USE THEIR NAME AS IF THEY LEFT SOME GREAT LEGACY.
YOU MISS THEM INSTEAD OF THANKING US.
WE'VE BEEN BURIED AND SNUFFED FOR TOO LONG. THE VOID HAS GIVEN US OUR LONG-WAITED CHANCE.
WE ARE OWED. YOU HAD YOUR CHANCE FOR PEACE--NOW IS THE CHANCE FOR--
S'CUSE ME! BEGAPARDON, EMPRESS!
MIGHT WE JUST BE LETTIN' 'EM GO? THIS ONCE? THEY'RE QUITE NICE.
GAVE ME A NAME. BWIRB'S THE NAME NOW, A PLEASURE.
MAYHAPS WE COULD BE LEADIN' WITH COMPASSION?
SCHLURCH
COMPASSION?
HOW MANY TIMES MUST WE MAKE THE COMPROMISE?!

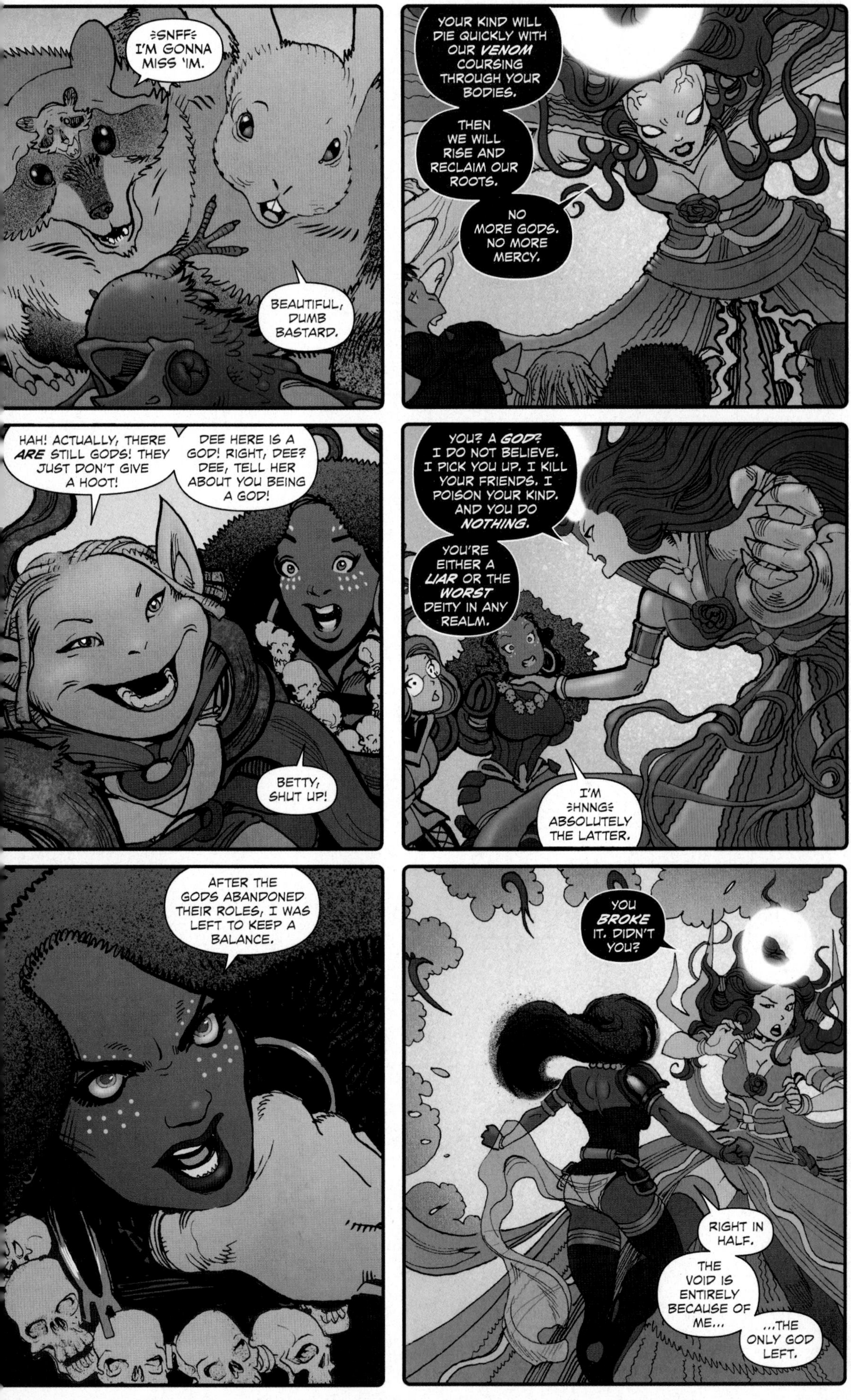

=SNFF= I'M GONNA MISS 'IM.
BEAUTIFUL, DUMB BASTARD.
YOUR KIND WILL DIE QUICKLY WITH OUR *VENOM* COURSING THROUGH YOUR BODIES.
THEN WE WILL RISE AND RECLAIM OUR ROOTS.
NO MORE GODS. NO MORE MERCY.
HAH! ACTUALLY, THERE *ARE* STILL GODS! THEY JUST DON'T GIVE A HOOT!
DEE HERE IS A GOD! RIGHT, DEE? DEE, TELL HER ABOUT YOU BEING A GOD!
BETTY, SHUT UP!
YOU? A *GOD?* I DO NOT BELIEVE. I PICK YOU UP. I KILL YOUR FRIENDS. I POISON YOUR KIND. AND YOU DO *NOTHING.*
YOU'RE EITHER A *LIAR* OR THE *WORST* DEITY IN ANY REALM.
I'M =HNNG= ABSOLUTELY THE LATTER.
AFTER THE GODS ABANDONED THEIR ROLES, I WAS LEFT TO KEEP A BALANCE.
YOU *BROKE* IT. DIDN'T YOU?
RIGHT IN HALF.
THE VOID IS ENTIRELY BECAUSE OF ME...
...THE ONLY GOD LEFT.

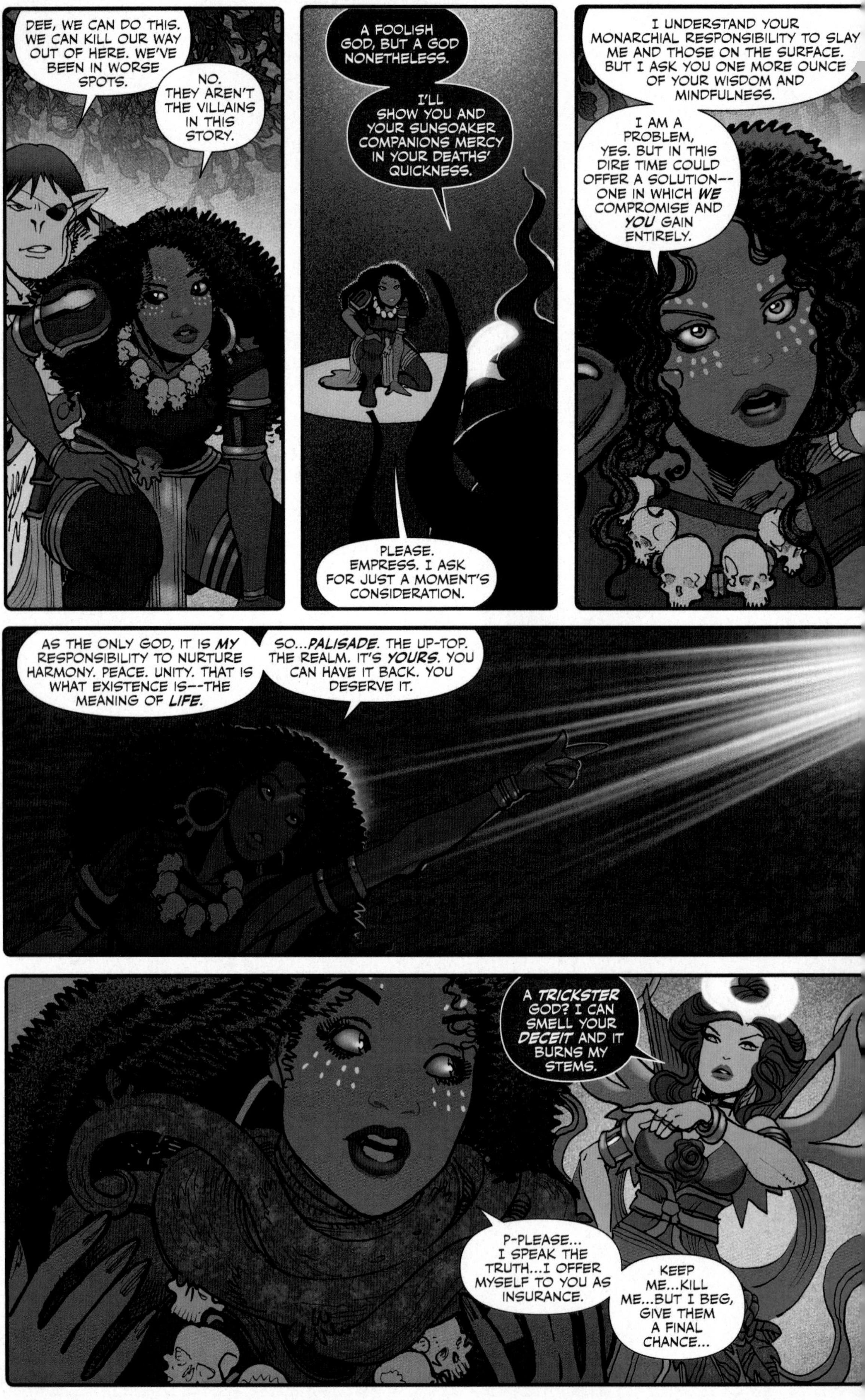
DEE, WE CAN DO THIS. WE CAN KILL OUR WAY OUT OF HERE. WE'VE BEEN IN WORSE SPOTS.
NO. THEY AREN'T THE VILLAINS IN THIS STORY.
A FOOLISH GOD, BUT A GOD NONETHELESS.
I'LL SHOW YOU AND YOUR SUNSOAKER COMPANIONS MERCY IN YOUR DEATHS' QUICKNESS.
PLEASE. EMPRESS. I ASK FOR JUST A MOMENT'S CONSIDERATION.
I UNDERSTAND YOUR MONARCHIAL RESPONSIBILITY TO SLAY ME AND THOSE ON THE SURFACE. BUT I ASK YOU ONE MORE OUNCE OF YOUR WISDOM AND MINDFULNESS.
I AM A PROBLEM, YES. BUT IN THIS DIRE TIME COULD OFFER A SOLUTION-- ONE IN WHICH *WE* COMPROMISE AND *YOU* GAIN ENTIRELY.
AS THE ONLY GOD, IT IS *MY* RESPONSIBILITY TO NURTURE HARMONY. PEACE. UNITY. THAT IS WHAT EXISTENCE IS--THE MEANING OF *LIFE*.
SO...*PALISADE*. THE UP-TOP. THE REALM. IT'S *YOURS*. YOU CAN HAVE IT BACK. YOU DESERVE IT.
A *TRICKSTER* GOD? I CAN SMELL YOUR *DECEIT* AND IT BURNS MY STEMS.
P-PLEASE... I SPEAK THE TRUTH...I OFFER MYSELF TO YOU AS INSURANCE.
KEEP ME...KILL ME...BUT I BEG, GIVE THEM A FINAL CHANCE...

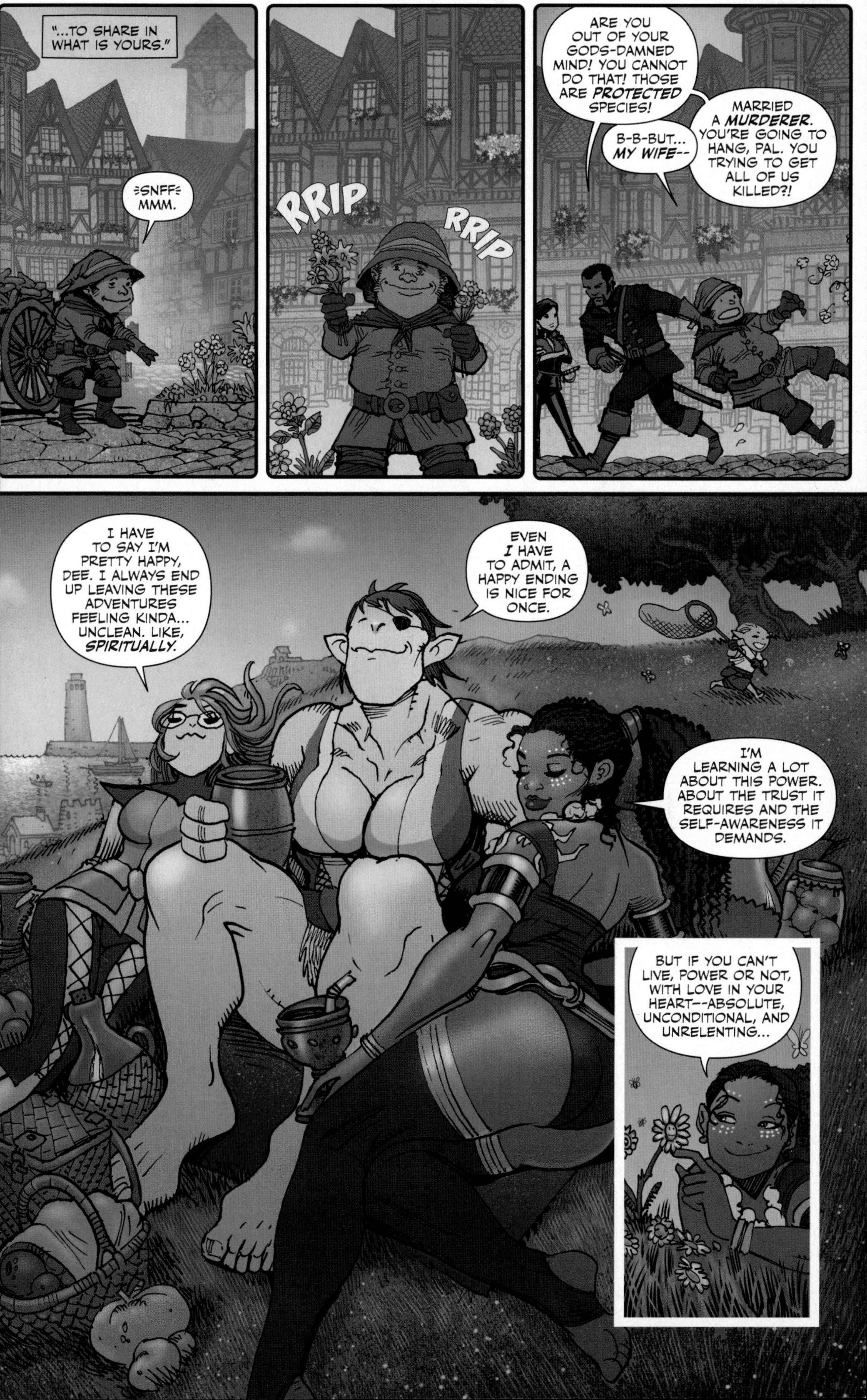
"...TO SHARE IN WHAT IS YOURS."
≡SNFF≡ MMM.
RRIP
RRIP
ARE YOU OUT OF YOUR GODS-DAMNED MIND! YOU CANNOT DO THAT! THOSE ARE PROTECTED SPECIES!
B-B-BUT... MY WIFE--
MARRIED A MURDERER. YOU'RE GOING TO HANG, PAL. YOU TRYING TO GET ALL OF US KILLED?!
I HAVE TO SAY I'M PRETTY HAPPY, DEE. I ALWAYS END UP LEAVING THESE ADVENTURES FEELING KINDA... UNCLEAN. LIKE, SPIRITUALLY.
EVEN I HAVE TO ADMIT, A HAPPY ENDING IS NICE FOR ONCE.
I'M LEARNING A LOT ABOUT THIS POWER. ABOUT THE TRUST IT REQUIRES AND THE SELF-AWARENESS IT DEMANDS.
BUT IF YOU CAN'T LIVE, POWER OR NOT, WITH LOVE IN YOUR HEART--ABSOLUTE, UNCONDITIONAL, AND UNRELENTING...

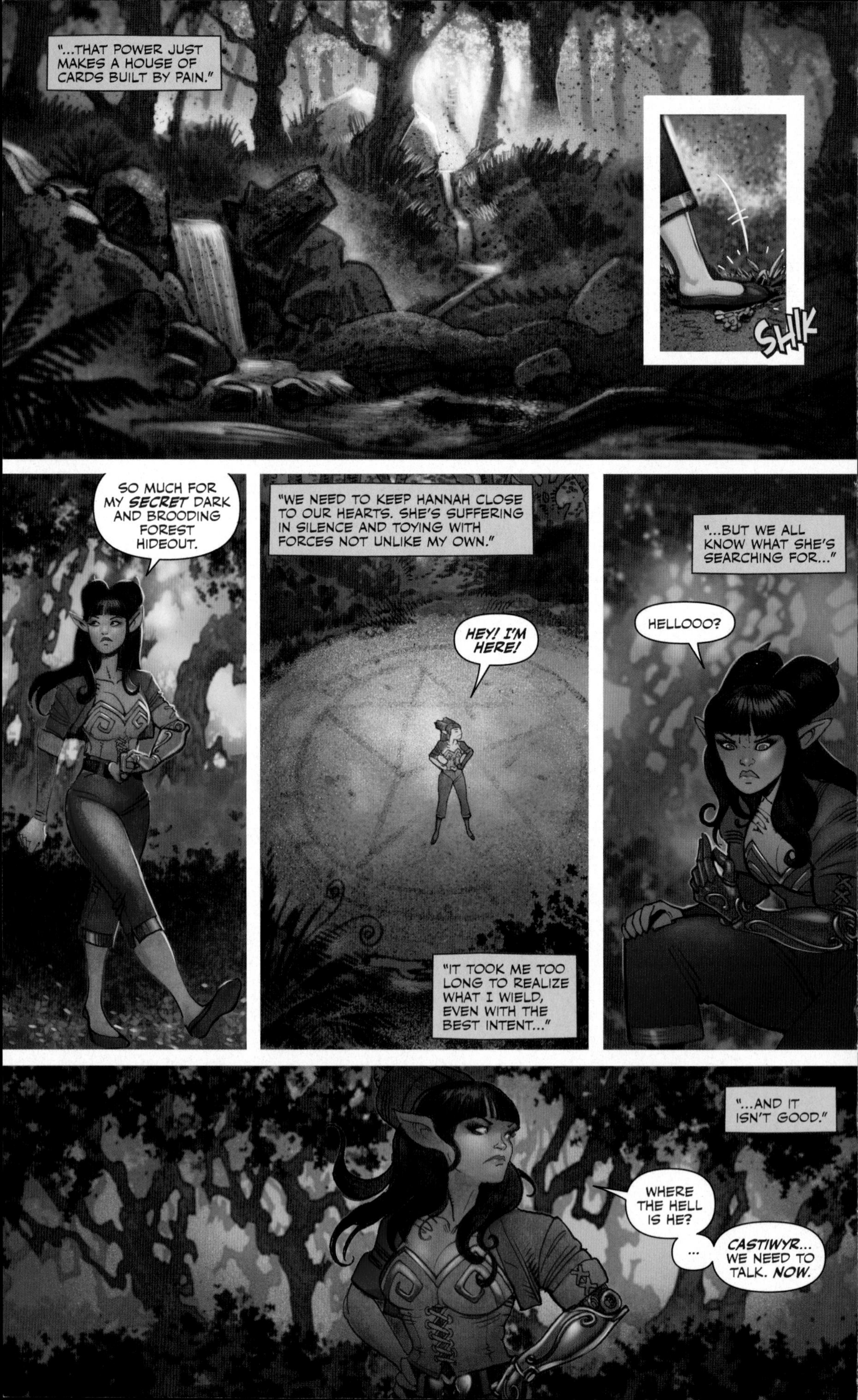
"...THAT POWER JUST MAKES A HOUSE OF CARDS BUILT BY PAIN."
SHIK
SO MUCH FOR MY *SECRET* DARK AND BROODING FOREST HIDEOUT.
"WE NEED TO KEEP HANNAH CLOSE TO OUR HEARTS. SHE'S SUFFERING IN SILENCE AND TOYING WITH FORCES NOT UNLIKE MY OWN."
HEY! I'M HERE!
"IT TOOK ME TOO LONG TO REALIZE WHAT I WIELD, EVEN WITH THE BEST INTENT..."
"...BUT WE ALL KNOW WHAT SHE'S SEARCHING FOR..."
HELLOOO?
"...AND IT ISN'T GOOD."
WHERE THE HELL IS HE?
...
CASTIWYR... WE NEED TO TALK. *NOW*.

CHAPTER TWENTY-FOUR

ISSUE #24 COVER

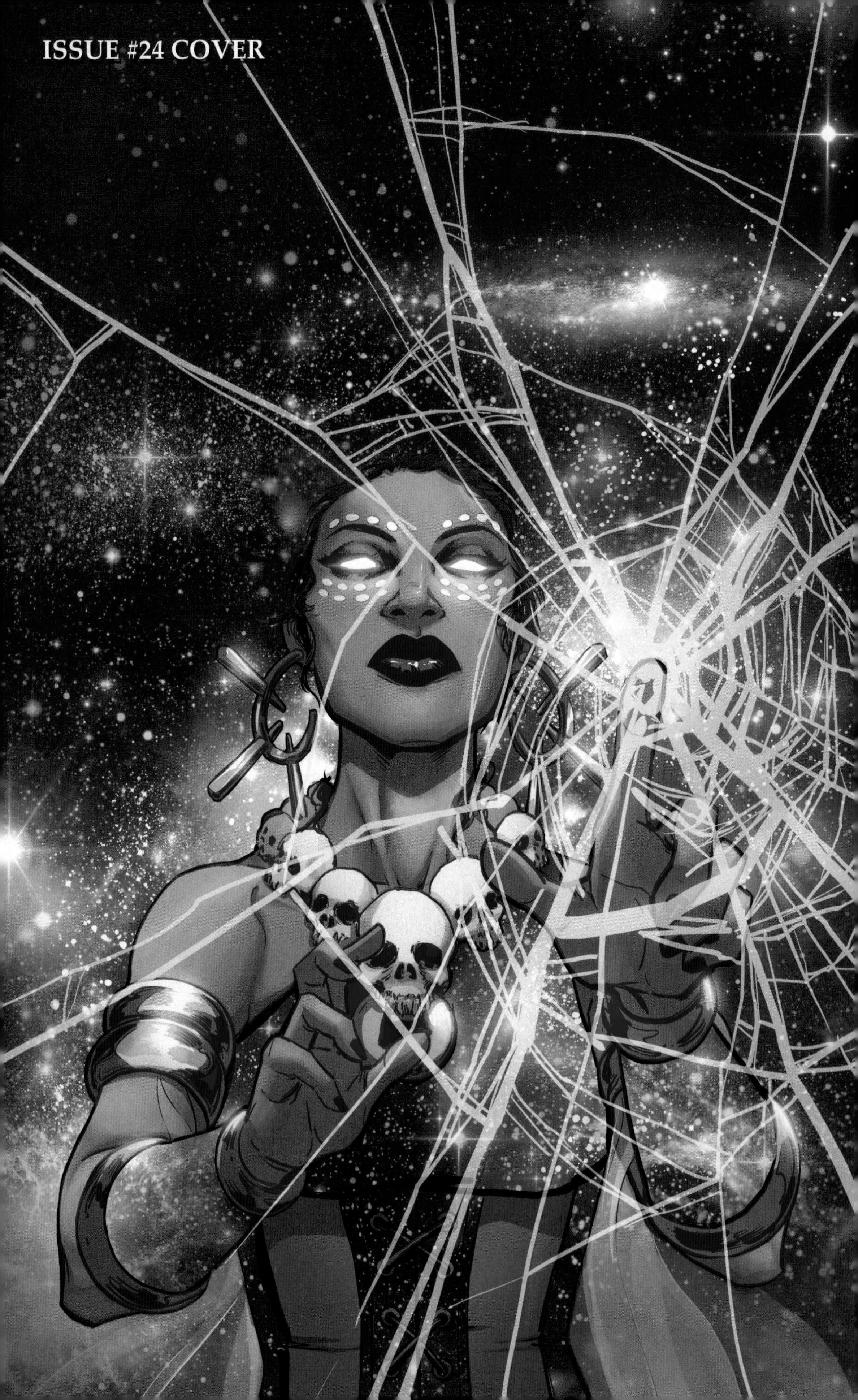

FUNNY, I DON'T REMEMBER HAVING TO DO THIS MUCH HOUSEKEEPING WHEN I WAS DRINKING...

...I MUST'VE CLEANED SO MUCH OVER THE YEARS, WOW.

SO, WHAT'S A *SOBER* SMIDGEON TO DO WHEN HER SISTERS ARE PASSED OUT?

BRAGA'S *BLUDDBARB PIE*, THAT'S WHAT.

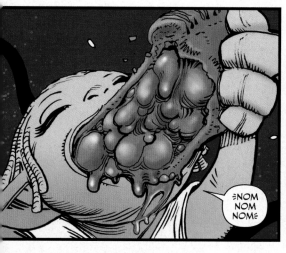

=NOM NOM NOM=

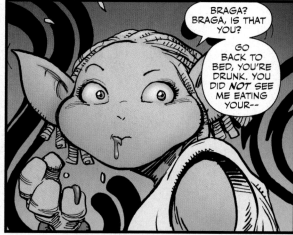

BRAGA? BRAGA, IS THAT YOU?

GO BACK TO BED, YOU'RE DRUNK. YOU DID *NOT* SEE ME EATING YOUR--

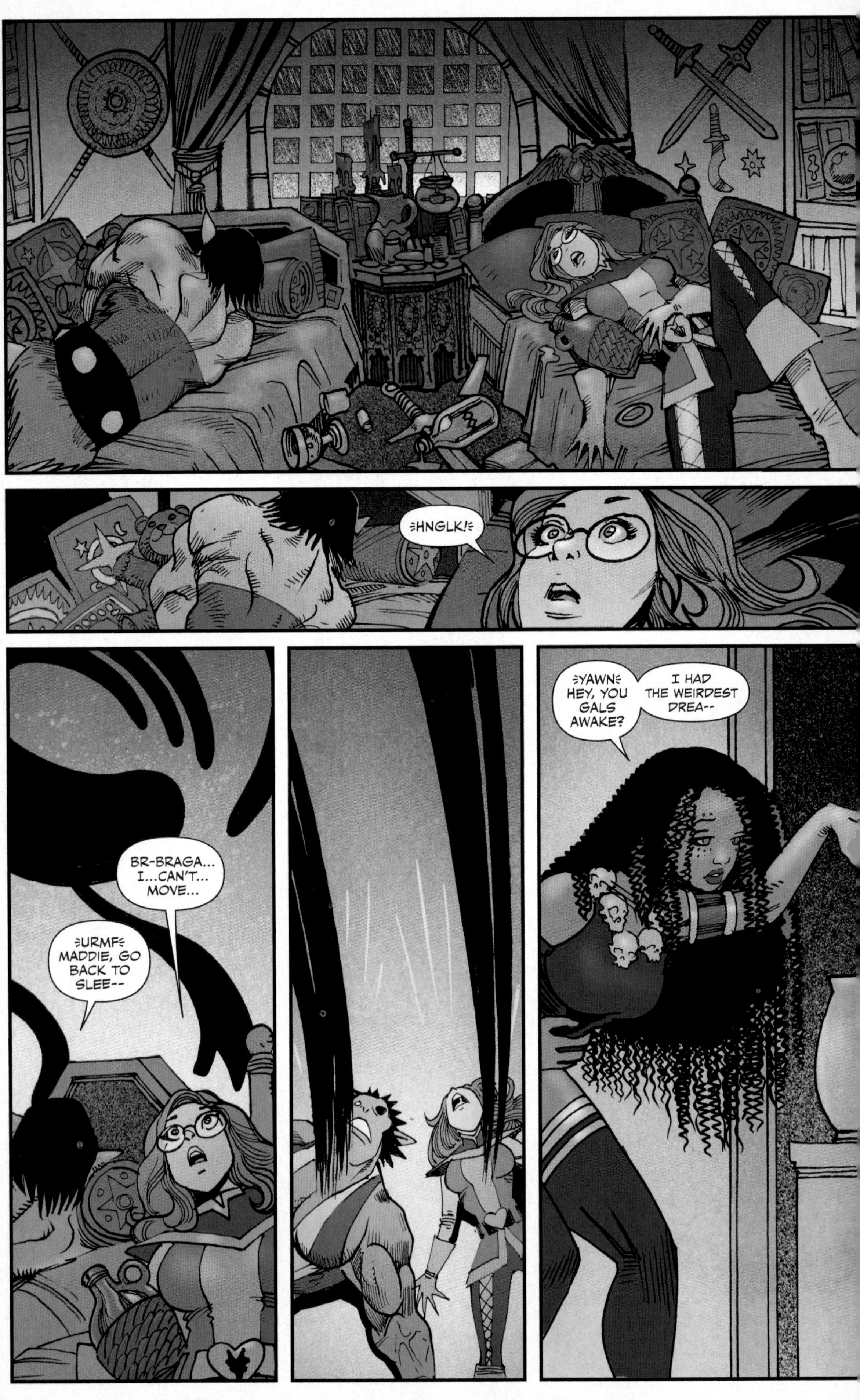

≈HNGLK!≈
BR-BRAGA... I...CAN'T... MOVE...
≈URMF≈ MADDIE, GO BACK TO SLEE--
≈YAWN≈ HEY, YOU GALS AWAKE?
I HAD THE WEIRDEST DREA--

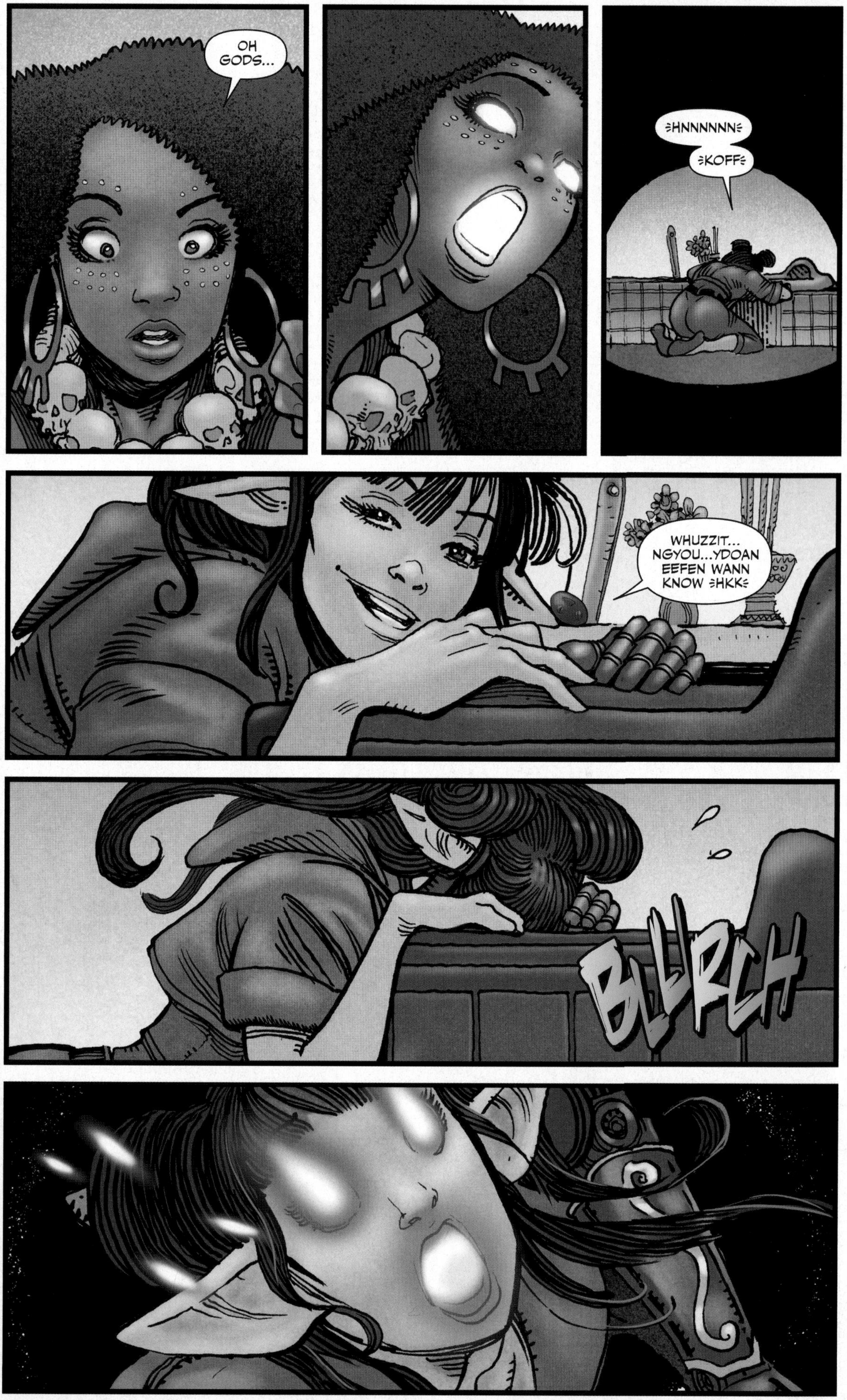
OH GODS...
HNNNNNN
KOFF
WHUZZIT... NGYOU...YDOAN EEFEN WANN KNOW HKK
BLURCH

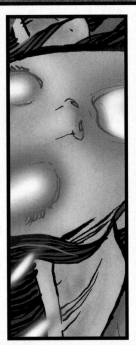
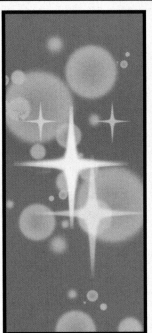

HOOOLY SHIT, GUYS... I THINK I FELL INTO THE TOILET.

WERE YOU *ALL* HOLDING MY HAIR?

WAIT... ARE WE IN THE *TOILET REALM*?!

I'VE ONLY SEEN THIS IN MY WILDEST DREAMS.

I WAS SLEEPING—BUT I WASN'T. I COULDN'T MOVE. SOMETHING WAS IN THERE WITH US.

I SAW IT TOO. IT TOUCHED US. AND NOW...

DEE, WAKE UP! WE'RE SADLY *NOT* IN THE TOILET REALM, AS IT WERE.

WHAT'S THE SCOOP, DEE? WHAT DO YOU SEE?

MY POWERS AREN'T WORKING HERE.

I'M *SIFTING.*

SPIRITUALLY LIVING THROUGH EVERY POSSIBLE SCENARIO FOR WHAT THE HELLS JUST HAPPENED...

OH. SOUNDS... FUN.

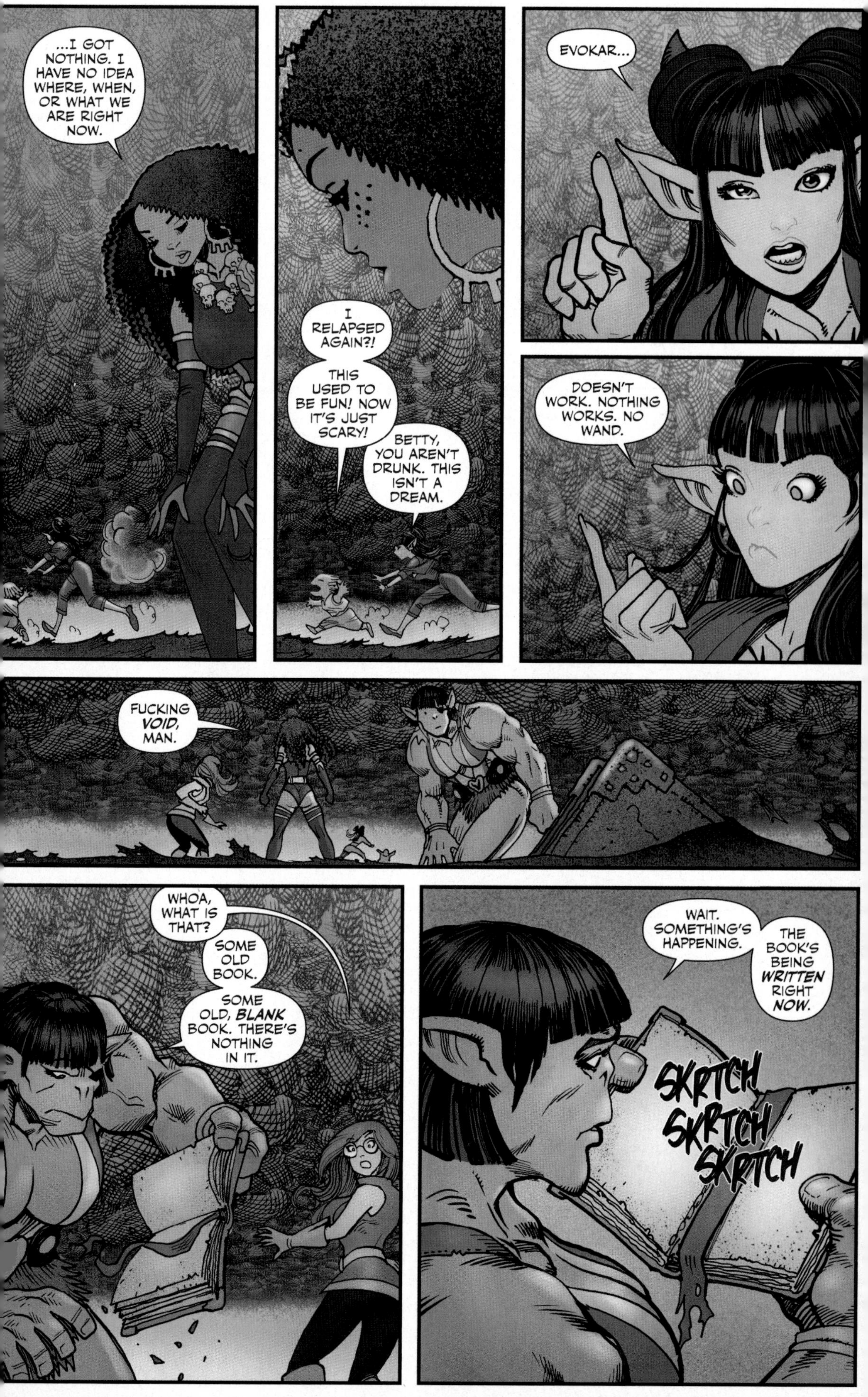

...I GOT NOTHING. I HAVE NO IDEA WHERE, WHEN, OR WHAT WE ARE RIGHT NOW.
I RELAPSED AGAIN?!
THIS USED TO BE FUN! NOW IT'S JUST SCARY!
BETTY, YOU AREN'T DRUNK. THIS ISN'T A DREAM.
EVOKAR...
DOESN'T WORK. NOTHING WORKS. NO WAND.
FUCKING VOID, MAN.
WHOA, WHAT IS THAT?
SOME OLD BOOK.
SOME OLD, BLANK BOOK. THERE'S NOTHING IN IT.
WAIT. SOMETHING'S HAPPENING.
THE BOOK'S BEING WRITTEN RIGHT NOW.
SKRTCH SKRTCH SKRTCH

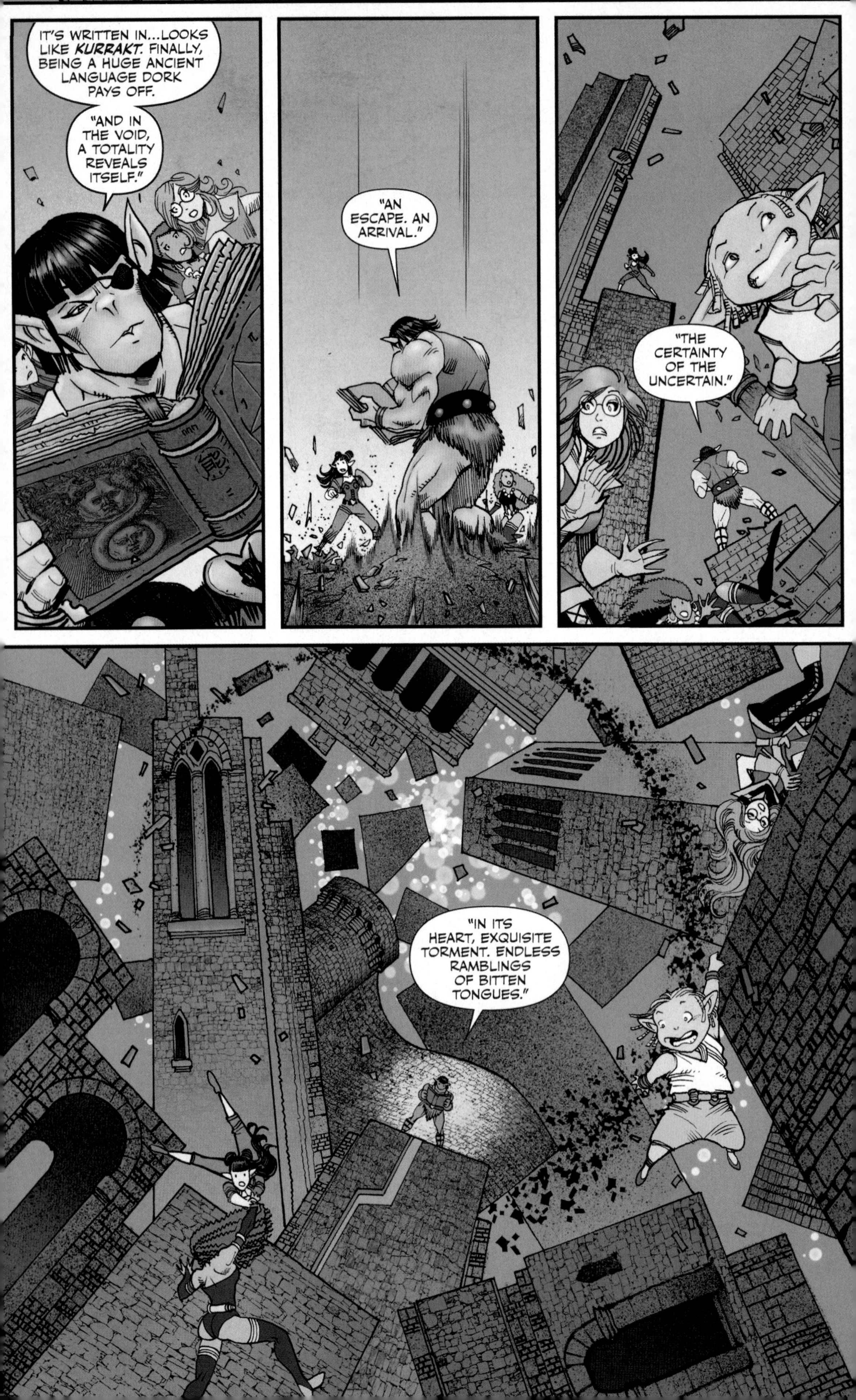
IT'S WRITTEN IN...LOOKS LIKE KURRAKT. FINALLY, BEING A HUGE ANCIENT LANGUAGE DORK PAYS OFF.
"AND IN THE VOID, A TOTALITY REVEALS ITSELF."
"AN ESCAPE. AN ARRIVAL."
"THE CERTAINTY OF THE UNCERTAIN."
"IN ITS HEART, EXQUISITE TORMENT. ENDLESS RAMBLINGS OF BITTEN TONGUES."

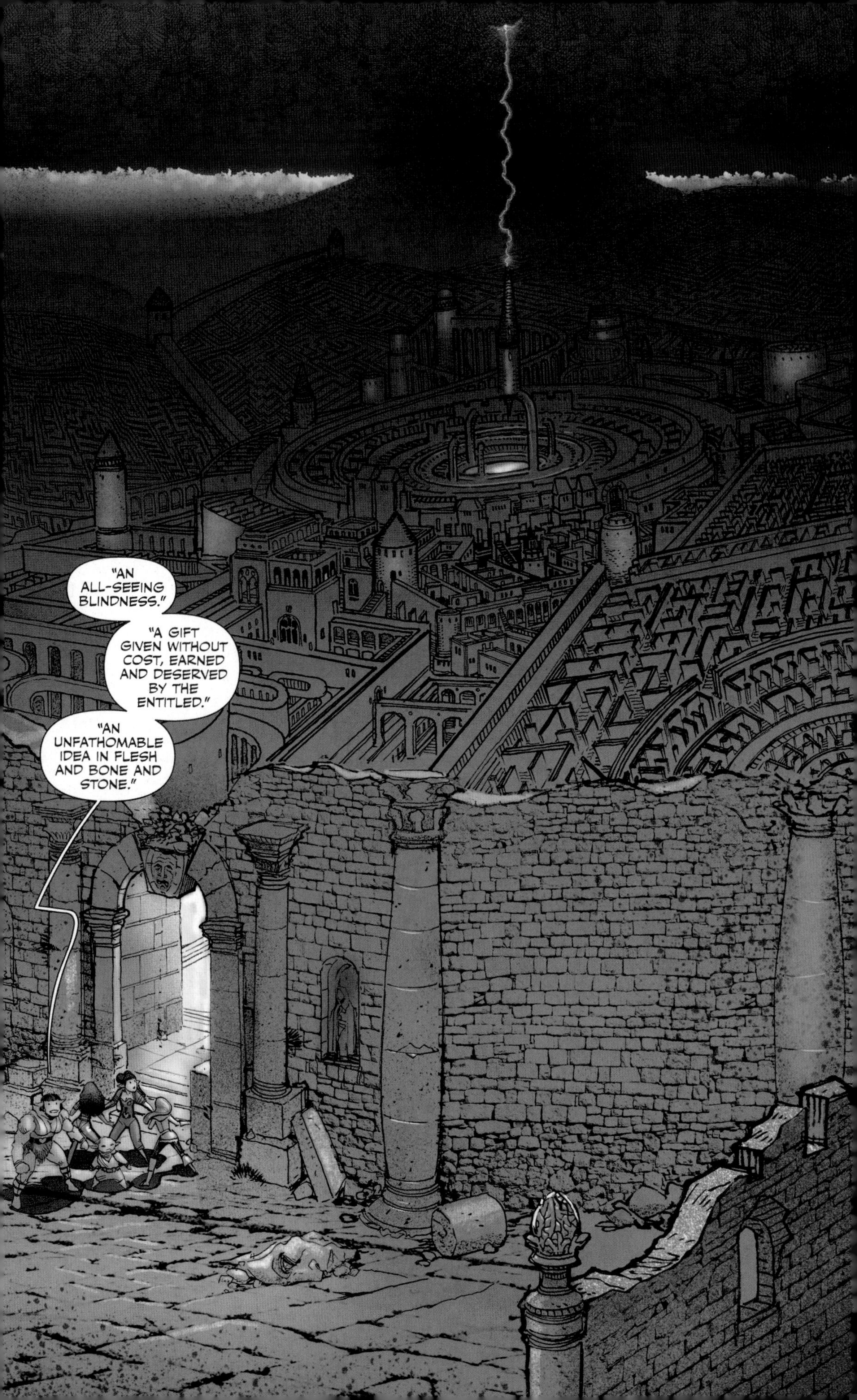
"AN ALL-SEEING BLINDNESS."
"A GIFT GIVEN WITHOUT COST, EARNED AND DESERVED BY THE ENTITLED."
"AN UNFATHOMABLE IDEA IN FLESH AND BONE AND STONE."

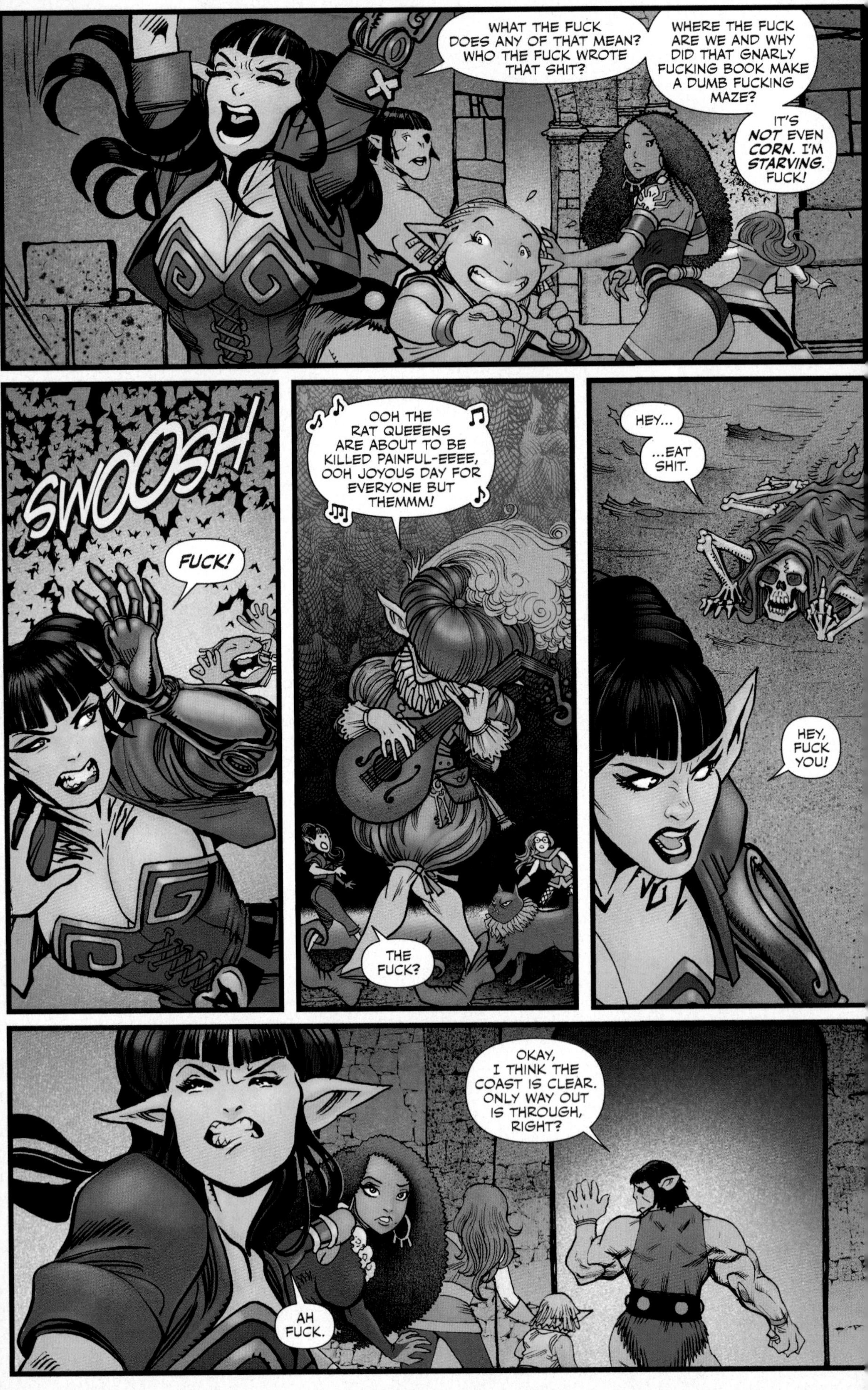
WHAT THE FUCK DOES ANY OF THAT MEAN? WHO THE FUCK WROTE THAT SHIT?
WHERE THE FUCK ARE WE AND WHY DID THAT GNARLY FUCKING BOOK MAKE A DUMB FUCKING MAZE?
IT'S NOT EVEN CORN. I'M STARVING. FUCK!
SWOOSH
FUCK!
OOH THE RAT QUEEENS ARE ABOUT TO BE KILLED PAINFUL-EEEE, OOH JOYOUS DAY FOR EVERYONE BUT THEMMM!
THE FUCK?
HEY...
...EAT SHIT.
HEY, FUCK YOU!
OKAY, I THINK THE COAST IS CLEAR. ONLY WAY OUT IS THROUGH, RIGHT?
AH FUCK.

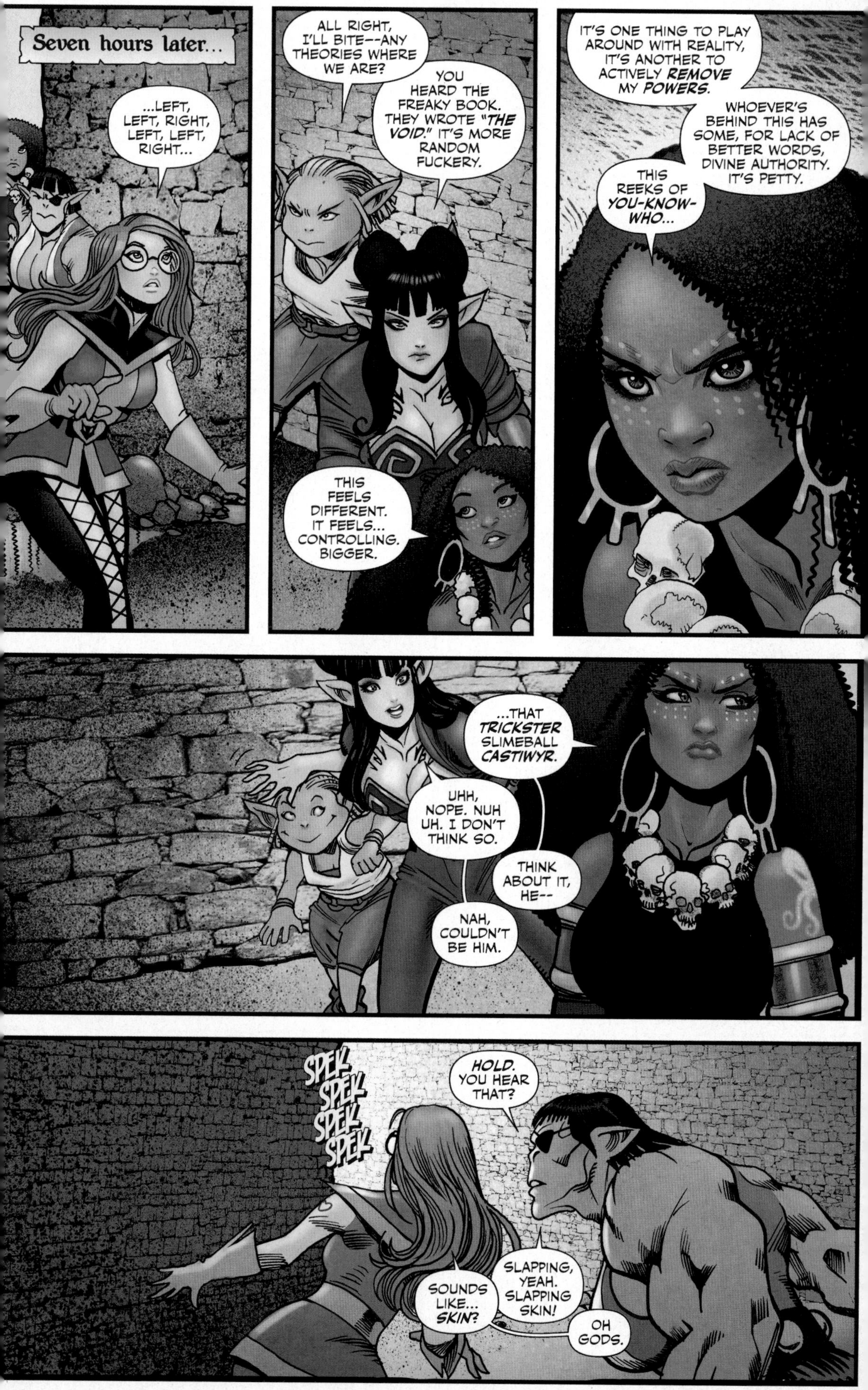
Seven hours later...
...LEFT, LEFT, RIGHT, LEFT, LEFT, RIGHT...
ALL RIGHT, I'LL BITE--ANY THEORIES WHERE WE ARE?
YOU HEARD THE FREAKY BOOK. THEY WROTE "THE VOID." IT'S MORE RANDOM FUCKERY.
THIS FEELS DIFFERENT. IT FEELS... CONTROLLING. BIGGER.
IT'S ONE THING TO PLAY AROUND WITH REALITY, IT'S ANOTHER TO ACTIVELY REMOVE MY POWERS.
WHOEVER'S BEHIND THIS HAS SOME, FOR LACK OF BETTER WORDS, DIVINE AUTHORITY. IT'S PETTY.
THIS REEKS OF YOU-KNOW-WHO...
...THAT TRICKSTER SLIMEBALL CASTIWYR.
UHH, NOPE. NUH UH. I DON'T THINK SO.
THINK ABOUT IT, HE--
NAH, COULDN'T BE HIM.
SPEK SPEK SPEK SPEK
HOLD. YOU HEAR THAT?
SOUNDS LIKE... SKIN?
SLAPPING, YEAH. SLAPPING SKIN!
OH GODS.

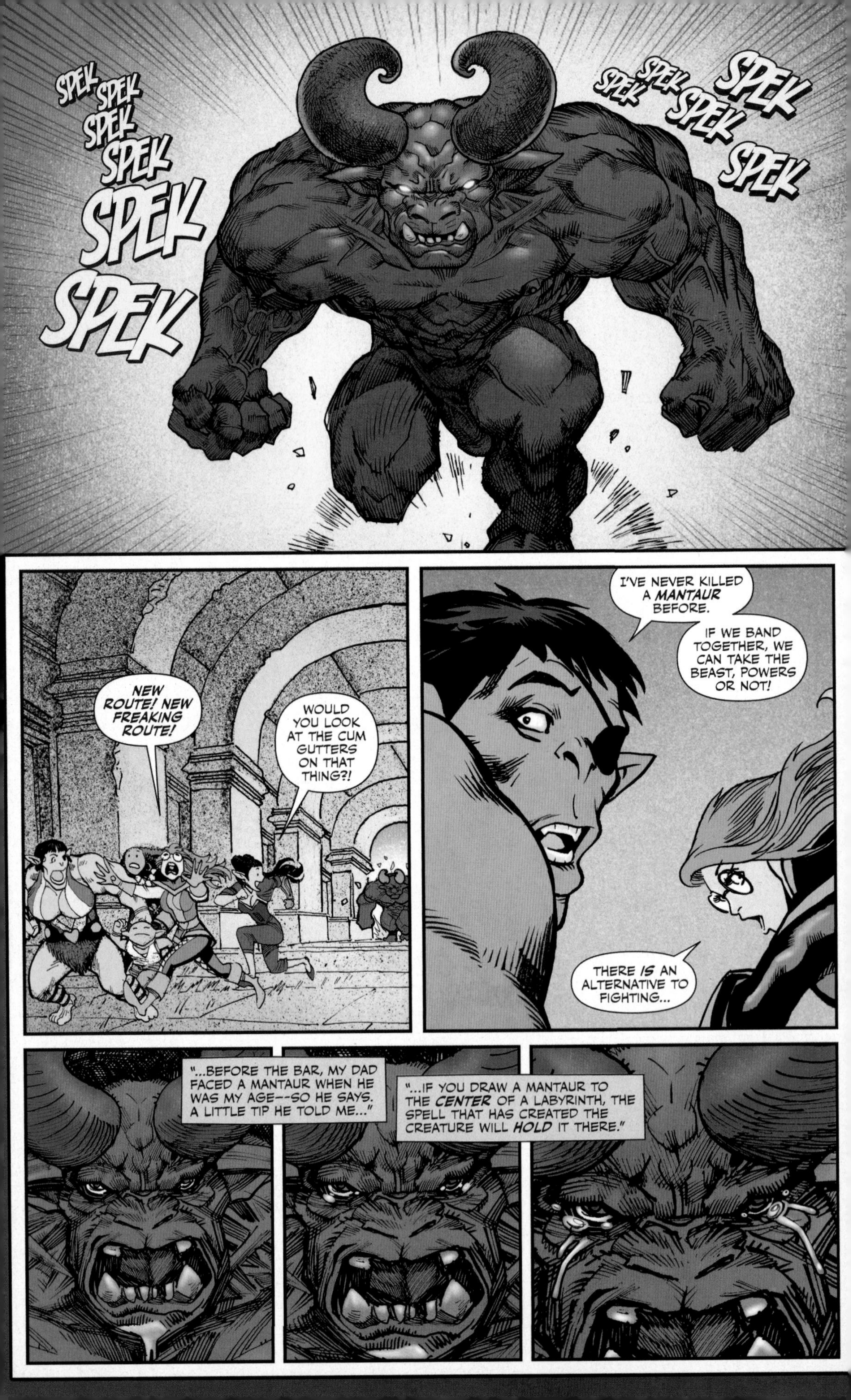
SPEK SPEK SPEK SPEK SPEK SPEK
SPEK SPEK SPEK SPEK SPEK
NEW ROUTE! NEW FREAKING ROUTE!
WOULD YOU LOOK AT THE CUM GUTTERS ON THAT THING?!
I'VE NEVER KILLED A MANTAUR BEFORE.
IF WE BAND TOGETHER, WE CAN TAKE THE BEAST, POWERS OR NOT!
THERE IS AN ALTERNATIVE TO FIGHTING...
"...BEFORE THE BAR, MY DAD FACED A MANTAUR WHEN HE WAS MY AGE--SO HE SAYS. A LITTLE TIP HE TOLD ME..."
"...IF YOU DRAW A MANTAUR TO THE CENTER OF A LABYRINTH, THE SPELL THAT HAS CREATED THE CREATURE WILL HOLD IT THERE."

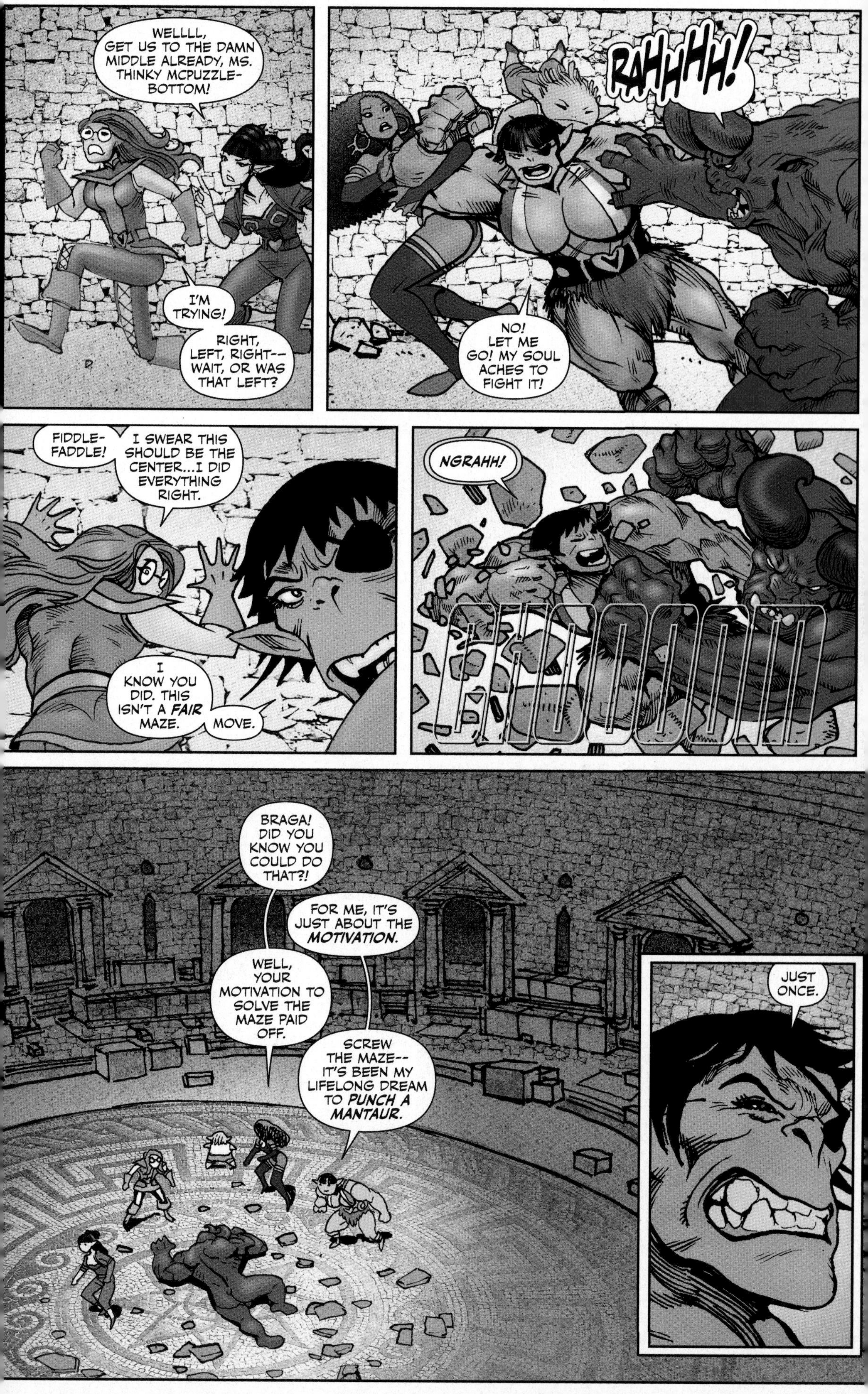
WELLLL, GET US TO THE DAMN MIDDLE ALREADY, MS. THINKY MCPUZZLE-BOTTOM!
I'M TRYING!
RIGHT, LEFT, RIGHT-- WAIT, OR WAS THAT LEFT?
RAHHHH!
NO! LET ME GO! MY SOUL ACHES TO FIGHT IT!
FIDDLE-FADDLE!
I SWEAR THIS SHOULD BE THE CENTER...I DID EVERYTHING RIGHT.
I KNOW YOU DID. THIS ISN'T A FAIR MAZE.
MOVE.
NGRAHH!
BRAGA! DID YOU KNOW YOU COULD DO THAT?!
FOR ME, IT'S JUST ABOUT THE MOTIVATION.
WELL, YOUR MOTIVATION TO SOLVE THE MAZE PAID OFF.
SCREW THE MAZE-- IT'S BEEN MY LIFELONG DREAM TO PUNCH A MANTAUR.
JUST ONCE.

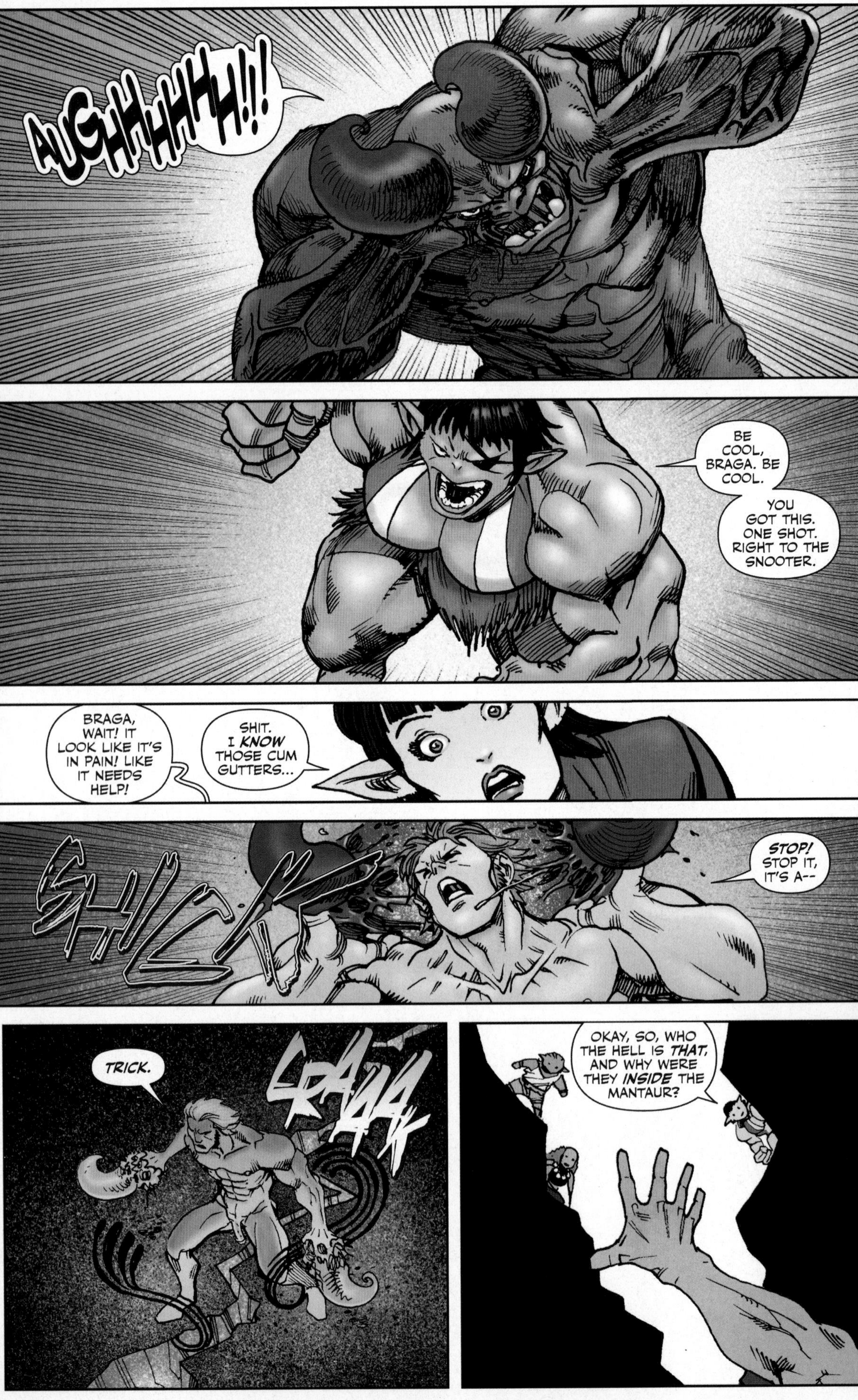
AUGHHHHH!!!
BE COOL, BRAGA. BE COOL.
YOU GOT THIS. ONE SHOT. RIGHT TO THE SNOOTER.
BRAGA, WAIT! IT LOOK LIKE IT'S IN PAIN! LIKE IT NEEDS HELP!
SHIT. I KNOW THOSE CUM GUTTERS...
SHLCK
STOP! STOP IT, IT'S A--
TRICK.
GRAAAK
OKAY, SO, WHO THE HELL IS THAT, AND WHY WERE THEY INSIDE THE MANTAUR?

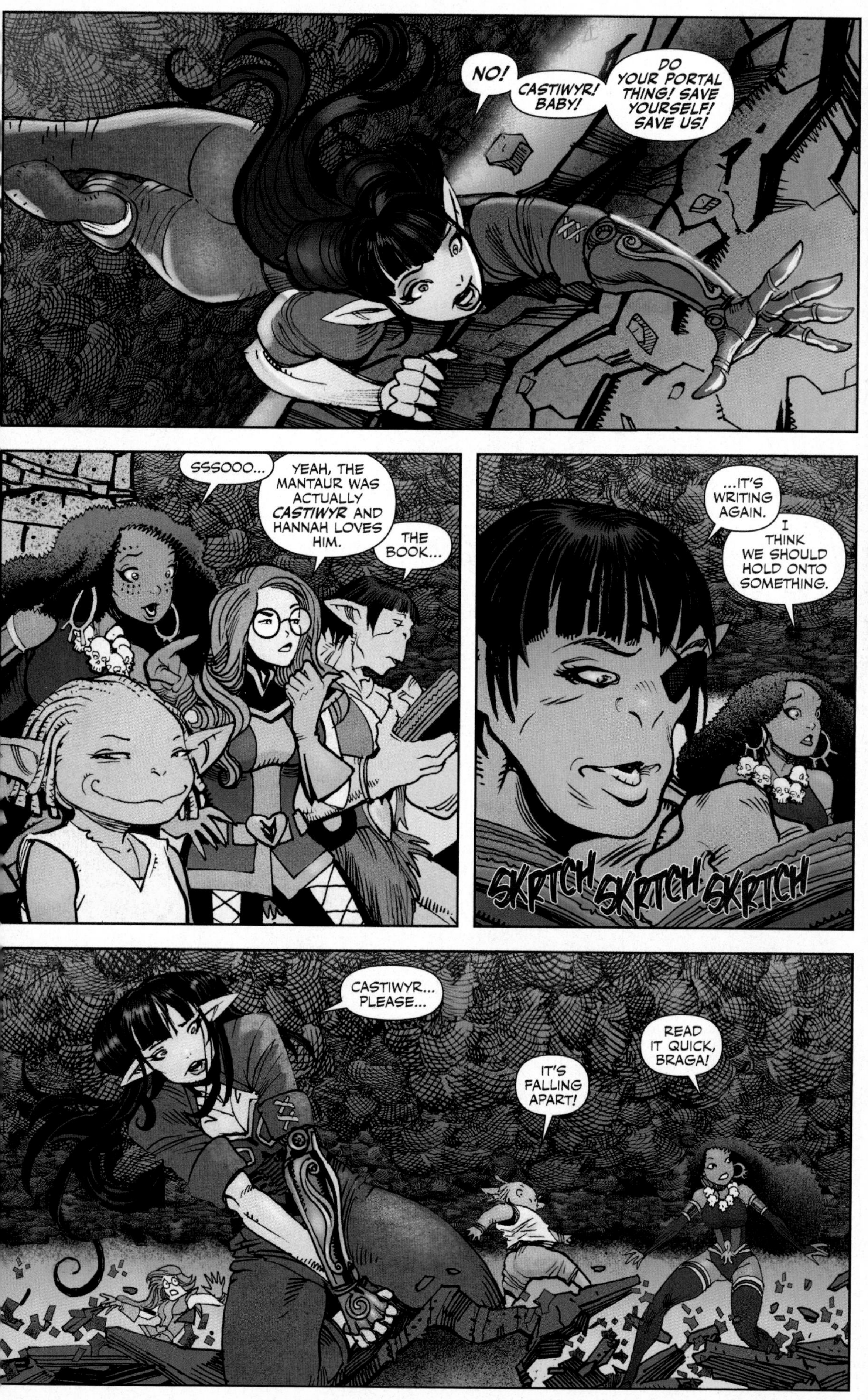
NO!
CASTIWYR! BABY!
DO YOUR PORTAL THING! SAVE YOURSELF! SAVE US!
SSSOOO...
YEAH, THE MANTAUR WAS ACTUALLY *CASTIWYR* AND HANNAH LOVES HIM.
THE BOOK...
...IT'S WRITING AGAIN.
I THINK WE SHOULD HOLD ONTO SOMETHING.
SKRTCH SKRTCH SKRTCH
CASTIWYR... PLEASE...
READ IT QUICK, BRAGA!
IT'S FALLING APART!

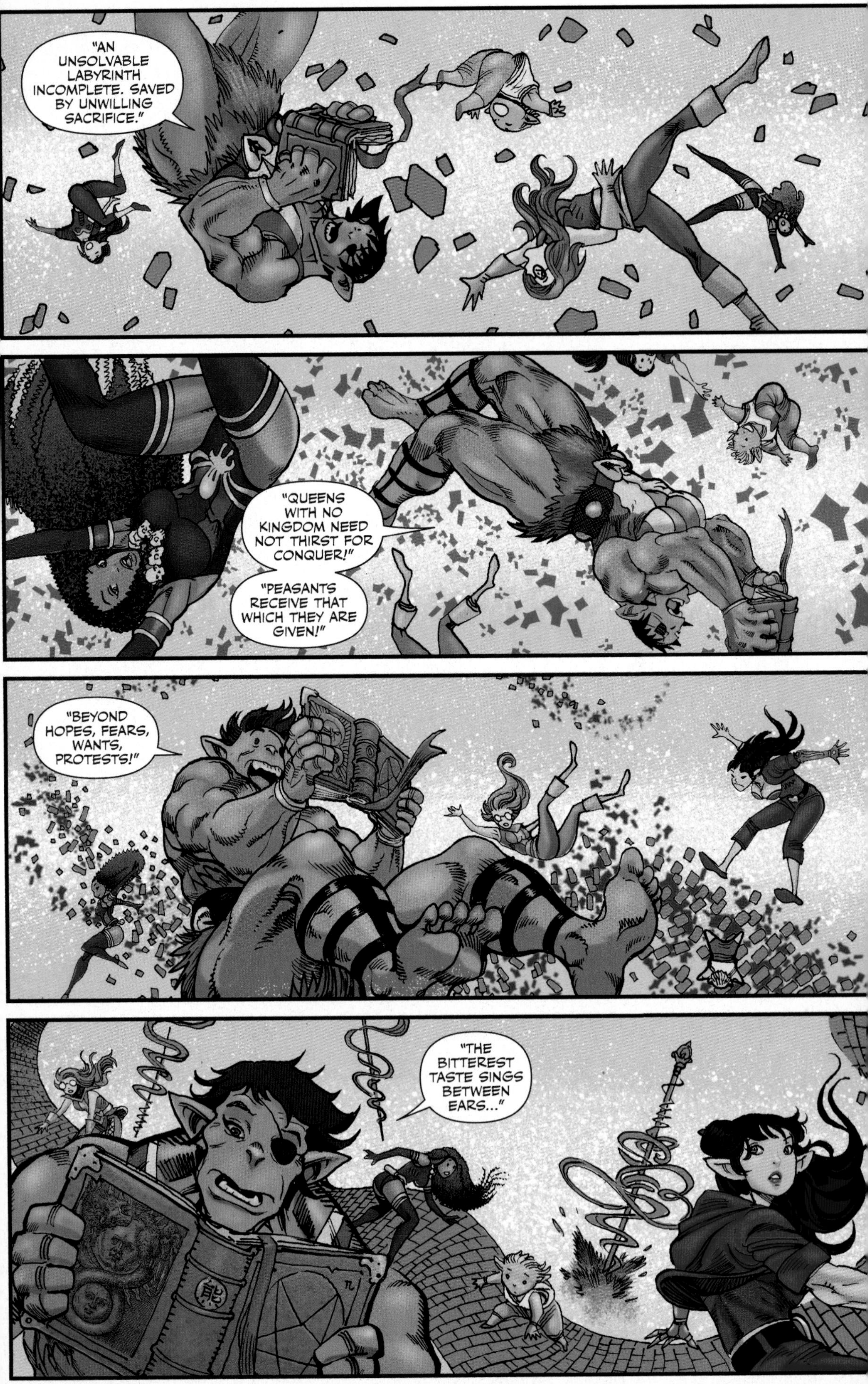
"AN UNSOLVABLE LABYRINTH INCOMPLETE. SAVED BY UNWILLING SACRIFICE."
"QUEENS WITH NO KINGDOM NEED NOT THIRST FOR CONQUER!"
"PEASANTS RECEIVE THAT WHICH THEY ARE GIVEN!"
"BEYOND HOPES, FEARS, WANTS, PROTESTS!"
"THE BITTEREST TASTE SINGS BETWEEN EARS..."

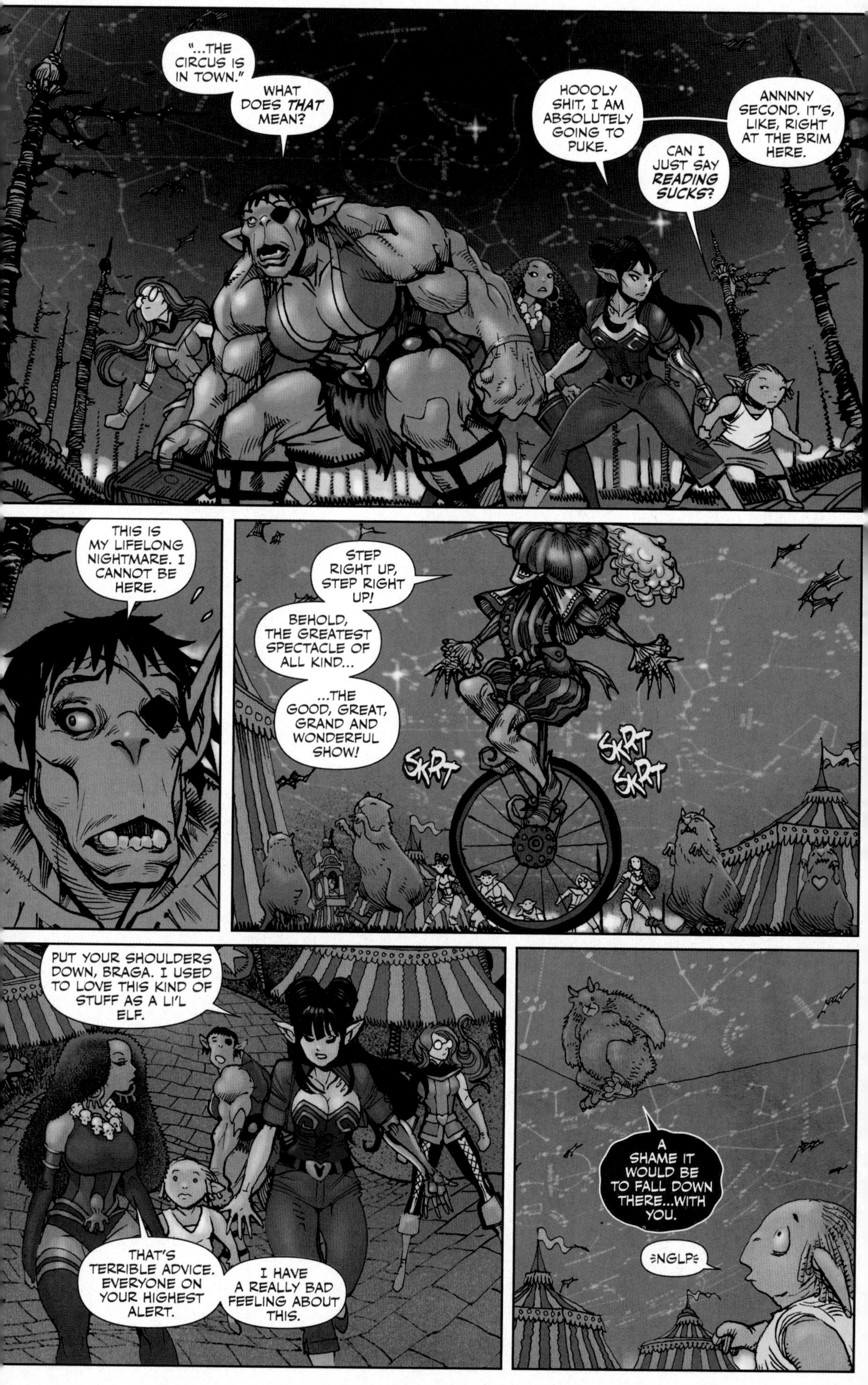
"...THE CIRCUS IS IN TOWN."
WHAT DOES *THAT* MEAN?
HOOOLY SHIT, I AM ABSOLUTELY GOING TO PUKE.
ANNNNY SECOND. IT'S, LIKE, RIGHT AT THE BRIM HERE.
CAN I JUST SAY *READING SUCKS?*
THIS IS MY LIFELONG NIGHTMARE. I CANNOT BE HERE.
STEP RIGHT UP, STEP RIGHT UP!
BEHOLD, THE GREATEST SPECTACLE OF ALL KIND...
...THE GOOD, GREAT, GRAND AND WONDERFUL SHOW!
SKRT
SKRT SKRT
PUT YOUR SHOULDERS DOWN, BRAGA. I USED TO LOVE THIS KIND OF STUFF AS A LI'L ELF.
THAT'S TERRIBLE ADVICE. EVERYONE ON YOUR HIGHEST ALERT.
I HAVE A REALLY BAD FEELING ABOUT THIS.
A SHAME IT WOULD BE TO FALL DOWN THERE...WITH YOU.
NGLP

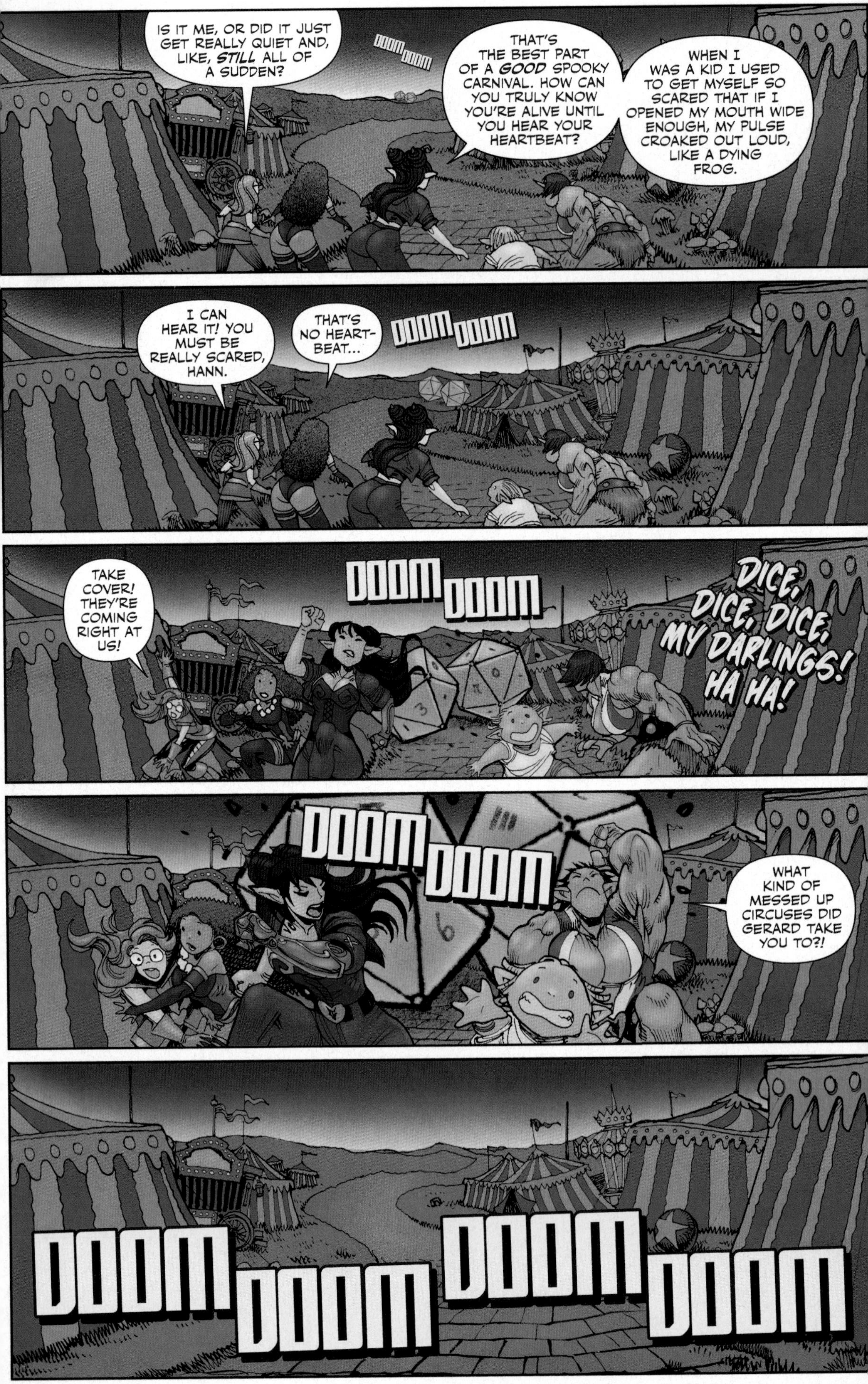

IS IT ME, OR DID IT JUST GET REALLY QUIET AND, LIKE, STILL ALL OF A SUDDEN?
DOOM DOOM
THAT'S THE BEST PART OF A GOOD SPOOKY CARNIVAL. HOW CAN YOU TRULY KNOW YOU'RE ALIVE UNTIL YOU HEAR YOUR HEARTBEAT?
WHEN I WAS A KID I USED TO GET MYSELF SO SCARED THAT IF I OPENED MY MOUTH WIDE ENOUGH, MY PULSE CROAKED OUT LOUD, LIKE A DYING FROG.
I CAN HEAR IT! YOU MUST BE REALLY SCARED, HANN.
THAT'S NO HEART-BEAT...
DOOM DOOM
TAKE COVER! THEY'RE COMING RIGHT AT US!
DOOM DOOM
DICE, DICE, DICE, MY DARLINGS! HA HA!
DOOM DOOM
WHAT KIND OF MESSED UP CIRCUSES DID GERARD TAKE YOU TO?!
DOOM DOOM DOOM DOOM

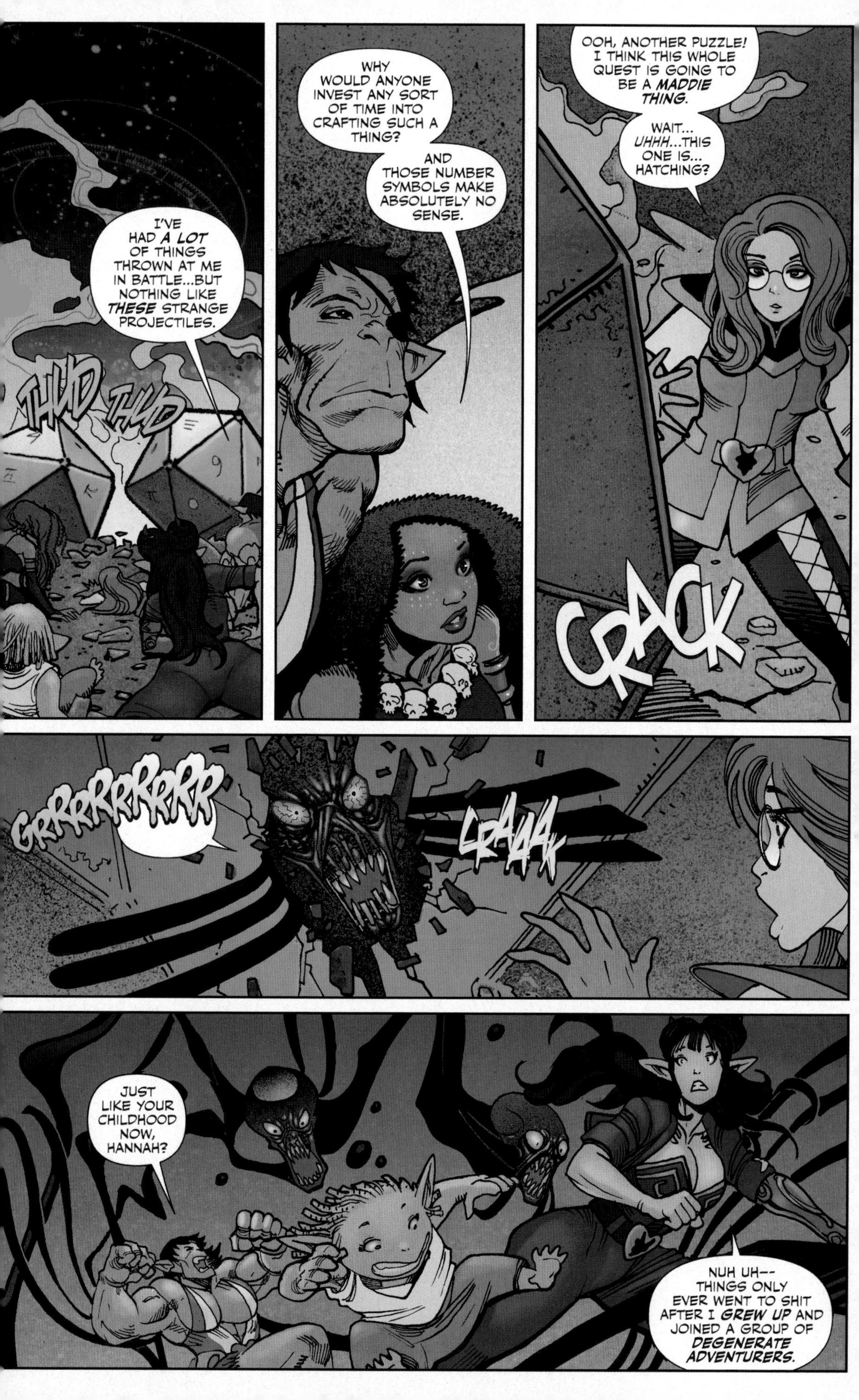

I'VE HAD *A LOT* OF THINGS THROWN AT ME IN BATTLE...BUT NOTHING LIKE *THESE* STRANGE PROJECTILES.
THUD THUD
WHY WOULD ANYONE INVEST ANY SORT OF TIME INTO CRAFTING SUCH A THING?
AND THOSE NUMBER SYMBOLS MAKE ABSOLUTELY NO SENSE.
OOH, ANOTHER PUZZLE! I THINK THIS WHOLE QUEST IS GOING TO BE A *MADDIE THING*.
WAIT... *UHHH*...THIS ONE IS... HATCHING?
CRACK
GRRRRRRRRR
CRAAAK
JUST LIKE YOUR CHILDHOOD NOW, HANNAH?
NUH UH-- THINGS ONLY EVER WENT TO SHIT AFTER I *GREW UP* AND JOINED A GROUP OF *DEGENERATE ADVENTURERS*.

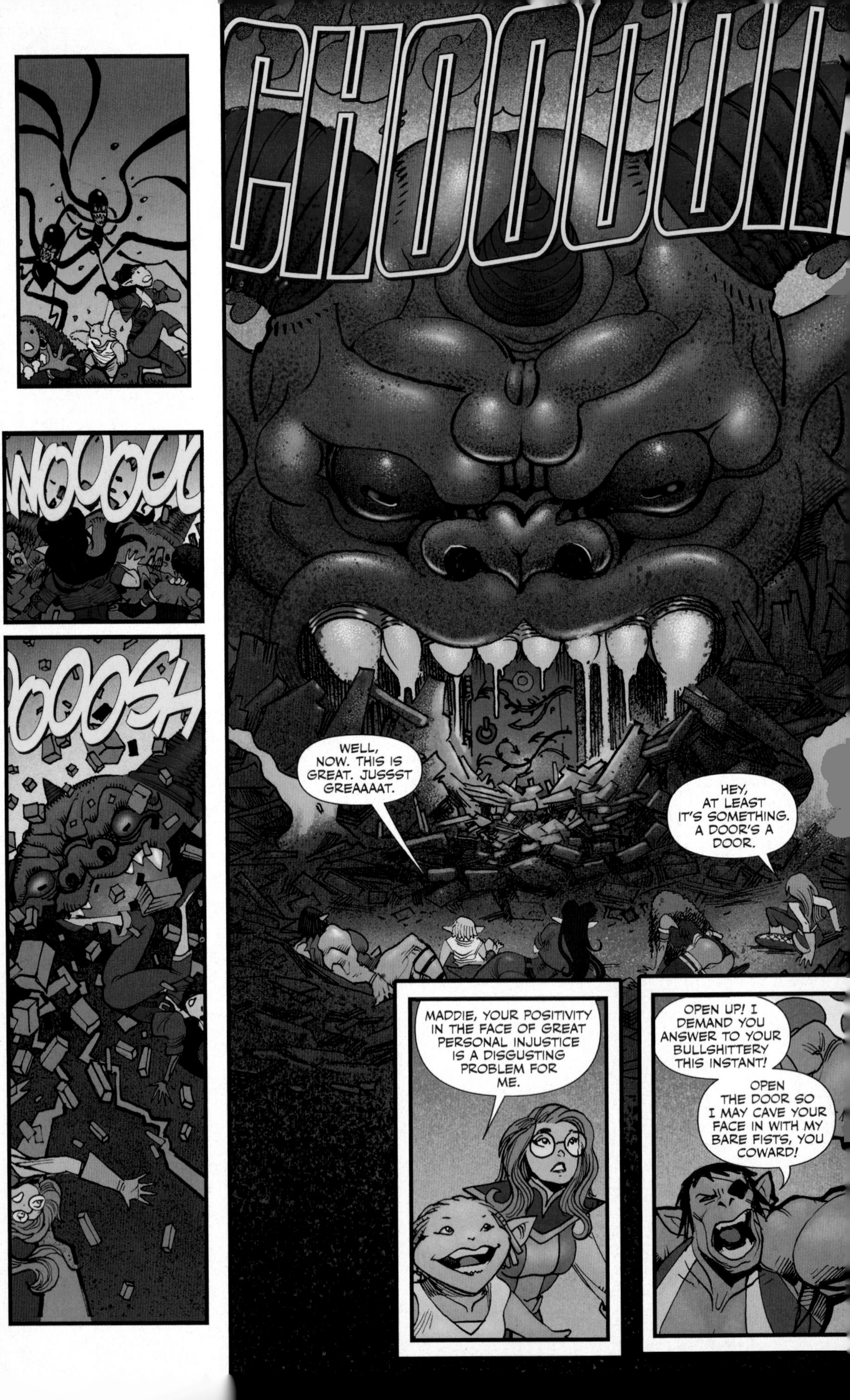
WOOOOO
OOOSH
CHOOOOM
WELL, NOW. THIS IS GREAT. JUSSST GREAAAAT.
HEY, AT LEAST IT'S SOMETHING. A DOOR'S A DOOR.
MADDIE, YOUR POSITIVITY IN THE FACE OF GREAT PERSONAL INJUSTICE IS A DISGUSTING PROBLEM FOR ME.
OPEN UP! I DEMAND YOU ANSWER TO YOUR BULLSHITTERY THIS INSTANT!
OPEN THE DOOR SO I MAY CAVE YOUR FACE IN WITH MY BARE FISTS, YOU COWARD!

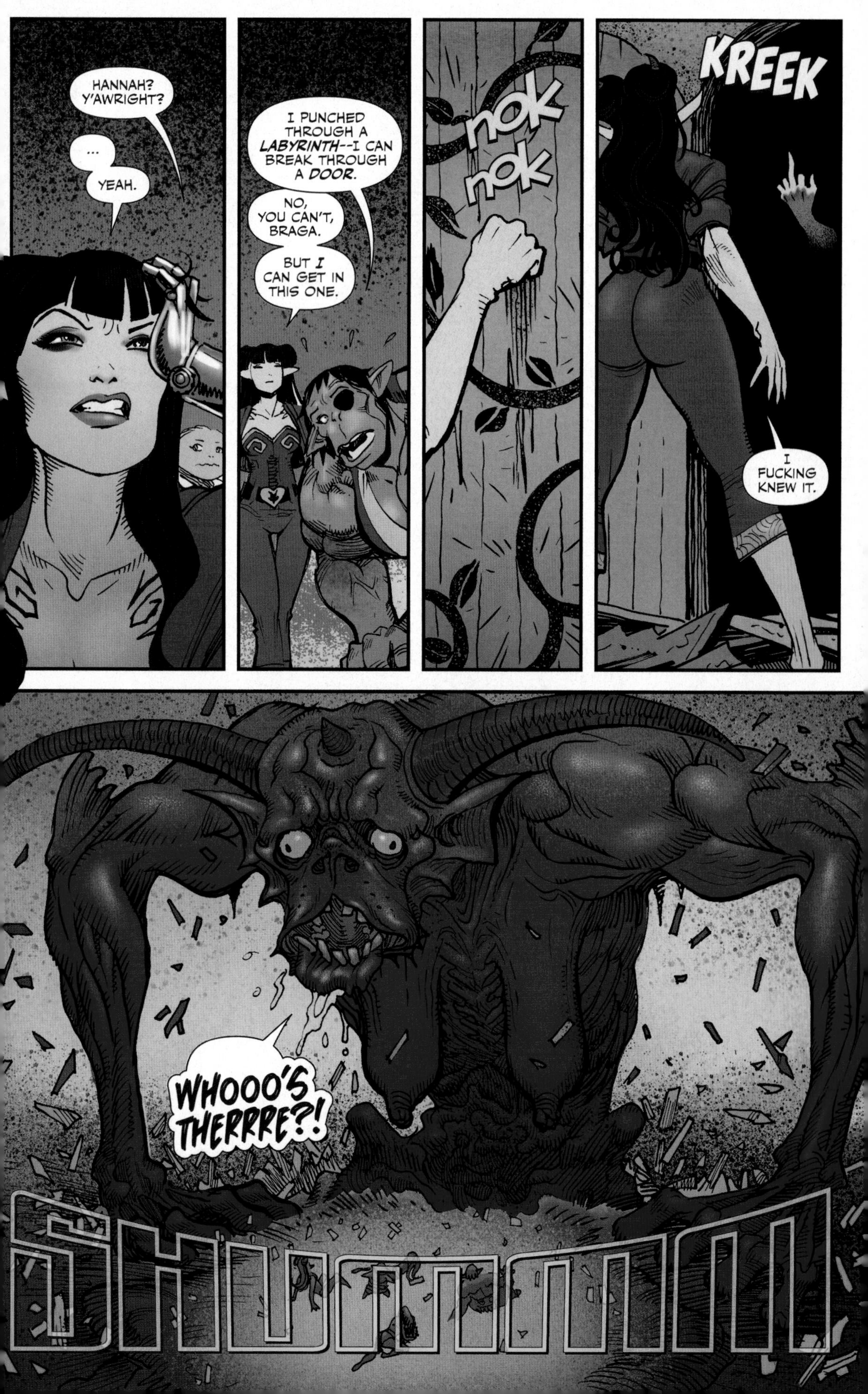
HANNAH? Y'AWRIGHT?
...
YEAH.
I PUNCHED THROUGH A LABYRINTH--I CAN BREAK THROUGH A DOOR.
NO, YOU CAN'T, BRAGA.
BUT I CAN GET IN THIS ONE.
nok nok
KREEK
I FUCKING KNEW IT.
WHOOO'S THERRRE?!
SHUNNNN

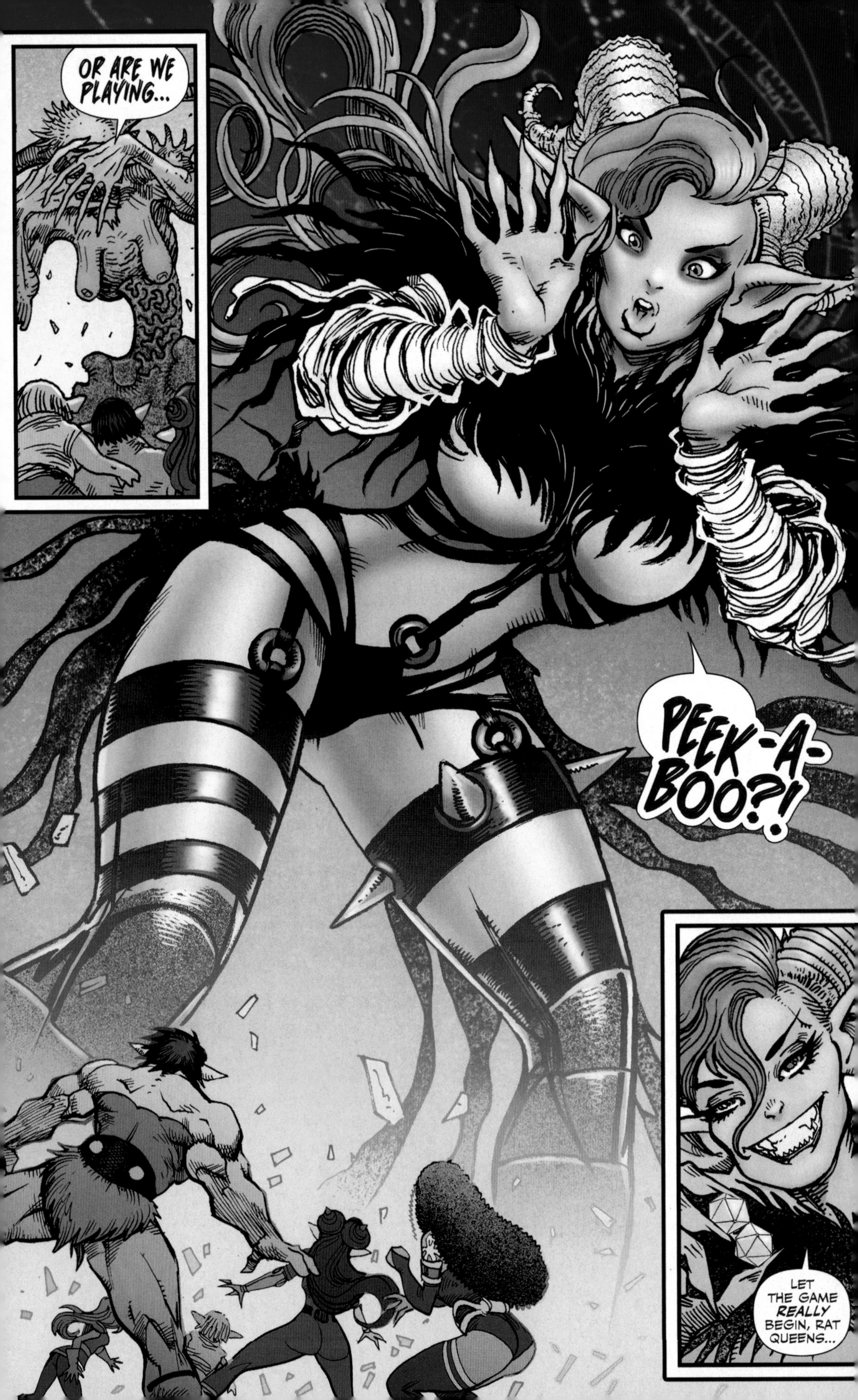
OR ARE WE PLAYING...
PEEK-A-BOO?!
LET THE GAME *REALLY* BEGIN, RAT QUEENS...

CHAPTER TWENTY-FIVE

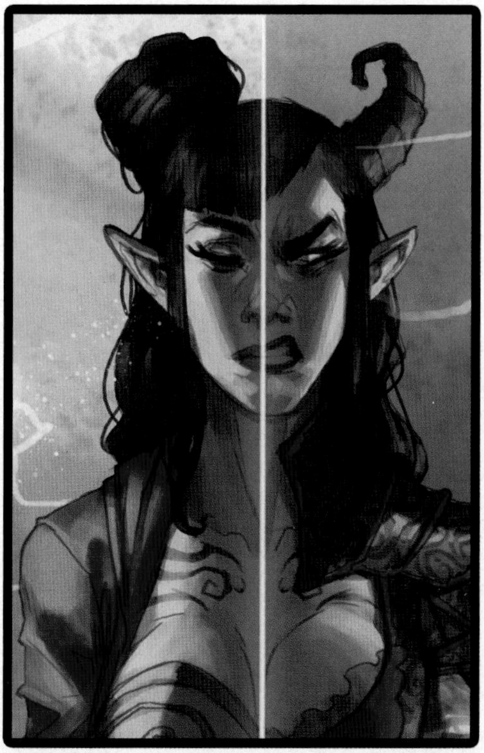

ISSUE #25 COVER

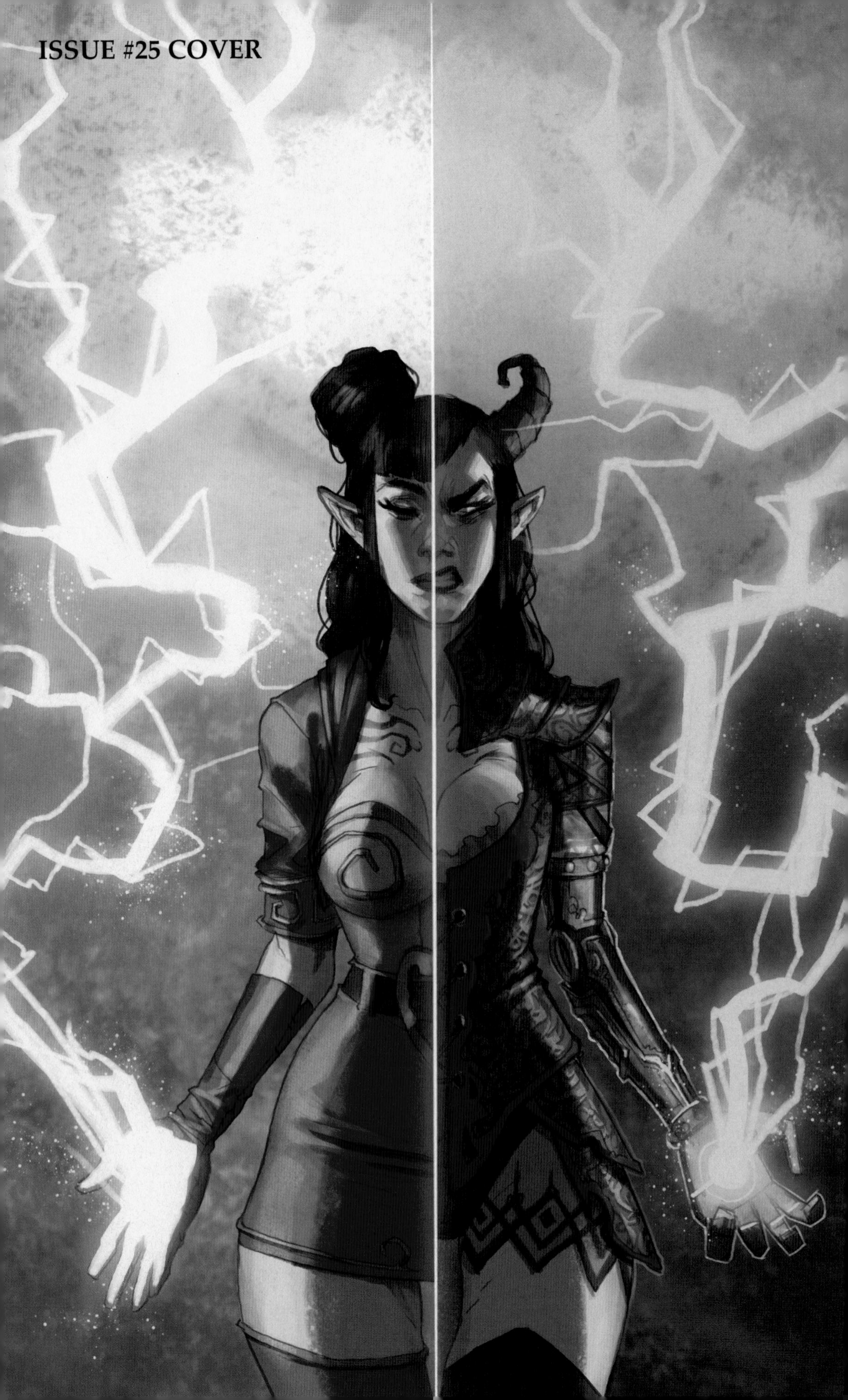

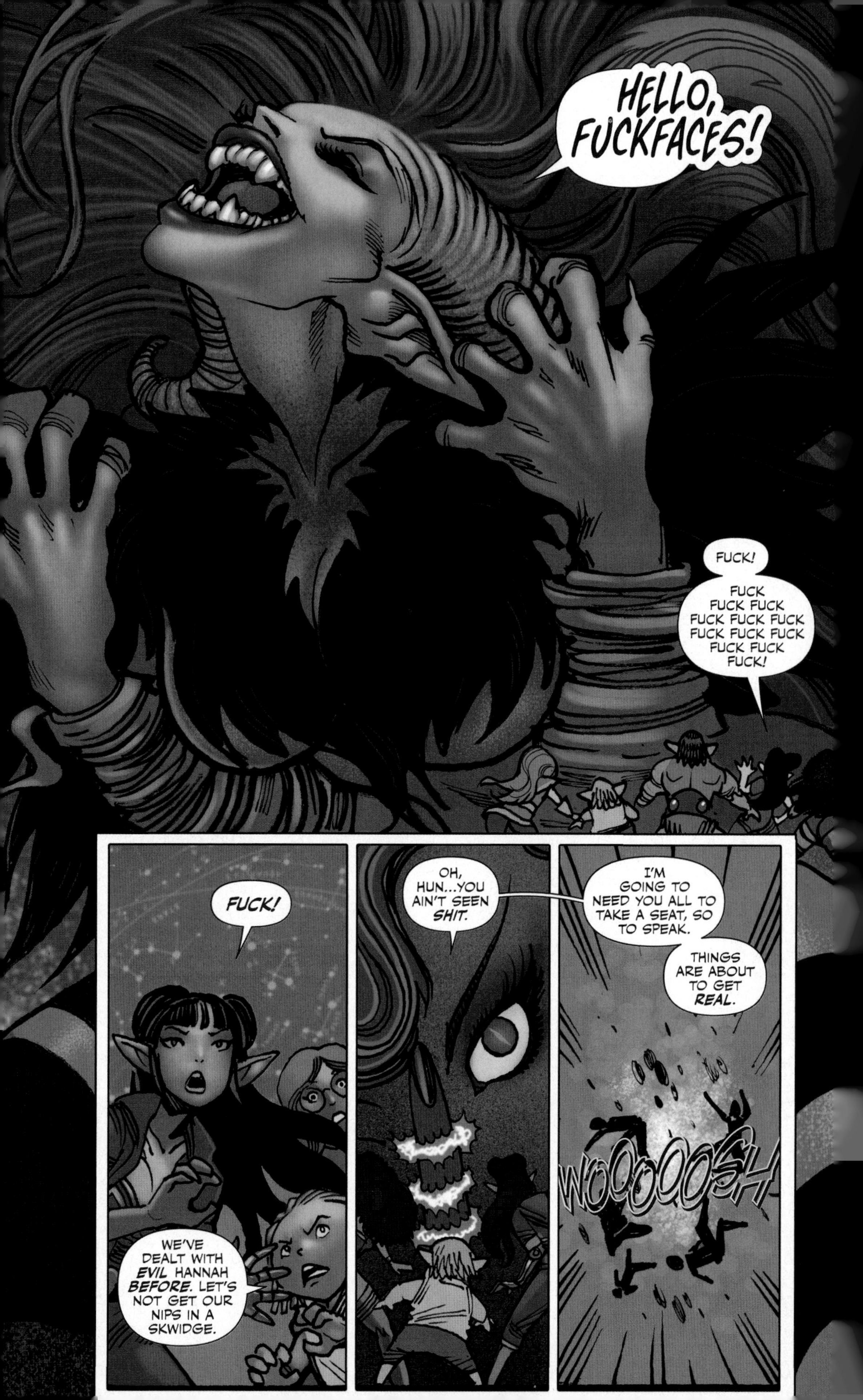
HELLO, FUCKFACES!
FUCK!
FUCK FUCK FUCK FUCK FUCK FUCK FUCK FUCK FUCK FUCK FUCK FUCK!
FUCK!
WE'VE DEALT WITH EVIL HANNAH BEFORE. LET'S NOT GET OUR NIPS IN A SKWIDGE.
OH, HUN...YOU AIN'T SEEN SHIT.
I'M GOING TO NEED YOU ALL TO TAKE A SEAT, SO TO SPEAK.
THINGS ARE ABOUT TO GET REAL.
WOOOOOOSH

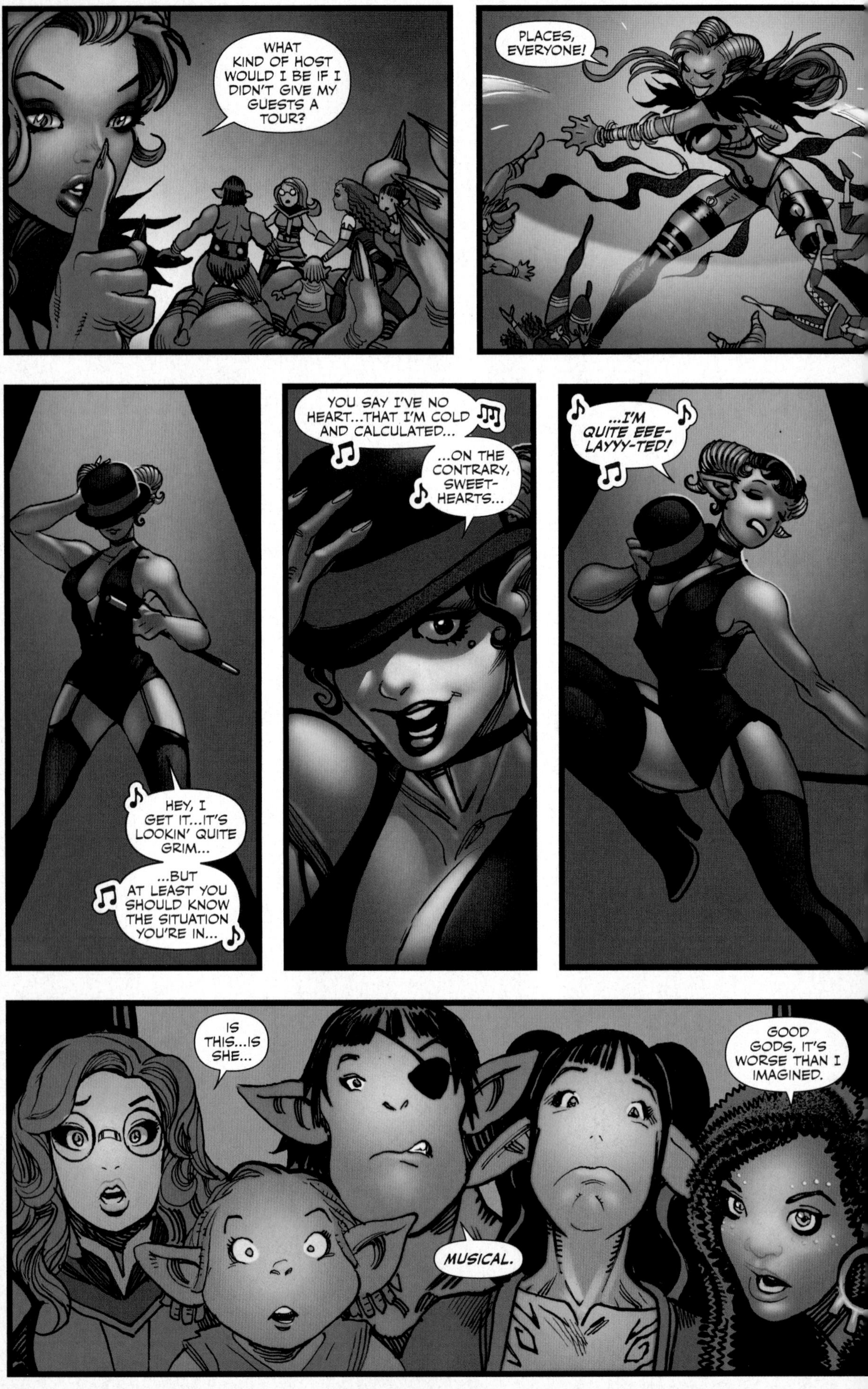
WHAT KIND OF HOST WOULD I BE IF I DIDN'T GIVE MY GUESTS A TOUR?
PLACES, EVERYONE!
HEY, I GET IT...IT'S LOOKIN' QUITE GRIM...
...BUT AT LEAST YOU SHOULD KNOW THE SITUATION YOU'RE IN...
YOU SAY I'VE NO HEART...THAT I'M COLD AND CALCULATED...
...ON THE CONTRARY, SWEET-HEARTS...
...I'M QUITE EEE-LAYYY-TED!
IS THIS...IS SHE...
MUSICAL.
GOOD GODS, IT'S WORSE THAN I IMAGINED.

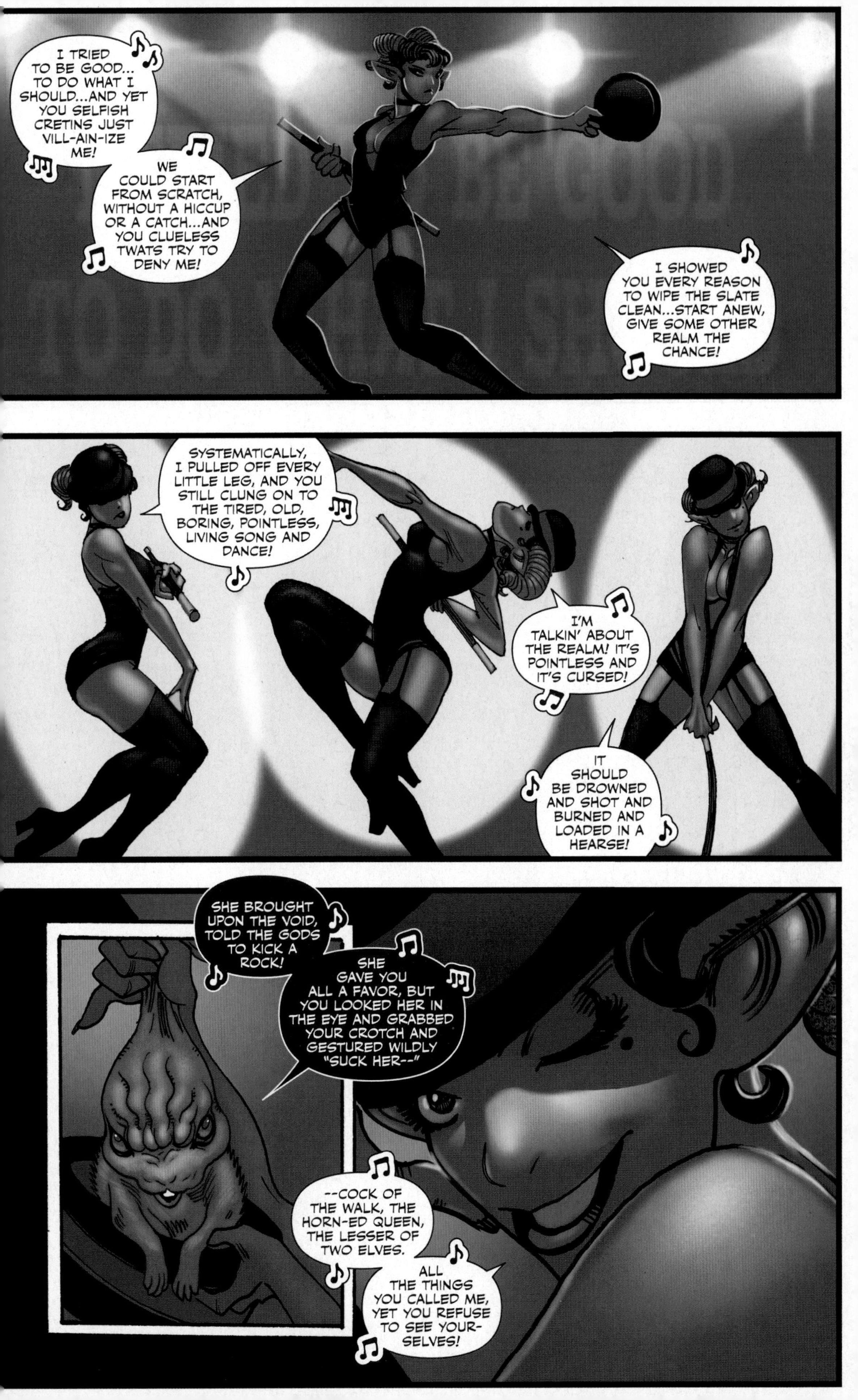

I TRIED TO BE GOOD... TO DO WHAT I SHOULD...AND YET YOU SELFISH CRETINS JUST VILL-AIN-IZE ME!
WE COULD START FROM SCRATCH, WITHOUT A HICCUP OR A CATCH...AND YOU CLUELESS TWATS TRY TO DENY ME!
I SHOWED YOU EVERY REASON TO WIPE THE SLATE CLEAN...START ANEW, GIVE SOME OTHER REALM THE CHANCE!
SYSTEMATICALLY, I PULLED OFF EVERY LITTLE LEG, AND YOU STILL CLUNG ON TO THE TIRED, OLD, BORING, POINTLESS, LIVING SONG AND DANCE!
I'M TALKIN' ABOUT THE REALM! IT'S POINTLESS AND IT'S CURSED!
IT SHOULD BE DROWNED AND SHOT AND BURNED AND LOADED IN A HEARSE!
SHE BROUGHT UPON THE VOID, TOLD THE GODS TO KICK A ROCK!
SHE GAVE YOU ALL A FAVOR, BUT YOU LOOKED HER IN THE EYE AND GRABBED YOUR CROTCH AND GESTURED WILDLY "SUCK HER--"
--COCK OF THE WALK, THE HORN-ED QUEEN, THE LESSER OF TWO ELVES.
ALL THE THINGS YOU CALLED ME, YET YOU REFUSE TO SEE YOUR-SELVES!

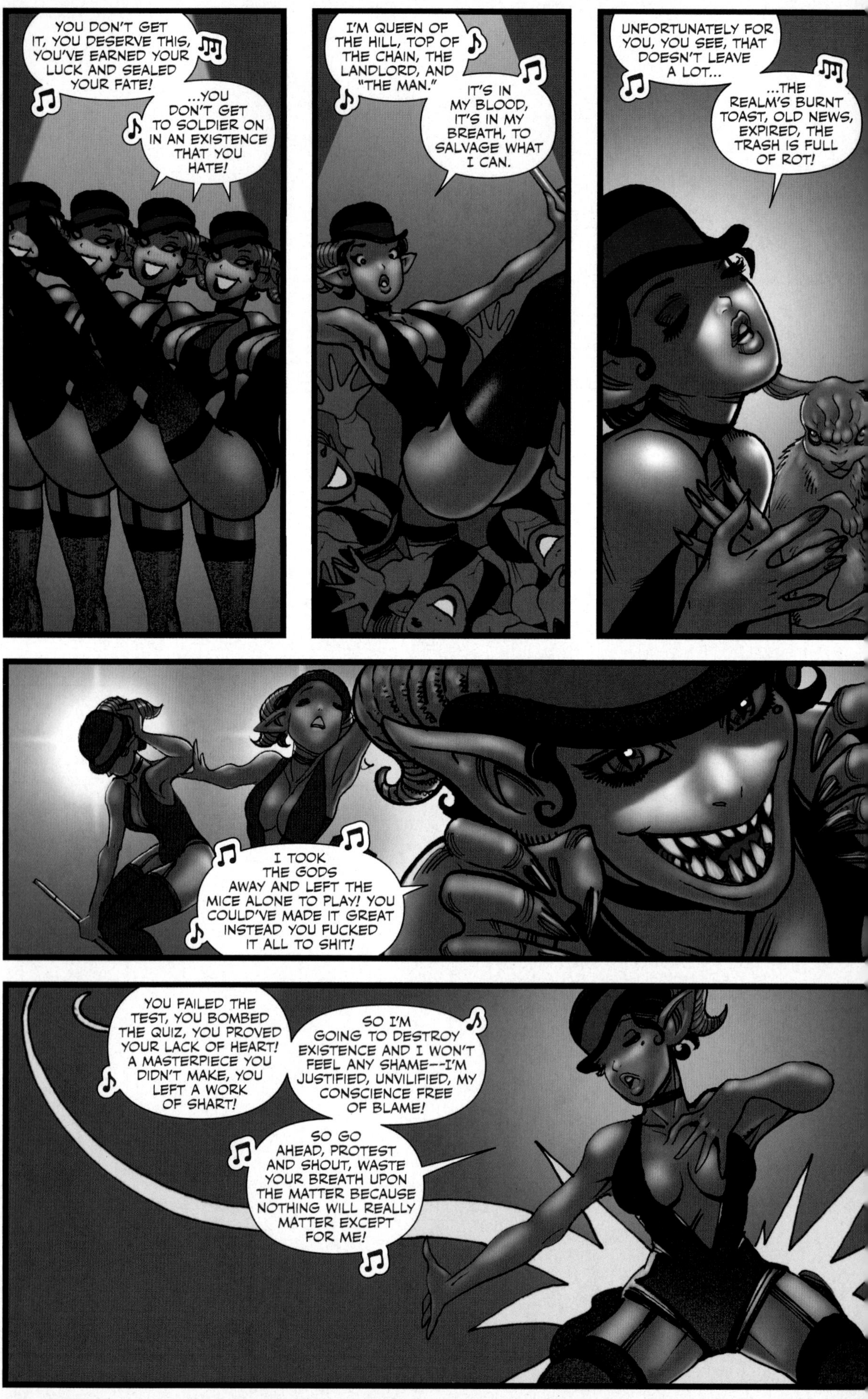

YOU DON'T GET IT, YOU DESERVE THIS, YOU'VE EARNED YOUR LUCK AND SEALED YOUR FATE!
...YOU DON'T GET TO SOLDIER ON IN AN EXISTENCE THAT YOU HATE!
I'M QUEEN OF THE HILL, TOP OF THE CHAIN, THE LANDLORD, AND "THE MAN."
IT'S IN MY BLOOD, IT'S IN MY BREATH, TO SALVAGE WHAT I CAN.
UNFORTUNATELY FOR YOU, YOU SEE, THAT DOESN'T LEAVE A LOT...
...THE REALM'S BURNT TOAST, OLD NEWS, EXPIRED, THE TRASH IS FULL OF ROT!
I TOOK THE GODS AWAY AND LEFT THE MICE ALONE TO PLAY! YOU COULD'VE MADE IT GREAT INSTEAD YOU FUCKED IT ALL TO SHIT!
YOU FAILED THE TEST, YOU BOMBED THE QUIZ, YOU PROVED YOUR LACK OF HEART! A MASTERPIECE YOU DIDN'T MAKE, YOU LEFT A WORK OF SHART!
SO I'M GOING TO DESTROY EXISTENCE AND I WON'T FEEL ANY SHAME--I'M JUSTIFIED, UNVILIFIED, MY CONSCIENCE FREE OF BLAME!
SO GO AHEAD, PROTEST AND SHOUT, WASTE YOUR BREATH UPON THE MATTER BECAUSE NOTHING WILL REALLY MATTER EXCEPT FOR ME!

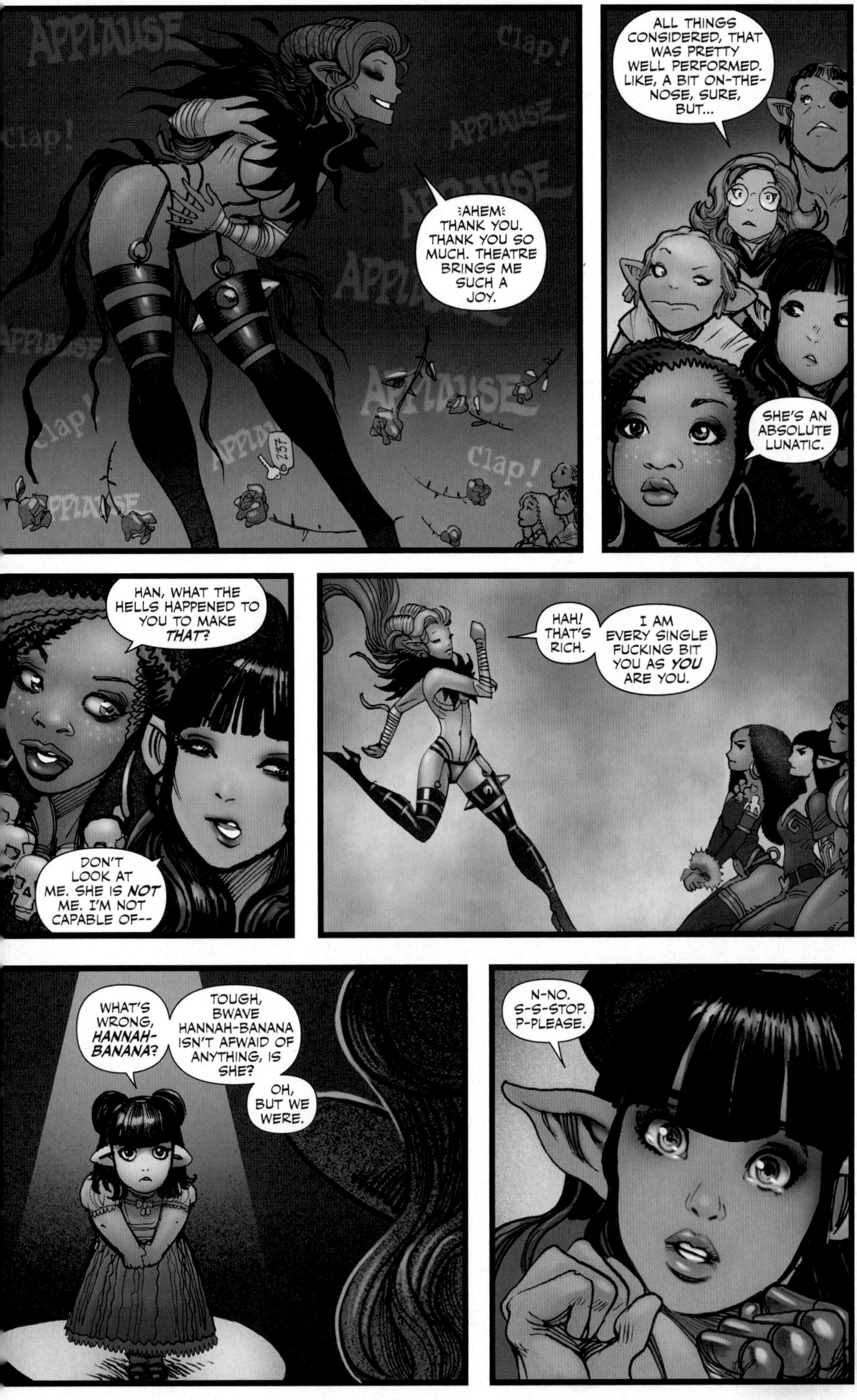
APPLAUSE
Clap!
APPLAUSE
Clap!
APPLAUSE
APPLAUSE
APPLAUSE
APPLAUSE
Clap!
APPLAUSE
Clap!
APPLAUSE
APPLAUSE
:AHEM: THANK YOU. THANK YOU SO MUCH. THEATRE BRINGS ME SUCH A JOY.
ALL THINGS CONSIDERED, THAT WAS PRETTY WELL PERFORMED. LIKE, A BIT ON-THE-NOSE, SURE, BUT...
SHE'S AN ABSOLUTE LUNATIC.
HAN, WHAT THE HELLS HAPPENED TO YOU TO MAKE *THAT*?
DON'T LOOK AT ME. SHE IS *NOT* ME. I'M NOT CAPABLE OF--
HAH! THAT'S RICH.
I AM EVERY SINGLE FUCKING BIT YOU AS *YOU* ARE YOU.
WHAT'S WRONG, *HANNAH-BANANA*?
TOUGH, BWAVE HANNAH-BANANA ISN'T AFWAID OF ANYTHING, IS SHE?
OH, BUT WE WERE.
N-NO. S-S-STOP. P-PLEASE.

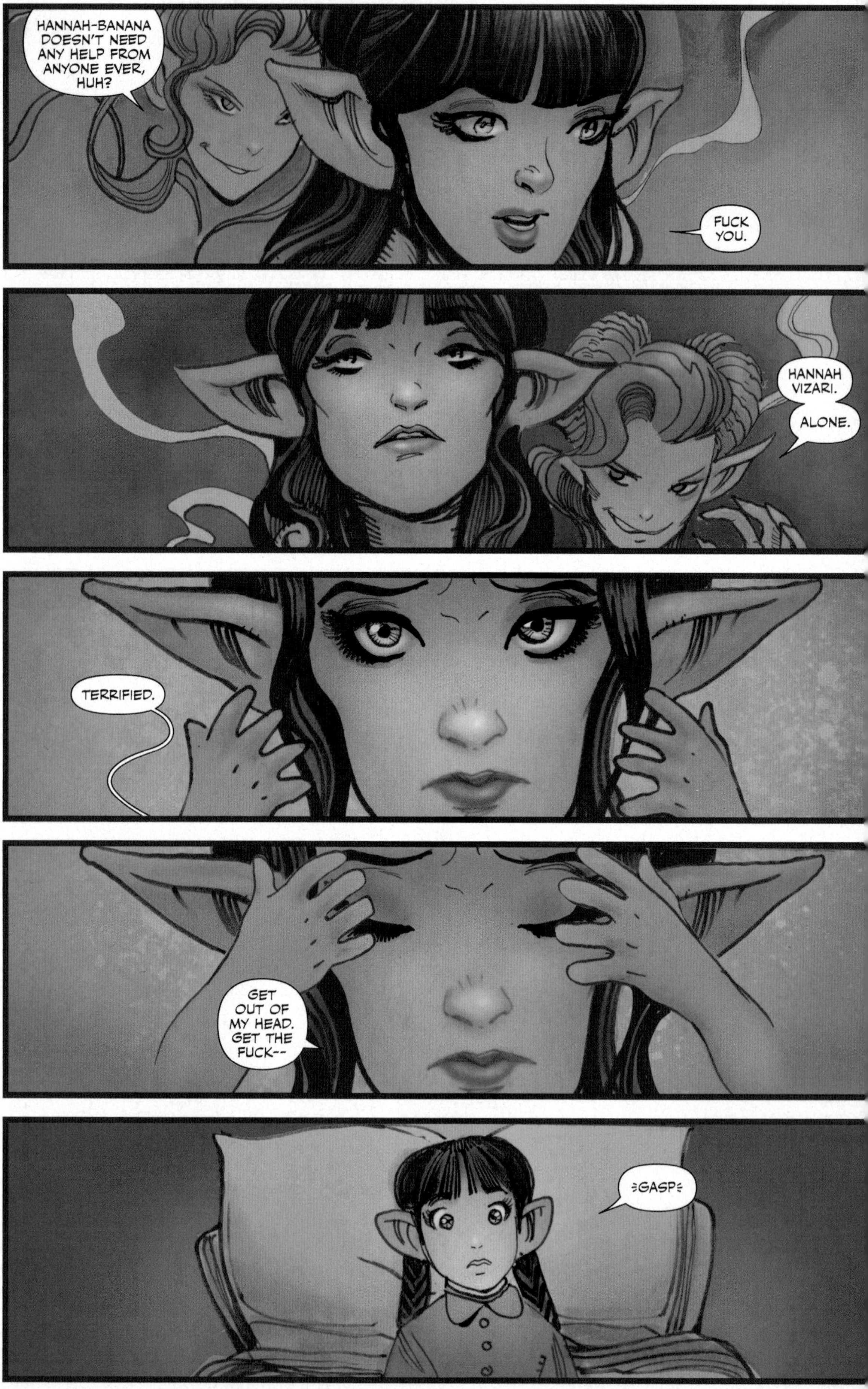
HANNAH-BANANA DOESN'T NEED ANY HELP FROM ANYONE EVER, HUH?
FUCK YOU.
HANNAH VIZARI.
ALONE.
TERRIFIED.
GET OUT OF MY HEAD. GET THE FUCK--
GASP

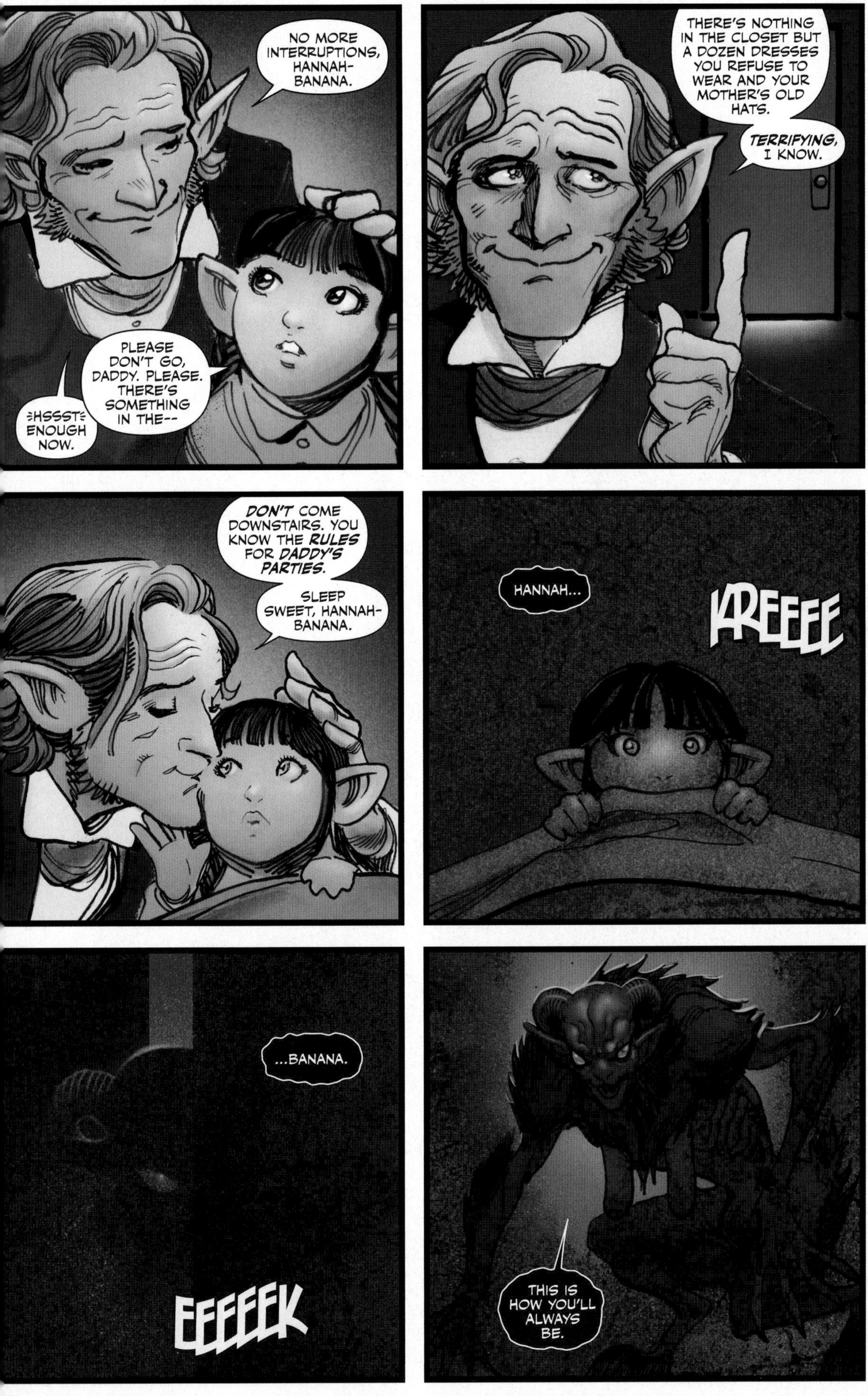

NO MORE INTERRUPTIONS, HANNAH-BANANA.
PLEASE DON'T GO, DADDY. PLEASE. THERE'S SOMETHING IN THE--
≠HSSST≠ ENOUGH NOW.
THERE'S NOTHING IN THE CLOSET BUT A DOZEN DRESSES YOU REFUSE TO WEAR AND YOUR MOTHER'S OLD HATS.
TERRIFYING, I KNOW.
DON'T COME DOWNSTAIRS. YOU KNOW THE RULES FOR DADDY'S PARTIES.
SLEEP SWEET, HANNAH-BANANA.
HANNAH...
KREEEE
...BANANA.
EEEEEK
THIS IS HOW YOU'LL ALWAYS BE.

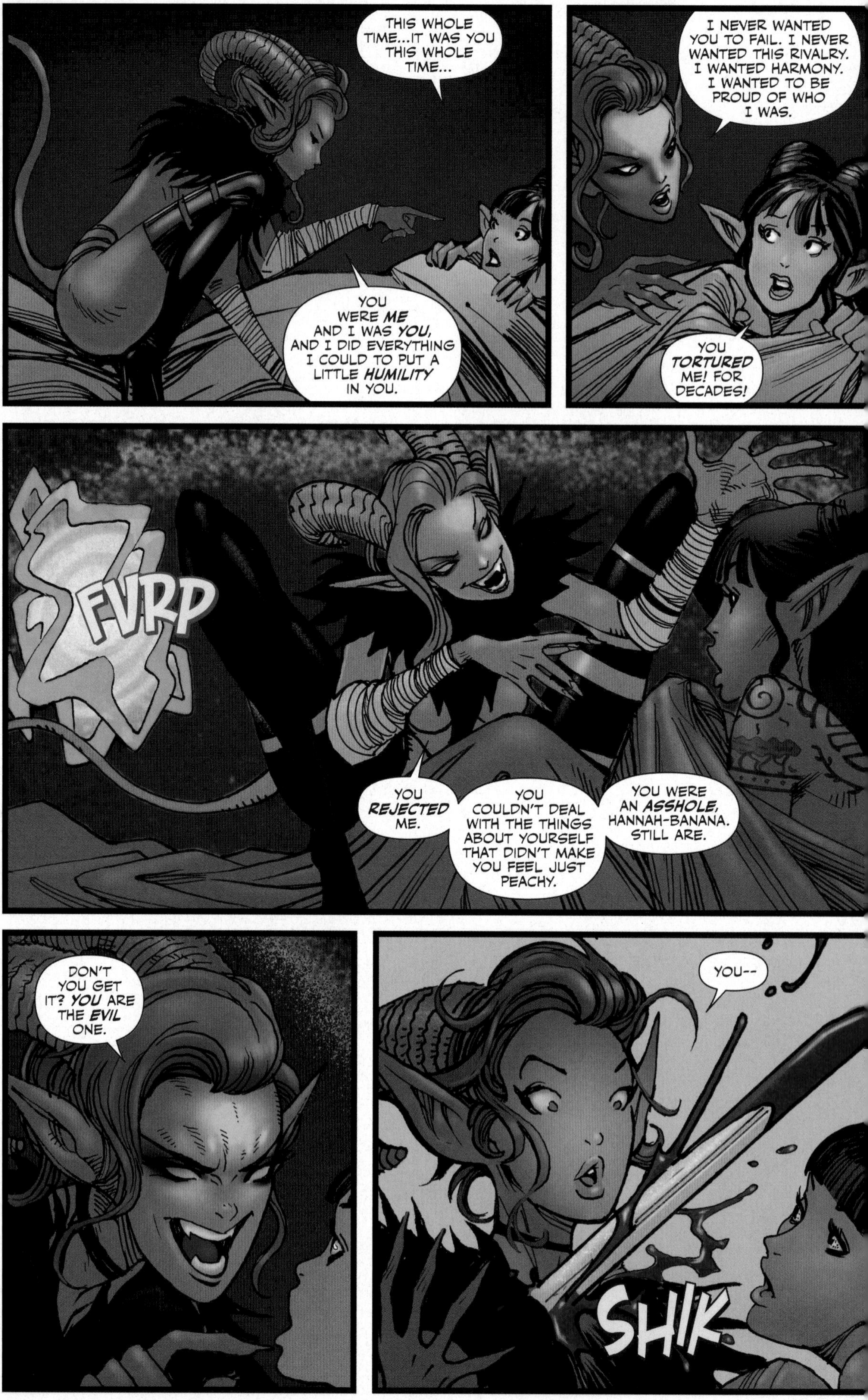
THIS WHOLE TIME...IT WAS YOU THIS WHOLE TIME...
YOU WERE ME AND I WAS YOU, AND I DID EVERYTHING I COULD TO PUT A LITTLE HUMILITY IN YOU.
I NEVER WANTED YOU TO FAIL. I NEVER WANTED THIS RIVALRY. I WANTED HARMONY. I WANTED TO BE PROUD OF WHO I WAS.
YOU TORTURED ME! FOR DECADES!
FVRP
YOU REJECTED ME.
YOU COULDN'T DEAL WITH THE THINGS ABOUT YOURSELF THAT DIDN'T MAKE YOU FEEL JUST PEACHY.
YOU WERE AN ASSHOLE, HANNAH-BANANA. STILL ARE.
DON'T YOU GET IT? YOU ARE THE EVIL ONE.
YOU--
SHIK

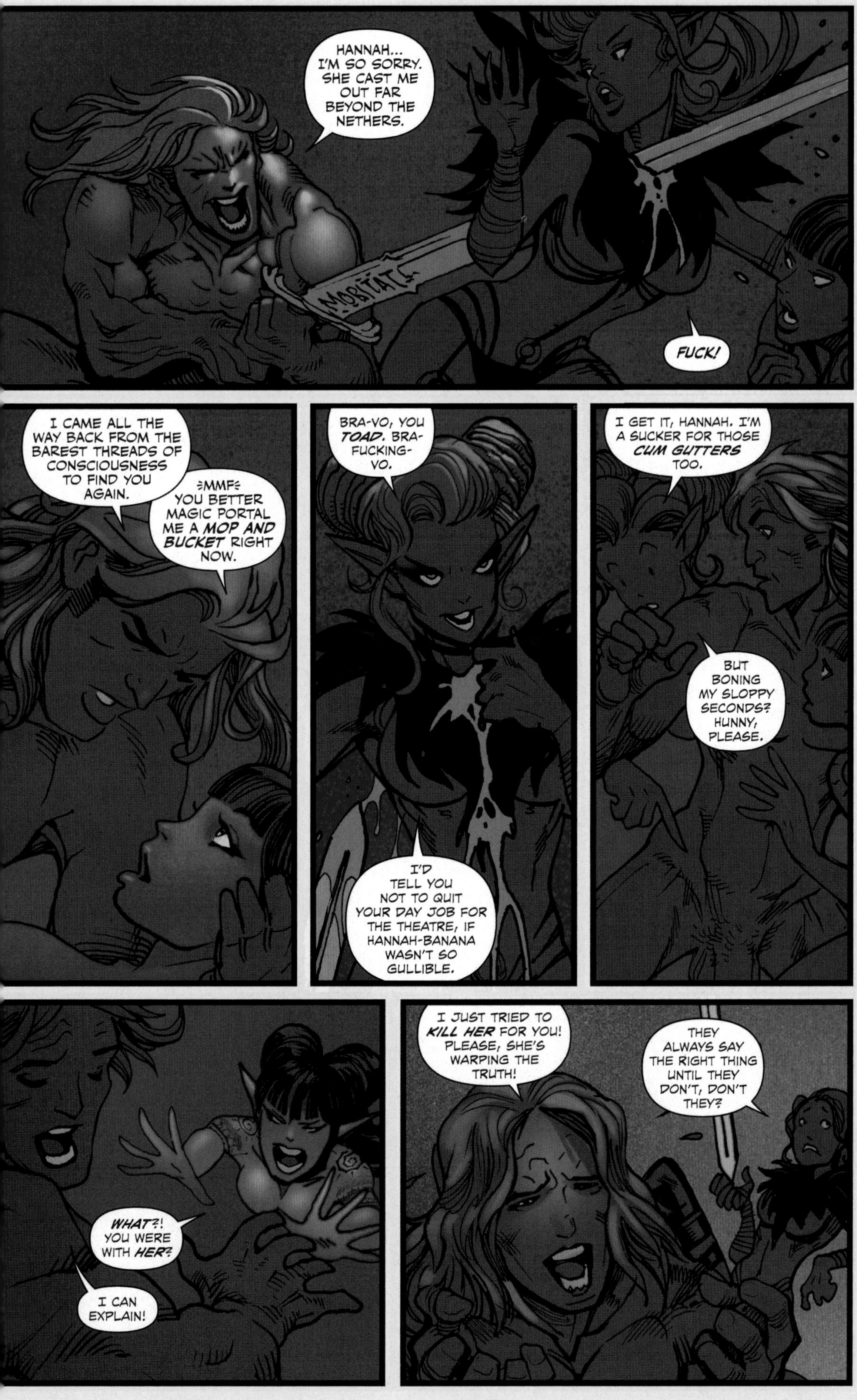
HANNAH... I'M SO SORRY. SHE CAST ME OUT FAR BEYOND THE NETHERS.
FUCK!
I CAME ALL THE WAY BACK FROM THE BAREST THREADS OF CONSCIOUSNESS TO FIND YOU AGAIN.
=MMF= YOU BETTER MAGIC PORTAL ME A ***MOP AND BUCKET*** RIGHT NOW.
BRA-VO, YOU ***TOAD.*** BRA-FUCKING-VO.
I'D TELL YOU NOT TO QUIT YOUR DAY JOB FOR THE THEATRE, IF HANNAH-BANANA WASN'T SO GULLIBLE.
I GET IT, HANNAH. I'M A SUCKER FOR THOSE ***CUM GUTTERS*** TOO.
BUT BONING MY SLOPPY SECONDS? HUNNY, PLEASE.
WHAT?! YOU WERE WITH ***HER?***
I CAN EXPLAIN!
I JUST TRIED TO ***KILL HER*** FOR YOU! PLEASE, SHE'S WARPING THE TRUTH!
THEY ALWAYS SAY THE RIGHT THING UNTIL THEY DON'T, DON'T THEY?

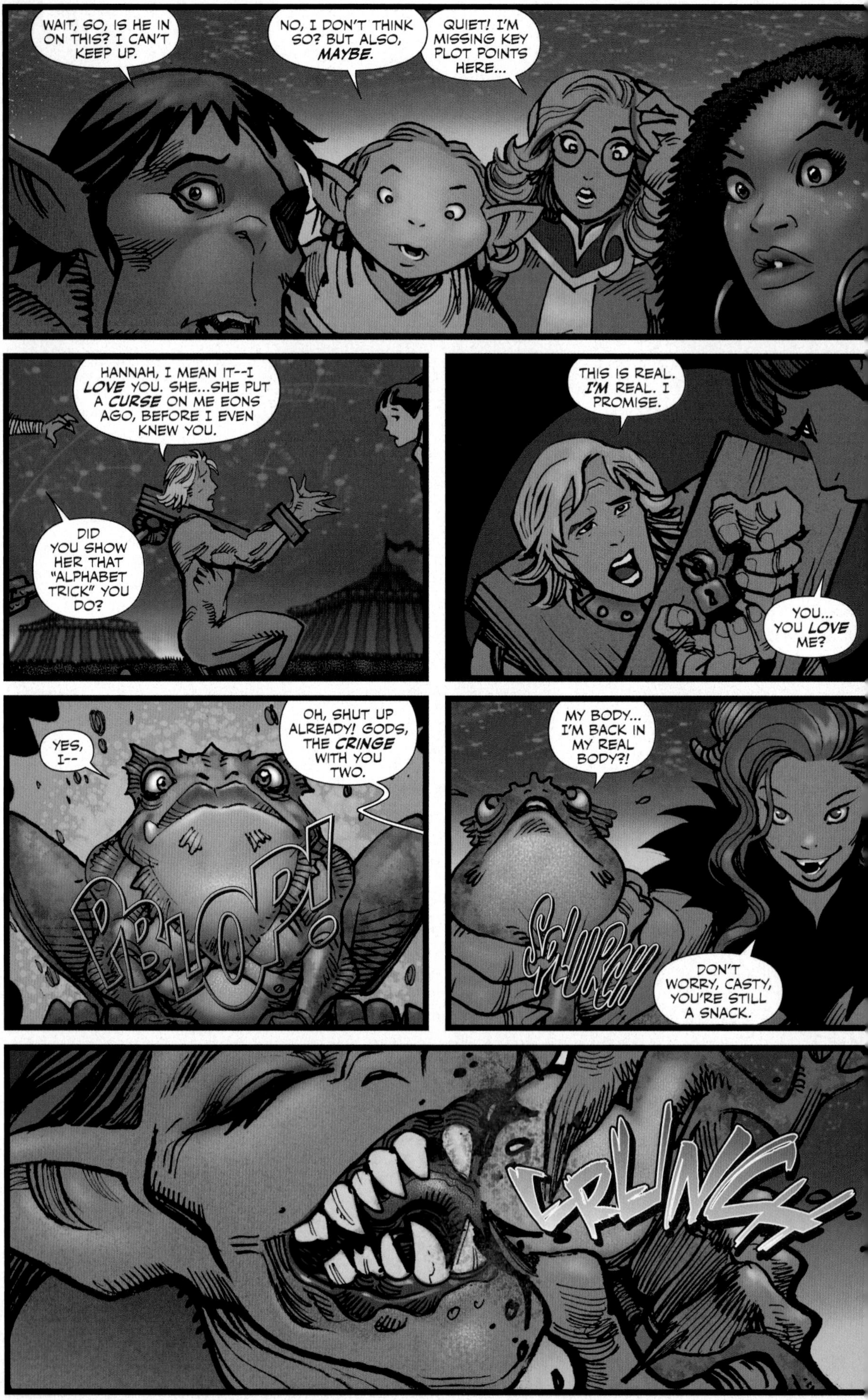
WAIT, SO, IS HE IN ON THIS? I CAN'T KEEP UP.
NO, I DON'T THINK SO? BUT ALSO, *MAYBE*.
QUIET! I'M MISSING KEY PLOT POINTS HERE...
HANNAH, I MEAN IT--I *LOVE* YOU. SHE...SHE PUT A *CURSE* ON ME EONS AGO, BEFORE I EVEN KNEW YOU.
DID YOU SHOW HER THAT "ALPHABET TRICK" YOU DO?
THIS IS REAL. *I'M* REAL. I PROMISE.
YOU... YOU *LOVE* ME?
YES, I--
OH, SHUT UP ALREADY! GODS, THE *CRINGE* WITH YOU TWO.
PBLOP!
MY BODY... I'M BACK IN MY REAL BODY?!
SCLURCH
DON'T WORRY, CASTY, YOU'RE STILL A SNACK.
CRUNCH

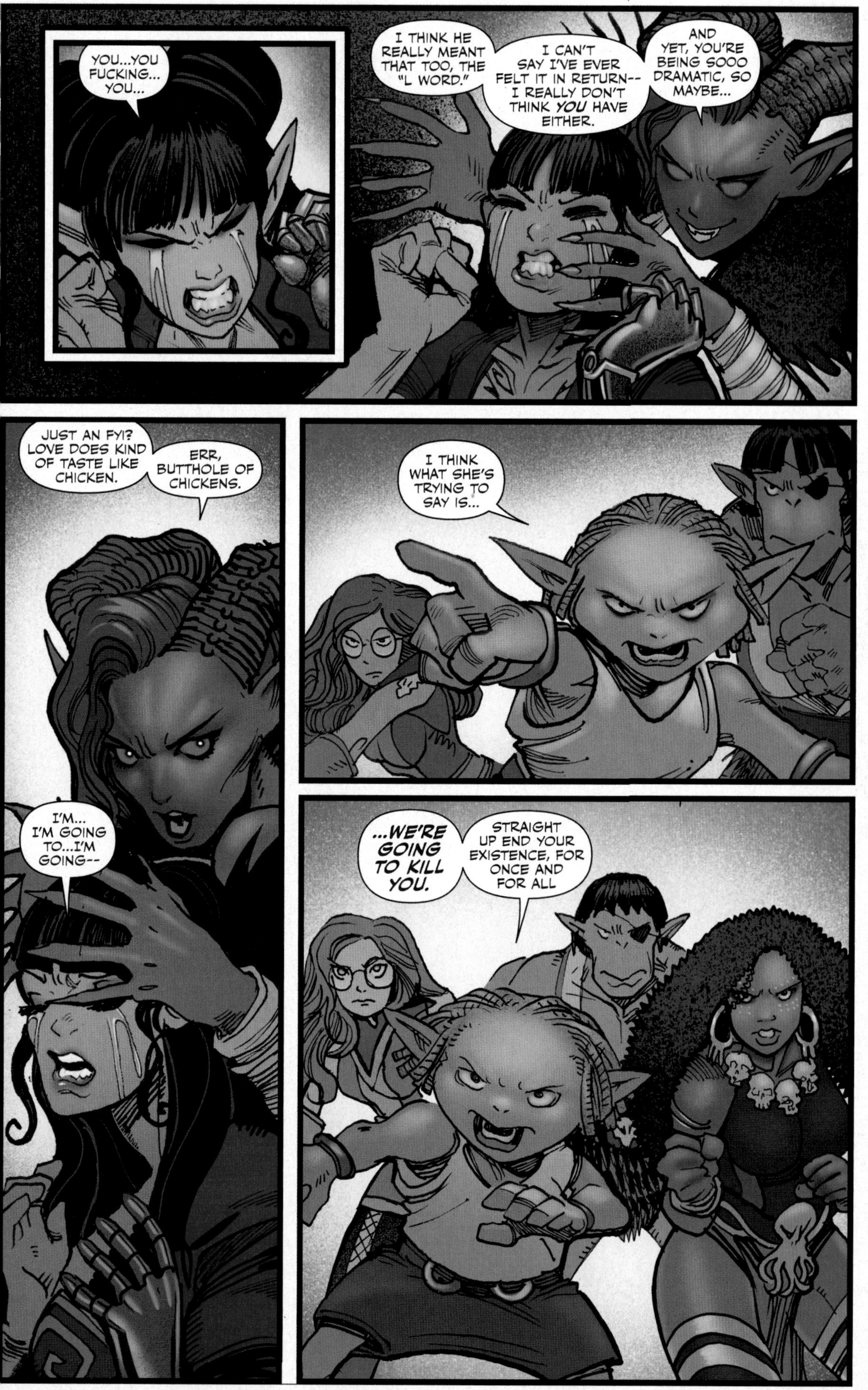
YOU...YOU FUCKING... YOU...
I THINK HE REALLY MEANT THAT TOO, THE "L WORD."
I CAN'T SAY I'VE EVER FELT IT IN RETURN-- I REALLY DON'T THINK *YOU* HAVE EITHER.
AND YET, YOU'RE BEING SOOO DRAMATIC, SO MAYBE...
JUST AN FYI? LOVE DOES KIND OF TASTE LIKE CHICKEN.
ERR, BUTTHOLE OF CHICKENS.
I'M... I'M GOING TO...I'M GOING--
I THINK WHAT SHE'S TRYING TO SAY IS...
...WE'RE GOING TO KILL YOU.
STRAIGHT UP END YOUR EXISTENCE, FOR ONCE AND FOR ALL

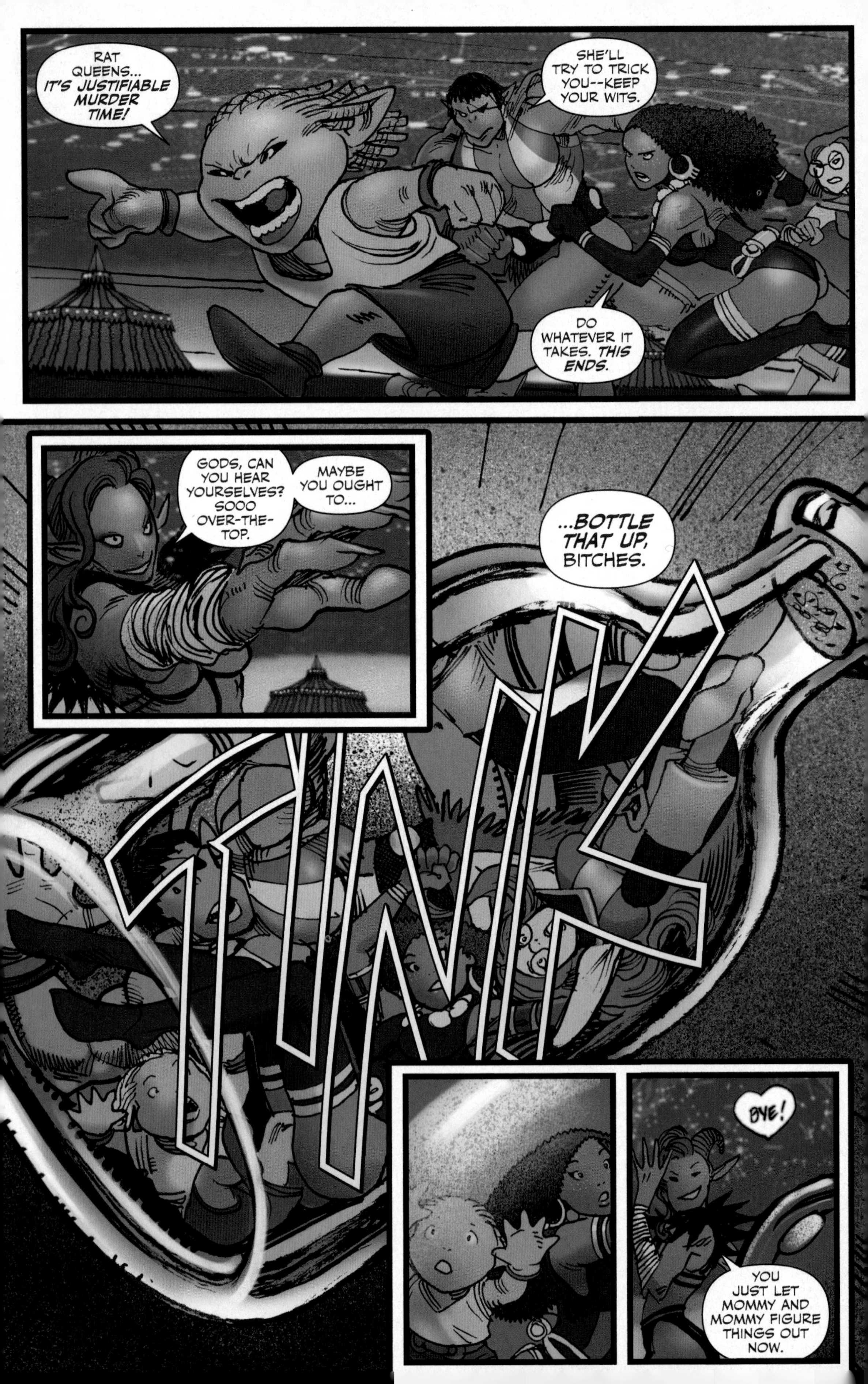
RAT QUEENS... IT'S JUSTIFIABLE MURDER TIME!
SHE'LL TRY TO TRICK YOU--KEEP YOUR WITS.
DO WHATEVER IT TAKES. THIS ENDS.
GODS, CAN YOU HEAR YOURSELVES? SOOO OVER-THE-TOP.
MAYBE YOU OUGHT TO...
...BOTTLE THAT UP, BITCHES.
TINK
BYE!
YOU JUST LET MOMMY AND MOMMY FIGURE THINGS OUT NOW.

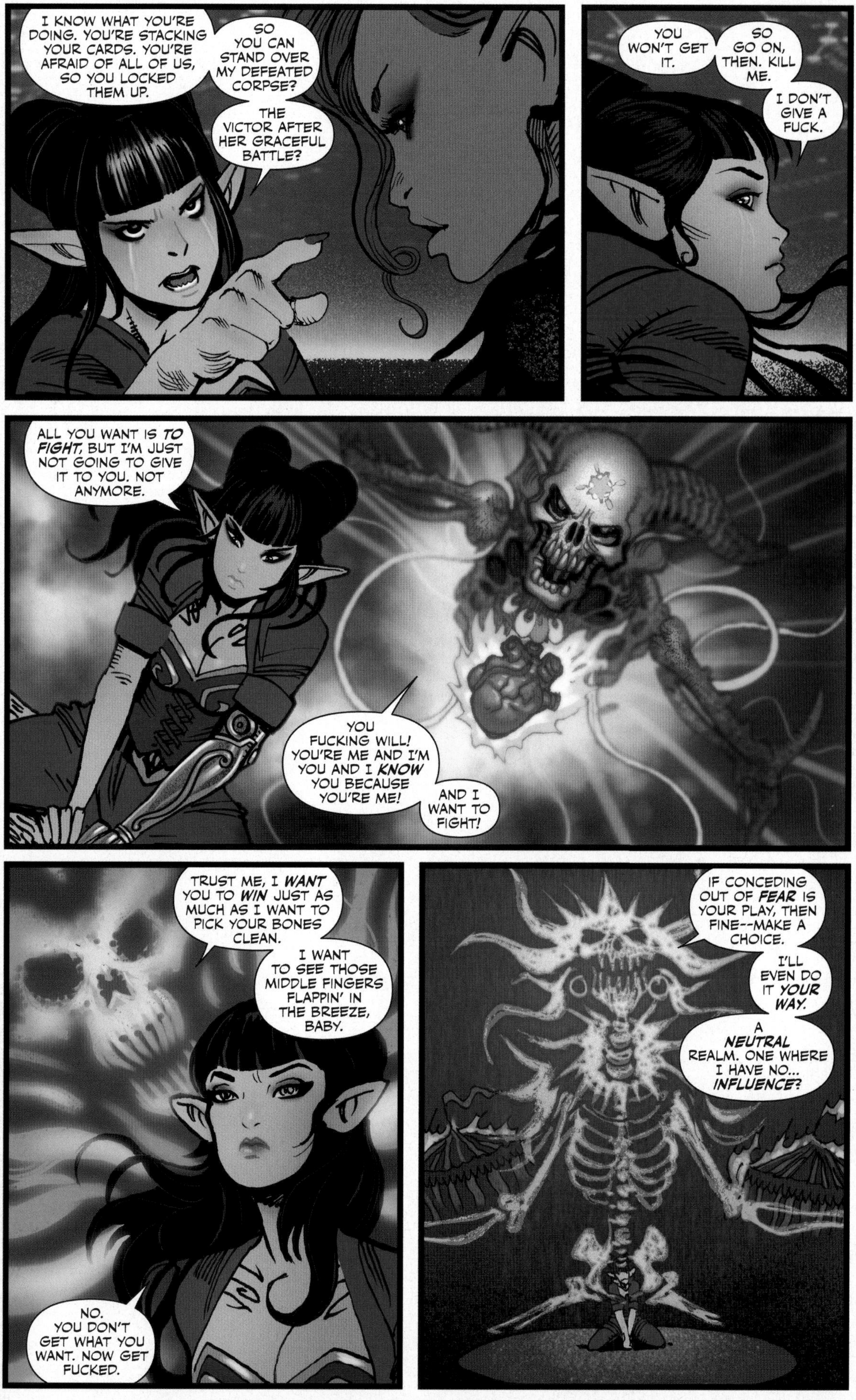
I KNOW WHAT YOU'RE DOING. YOU'RE STACKING YOUR CARDS. YOU'RE AFRAID OF ALL OF US, SO YOU LOCKED THEM UP.
SO YOU CAN STAND OVER MY DEFEATED CORPSE?
THE VICTOR AFTER HER GRACEFUL BATTLE?
YOU WON'T GET IT.
SO GO ON, THEN. KILL ME.
I DON'T GIVE A FUCK.
ALL YOU WANT IS *TO FIGHT,* BUT I'M JUST NOT GOING TO GIVE IT TO YOU. NOT ANYMORE.
YOU FUCKING WILL! YOU'RE ME AND I'M YOU AND I *KNOW* YOU BECAUSE YOU'RE ME!
AND I WANT TO FIGHT!
TRUST ME, I *WANT* YOU TO *WIN* JUST AS MUCH AS I WANT TO PICK YOUR BONES CLEAN.
I WANT TO SEE THOSE MIDDLE FINGERS FLAPPIN' IN THE BREEZE, BABY.
NO. YOU DON'T GET WHAT YOU WANT. NOW GET FUCKED.
IF CONCEDING OUT OF *FEAR* IS YOUR PLAY, THEN FINE--MAKE A CHOICE.
I'LL EVEN DO IT *YOUR WAY.*
A *NEUTRAL* REALM. ONE WHERE I HAVE NO... *INFLUENCE?*

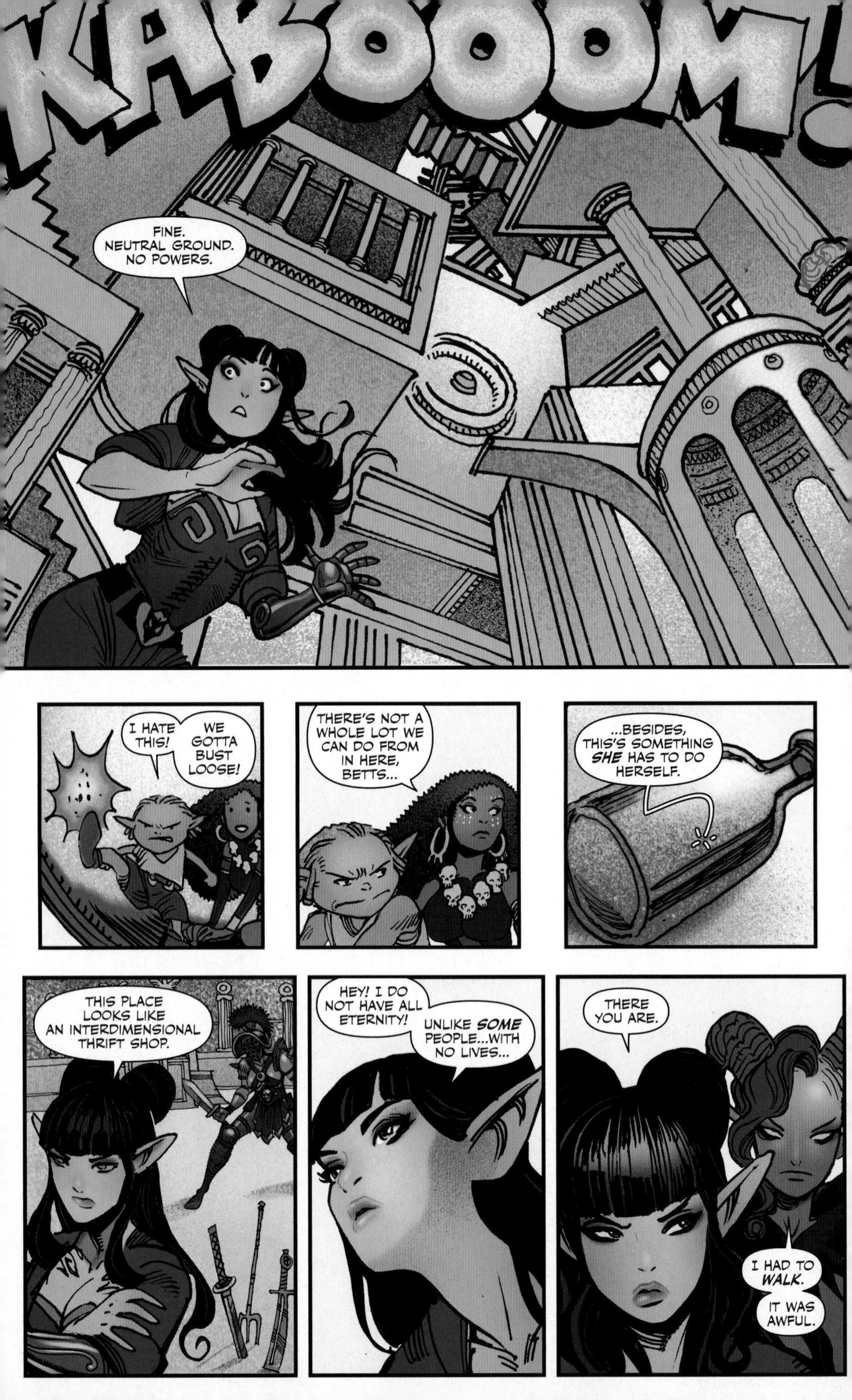
KABOOOM!
FINE. NEUTRAL GROUND. NO POWERS.
I HATE THIS!
WE GOTTA BUST LOOSE!
THERE'S NOT A WHOLE LOT WE CAN DO FROM IN HERE, BETTS...
...BESIDES, THIS'S SOMETHING SHE HAS TO DO HERSELF.
THIS PLACE LOOKS LIKE AN INTERDIMENSIONAL THRIFT SHOP.
HEY! I DO NOT HAVE ALL ETERNITY!
UNLIKE SOME PEOPLE...WITH NO LIVES...
THERE YOU ARE.
I HAD TO WALK.
IT WAS AWFUL.

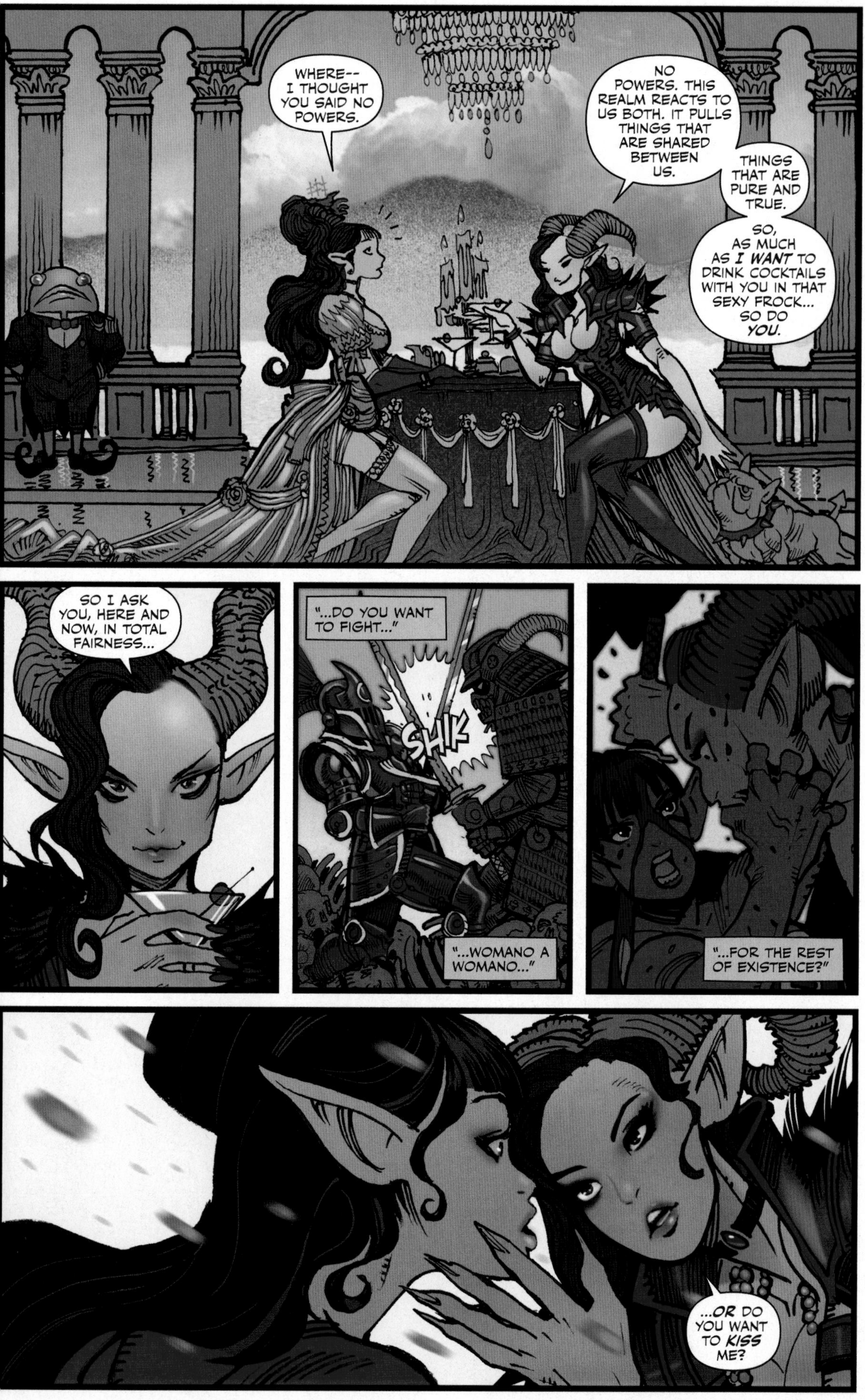
WHERE-- I THOUGHT YOU SAID NO POWERS.
NO POWERS. THIS REALM REACTS TO US BOTH. IT PULLS THINGS THAT ARE SHARED BETWEEN US.
THINGS THAT ARE PURE AND TRUE.
SO, AS MUCH AS *I WANT* TO DRINK COCKTAILS WITH YOU IN THAT SEXY FROCK... SO DO *YOU.*
SO I ASK YOU, HERE AND NOW, IN TOTAL FAIRNESS...
"...DO YOU WANT TO FIGHT..."
SHIK
"...WOMANO A WOMANO..."
"...FOR THE REST OF EXISTENCE?"
...*OR* DO YOU WANT TO *KISS* ME?

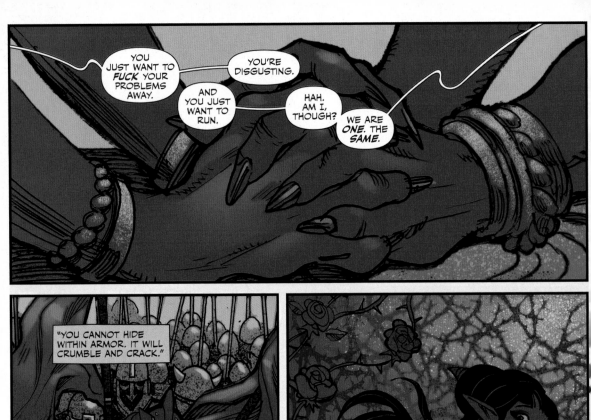

YOU JUST WANT TO *FUCK* YOUR PROBLEMS AWAY.

YOU'RE DISGUSTING.

AND YOU JUST WANT TO RUN.

HAH. AM I, THOUGH?

WE ARE *ONE*. THE *SAME*.

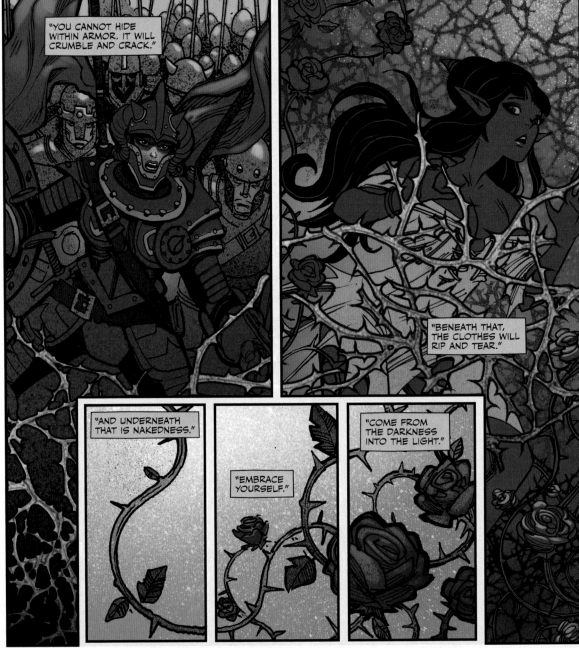

"YOU CANNOT HIDE WITHIN ARMOR. IT WILL CRUMBLE AND CRACK."

"BENEATH THAT, THE CLOTHES WILL RIP AND TEAR."

"AND UNDERNEATH THAT IS NAKEDNESS."

"EMBRACE YOURSELF."

"COME FROM THE DARKNESS INTO THE LIGHT."

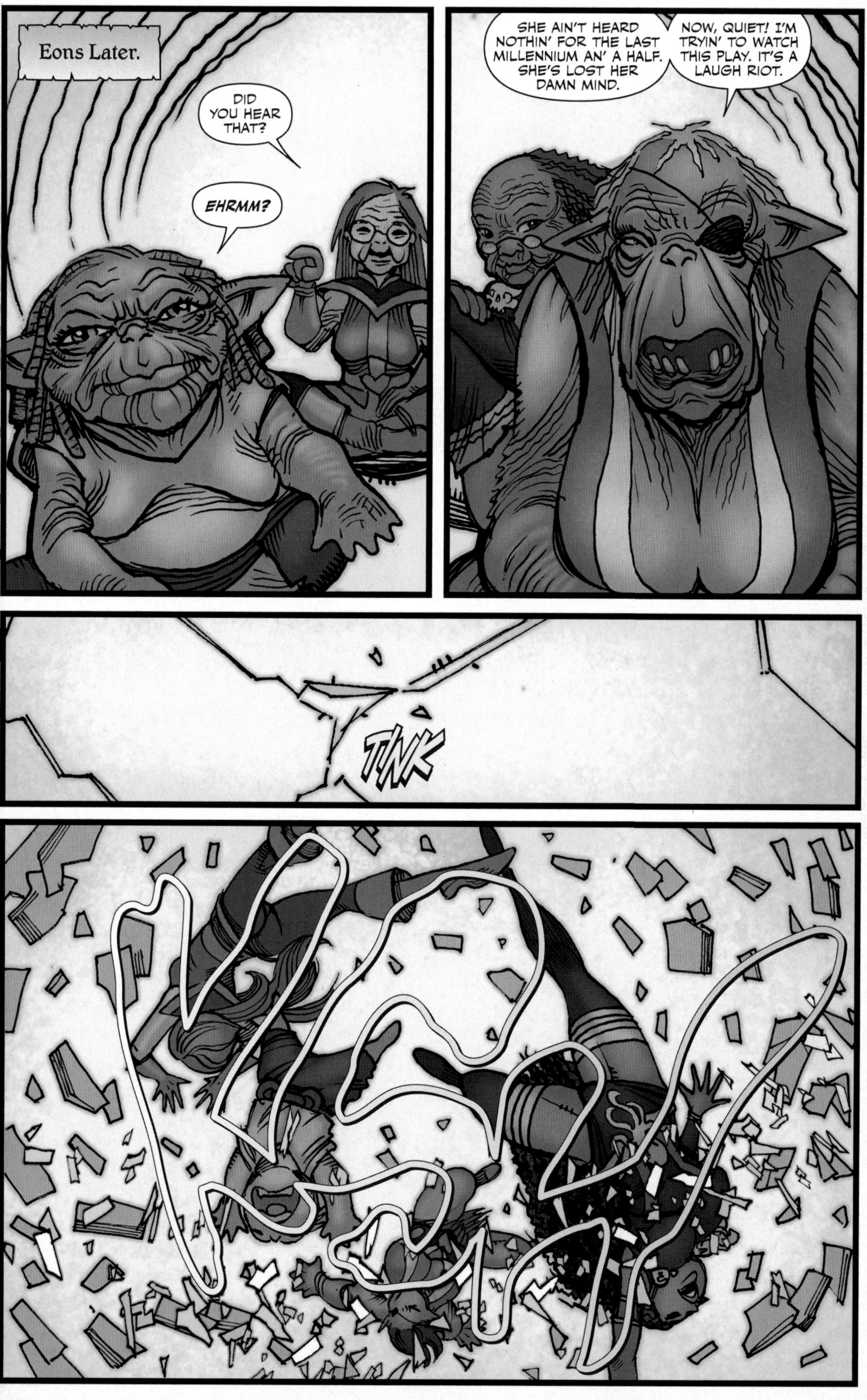
Eons Later.
DID YOU HEAR THAT?
EHRMM?
SHE AIN'T HEARD NOTHIN' FOR THE LAST MILLENNIUM AN' A HALF. SHE'S LOST HER DAMN MIND.
NOW, QUIET! I'M TRYIN' TO WATCH THIS PLAY. IT'S A LAUGH RIOT.
TINK

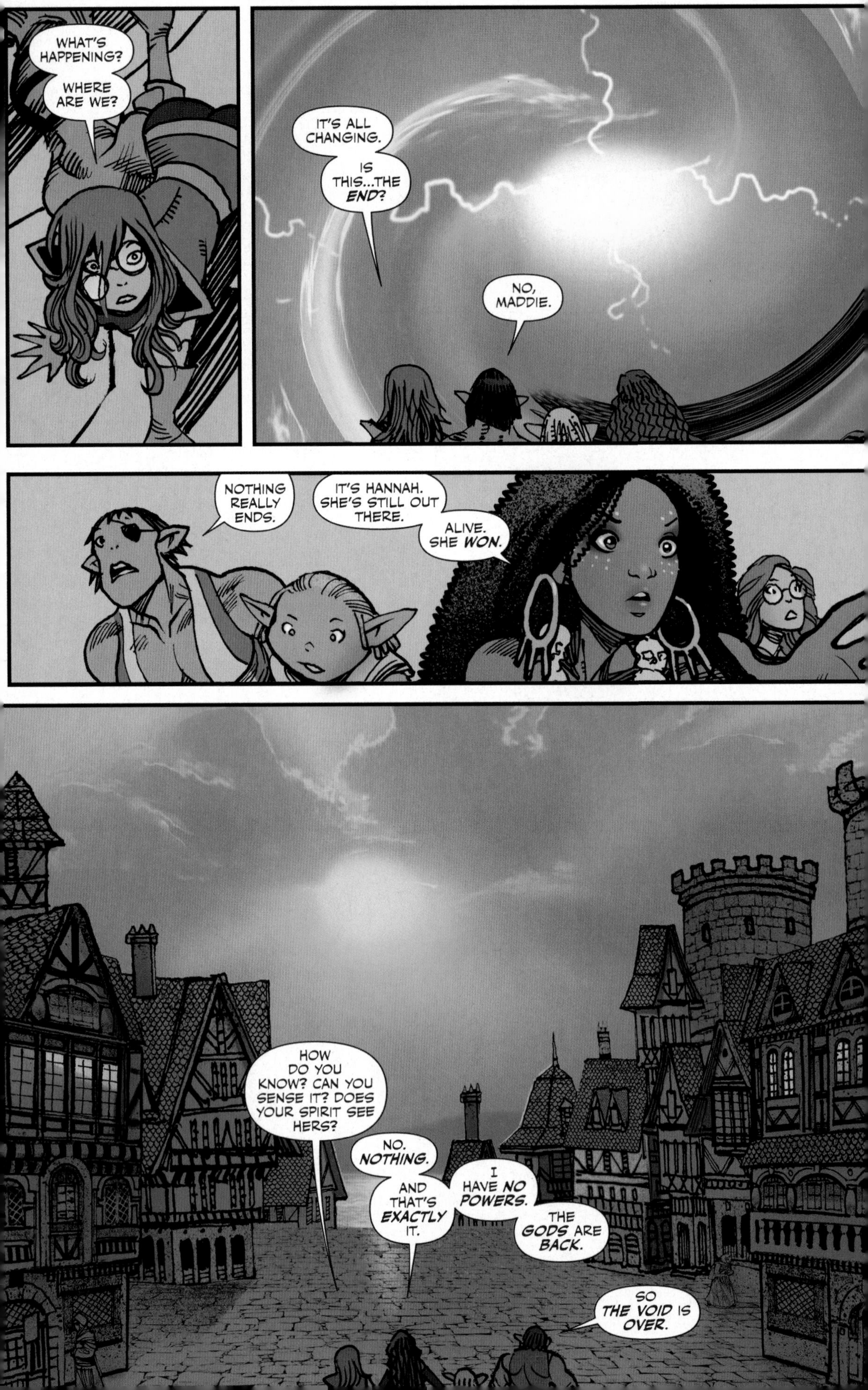

WHAT'S HAPPENING?
WHERE ARE WE?
IT'S ALL CHANGING.
IS THIS...THE END?
NO, MADDIE.
NOTHING REALLY ENDS.
IT'S HANNAH. SHE'S STILL OUT THERE.
ALIVE. SHE WON.
HOW DO YOU KNOW? CAN YOU SENSE IT? DOES YOUR SPIRIT SEE HERS?
NO. NOTHING.
AND THAT'S EXACTLY IT.
I HAVE NO POWERS.
THE GODS ARE BACK.
SO THE VOID IS OVER.

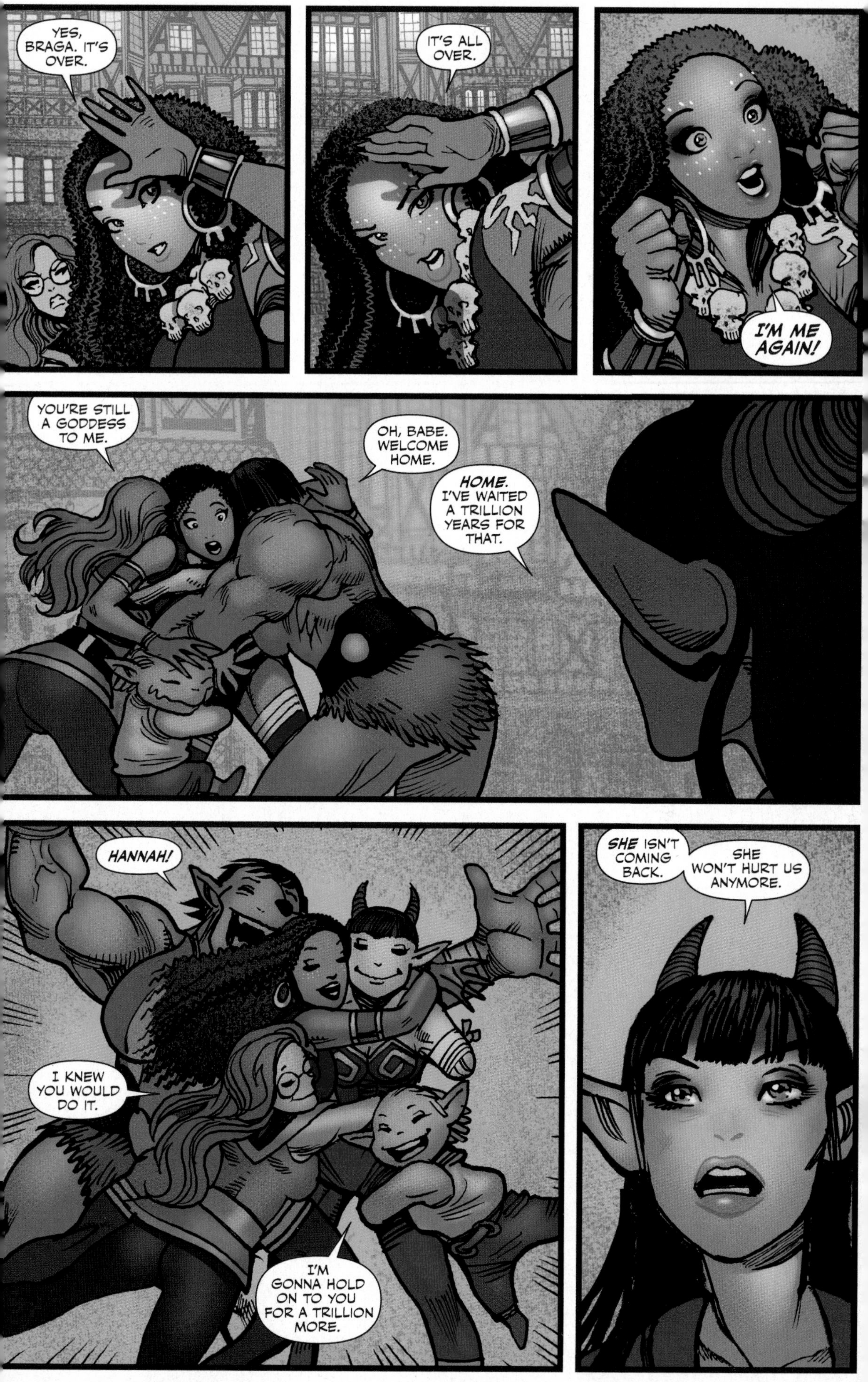
YES, BRAGA. IT'S OVER.
IT'S ALL OVER.
I'M ME AGAIN!
YOU'RE STILL A GODDESS TO ME.
OH, BABE. WELCOME HOME.
HOME. I'VE WAITED A TRILLION YEARS FOR THAT.
HANNAH!
I KNEW YOU WOULD DO IT.
I'M GONNA HOLD ON TO YOU FOR A TRILLION MORE.
SHE ISN'T COMING BACK.
SHE WON'T HURT US ANYMORE.

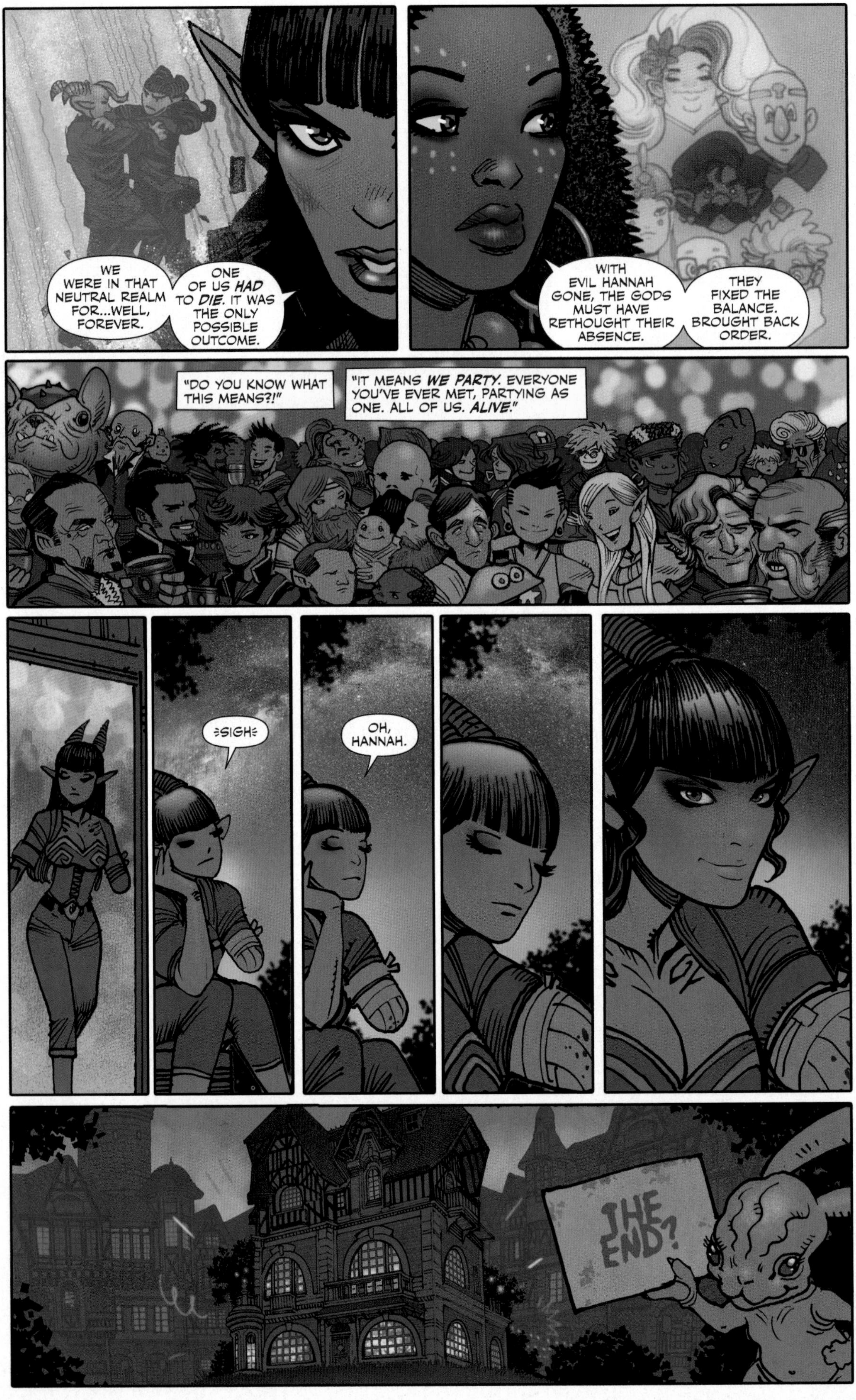
WE WERE IN THAT NEUTRAL REALM FOR...WELL, FOREVER.
ONE OF US HAD TO DIE. IT WAS THE ONLY POSSIBLE OUTCOME.
WITH EVIL HANNAH GONE, THE GODS MUST HAVE RETHOUGHT THEIR ABSENCE.
THEY FIXED THE BALANCE. BROUGHT BACK ORDER.
"DO YOU KNOW WHAT THIS MEANS?!"
"IT MEANS WE PARTY. EVERYONE YOU'VE EVER MET, PARTYING AS ONE. ALL OF US. ALIVE."
SIGH
OH, HANNAH.
THE END?

EXTRAS

SKETCHES, LAYOUTS, and MORE
by MORITAT

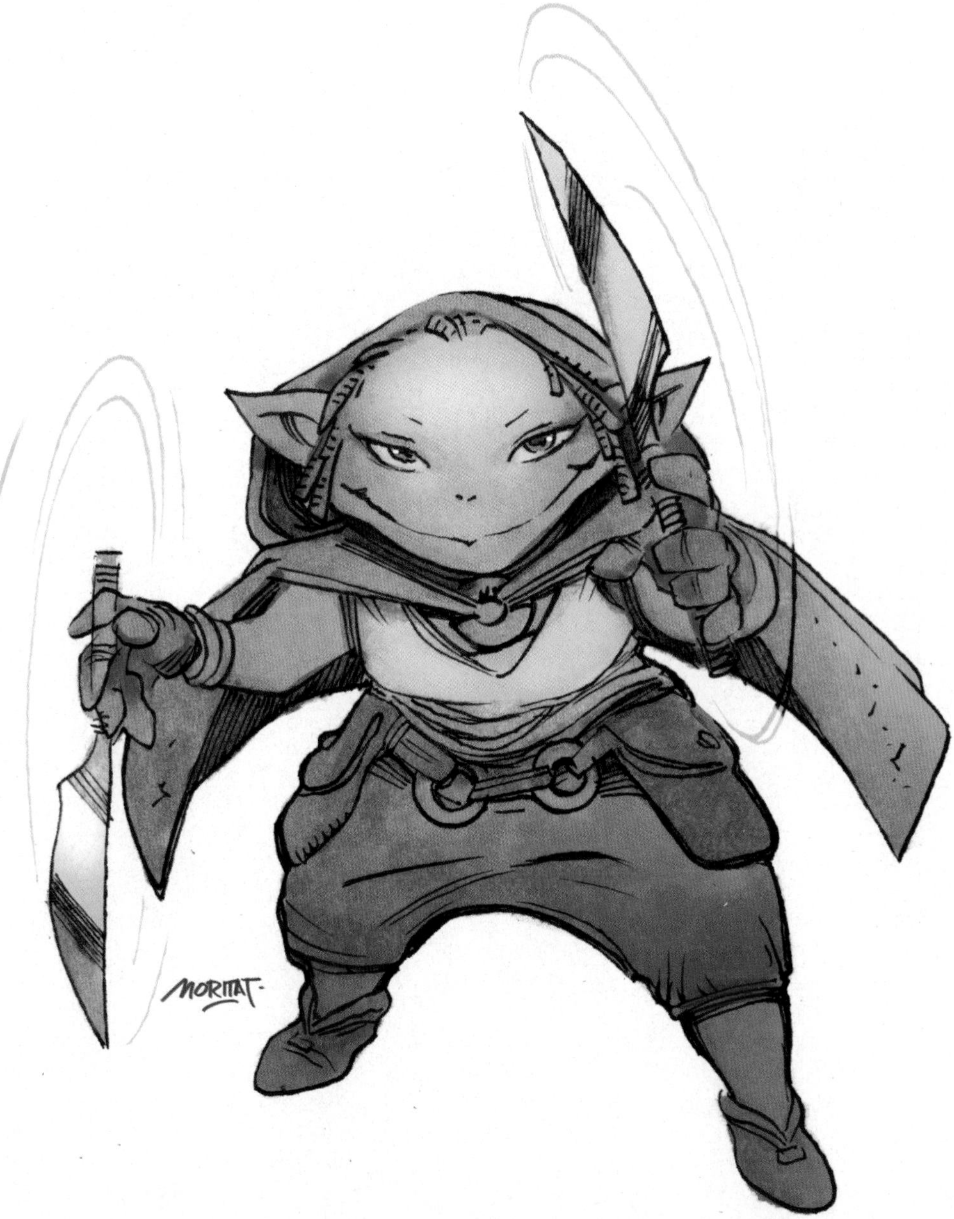
MORITAT

CHARACTER SKETCHES

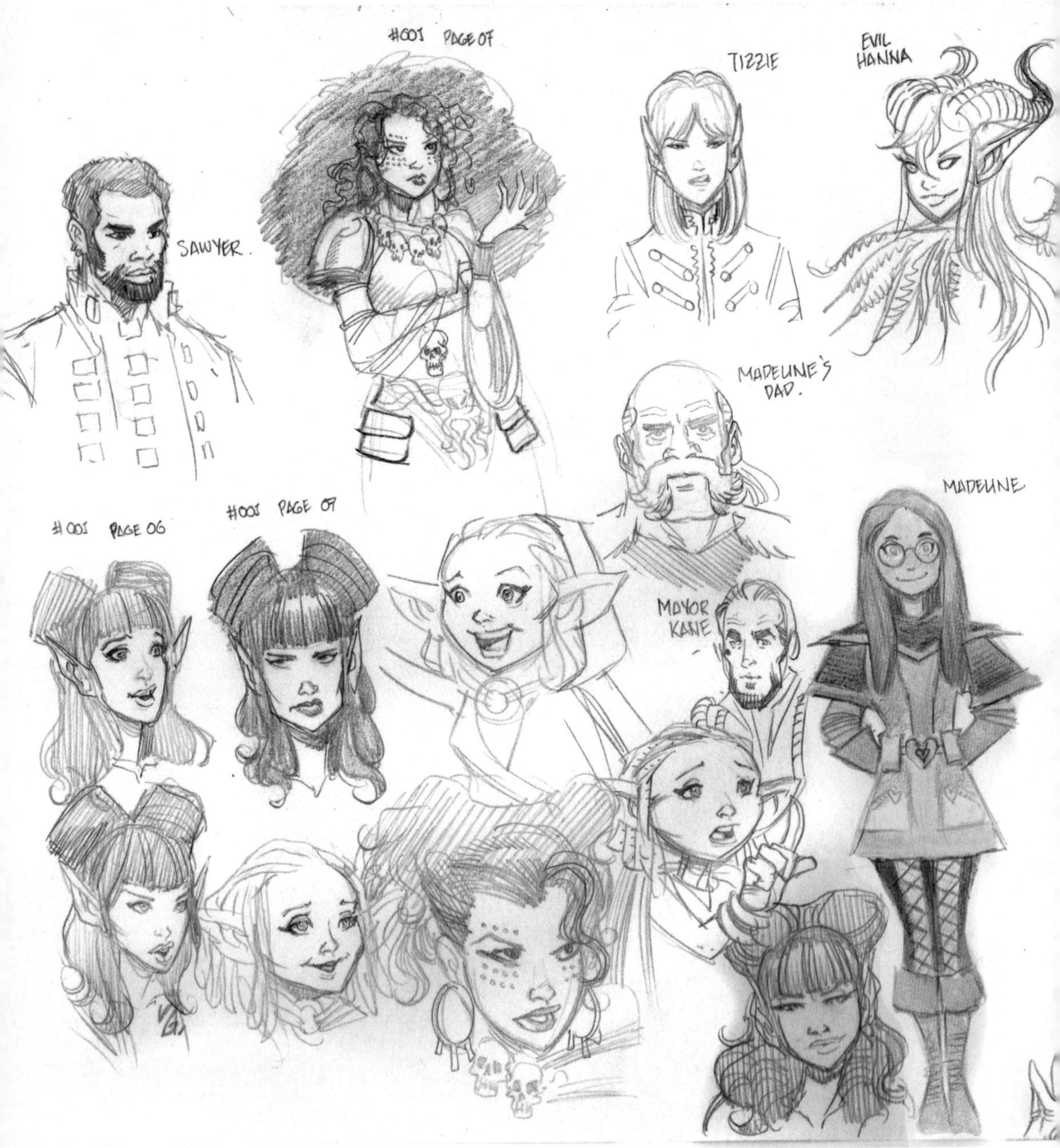
#001 PAGE 07
TIZZIE
EVIL HANNA
SAWYER.
MADELINE'S DAD.
MADELINE
#001 PAGE 06
#001 PAGE 07
MAYOR KANE

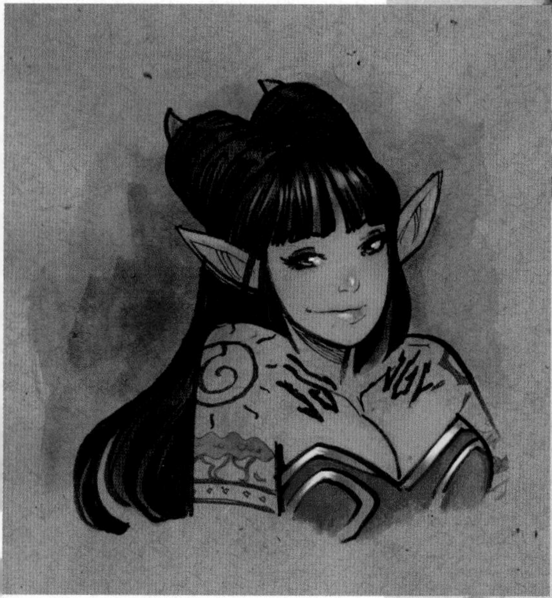

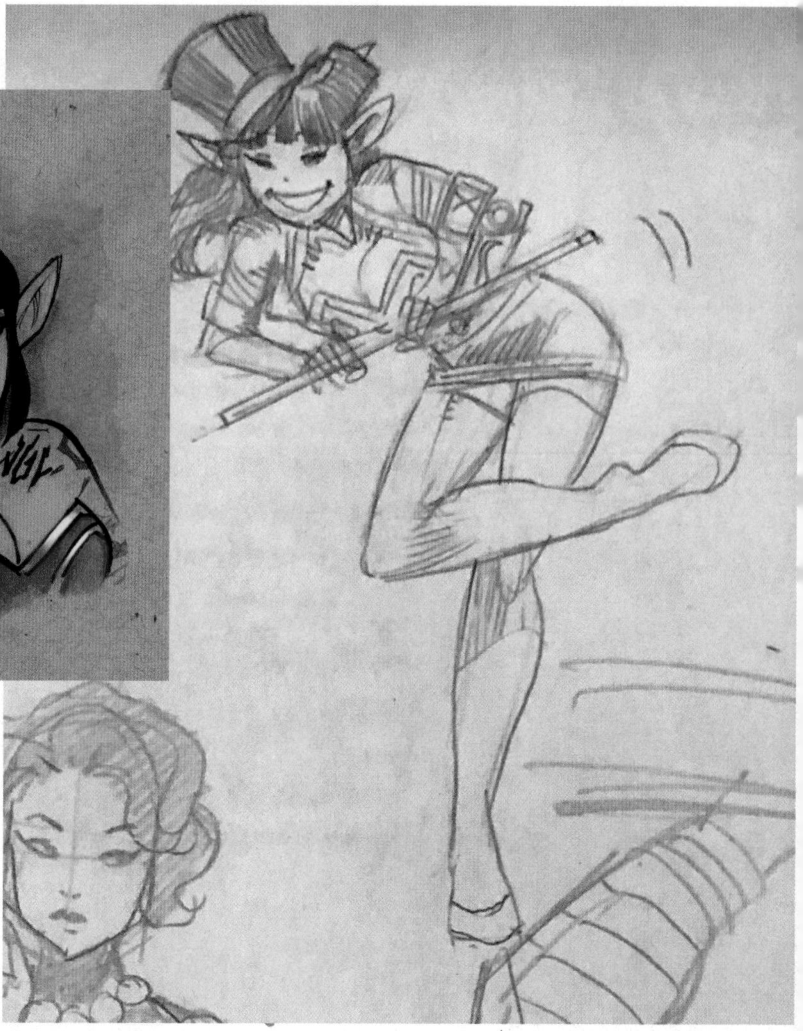

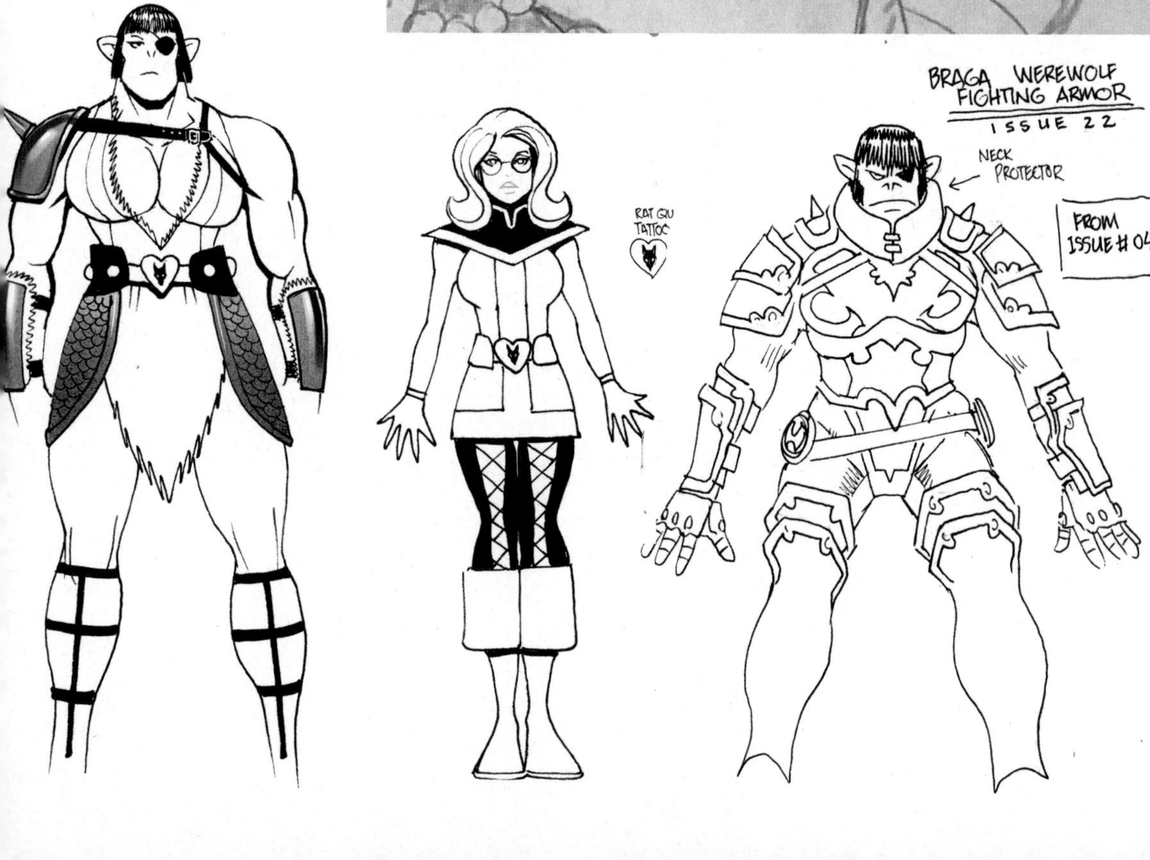
BRAGA WEREWOLF FIGHTING ARMOR
ISSUE 22
NECK PROTECTOR
FROM ISSUE # 04
RAT GU TATTOO

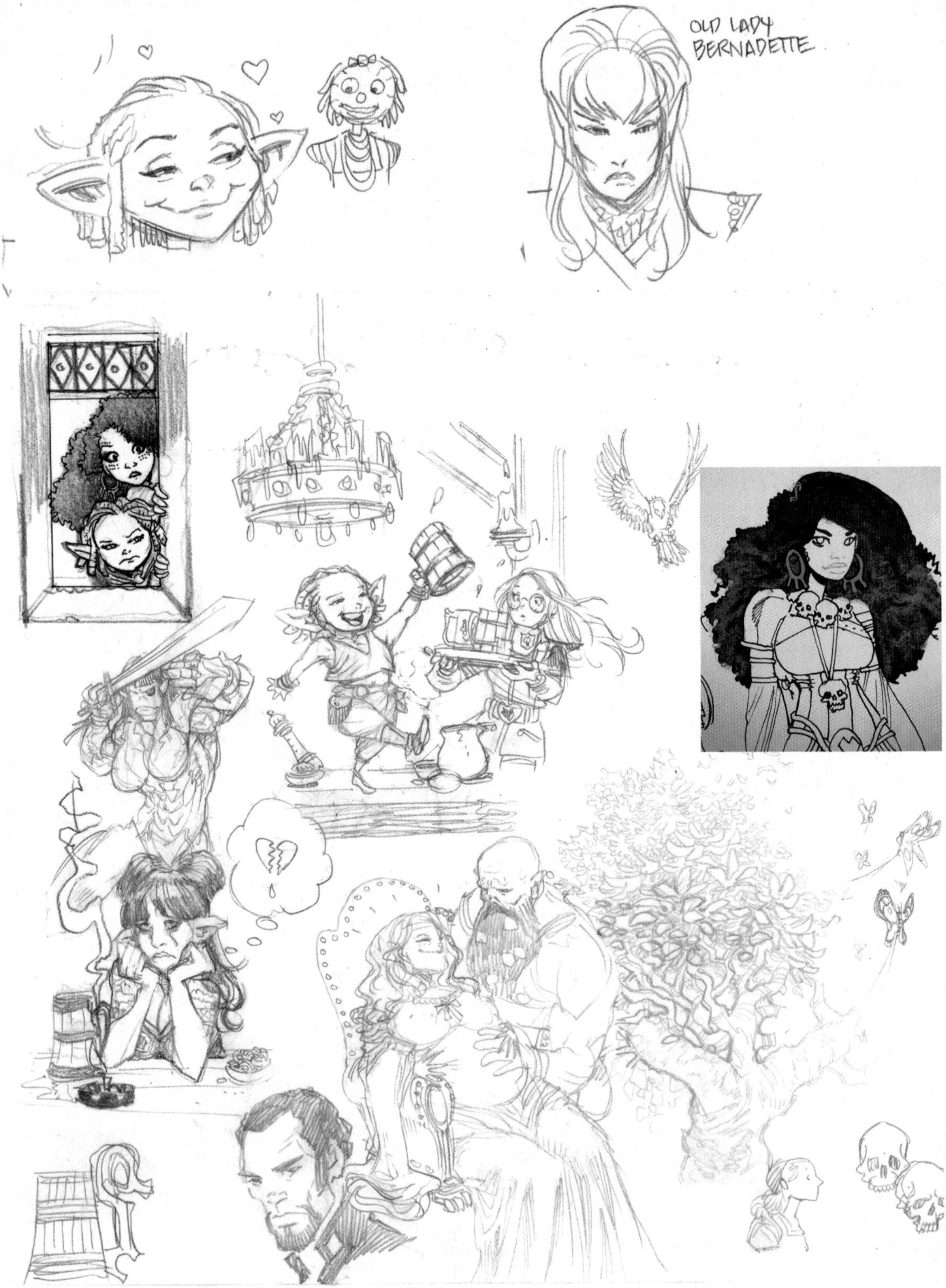
OLD LADY
BERNADETTE

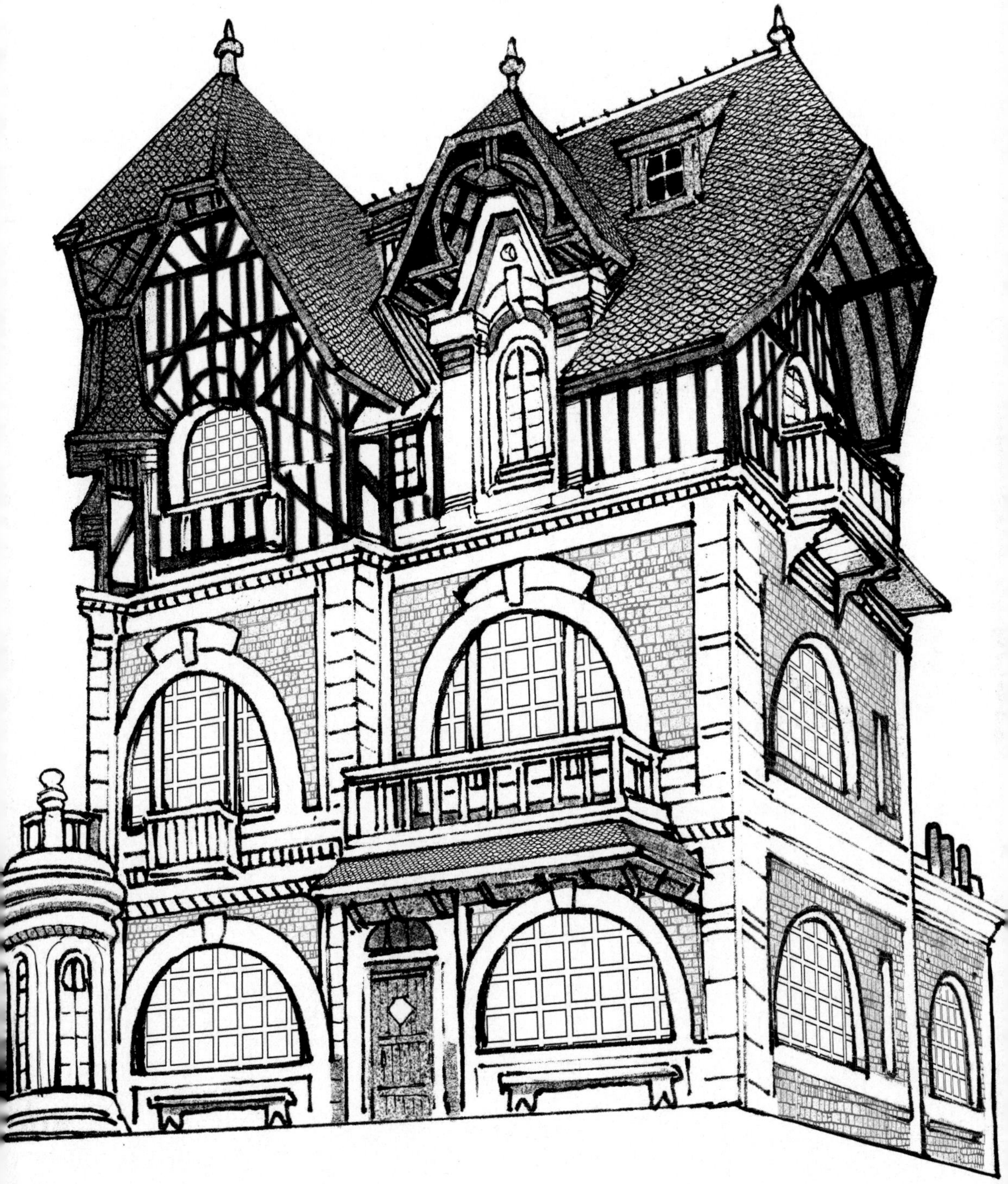

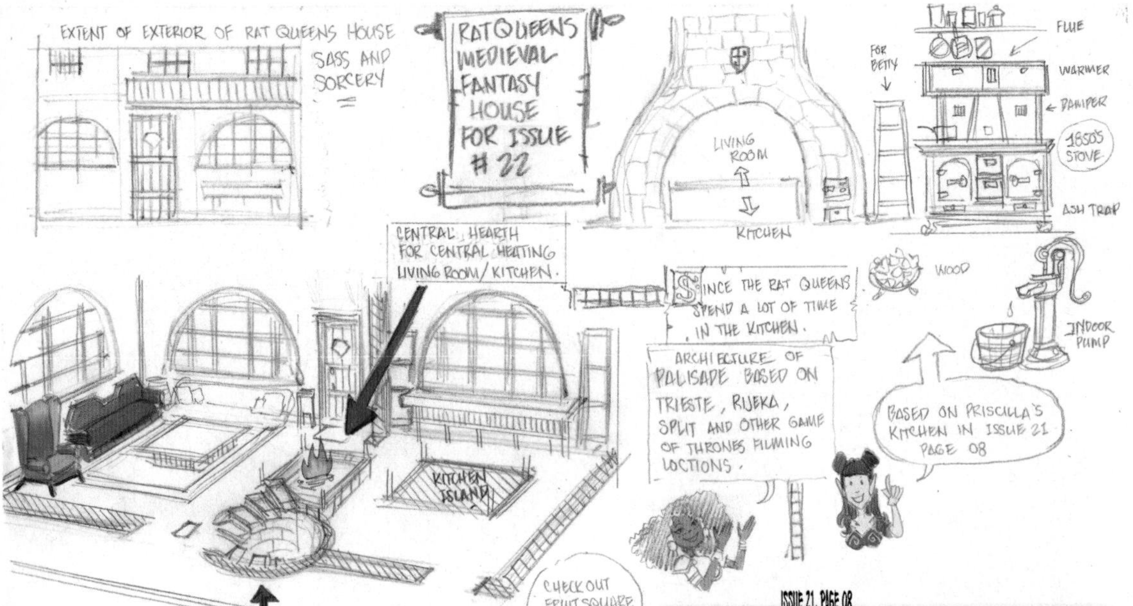
EXTENT OF EXTERIOR OF RAT QUEENS HOUSE
SASS AND SORCERY
RAT QUEENS MEDIEVAL FANTASY HOUSE FOR ISSUE #22
LIVING ROOM
KITCHEN
FOR BETTY
FLUE
WARMER
DAMPER
1850'S STOVE
ASH TRAP
CENTRAL HEARTH FOR CENTRAL HEATING LIVING ROOM / KITCHEN.
SINCE THE RAT QUEENS SPEND A LOT OF TIME IN THE KITCHEN.
WOOD
INDOOR PUMP
ARCHITECTURE OF PALISADE BASED ON TRIESTE, RIJEKA, SPLIT AND OTHER GAME OF THRONES FILMING LOCTIONS.
BASED ON PRISCILLA'S KITCHEN IN ISSUE 21 PAGE 08
KITCHEN ISLAND

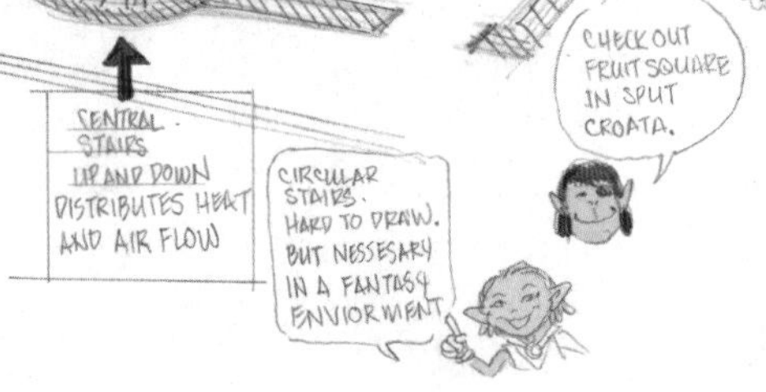
CHECK OUT FRUIT SQUARE IN SPLIT CROATA.
CENTRAL STAIRS UP AND DOWN DISTRIBUTES HEAT AND AIR FLOW
CIRCULAR STAIRS. HARD TO DRAW. BUT NESSESARY IN A FANTASY ENVIORMENT

ISSUE 21, PAGE 08

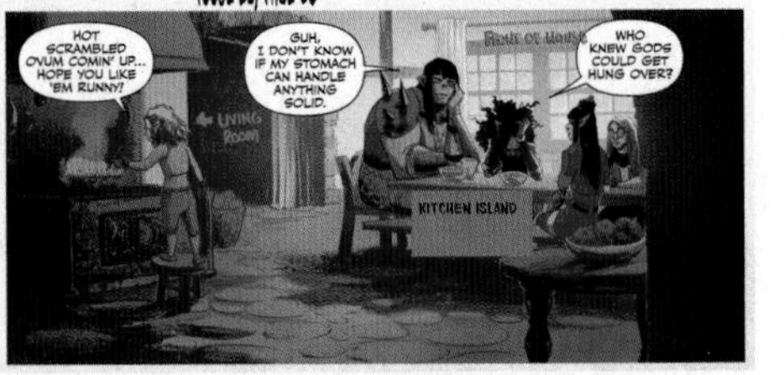
HOT SCRAMBLED OVUM COMIN' UP... HOPE YOU LIKE 'EM RUNNY!
GUH, I DON'T KNOW IF MY STOMACH CAN HANDLE ANYTHING SOLID.
WHO KNEW GODS COULD GET HUNG OVER?
LIVING ROOM
KITCHEN ISLAND

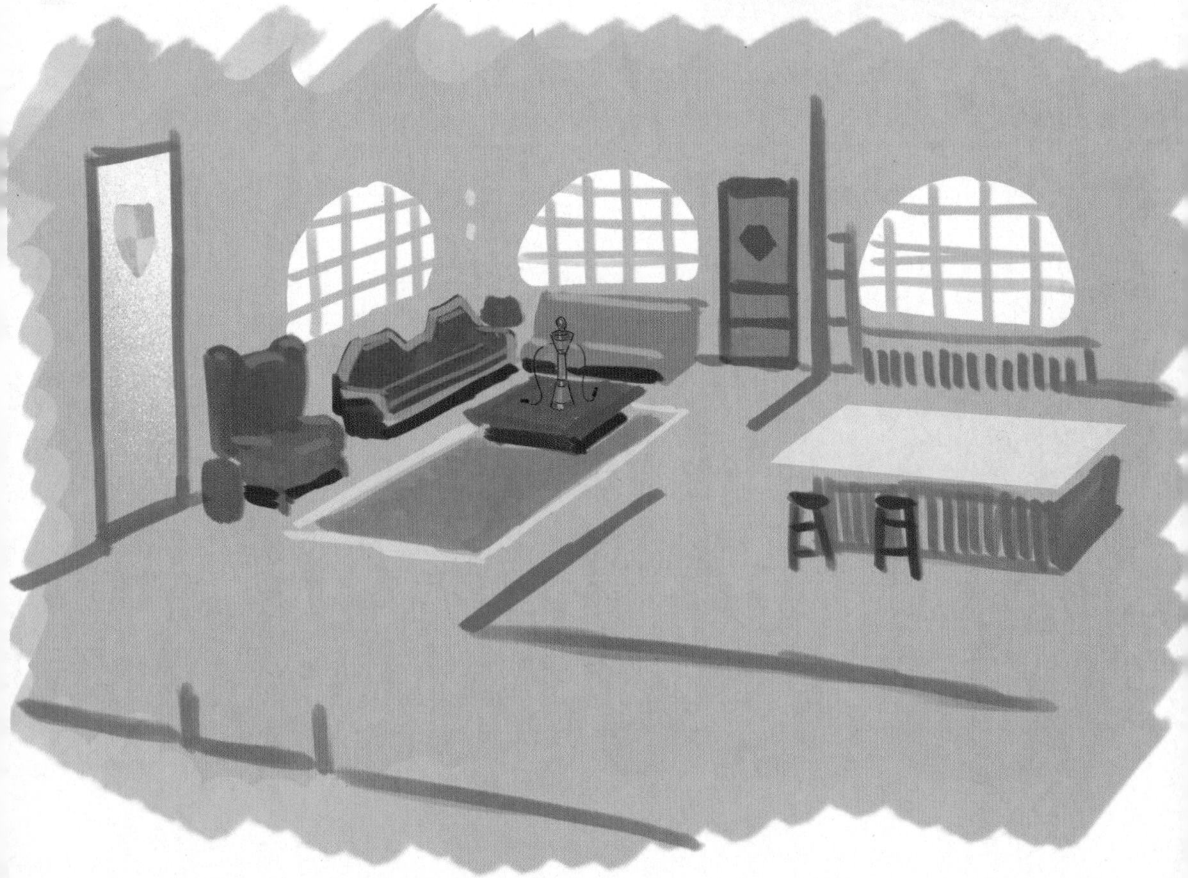

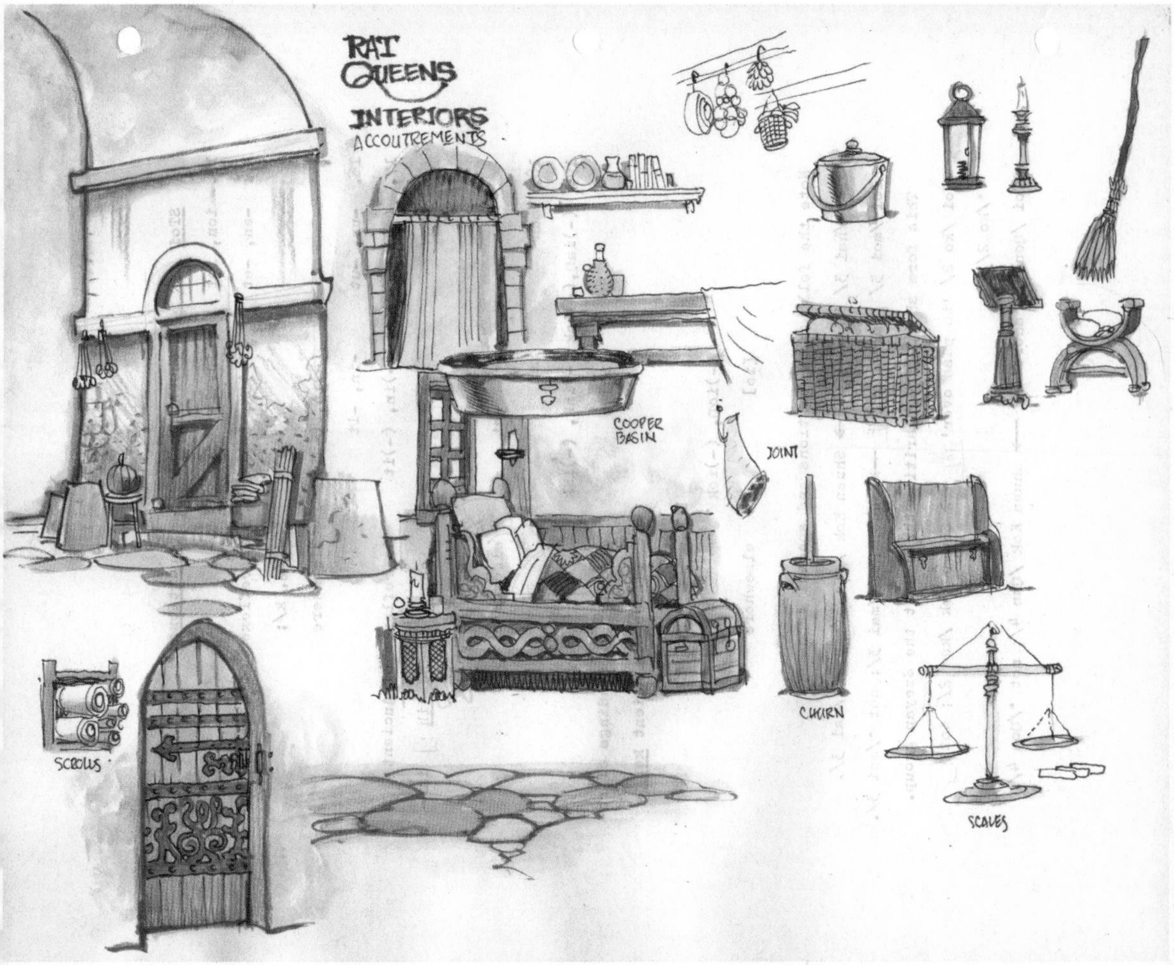
RAT QUEENS
INTERIORS
ACCOUTREMENTS
COOPER BASIN
JOINT
CHURN
SCROLLS
SCALES

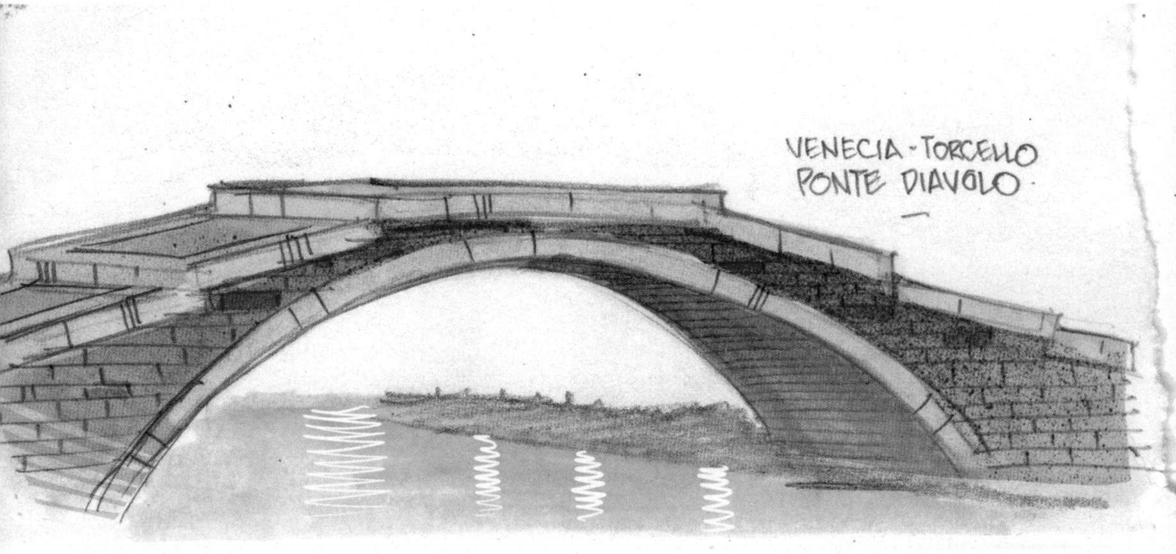
VENECIA - TORCELLO
PONTE DIAVOLO

RAT QUEENS #22 PAGE 01.

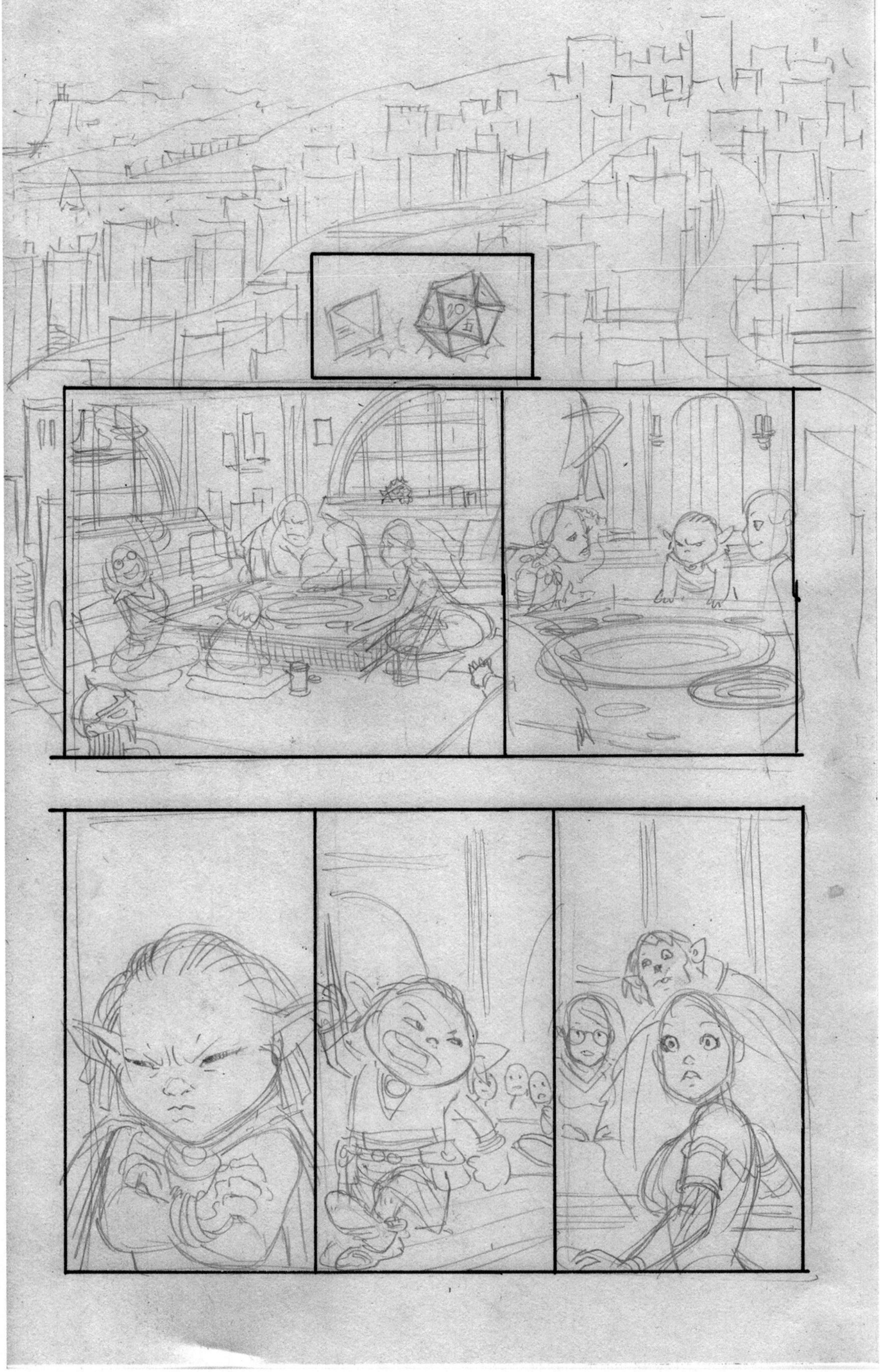

DEE (original drawing used in #25 Cover B collage—page 4)

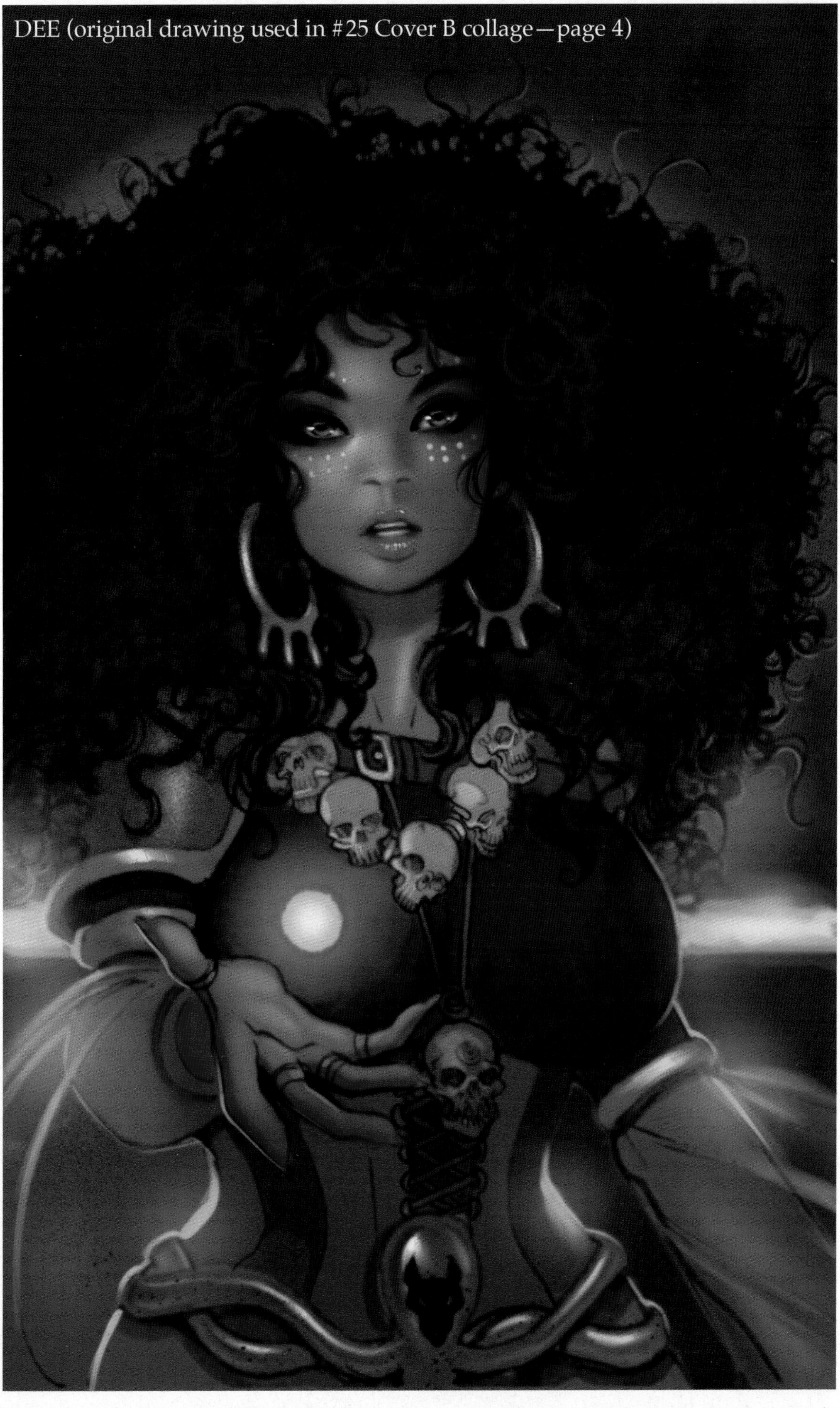

We would like to thank the following for their contributions to Rat Queens...

On the main series and specials...
Tamra Bonvillain, Ed Brisson, Max Dunbar, Ryan Ferrier, Kelly Fitzpatrick, Tess Fowler, Owen Gieni, William Kirkby, Marco Lesko, Moritat, Micah Myers, Priscilla Petraites, Stjepan Sejic and Casey Silver

On extra covers and back-up features...
Sweeney Boo, Kyle Charles, Tim Daniel, Leila del Duca, Colleen Doran, Jenny Frison, Kerrie Fulker, Chris Gutierrez, Jonathan Hickman, Leigh Hyland, Tyler Jenkins, Mindy Lee, Joseph Michael Linsner, Michael Avon Oeming, Ben Rankel, Riley Rossmo, Patrick Rothfuss, Fiona Staples, Nate Taylor and Chance Wolf.

Our ever patient editors
Melanie Hackett and Laura Tavishati

Special thanks to
Marc Lombardi, Erika Schnatz and
Shannon Marie Woodhouse

and, especially to

Kurtis J. Wiebe and Roc Upchurch

Eight years and forty-five issues,
it's been one hell of a ride!

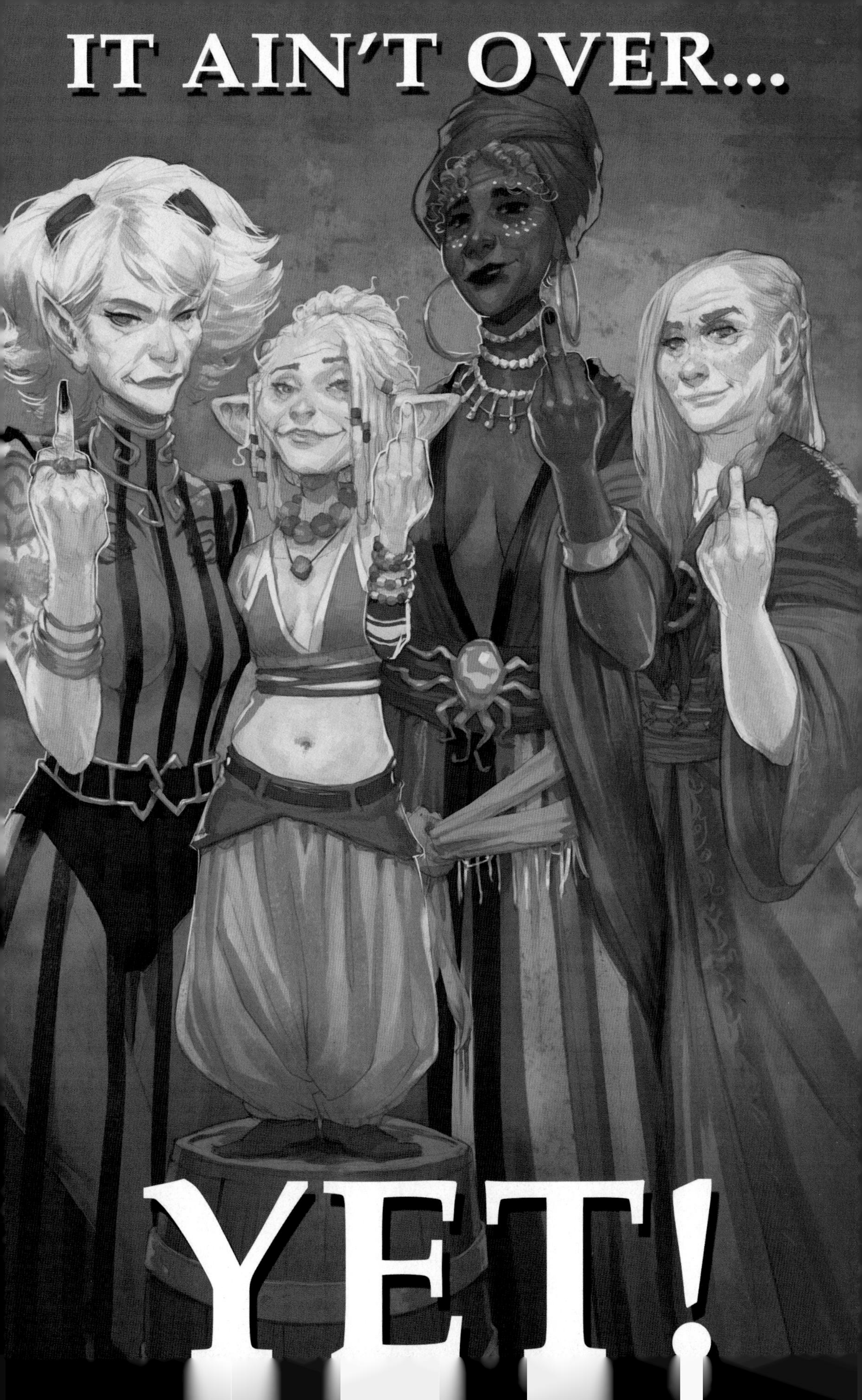
IT AIN'T OVER...
YET!

COMING IN 2021

THE

KURTIS J. WIEBE and ROC UPCHURCH
FINISH WHAT THEY STARTED!

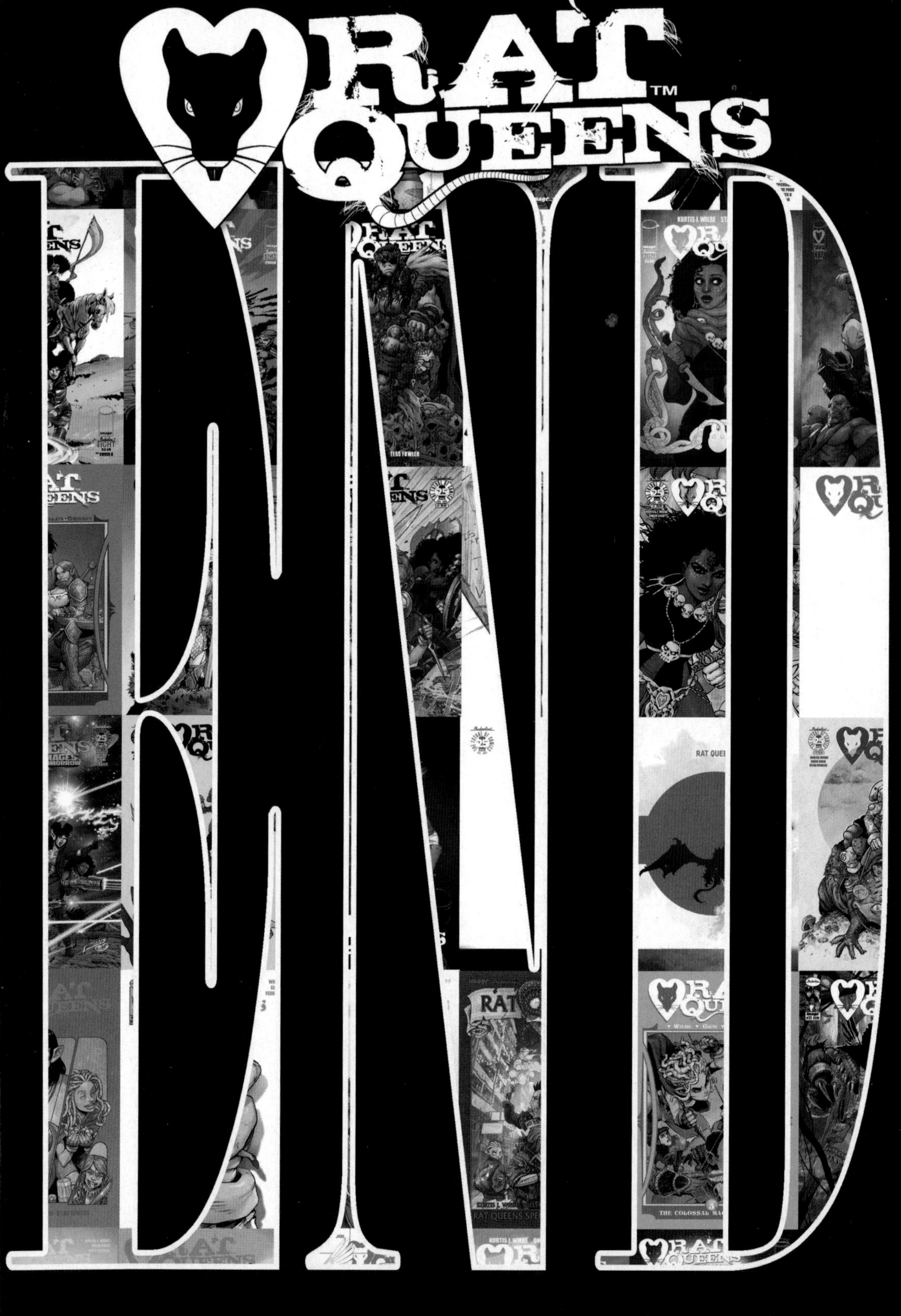
RAT QUEENS™
END

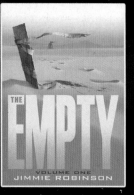
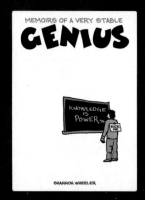

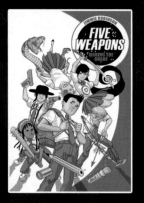